Play to Live
by D. Rus

Book 1
AlterWorld

Play to Live

Sensitive information
Eyes only
Destroy after reading

From a memorandum to President of the Russian Federation:

At year's end 203X, we have lost 82,000 of the population to the 'perma mode effect' which is 3.2 times more than in the previous year. However, it should be noted that overall, the disappearance of the above nationals improves the country's gene pool and eases the burden on our economy. Over 89% of those who chose to become perma-stuck in virtual reality on their own free will were elderly, handicapped or terminally ill, plus a considerable group of society dropouts including immature individuals and other misfits. In terms of economy, they're dead wood.

After introducing the 16th amendment to the Internet and Virtual Reality Act which limited FIVR (Full Immersion Virtual Reality) exposure to four hours a day, the number of individuals permanently stuck in MMORPG (Massively Multiplayer Online Role-Playing Games) has fallen to 2.600 a year. Even though the USA and Western Europe toe the line at three hours of FIVR exposure a day, we don't deem it necessary to follow their example, especially in apprehension of the Silicon Lobby's reaction. But we do suggest taking some preventative measures that would diminish the flow of nationals seeking to 'go perma mode' willingly, with the eventual possibility of reducing it to zero. These are the measures we propose:

1. To introduce legal limits to authenticity levels of FIVR worlds.

2. To define permissible configuration types and top options available for FIVR capsules.

3. To arrange for regular instances of signal deterioration including pseudo accidental cutouts, every X hours.

4. To limit or ban FIVR connections to the worlds with over 40% authenticity for certain categories of nationals, such as: government functionaries, members of the military, key scientific workers and those in possession of secret clearance.

Chapter One

"A month. One month of relatively active life. I'm afraid, this is all you've got left," the doctor removed his glasses and rubbed his tired eyes.

I knew of course that his profession would make anyone a cynic. And still he didn't seem to be delivering the news lightly.

The doctor shook his head, his hair gray before his time. "Yes, a month," he pursed his lips, hesitating, then blurted,

"It'll be the question of what runs out first: your health reserves, your will to live in ever-growing agony—or your ability to finance therapy and medications. I hope you'll excuse me for being so blatant. I'm very sorry. Normally, we don't inform our patients in case of a Class A diagnosis. We contact their relatives, but you don't seem to have listed any. What a shame. I don't think that spending the next month in and out of surgeries will be worth your while. We just can't do anything for you. An inoperable brain tumor is indeed the end of the line. Today's medical science just isn't good enough. I'd rather suggest you put your affairs in order. Pay off your debts. Go on holiday with your friends or someone you love."

He continued talking but his voice didn't register any more. I stared at his hands fiddling with some paperwork. I wasn't going to die, surely! What cancer was he talking about? My life had only just started to work out!

The phrase echoed in my mind. *Today's medical science just isn't good enough.* What about the science of the future, then? Will it be good enough?

The thought struck me, giving me new hope. I sprung to my feet. The chair creaked, having heard yet another death sentence. It must have witnessed more of those than Old Sparky. I mumbled my goodbyes and headed for the door. Ignoring the elevator, I flew down the steps three at a time, ran across the crowded parking lot and slumped into my Hyundai's seat.

I pulled the cell out of its case and started the browser. What was it that I'd heard on the radio on my way to work? *The first in Moscow...We sell immortality... a chance to live forever... to see the future with your own eyes...* Implanted by some marketroid team, the buzz words sat firmly in my brain, and still I couldn't remember the name of the thing – a center or something.

My head smarted with the effort, sending colored circles dancing before my eyes. I winced and sat still, waiting for the spasm to go, then felt for the painkillers in my pocket. When had I last taken them? Was it with my breakfast at ten o'clock? If it was, I'd better make the pills last another couple of hours. The doctor had already taken me to task saying that all that constant OD-ing was ruining my liver. Had he been trying to be funny?

What was their name, dammit! Was it *Chrome*? *Chronyl*? Or... *Chronos*? Exactly. Chronos. I Googled their office number.

"Chronos life extension, how can I help you?" chimed a young female voice, soft and eager.

"I, er," I faltered. "I mean, hi. It's about your cryonics program. Can I make an appointment or something?"

"Absolutely. I'm feeding you our location."

Forty minutes later, I parked up by a state-of-the-art business center. Their high-speed elevator gave me a bout of childish delight replaced by a new spasm of agony. I gave up and swallowed another pill with best wishes to my liver. It shouldn't get any ideas about being transplanted, once I croaked, into some lucky alcoholic billionaire.

The client manager was too young and too pretty. A strategically undone button on her business blouse added to her cleavage and hindered my concentration. But despite her tender age, she spoke in a competent voice and her eyes filled with compassion and purpose as we talked.

"We've been in business since 1960s in the US alone. Now we're offering a large spectrum of cryonics services in dozens of our centers all over the world. It's our fifth year worldwide, so you've come at the right moment to enjoy our anniversary discounts."

"Excuse me," I butted into her pitch. "Could you please tell me about the procedure? And, er, about your price range."

"Absolutely. Once the contract is signed and the payment clears our bank, we fit you with a sensor which feeds your data to our ER team. If your condition becomes critical, the team will remain on standby twenty-four-seven. Once you're pronounced legally deceased, they begin the cryonics procedure in order to-"

"Wait a sec," I faltered. "What do you mean, legally deceased? Are you going to wait till I die?"

The manager gave me an understanding nod. She'd obviously heard the question hundreds of times. "We can't freeze you alive, can we? Legally, it would be murder. So first we need to obtain a proper death certificate. Following that, our team of experts will perfuse a client's tissues with our cryoprotective solution and begin freezing his body before transporting it to our cooldown facility where it is stored under liquid hydrogen in an individual cryostat container. The body remains there for the duration of the contract – usually, until the arrival of a resuscitation technology."

She beamed, delivering the good news, as if they'd already brought me back to life. I wasn't so impressed, though. The prospects of me waiting for myself to die didn't sound like a promise of immortality.

"So how much would it be in total?"

The girl produced the price list. Zeroes flickered before my eyes.

"Our anniversary campaign," she raised her finger, "allows us to drop the bottom line twenty percent. The complete package will cost you seventy thousand dollars."

She saw my raised eyebrows and hurried to add, "There is an option to only have your head stored for as little as twenty-five thousand. And for just six thousand we can preserve your DNA sample which will allow the science of the future to grow your clone. Our analysts believe that it might preserve part of your personality."

I stared at her. What was she saying? All they seemed to be doing was milking terminal patients for their last buck. Having said that, wasn't official medicine doing the same? Their job was making more money, not helping us recover.

"I... I'll think about it."

I stood up, ending her rosy pitch of incredible generosity. For a brief moment, the girl lost her sales drive and looked straight at me as she offered me her hand. "I have a funny feeling you'll be all right... Max. Just don't give up. I'll see what I can do and I'll give you a call. I might bring the bottom line down a bit."

"Thanks," I said, looking for her name tag. "Thank you... Olga. I'll be all right."

I gave her another smile as I let her soft palm linger in my hand. Wistfully I released my fingers, turned round and strode out of reception. Interesting girl. A dark horse. Yesterday I'd have probably tried to get to know her better. You never know, it might have worked. But today... damn this cancer!

In any case, I had to look into it further. At least this cryonics stuff gave you half a chance. I couldn't afford to dismiss any ray of hope, however ephemeral. The alternatives were too bleak to even start to contemplate. Had I had enough money, I'd have risked it: you couldn't take your wallet with you, anyway. But I'd never been lucky enough to see so much dough, let alone possess it.

For the last two years, I'd finally gotten my act together. I'd prized my ass off the computer chair and began looking around, learning to mix and fit in while keeping my eyes on the ball. Funnily enough, my hobby had become my career—who was it that said, *Find a job you love and you'll never have to work again?* Basically, I'd started a hardware repair shop. I didn't underprice myself, but I enjoyed doing quality work and always fixed a few extra bits the customer hadn't paid me to do. Word-of-mouth marketing had me as a new and upcoming expert and the money flow grew deeper and wider. Not that my savings account had grown any healthier: I had too much to catch up on after all the years of vegetation. I got myself a new wardrobe and a two-year-old Hyundai. I could finally afford to take a girl out or help Mom financially. All that allowed me to feel human again, but I hadn't arrived at the savings stage yet. My little business had grown to the point where I started thinking about hiring an assistant when trouble came from the least expected place.

Anyway. Back to the drawing board. I needed money. My immediate goal was to leave Mom with as much as I could. After Dad had died in that wretched car accident, she'd been in a bad way, what with her heart and leg problems. She was a brick, was Mom – she'd even moved into Granddad's old country house not far from Moscow. If you believed her, the country air did her good. But her miserable disability pension came nowhere near my recent assistance. Without my help, Mom would soon be living hand to mouth: clutching a few pennies by the grocer's doors, counting them over and over as she calculated whether she had enough for some bread and a carton of milk or whether she'd have to wait and leave milk till Sunday?

My ultimate goal, however, was to find enough money for this cryonics thing. I needed a chance. I could always lie down and die if it came to that. Now where would I get hold of a hundred thousand dollar bills? Could I maybe rip off a get-rich-quick scammer or corrupt functionary? I had no qualms whatsoever about doing so, but even then you had to agree that moneybags weren't that easy to approach these days. Without proper training, you couldn't really penetrate their guarded residences. I was likely to get busted before I even started and spend the last weeks of my life behind bars – if their bodyguards didn't put me to rest in a local graveyard before that.

Next. Could I win some money in a lottery? Or in a game? Chances were minimal but you can't win if you don't try. I made a mental note to set aside a few hundred for a casino. Let's see if Lady Luck had the hots for me.

Now. What else? Where could you find lots of money in one place? A bank sounded about right. So should I maybe go around shoving scribbled notes to unsuspecting tellers, *Put all the money in a bag—I have a gun*? Wonder if they're trained to deal with that sort of emergency? Bullshit. So they'll offer you a few handfuls of whatever they happen to have in the till, big deal. Even if you manage to escape unscathed, you'll have to rinse and repeat the whole procedure a couple dozen times.

Besides, Mom would end up taking the money back to them. Which was where they'd fleece her for every penny she'd ever had. Having said that, why raid a bank when you can nicely apply for a loan? I was an old respected customer, successfully self-employed. All I needed to do was to bring along lots of paperwork confirming my healthy income. So that's what I'd do, then: straight back home to pick up the papers. And the business plan I'd drafted the other day would come in handy, too.

The teller sent me directly to the manager. He was the one dealing with large loans and he turned out to be a lively gray-haired gentleman with a definite Jewish air about him. He listened to me rather skeptically and began leafing through my paperwork, pouting his lips. He must have come to a decision as he nodded.

"Very well, young man. We seem to have finally left the credit crisis behind us. The President is all for supporting small businesses and we'd be stupid not to listen to him. In your case, I believe I can see some potential. If you keep applying your head as you've been applying your hands, you might get something out of it in the end. A hundred thousand is a bit too tall, don't you think? You just won't need it so we're not giving it to you. But twenty... say, thirty thousand – I think we could manage that. So let's see what we can expect back from it."

The manager moved the keyboard closer and tapped away. Every now and then he'd stop and move his lips, peering at the text on the screen. Then he frowned and leaned closer to the monitor. I tensed, sensing things weren't going as planned. The manager looked up at me. Shook his head. Then he pushed the keyboard away and sat back.

"Tsk, tsk, tsk. I have to admit I thought better of you, young man. I'm sorry about your situation, I really am. So here you are asking me for help and I'm quite prepared to give you some money like you were my own son. And all you're doing you're setting Jacob Finkelstein up for an unrecoverable loan? Feh! Didn't you know that your ID card had access to your medical records? In case of interest, all one needs to do is apply for them. And our interest in you is quite understandable, don't you think?"

The man looked quite upset. I wished the earth could swallow me whole, like when I'd wetted my pants back at the nursery school. Being caught *in flagrante*, red-handed... As far as crooks went, I was pretty lousy – I lacked the nerve. My cheeks burned as I rose from the creaking chair.

"I just meant to leave some money to my mother. She's sick, you know... I'm sorry," I mumbled, avoiding his stare.

I stepped toward the exit when the manager barked, "I'm not finished with you yet!"

He waited for me to turn back to him and went on, "I can't say I don't sympathize with your situation. But it doesn't mean I can allow you to defraud me. You're blushing – that's a good sign. So allow me to give you some advice. Every bank has access to your data and that includes gray-market dealers too. So I suggest you give them a miss. All they'll do they'll make sure you don't live as long as you had hoped. Even a retailer won't offer you a consumer credit over ten thousand rubles without checking his computer first. You know what I mean? *Under ten thousand, in major retail stores.* You understand?"

He looked me straight in the eye as he enunciated the last words.

Had I understood him? You bet.

"Yes," I said softly. "*Under ten thousand, in major retail stores.*"

The man lowered his eyelids, pushed the forgotten paperwork pile across the desk toward me and nodded at the door. "You can go now. God help you, young man."

* * *

Strictly Confidential

To Security Service Curator General Alesiev V.A.

The experiment results report No 118/2

Location of the experiment: The detention room of the Federal Security Agency
Subjects: 20 detainees of various age, ethnicity and gender
Exposure world: Virtual Eden 6.51
The experiment results showed that the first incident of 'getting perma-stuck' took place after five hours of uninterrupted exposure. The last one occurred on the seventh day. The following eighteen days of virtual exposure did not bring about any further results. Seventeen of the subjects proved susceptible to the perma mode effect. Their bodies sank into a coma-like state. All attempts to resuscitate them by use of pain shocking, drugs and CPR procedures didn't render any result.
At this stage we can conclude that the perma mode is irreversible. The FIVR-located personalities of

affected individuals—the so-called 'perma players'— did not show any reactions to the termination of their respective host bodies.

Upon completion of the experiment, all bodies were buried at the FSA disposal site (lots 411-431). The FIVR server infocrystals were recycled in accordance with Procedure 719.

Chapter Two

For the next five days I was really busy. The feeling of time slipping through my fingers pushed me harder than any number of motivational coaches. Had I lived my whole life as if every day was the last, I'd have been driving a Bentley before I turned thirty.

For a start, I raked together whatever cash I had. That included collecting a couple of pretty well written-off debts. One of the debtors was reduced to hiccupping, amazed at my aggressive stance. It didn't amount to much—about three grand give or take, of which four hundred and a whole precious day were wasted on repeat exams in a private clinic. All they did was confirm the initial diagnosis. The only difference was that their doctor insisted that I be admitted straight away for some proper care and a possible few extra weeks—or months—to live. I told him very nicely that I'd think about it, then legged it. Vultures.

I splurged five hundred more on a casino. Actually, I was on the point of winning a couple grand, but that wasn't what I'd come there for so I kept betting on color doubling up after each loss. In theory, provided there were no limitations to the size of your bet or your wallet, you might just end up in the black if you quit in time. But my particular wallet had quit after having backed black seven times while the wheel kept throwing up just reds. The croupier suppressed a smirk. As if I didn't know that he could come up with any number he pleased. What he didn't know was that I was staking my life, not just my money. But it wouldn't have changed jack shit.

For three more days I was doing the rounds of the retail stores buying on credit cell phones, game consoles and other such electronic junk. In the evenings, I'd drive to the market and flog it for a third of the real price.

Now I sat in a burger joint, my aching legs stretched out under the table, my stomach reluctantly digesting whatever artery-cloggers they had on the menu. Pointless trying to lead a healthy lifestyle. I was entitled to whatever I fancied, be it food or activity. Should I smoke a cigarette? Shame really, considering how much effort I'd put into doing cold turkey only a year ago. Right. What was on my agenda for tomorrow? First thing I needed to pop by the lawyer's and get a letter about parents not assuming responsibility for their children's consumer credits. Just in case a bailiff paid Mom a visit after my death.

I didn't like the way it sounded. After my death, bah. From the lawyer I had to go back home and sort through my digs. I had to decide what to give away and what to take to a boot sale. The rest was going straight to the dump. I didn't want strangers – or Mom even, for that matter – to rummage through my underpants and dusty mementos. I also needed to go through my photos and paperwork and trash the more personal items. Then, back to my retailers to ruin their insurance statements by a few more cents.

My iPhone vibrated over the slippery table top, gradually sliding to the edge. I didn't recognize the number so I kept watching the gadget's suicide attempt. On the ninth beep it plunged and leapt down onto the tiles.

I caught it halfway to the floor giving a wink to the picture of a pretty young mother complete with kid who observed my actions from the phone screen. "Yes."

'Max? Hi. This is Olga from Chronos."

I glanced at the clock. It was well past eight. "You seem to be working long hours. Be careful they don't run you into the ground."

I heard a short polite laugh. "Not at all. I'm already finishing. You're the last on my call list," her voice grew serious. "So, have you decided anything?"

"I'm afraid I haven't," I shook my head as if she could see it. "It's too expensive. No way I can afford it. Some other time, maybe? Some other life?"

"I see."

Was it my imagination or was the sympathy in her voice genuine? Or was it still her sales pitch?

"Max, I... I'm not sure you know but our company has access to our potential clients' medical records. In case something needs checking, you understand..."

I winced. In this electronically-controlled world, privacy was quickly becoming obsolete.

"So I know all about your situation. My mom died of cancer three years ago, too," she faltered and sniffled. I could see her wiping the corner of her eye with a Kleenex trying not to smear her mascara. "This was what influenced my decision to work for Chronos. But there's something I want you to know...

Max," her voice grew stronger. "Cryonics isn't the only solution. There's another option, too."

I pricked up my ears. "Which is?"

"Have you ever tried playing computer games? Those online multiplayer ones?"

I winced again. "I used to. A lot. Really a lot."

"Are you a professional gamer, then? You know all about these things, do you?"

"No, I don't," I crumpled the paper napkin and shoved it into an unfinished soft drink. "You need to earn serious money to be called a pro. You must use your skill to help push the product, or at least to farm elite items to sell, or rush newbies. I was a regular hardcore shithead, excuse my French. Spent twelve hours a day playing. I've pissed away my friends, my girl and my studies. Only when my Dad died in a car accident and my Mom was left on my hands handicapped for life, only then did I manage to pull myself away from the monitor. I freaked out and formatted the disks. Since then I don't even read gaming news for fear of a relapse."

Olga sniffled again. I made a mental note not to go ballistic every five seconds. I was getting too easy to wind up. My nerves were like live wires.

"I'm sorry, Olga. I'm just tired. And it still hurts me to talk about it. So what's that option you mentioned? What's that got to do with gaming?"

"Have you ever heard anything about going perma mode? You haven't. That's funny. It's all over the news these days. Even on television. Officially, the problem doesn't even exist. State TV won't touch it with a barge pole. But us – despite all our aggressive marketing tactics, our customer database has dropped seventy percent. That's sensitive information, of course, so I haven't told you anything-"

"Just spit it out," I butted in. "I don't give a damn about your sensitive shit. What's this perma stuff you're on about?"

"Please understand, I'm not an expert. I don't think I can explain it correctly. Look it up. It's all over the Internet."

"I will. Thanks for the tip. I owe you one. Do you like champagne?"

"I prefer flowers."

"Agreed. Flowers and champagne," I couldn't help smiling.

I thanked her some more and mumbled a hasty goodbye. Then I jumped into my trusty Korean tin can and headed back home, the new hope forcing my foot down. In less than an hour, I was sitting in front of my computer screen taking in search results.

The Internet community was in a frenzy. Apparently, about two years ago, gaming blogs, portals and clan forums had been flooded with the first scary reports as more and more people had become stuck in a game for good. Nothing could sever the person's connection with the game server, not even unplugging the Internet and shutting down the capsule. Later, it turned out that the person's mind didn't need a connection as it bled into the game world leaving its empty shell outside, devoid of identity.

No one was sure of the existence of those unlucky enough to *get perma stuck* (or *go perma mode,* or *get digitized,* as some had put it) within a basic game of chess or Tetris. Nor would you envy those whose mind was locked inside various tanks, fighter planes and other combat simulators. No matter how much you loved your fighting gear, getting burned alive dozens of times a day scorched inside a tank's red-hot hull had become many a gamer's personal hell—literally.

Luckier were those perma-stuck inside full-feature worlds of multiplayer online games. Billions of square miles of their premises offered a well-developed social structure and a life virtually indistinguishable from reality. Apparently, quite a few victims were happy enough to escape there. No need to work or study, no worries about tomorrow, no staring into the mirror contemplating your flabby body and spotty (or, alternatively, wrinkled) face. Within FIVR, you were tough and strong. You were your own master. Certain population categories had come to appreciate a virtual life over their current existence.

The handicapped and terminally ill would attempt to go perma mode in the hope of obtaining new healthy bodies for themselves, however virtual. Some of the more computer-literate senior citizens took their places inside FIVR capsules looking forward to immortality, especially desirable when life is already slipping through your fingers. They were joined by those on death row. Star-crossed lovers, too, instead of hurling themselves from a cliff in one final embrace, chose a suitable world to get stuck in. Tolkien's fans and historical reenactors with their dreams of being reborn as Elves, dwarfs and mages entered capsules in an ecstasy of anticipation. The statistics pointed at a growing suicide epidemic raging among the unlucky seventeen percent immune to the perma mode effect. They craved being digitized. The timing was fatally right.

Governments sounded the first alarms. New laws restricted the duration of full-immersion capsule time. The state monitored every game server containing even a single perma player. Official statements promised that such servers would never be disconnected.

No idea how I'd managed to miss all that hoo-hah. My fingers trembled as I kept digging deeper and deeper into the Internet. Cigarette butts floated in empty coffee cups after I'd rummaged the cupboards for a long-forsaken pack of Camel.

I met the morning by the open kitchen window, drawing on the last cigarette. My eyes watered. The coffee I'd drunk was now churning in my stomach. But everything inside me cheered at the news. This was it. This didn't involve paying a king's ransom for being deep-frozen like a drumstick. This was an honest-to-God hole to escape into giving the Grim Reaper the finger.

I still had a lot to do. There were technicalities to consider: which capsule would allow me to bypass the preinstalled timer restricting immersion type and duration? Numerous freshly-baked perma forum gurus recommended aiming for a week or two of full immersion, but how was I supposed to last all that time without food, water and medication? Lots of people had successfully answered those questions for themselves: all I had to do was dig for more info and process it wisely choosing the solutions that suited my particular situation. A dozen manuals and video guides were already downloading. The links to several dodgy sites that sold FIVR jailbreak chips were already sitting in my Favorites. Open browser tabs glinted with scary-looking pictures of multi-stage IV drips and saline canisters. Things had begun to cook. The technicalities proved doable, after all.

I still had to choose the world to go to. I had to decide who to play and how to do it. I had tons of sites and forums to peruse. If you set aside two weeks for the attempt itself, it left me with five to seven days to do the research. Way not enough. It was hit or miss. Time to bet on zero!

* * *

From Wikipedia:

AlterWorld is an MMOG (massively multiplayer online game) first released in May 203X.

Number of players: 48,000,000, with an increase of 1,400,000 new players each month.

Connection type: 2/3D FIVR capsule. Immersion types: full/restricted.

World size: 552,126 square miles, with an increase of 4,633 square miles each month.

New territories, NPCs, mobs and quests are generated by an AI group controlled by AI Ray31.

World administrator: AI Crimson9

Deposit and withdrawal of real funds and virtual property sales topping $42 billion a year.

Chapter Three

The cooler fans whirred. Massage rollers stirred. With a hum, the seat heating kicked in. The FIVR capsule was waking up from sleep mode. The initial checks flashed before my eyes. Self-test. Operator connected. A 3D Desktop menu unfolded in front of me.

I mentally knocked on wood and started AlterWorld's game client. A second's delay as it ran an automatic upgrade. I fed my credit card information into the registration form and, ignoring the endless scroll of the world's description, headed straight for the character generation menu.

Choose character.

"High Elf."

For your information: High Elves are recommended for experienced players only. The High Elves' religion of Gods of Light makes them a legitimate prey for all the supporters of the Fallen One. Furthermore, the City of Light which is their capital and start location borders on the Dark Lands. Although the city itself is well-fortified against the Fallen One and his henchmen, the neighboring locations can already bring encounters with beings of the Dark. Are you sure you want to choose this race?

"Confirm."

Congratulations! You receive +1% racial bonus to Intellect at each level.

This what might seem like a negligible bonus had compelled me to choose an Elf. An extra 100% Intellect could tip the scales in my favor already at level 100. Even though it definitely complicated my way to the top levels, it stood to reason that the time spent leveling up was nothing compared to top-level playing. The end reward was large and quite tangible, worth every bit of the creators' pain in the butt. Because, let me tell you, the top levels do not end the game. This is only where it starts.

Choose class.

"Warlock."

For your information: Warlocks are the Fallen One's secret worshipers and are attracted to the Dark forces. Other Light races tend to shun them. Certain NPC characters may refuse to interact with you. Quite a few vendors might jack up their prices when dealing with you.

On reaching level 10, a Warlock will have to decide on a specialization. You will be asked to choose between Necromancer and Death Knight. Both are despised by the Powers of Light. Many quests and locations will be closed to you. If you still want to play for the above classes, we suggest you choose a Dark or neutral race.

"No way!" I shouted at the interface. "Necro is my favorite toon since the day I was born! I don't want to be the umpteenth Archer Elf. I don't give a toss about your politically correct standards. *'We advise, we suggest, you had better...'* Yeah, right. I'm going to screw your template. I'll be the first Dark Elf among your cute-and-cuddly Paladins. *Confirm!*"

Congratulations! You receive +1% class bonus to Intellect and +1 to Spirit at each level.

Choose your starting characteristics. You have 25 points. Use them wisely. Once the character is created, no further changes are possible.

The descriptions of the five basic attributes hovered before my eyes.

Strength: increases attack power and the chances to block and parry. Controls the amount of weight a character can carry. Weight overload may lead to speed loss.

Intellect: increases the character's ability to learn non-combat and magic skills. Increases spell power and mana pool (1 Intellect point gives 10 mana points). Boosts mana regeneration.

Agility: increases movement accuracy, improves evasion and chances to score a critical hit in both close and long-range combat.

Spirit: boosts Life/mana regeneration.

Constitution: gives hit points (1 Constitution point gives 10 Life points).

A miserable chain of zeros glowed against all of the above characteristics. Oh well. Every junkie knows that the preparation process is just as sacred as the shooting up. Off we go, then. The dumb housewife solution would be to set all the parameters to five and enjoy the perfect balance. Won't do. Specialization is the key. Better to be the best in one area than average in everything. I much preferred a surgeon's knife of specialization to the Jack-of-all-trades' monkey wrench.

So. What is our ultimate goal? Who is a Necro? He's a caster: a character with the ability to cast spells as his preferred method of attack. He can also summon various forms of the undead, such as skeletons, zombies, demons and so on and so forth. Virtually a small group consisting of a mage and his pet tank.

All the damage is done by casting spells at long range, no hand-to-hand combat, no risk of the opponent delivering direct blows. Which means that Strength, Agility and Constitution are secondary to the part.

Now the Spirit is vital, even though you don't regen much mana in the course of the combat. All the meditation only starts once it is over. Sure it's a pain wasting three full minutes sitting on your backside, but not as bad as running out of mana in the middle of a fight. All right, that little was clear. Let's start from the end:

Agility, 0

I just hoped I wouldn't be all thumbs. Zero agility wasn't for that, anyway. It only meant that I wasn't getting any racial bonuses.

Strength, 3

I needed some to lug around my gear and the loot dropped by monsters. It wouldn't be cool to rush to the store every time I got myself a dagger or some ore.

Constitution, 5

I didn't want them to blow me over with a feather. So I went for it, even though it meant having a hard time parting with every point.

Spirit, 6

I needed every drop of mana I could get. My life would be hanging by a thread thousands of times, depending on whether I had enough mana for that one final spell.

Intellect, 11

I splurged every remaining point on it. You just couldn't have enough mana. It was either not enough or more than you could handle.

Accept new characteristics. Are you sure?

"Confirm."

Congratulations! Welcome to the character visualization menu. Choose your avatar's appearance.

The figure of an Elf turned slowly before my eyes. It was male by default which saved you a couple of unpleasant surprises in the process of virtual sex.

I played with the scroll boxes choosing a build similar to my own. Okay, so I did add a bit of muscle here and there and made the six-pack more pronounced. Who wouldn't? With any luck, I'd end up living in this body happily ever after.

I turned to the facial options. The avatar had my face—also by default. These days even pocket calculators came with cameras so I shouldn't have been surprised to have found one inside the capsule. The menu offered a lengthy choice of premade portraits in various stages of cuteness or brutality. I ticked a few and started clicking the randomizer. Surprisingly, I liked one of the resulting images. It was a rougher version of myself: a rugged soldier with a seen-it-all air about him. I pushed the slider closer to the virtual thirty years old, added a few gray strands for believability and saved the character.

Choose a name.

Good question. Wouldn't be nice to walk around a fantasy world with Max as a moniker. I clicked through the name generator until I decided on Laith. In Elven, *La* stands for "night" and *Ith* means "a child". Child of Night. I had to take my character seriously. The deeper the immersion, the higher the chances of going perma.

"Laith."

Welcome to AlterWorld, Laith. You're facing an eternity's worth of infinite possibilities.

While I tried to fathom out that last bit, the virtuality faded, enveloping me in thick darkness. I waggled my head peering into nothing.

Sounds came first. The trees rustled. A grasshopper chirped. A bird whistled. Then the world gained light and color, smothering me with its beauty. A forest breathed around me. No; not just any old forest: *the forest*. Have you ever been to an Elven forest? I hadn't. But you'll know it the moment you see it. A little brook murmured nearby; butterflies fluttered their wings amid sunrays dancing in the foliage. The depth and intensity of the image left you speechless. I crouched and ran my hand across the carpet of flowers and grass.

"Hi there, new world," I whispered. "I'm afraid we're stuck here together for a long time."

A long-eared hare sprang out into the opening. As I stared at it, a prompt popped up:

A young rabbit. Level 1.

Okay, a rabbit, not hare. Same difference. Enjoy your freedom, buddy, while I'm in a good mood and have better things to do with my time.

Only then I noticed the game interface. Semi-transparent chat boxes; the life, mana and experience bars; the belt with quick spell access slots empty as yet. I played with the transparency levels and shuffled the icons around. I had plenty of time to adjust it all to suit my own needs.

Talking about myself. My rags were just about that—rags. A light-colored canvas shirt and a pair of gray canvas pants. As far as Elves went, I was a bum. Never mind. Just give me some time to level up a bit, and I'll be wearing Versace tights, or whatever they crave here.

I opened the character menu and saw that my clothing was purely decorative. It didn't offer any extra stats or even armor points. I opened my shoulder bag and discovered a water flask and a piece of bread. Another prompt popped up:

Food plays an important role in the AlterWorld territories. A hungry character's ability to restore life and mana may dwindle to a stop. Keep an eye on your avatar's satiety levels. Some food and drink may bring extra boost bonuses. In order to be able to make your own food, you need to practice the cooking skill. See Wiki for more details on bonuses and skills.

For a second, I regretted letting the rabbit go unscathed. A roast is always better than a moldy roll. Never mind. There had to be more game out there.

My eye was caught by a blinking FIVR connection icon. I opened the menu and grinned with delight.

Ping: 3 milliseconds. Packet loss: 0%. Connection type: 3D. FIVR time restrictions: none."

Yess! It worked. Deep inside, I'd had a nagging feeling that either the chip or the patch would let me down despite all the testing, throwing me out of FIVR four hours later. That would be the end. Bye, world. Hello, tombstone.

The next thing I saw was the lit-up pictogram of the quest tab. I switched over to it and discovered a new quest.

Greetings, young Warlock! A long and hard road lies in front of you. Few have mastered it. But a journey of a thousand miles begins with a single step. You're about to make this first step. There is a cave not far from the place where you first arrived in this world. Old Grym lives there, a hermit. Local peasants think he's mad and shy away from his company. But Grym is still the Fallen One's faithful servant. He will help you. Follow the deer trail to go east. It will take you to your destination.

Aquilum, The Dark Guild Master of the City of Light.

A guild master without a guild. Okay. When I'd chosen the race, I'd also studied the city map. I could bet my bottom dollar there'd been no Dark Guild on it. Unfortunately, time was an issue so I had to leave Googling it till later. Shame. I had to play blind – no guides, no manuals or prompts. Just like in the good old days.

Having said that, many an unexpected surprise could open to the newly initiated. We'd just have to see. In the meantime, all eyes east. Time to hop down the bunny trail.

I checked the interface for its built-in compass and walked, unhurried, down the barely discernible trail. The total absence of weapons and spells worried me a little. Failing everything else, I could do with a stick but the forest was clean and neat like a parkland—not a broken branch in sight.

I didn't have to walk long. Another couple hundred paces, and the trees gave way revealing a gloomy opening. Gray grass crunched underfoot. Ancient trees rose skywards, their trunks silver with moss. The sun had disappeared behind some stray cloud.

Yeah. Welcome to a Necro's lifestyle. I squinted at the scene. And the worst was still to come: graveyards and zombies, and the tombs of the undead.

I wondered if I'd jumped the gun with my character choice considering the local visualization levels. Should I exit while I still could and change my colors to some sort of daisy-picking, tree-hugging Druid? Deep in thought, I kicked a toadstool or some such mushroom and volleyed it right into the wide hollow of a gnarled oak tree.

"Never mind," I murmured, looking around. "No good changing horses midstream. I'm an evil warlock, and no mistake. Where's that cave of his? Come out, you old schemer! We've got business to discuss!"

And there it was, his cave: a cliff green with age hiding in the shade of a straggling fir tree. The entrance was wide enough for me not to have to duck. I made a shaky step or two, guided by the fire gleaming within its bowels. Another step, and I entered a large room dimly lit by a single wax candle. The light played games with the shadows, not letting me see properly. Then a shadow stirred in the corner and stared at me with two odd-color eyes.

"Grym the Hermit?" I asked, not quite sure, and stepped back, feeling the air around me for something heavy enough to pass for a weapon.

The dark shape in the corner grumbled and stepped toward me.

"You bastard," my fingers finally closed around something handy by the wall. I raised the object and took a swing. "Name yourself, O monster! Which eye you'd prefer to keep, the blue one or the yellow one?"

The shadow gave a skeptical chuckle and stepped into the light. A goblin, short and gray-haired, shook the cobwebs off his patched robes and looked over me.

"Put the broom back, young warrior," he said in a thin voice.

Shuffling his worn-out sandals, he walked around me, shaking his head with disapproval. "So! The young Elf has decided to defect and follow the Fallen One? Are you craving adventures or something? What do you want to prove? Many an immortal has visited me here but few have reached true power. They'd hover around for a few weeks before disappearing from sight. They have no will – no passion."

I lowered my head to him. "Sir Grym, one does not choose one's parents. It's not my fault I was born an Elf. It was my own choice to follow the path of a warlock and with any luck, I shall prove it to you soon."

The goblin's grim stare bored a hole in me. "It might happen sooner than you think, young clown," he hissed in my face.

He swung round, reached for a heap of old rags and produced a bundle, wrapped in purest white cloth.

"In the name of the Fallen One who demands a sacrifice! Cut her heart out!"

The goblin pulled the fabric away and the cave echoed with a baby's cry. Tears welled in her bright blue eyes.

I recoiled. Something clanged against the stone. I looked down at a curved dagger now gleaming in my hand.

New quest alert! Demonstrate your loyalty to the Fallen One.
Quest type: general
Execution conditions: may vary
Reward: unknown

They were all raving mad here. Conditions may vary? My knuckles cracked as I squeezed the dagger. "How about a goblin's heart instead? Will it do for my demonstration of loyalty?"

I stepped forward and stabbed the sickening face. At least I tried to. The air around me thickened and I froze in the awkward pose of a dueling musketeer.

You've been immobilized. Spell cast: Chains of Bone.

The goblin sniggered and waved his hand. The baby bundle disappeared. I collapsed in a heap on the floor. The dagger clattered on the stone and skidded away.

You've been knocked down. Damage sustained: 12 Life points.

"Cool down, young Elf. It was naught but an illusion. You shouldn't listen to everything your priests tell you. We need no butchers here. The Fallen One isn't the dark side. He's just one of the Pantheon who lost his battle for the right to have his place in the Temple of Heaven."

Quest completion alert: Demonstrate your loyalty to the Fallen One. Quest completed!
Reward: Twilight Blade.
Your relationship with the Dark Alliance has improved!
Your relationship with Grym has improved!

"Arise, Warlock," Grym helped me back to my feet. "And pick up that dagger over there. It's not an illusion. Don't be scared: there's no blood on it. I'm pleased with you. Haven't been so pleased for a long time. And still you'll have to walk the walk, not just talk the talk."

New quest alert! Demonstrate your loyalty to the Fallen One II
  Quest type: unusual
  Execution conditions: may vary
  Reward: unknown

I couldn't believe it. The old fusspot just wouldn't stop, would he? Should I try my new dagger out on him? Then again, he might come up with something better than the immobilization trick. I reached for the dagger and concentrated.

Twilight Blade. Binds on Pickup. Thrust weapon. One-handed.
  Damage 1-8. Speed 1.8. Durability 80/80.
  Effects: 7% Tremble Hand debuff probability in attack slowing counterattack 24%.

Not bad for a letter opener. Some newb rogue would pay a nice pile of gold for a sticker like this. A couple of them could have enough DpS to last me through the first ten or fifteen levels. The effect was a dream, stripping your opponent of a quarter of his power. Not that I really needed this sort of gizmo. I didn't think I'd have to do much tanking, apart from possibly the first few levels when I might have to perform a bit of blade-rattling. After that, casters like myself with no armor and negligible life would come down after just five or six hits from average mobs, so I could forget close combat.

I attached the dagger to my belt and lowered my head in a bow. "I thank you for your lesson and your gift, Sir Grym. What I would like to know is where could I study Warlocks' magic skills?"

The goblin cocked his head and rubbed his chin in thought. "I could help you as far as my knowledge goes. You do have a gift for magic and I could give you access to it. Come back when you gain some strength. Now go. I am tired."

The goblin turned his back while a mysterious force grabbed my elbows and dragged me along the passage before pushing me out.

"Wait up! I need to ask you about the Guild..." I tried to shove my head back inside but the invisible taut wall pushed me away.

Grym the Hermit is busy. He doesn't want to see you. Come back when you reach Level 5.

Bastard. I ignored the alert box but another one chimed in its place:

Quest completion alert: Meet Grym the Hermit. Quest completed!
Reward: Magic abilities unlocked.

Skill Tree Available: Blood Magic
Skill Tree Available: Summoning
Skill Tree Available: Death
You have 3 Talent points available!

Much better. I slumped onto the grass and started opening the menu windows.

Main growth options: raising the undead or summoning otherworldly monsters. The former started off as weaker and also called for summoning ingredients, but theoretically, had a higher leveling potential. The summoning line had a choice of skills on higher levels that would increase your raised monsters' power. It also offered quite a few buffs and bonus items for your raised pets.

Summoned creatures tended to be stronger than the raised ones until at a certain point they hit their limit. Not quickly, but somewhere in the area of level 200 things would come to a complete halt. Beyond the Archdemon there was nothing left to summon. Of course, he had his own buffs and skills but the statistics showed that a top master specializing in summoning showed a 6% higher win rate in combat. Which was nothing to sniff at. For me at least. The bulk of players lived online as they did in real life: *I want it all and I want it now, and let tomorrow worry about itself.*

I made my choice, minus one Talent point.

Congratulations! You've learned the spell: Summoning the Undead
     Cast time: 4.5 sec
     Mana expenditure: -30 (+15 for each caster level)
     Ingredient: The Soul Stone
     Properties: Raises the undead. See Wiki for more details.

I followed the link. Never a bad idea to find out as much as you can about your main weapon. As it turned out, the only way to get hold of a Soul Stone was to have it dropped by a slain opponent. You couldn't buy or steal it, nor trade it with another player: you could only get it by killing a monster – or have it killed by your group. In the latter case, the chances of the corpse dropping the stone shrank progressively, depending on the number of group members and, most importantly, their level gap.

The power of the raised creature was relative to its level when still alive. Plus item bonuses, buff bonuses, minus a certain quotient depending on the player's class and level. Mana expenditure, too, was related to the char's growth. That was clear enough. The spell itself remained unchanged but what took 30 mana at level 1 demanded 1530 mana at level 100.

Now the Blood Tree. This was where we were soon going to have a variety of DoTs, auras and debuffs.

DoTs were a Necro's second most powerful weapon. Unlike wizards or mages, a Necro couldn't deal a large instant damage. But he could cast a bunch of spells which would reduce the target's life fast enough. And the spells themselves, apart from dealing basic damage, could have some very nasty extras, from slowing life and mana to poisoning or even draining them. Lots of little tactics and combinations made it perfect for anyone clever enough both with his head and his hands.

At the moment, I had two such spells available: a slowing one and a stronger poisoning one. The latter could deal more damage which was a good thing but still I was going to take the first one. As I leveled up, the slowing effect would grow, ultimately freezing the target 60-70%, and that could save my skin quite a few hundred times. Good thing.

Congratulations! You've learned the spell: Thorny Grass.
Cast time: 1.5 sec
Mana expenditure: 15
The spell deals 5 points magic damage every 4 sec for 16 sec. Slows an enemy target 11%. See Wiki for more details.

Excellent. I had one more Talent point left. Moving to the Death Tree.

At the moment, I had two spells available and I was dying to get both.

The first one was Life Absorption which, apart from damage, drained the target's life. The damage wasn't much but it ignored the player's magic resistance and, most importantly, helped me heal. And you couldn't underestimate the importance of healing for solo classes.

The second one was Bone Shield. It created a magic shield capable of absorbing a certain amount of damage.

I gave it a good thought and decided to go with the healing one. The shield I could still take a bit later on one of the next levels. From what I could remember from the official guidebook, I would receive 3 more talent points at level 5, and then one point for each level once I chose my specialization.

Congratulations! You've learned the spell: Life Absorption.

Cast time: 1.4 sec

Mana expenditure: 14

The spell deals 8 points of magic damage to an enemy target simultaneously giving you 8 XP points. See Wiki for more details.

I moved my newly acquired spells into quick access slots. Having finished, I jumped to my feet and shook the dirt off my pants. Great worldbuilding. The developers showed amazing attention to detail.

The leaves rustled. The sound of footsteps came from the trail. In a moment, a beefcake Elf walked out into the open, his recognizable celebrity face distorted with fear, his childlike eyes wide open. He carried no arms and wore the same kind of sack shirt as myself. I took my hand off the dagger. "Be welcome, O young Warlock!"

The Elf's eyes opened wider. "Are you Grym the Hermit?"

Can't he read or what? "I'm his younger twin. Go in, be my guest," I pointed at the cave. "He's expecting you."

"TY," the young Elf forced out sliding past me toward the entrance.

I shook my head, unbelieving. How mature. I just hoped the developers took the players' age into account. That way, he'd have to prove his loyalty by slaughtering a rabbit. Alternatively, he could get a snail and a hammer—all that snot and gore hitting the cave walls.

Nah, I was going too far. Most likely, the FIVR capsule's parental guidance was blocking out all gore, pain and erotic sensations and activating the profanity filter.

Right. Time to get going. I'd been in the game already for an hour and a half and hadn't risen beyond a level one newb. Not good. Judging by the map, the city's East Gate was only ten minutes' walk away. The new players' starting locations were situated behind the city walls allowing endangered newbies to escape to the safety of the guards, if needed. I could do a bit of hunting while heading toward the city. These backwoods had to have more rabbits and other game to offer than the newbie-infested city limits.

Chapter Four

My first attempt at hunting very nearly became my last. I saw a small rabbit just off the trail. The pop-up prompt helpfully informed me that the rabbit was young: level 1. Sounded like my size. Without the Soul Stone, I couldn't raise a pet for myself. Never mind, I could manage. Level 1 casters often had to do a lot of tanking.

I selected the bunny as target and activated the Thorn Grass. The earth bubbled around the poor creature entangling its paws with the thorny blue foliage. The life bar above the rabbit's head shrank about ten percent. The bunny emitted a shriek—a call, rather—and bounded toward me. Simultaneously, a God-awful beast of a rabbit cleared the nearby shrubs.

An adult rabbit. Level 3.

Whatever. It was going for me. Embarrassing, really: to be killed in your first fight—by a rabbit.

Rabbit or no rabbit, I hurried to move the target to the big bastard and cast a slowing DoT. A resist. The target couldn't care less about the spell. A magic resistant rabbit—what kind of world was that? Another try, and I managed to slow it down a bit.

You've been bitten! Damage sustained: 6 points. Source: the young rabbit's teeth. Life: 54/60.

The young rabbit's missed! He attempted to punch you but failed!

Indeed, the young 'un had caught up with me and was now busy trying to hurt me. I drew the dagger and slashed the bunny in the face. His life bar shrank some more. I activated Life Absorption.

The Young Rabbit has sustained 8 points Damage.
You've received 8 points Life. 60/60.
You've been bitten! Damage sustained: 17 points. Source of damage: the Adult Rabbit's teeth. Life 43/60.
You've been bitten! Damage sustained: 5 points. Source of damage: The Young Rabbit's teeth. Life 38/60.
You've been clawed! 12 points Life lost to the Adult Rabbit's claws. 26/60.

Shit. Time to leg it. I still had the slowing spell on both bunnies—enough time to run off a couple dozen paces, turn round and cast Absorption twice.

The Young Rabbit has sustained 8 points Damage!
You've received 8 points Life. 34/60.
The Young Rabbit has sustained 5 points Damage!
You've received 5 points Life. 39/60
You've received Experience!

Die, you bastard!

My attempt to slow down the mature rabbit resulted in more aggro and two more bites. My life dropped into the orange zone so I had to retreat double quick. Had it dropped into the red, my speed would have dropped accordingly and no way I could've escaped. But even so my advantage was minimal. I just couldn't shake the big bunny off for enough time to cast the spell safely.

After another hundred paces, the forest parted. We scrambled out into a clearing. Far beyond, I could make out the city walls and dozens of players swarming below as they interacted with each other, doing a bit of leveling. I marked the position of the gate towers and the paved road and bolted for the main gate, counting on the guards. Surely they would stick up for a player and not let a mob into town. A monster rabbit, never thought I'd live to see the day. Total embarrassment.

Shame about the experience lost: I could kiss it goodbye if the guards finished the mob. But I spoke too soon. The big bunny shrieked. I looked behind me and yanked the brakes on. Some level two rogue stepped in the bunny's way and prodded him with two short swords.

Now I had to think fast. Whoever inflicted more attack damage on him would get the experience.

I began casting the Life Absorption double quick. An extra bit of healing wouldn't go amiss.

You've received Experience!

Got him. By then the young rogue was almost finished, too. Either the bunny had critted him or the kid had already been low on life when he'd aggroed him.

I dragged my feet toward the rogue sitting on the ground next to the bunny and tending to his wounds.

"Thanks, man."

"Thanks don't fill a purse," he answered with a smile as he unwrapped another bandage.

"You can't be Russian, surely?" Naturally, the game translated the entire content into the player's mother tongue, but that was a bit too good.

"Ukrainian," he offered a blood-stained hand. "Cyril a.k.a. Cryl, Elf rogue level two."

"I'm Max. You can call me Laith. A new Nec," I shook his strong fingers looking over the gradually disappearing blood stains.

Having said that, it really had hurt when the bunnies were making a quick job of me. Blood had splattered everywhere. Not an agonizing pain, but pain nevertheless. In the heat of the fight, I'd taken it for granted forgetting I was stuck inside the FIVR. The high pain threshold and overall acuteness pointed at the *profound* FIVR immersion. Actually, the officials recommended to switch to a basic 3D type at the first signs of pain. The deeper the immersion, the more real it is for your brain and the higher the risk of getting perma-stuck. The likes of myself were discouraged from visiting virtual worlds with high authenticity levels. But in this case, you couldn't please me more. My hyper sensitivity increased my chances tenfold.

In the meantime, Cryl was done with his bandages which brought his life up to fifty percent.

"A Nec, you said? In all frankness, you're either a masochist or an idiot. Then you may be someone with lots of patience and an ambition to match."

I smirked. "You forgot lots of spare time. But I could use some patience, sure."

"Good to know that," Cryl was already stomping his feet impatiently, looking for a new challenge. "Any plans? I still have two hours left until forced logout. Fancy grouping up?"

A message alert popped up.

Cryl the rogue has invited you to join his group.

Mechanically I adjusted the interface to semi-transparent as I gave it some thought. On one hand, I had to go to town and get myself settled down. I wasn't an on-and-off player—I was about to stay here. No innkeeper would rent me a room for free: I needed to get hold of some money for lodgings, food and some clothes. On the other hand, I still had plenty of time till sunset and even though a rogue wasn't the best choice for a tankless group, it was probably more fun together. I wanted to get a better look at him. You never know, we could become friends.

You've joined a group! Group leader: Cryl. The loot rule: Master Loot.

Cryl rubbed his hands. "Excellent. If we could just get ourselves a warrior tank and a healer, that would be awesome."

He yelled at the top of his lungs, "We need a tank and a healer, levels one to four. For the Gnoll Hill."

He turned to me and winked, lowering his voice, "Preferably young females. Preferably those who haven't yet armored themselves up to their eyebrows. AlterWorld must be the place. You wouldn't meet so many scantily clad cuties at a Miss Universe final."

He laughed so infectiously that I smiled, too. Funny guy.

In actual fact, the overstrung spring inside me was relaxing, I could feel it. Since I'd learned about my diagnosis, it had been a race against time. I kept pushing myself, too scared of dying on my apartment floor just two feet away from the phone. Having said that, what would I have done with it? Now the peaceful beauty of my new world poured inside me filling my drained soul and washing out all the stress and weariness. I closed my eyes, took a deep breath and smiled as I exhaled.

"You're not stoned, are you?" Cryl sat up.

"No. Not at all. It's just so... beautiful. What about those gnolls?"

"They're some awesome mobs. The caves are their main dungeon, three floors, levels 10 to about 25. Too early for us. But around the caves, there're tons of petty gnolls there, like workers, gatherers and messengers. Those guys are begging to be killed. They might drop a bracelet which you can sell to other players or to the Caravan Guards' Master. Each bracelet gives you the same experience as you get if you kill a gnoll. Donators—I mean those who invest real cash into the game—buy them like hot cakes. They'd rather spend an hour screaming their heads off to buy bracelets by the dozen, and then bingo! they're already level 10 or even 20, no need to waste rabbits. Talking about rabbits. You'd better check yours before it stinks."

All the rabbit dropped was two strips of rabbit meat. I could sell it to a shopkeeper or start to level the cooking skill. I was curious how much I could make by the end of the first day.

The location chat was busy:

I'll pay 1 gold for Red Bear ID. PM me.
WTS Blue Gladiolus or trade for top Druid gear.
Lvl 8 Mage LFG
WTB gnoll bracelets. Gray 20 copper, black 50 copper, red 2 silver. Preferably in bulk.
WTS +350 xp buff, duration 3 hr. Price: 1 gold. I'll be sitting by the East Gate.
Janis is PK! He's by the creek, go kill him!
You PK! You killed me first!

Cryl guffawed. "Kidz!"

"Yeah. Useless truants. It doesn't look as if we can find anyone. Let's just go and then decide."

"Okay. Let's go."

Seven minutes of brisk walking along the forest edge brought us to a low hill range. The foothills were teeming with players—groups and solos—busy pulling monsters and attempting to take them apart.

As we watched, a low-level warrior pulled a train of three gnolls and a level 8 gnoll overseer. In less than a minute, the whole party was lying dead having only nailed two of the lower gnolls. Greedy-eyed, we watched the monsters leave. The overseer, badly crippled as he was, was too tough for us.

"Cryl? You don't happen to have any distance weapon, do you? To pull a mob or two?

"I don't," he tut-tutted. "In theory, I can use slings and crossbows. Only I haven't saved enough yet to get myself any. I bought a dozen bandages and that was the end of my dough."

"I see. In that case, I'll be pulling them with DoT and then hand them over to you. Wait here."

I ran up the hill and looked around. About a thousand feet away I noticed a cave opening, surrounded by a low stockade with some dirty flags flapping over it. The ground around me was streaked with trails which were swarming with gnolls. The closest to me was a hurried level 3 messenger. I selected him as target and activated the Thorn Grass. The gnoll swung round, hissing, and trotted toward me. I cast Life Absorption and scrambled down the hill, taking cover behind Cryl's back.

He descended on the mob, stabbing him wherever he could reach. But he couldn't pull him off me fast enough as I'd aggroed the mob too much. Ignoring his opponent, the monster went for me.

You've been hit by Messenger Gnoll! Damage sustained: 16 points. Life 44/60
You've been hit by Messenger Gnoll! Damage sustained: 12 points. Life 32/60

It did hurt. I drew my dagger and we started slicing the mob up between the two of us. At the same time I was trying to cast Life Absorption. Twice the mob's hits made me lose concentration until finally the spell went through. I only had 20 Life left when the gnoll yelled something and passed away.

You've received Experience!

Just. I was no tank any way you looked at it. Cryl crouched by the body and lay one hand on it.

With a clank, the mob's money divided between the group members. I was now two coppers richer.

"He's got a letter on him too, binds on pickup," Cryl said. "Some low-level quest or other. Want it?"

"You can have it. He's not our last messenger."

We sat quiet for a couple minutes restoring life and mana while Cryl was changing his bandages.

"That's it, the bandages're finished," he said with regret. "I only raised the skill to 3 points. I have to heal 4 hits at a time."

"You shouldn't have started. It will cost you too much at the first levels," I watched a small group who had arrived running in their underpants and were now busy touching their graves and picking up their gear that appeared in place of tombstones.

I rose. "You ready?"

I waited for his affirmative and flew up the hill. This time I chose a single gnoll worker lugging a basketful of earth. DoT, two Life Absorptions, a quick hand-to-hand and finally, the welcome experience message. This time it was much easier: the worker had less life than the messenger so he packed up in no time.

Cryl bent over him, surprised. "Listen, he's got this Soul Stone here but it won't let me touch it. WTF?"

"Oh. Jeez, it has to be mine," I hurried to the body and picked up a nondescript little blue rock.

The Soul Stone. Contains the soul of a level 4 gnoll. To raise him, use the Summoning the Undead spell.

I moved the spell to the quick access panel, clenched the stone and cast the spell. With thunder and lightning the stone crumbled to dust. The earth parted right in front of the crouched Cryl's nose, letting out a Gnoll Zombie. The kid yelped and rolled out of its way. "You could've told me!"

"I'm telling you now," I guffawed. "Meet Rover, my pet. He'll be our tank."

I spent some quality time in the raised creature's custom settings. I renamed the zombie Rover and entered a few commands: as you'd guess, mainly *Attack! Heel! Off!* and others in the same vein. I ended up with a level 3 pet—not too bad considering that the stone fell out of a level 4 monster.

"Now it'll be easier. Sit!" I told Rover and ran to pull another gnoll.

The zombie was nothing to complain about. He made a decent tank pulling the aggro to himself and not letting the mobs kick our poorly armored asses. His hits were mediocre, 5 to 7 points, but he could take the heat and absorb damage. The farming process—that is to say, monotonously grinding mobs—started to fall into a pattern.

The next three mobs we ripped apart no problem. We even got another messenger, this time level five. After his death, a blue shimmering mist enveloped our bodies and the two of us gasped in unison.

"Ding!" I said.

"Up!" Cryl yelled.

Congratulations! You've reached Level 2!
Racial bonus: +1 to Intellect
Class bonus: +1 to Intellect, +1 to Spirit
5 Characteristic points available!

I opened the char's menu. After a second thought, I added 3 points to Intellect, 1 to Spirit and 1 to Constitution. Would do for the time being.

Intellect had already reached 16 which gave me 160 points mana—not bad at all for level 2.

"You finished with yours?" I asked a vacant-looking Cryl.

"Five more sec. You can start pulling."

"Okay," I nodded and began climbing the hill feeling I'd been living there for ages.

Whereby I immediately stumbled into two gnoll gatherers.

"é*@&!" the toothy bastards yelled, lunging at me.

" é*@ç$!!" I yelled back, tumbling down the hill. "I'm bringing a train! Two gnolls! Rover, attack!"

I set him loose on the farthest monster. Now I had to deal with just one. "This one's ours," I shouted to Cryl.

He nodded and stepped in the mob's way. After some quality clashing of steel and humming of spells, the gnoll collapsed.

You've received Experience!

While I'd fought, I kept casting Life Absorption as the quickest way to deal damage. So now my life bar was still at 100% while Cryl's hit indicator hovered in the orange zone.

The next moment, my zombie groaned and crumbled to dust. His gnoll, albeit rather bruised, turned round and went for us.

"Wait, step aside. Let me first," I told Cryl and lunged forward burying my dagger in the gnoll's eye.

You've dealt 14 points critical damage to Gnoll Gatherer!

Immediately I stopped his clawed paw with my face. His next punch landed on my liver. Jeez, it hurt.

Cryl joined in from behind my back, adding a lovely aggro-generating bunch of hits. The monster swung round to face him which allowed me to step back and cast Life Absorption again.

More hits. A flash of magic.

You've received experience!

Got him.

"Great job, man," I offered Cryl my hand. "You did it by the book."

He shook my hand, his face serious. "So did you, cutie. No fuss, just got the job done. You're a legend."

We smiled to each other.

"I hope one of them at least happens to have another Soul Stone," I said. "My zombie has given up the ghost."

"Let him rest in peace. He saved his master's life. Lived like a dog, died like a hero."

"Must be his karma," I mused watching Cryl crouch by the bodies.

More coin-rattling. I now was five coppers richer.

"When it rains it pours," Cryl cheered up. "This one has a Stone and a gray bracelet, call it twenty more coppers in the till. Oh. The other one's empty."

"You can have it all. I'll have the next one. But give me the stone, please. Time to resuscitate our hero."

The hero didn't live up to his fame. The raised zombie was level 2. I really needed to get myself some stuff with pet leveling bonuses. Never mind. I'd have to change the pet when I got another stone, as simple as that.

Two minutes for regen, then I rushed off to get us another gnoll.

The farming process continued without a glitch. I kept pulling a gnoll or sometimes two. The loot was meager to say the least: a few coppers apiece plus miscellaneous trash like rusty daggers, some ore, and all sorts of statless items. Once or twice we had a couple of quest bracelets albeit gray ones. To get anything cool you had to head deep into the caves.

Two hours into the game, we were level 5. Each had a couple hundred coppers and a dozen bracelets to show for our trouble. On top of that, I got myself twelve Soul Stones although now the raised zombies' levels 2 to 4 didn't look like much compared to my level 5.

We were meditating after a complex fight with two more gnolls when a high-level Druid dashed past right between us.

"Train!" he yelled and disappeared, speed-buffed.

"What did he say?" Cryl turned to me. Then we were swallowed by a mob crowd chasing the druid.

No idea where he'd pulled so many. He must have fallen out of a cave and bolted for the city not bothering about the low-level guards. It had worked for him. But not for us.

They spent us in five seconds flat. Still sitting, I took two crits to my back, jumped to my feet for a second and collapsed again. A crimson haze clouded my view.

Warning! You have died in battle. In a moment, you'll be respawn in your last bind point.

You can change the bind point using a special spell or artifact. A grave containing all your gear and the contents of your bag will appear in place of your death. Only you can pick them up. If you don't reach your grave within three hours, it'll be teleported to the nearest city graveyard.

* * *

Strictly Confidential
From the Edict of the President of the Russian Federation On Creating the Sharazhka Classified Experimental Facility

Installation Bunker 9 to be used as the server farm.

Deploy Eden 17 Office Deluxe as the experimental virtual environment software.

Register and assess all nationals categories 4, 4a, 7 and 11.

Shortlist all C1-listed nationals such as researchers, analysts and top engineers.

Lay the groundwork for potential digitizing of all the individuals over 65 years of age and those with serious health problems.

Chapter Five

When the crimson haze had dispersed, I found myself back at the forest opening where I'd entered AlterWorld. It wasn't quite the same, though. The forest had become black and white. My ears didn't detect a single sound. I was hanging suspended inside a slowly rotating crystal sphere. A countdown blinked before my eyes,

Resurrection in 5... 4... 3...

With every count, the world gained in intensity and depth. At zero, the sphere burst with a jingle sending an avalanche of sounds, smells and colors.

I shook like a wet dog and congratulated myself on my safe homecoming.

I wasn't too upset about my sudden death. I'd lasted five levels which wasn't bad for a newb: they normally died in droves in the beginning. I was a bit annoyed with the power-happy idiot who'd dragged his train across the whole location right over the low-level players' heads. The guards by the city gates would make a quick job of the gnolls. But how many others had they destroyed on their way? Even worse, they could lose their enemy and fall behind halfway, then walk back to the caves and attack the young hunters from behind.

I squinted at the location's chat room window and grinned. The place was rife with swearing as everyone cursed the idiot runner.

I hadn't lost my hard-earned experience, though. Up until Level 10, the game was in evaluation mode and didn't even demand paying. There was no penalty for character death and the player was temporarily immune to PK—that is, couldn't be killed by other players. By the same token, he or she couldn't choose specialization, either. Nothing new there: a drug dealer often offers the first fix for free. Admins had to have their pound of flesh. It wasn't for nothing that the corporation's annual profits were on a par with an average country budget.

My group chat was flashing. Cryl didn't mince words. "Did you remember the motherfucker's name? I'll blacklist him. I'll kill him every time I see him!"

"Relax. This is game in progress. Plenty of this sort of stuff. Leave it. What you gonna do now?"

"Dunno. It's eight minutes till forced logout. I'll have to play 3D, and I hate it. After FIVR, it feels as if you're handicapped. I might check the shops to get rid of the loot and pop into the guild to get my Talent points from the Master. And you?"

Good question. I'd made level 5. I needed to go see Grym. Then I had to do the corpse run to retrieve my gear. And it was high time I started thinking about somewhere to spend the night. Enough leveling. Time to get some daily bread.

"Same, more or less," I answered. "I've added you to my friends list. Until next time. It's been a pleasure playing with you."

"Likewise. I've added you, too. What time are you online, normally?"

Oh. I didn't want to lie to him. Nor did I want to talk about my hopes and plans. You never know. "I'm taking some downtime, sort of. I'm online whenever I want. Knock and it'll be opened, if you know what I mean."

We exchanged smilies and I left the group.

I inspected the white diaper that seemed to be an integral part of my body and lovingly felt my six-pack abs. They looked great. Freebies always do. How many years had I been dreaming of something like that? This is what made the virtual reality so appealing: it made the impossible possible as your dreams came true making you river deep, mountain high. Millions of slim fat girls, billions of pretty uglies...

I swatted a mosquito on my neck (what's wrong with those developer people? Or was it AI's idea?). Using a compass to find my bearings, I walked to the hermit's cave.

As I went, I killed half a dozen rabbits. The level-one monsters gave no experience but added a few points to your hand-to-hand skills and dropped enough meat and pelts in the bargain.

This is how Grym saw me this time: in my underpants, lugging an armful of pelts and meat in front of me. Seeing his eyebrow raised in silent question, I attempted to restore my plummeting authority. I bowed and laid the game on the table.

"This is all for you, dear Grym. You live alone and spend a lot of time reflecting on lofty subjects. I don't think you have time left to hunt. These pelts could make a nice cloak, too."

Skeptical, Grym poked at my offerings and wiped his finger on his robe. "I thank you. You could use a cloak yourself, by the looks of it. Did someone wrong you? Has our forest been sheltering robbers? What's all this about you walking around in your undies?"

I gestured vaguely. "It's complicated. A lady's honor..."

Grym guffawed. "I knew I could help you."

He rummaged through some heaped-up rags and produced a scuzzy bundle. Unfolding it, he shook it a few times raising a cloud of dust and handed me the garment. "There! At least you'll have something to cover your privates."

Your relationship with Grym the Hermit has improved!

You've received an item: Wind-Patched Cloak
Item class: Unusual
Durability: 8/40
Armor: +5
Intellect: +2
Appearance: -10

Well, well. That was a poisoned chalice. Despite its excellent characteristics, wearing it in public could prove not just embarrassing but also harm me in quite a few ways. They could easily bar my entry to the city or raise shop prices. Even deny me a quest, whatever.

"I thank you, dear Grym. I have another question to ask you. My hunt has been a success and I've acquired a bit of experience. Could I stay to become your apprentice?"

Grym nodded. "I can see you didn't waste your time here. Indeed, you deserve a reward."

Congratulations! You've received 3 Talent points!

"Now go. I need some rest. Come back when you've doubled your strength."

The familiar gust of wind grabbed me under my arms and led me out gently but insistently. I'd forgotten to ask him about the guild—again. Not expecting much, I tried to wriggle my way back in, but received a message to come back once I reached level 10.

I neatly folded the filthy cloak, placed it onto the wet grass and sat down. The idea struck me with its significance. I was supposed to become one with the world. Only why had I put the cloak under my backside? Was I afraid of getting virtual hemorrhoids or of soiling my snow-white underpants?

I'd done it mechanically, just the way I'd have done it in real life. How wonderful was that? Come on, brain, keep growing into this reality. This wasn't a game anymore, this was our new home. Keep going.

I opened the Magic Talents panel and stopped, thinking. I needed to summarize today's experience. I was quite pleased with the Necro. The pet was great, Life Absorption did the trick and the DoTs were awesome. Still, I'd have loved the spell to deal more damage and heal me better accordingly. So I had to invest an extra point into it.

Congratulations! You've learned the spell: Life Absorption II.
Cast time: 1.7 sec
Mana expenditure: 22
The spell deals 15 points of magic damage to an enemy target simultaneously giving you 15 XP points. See Wiki for more details.

At the moment, I was still unable to improve the summoning spell. Once I was level 10 and had chosen specialization, the summoned creature would be losing one level per player's every five. At the same time, once a Necro reached level 10, he had a new skill tree branch open, dedicated to pet leveling. It could give the pet a considerable boost. A Death Knight, however, could only have that branch open after level 30 which meant that for Death Knights, pets became superfluous. So most Death Knights would level into some sort of armored high-DpS tanks while more group-oriented ones became the same with a higher potential of casting curses and mass debuffs.

I kept switching between branches and reading descriptions until finally I opted for two Death Skill spells. That gave me a damage-absorbing buff and control magic in the shape of a freezing spell.

Congratulations! You've learned the spell: Bone Shield.
Cast time: 2.9 sec

Mana expenditure: 23

This personal buff creates a magic shield that absorbs 40 points Damage. Duration: 20 minutes.

Congratulations! You've learned the spell: Deadman's Hand.

Cast time: 1.5 sec

Mana expenditure: 19

Freezes target for 2 sec

I moved my new skills to the quick access panel. There were still plenty of slots left, enough for ten spells. In the future, however, I might need to think carefully to decide which spells to stash away and which to have at hand at all times.

I tested them straight away. First I activated the shield. A mesh sphere snapped open around me and, spinning, disappeared, replaced by a new buff icon just out of focus.

In search for a target to test my control magic, I headed for the Gnoll Hill. I still had to pick up my stuff. After a couple dozen paces, I met another bunny rabbit.

I selected it as target and glanced at the spell icon to activate it.

The ground bulged. A decaying hand reached out and grabbed the bunny's leg. The rabbit screamed and struggled, trying to free itself. Really, this spell stuff could leave you scared for life.

The rabbit finally pulled itself free. It covered the distance between us in three long leaps and clawed me with a vengeance. A familiar knock was followed by a combat chat report telling me that the

Bone Shield had absorbed 6 points Damage. It worked.

The shield lasted five more hits. Not much, but this was only the first step. Later, when I invested more points in it, I could expect more impressive results. Most importantly, the shield absorbed all damage allowing you to concentrate on casting the spell despite the hits received.

I finished the bunny off, picked up the pelt, refreshed the Shield and trotted toward the Gnoll Hill. You couldn't miss it. My tombstone flashed like a beacon on the interactive location map. I selected it as destination and set off, following the compass which showed direction and distance left. How's that for GPS?

The scenery had now changed. The forest parted, letting me through toward the hills. Wary of entering the aggro zone bustling with mobs, I gave a nearby gnoll gatherer a wide berth and crouched by my grave. I knew of course that back in the real world I was probably heading toward the same end: a small wonky tombstone with my name on it. Surreal, wasn't it, me sitting here admiring my own sepulcher. I reached out to shake off the dust and dirt. The stone vibrated under my touch.

Laith, Level 5. The grave will be teleported to the City of Light North Graveyard in 2 hrs. 12 min. Would you like to collect your possessions?
Yes/No

Yes. The tomb crumbled leaving behind a bag with my stuff. I kicked the gray handful of dust. I'd live.

The moment I crouched over my bag, a female player ran up the hill pulling a train of four gnolls. She rolled down the slope and turned to face the mobs. Despite her level 11, she seemed to have bitten off more than she could chew: a level 7 overseer and three level 5 workers.

The Elfa didn't seem to know what she was doing. Such low-level mobs wouldn't give her much loot or experience.

A growl came from behind her back. A messenger gnoll rushed to his buddies' aid and joined in the scuffle. The Elfa noticed the new threat and shook her head in dismay. Our eyes met. She sized up my embarrassing level-five frame, bit her lip and hurled herself back into what now looked like a hopeless fight.

I dug deep into my bag and produced the dagger and a couple Soul Stones. Too little time to rummage through the rest of it. My mana was at 75%. Not much but I couldn't allow a lady to be wasted in front of me. I'd done enough eye-averting in real life pretending I had no business in other couples' fights.

I raised the pet—only a level 3 zombie, dammit. Had neither time nor mana to raise another one. Rover, attack! Try to pull a gnoll or two, pup, even if for a moment.

The gnoll who until then hadn't received a single hit and hadn't gained any aggro, switched to the zombie with ease. I chose the weakest messenger and cast the DoT. Then, clutching the dagger and the spare Soul Stone, I lunged into close combat.

The Elfa didn't appreciate my efforts. She swung her bangs out of her eyes and snapped, "Run, you idiot!"

"Relax, babe. We'll do 'em," I shouted back. She shrugged and continued fighting.

Now it went quicker. A gnoll collapsed, slain by the girl. The zombie groaned and gave up the ghost. My opponent followed. We were two against four.

Throughout the brief fight I kept casting Life Absorption, aiming to kill my gnoll as fast I could. Which was why I came out of it with full life but only 25% mana. The gnoll worker—who'd kicked the shit out of my pet without losing more than 20% hits—now turned his attention to me. I received a couple of hearty blows before I could cast Deadman's Hand, draw out and raise a new pet. Success. Level 4.

Rover, attack! His mana dropped to zero. I waited a few seconds for the pet to gain some aggro, sneaked up behind the gnoll and put my Grym-awarded hole puncher to good use.

When we had done away with all of the Elfa's enemies but one, her life bar was already blinking in the red zone. The girl was finished. Still, she was full of surprises. She raised her sword and shield and activated some spectacular skill, completely restoring her life. Apparently, she wasn't a warrior but rather some hybrid class. With her heavy steel armor, the sword and the shield, could she be a paladin? The amazing skill had to be Holy Hands which allowed you to heal completely once every twenty-four hours. I remembered reading about it at some forum or other. She could have probably done without me. Then again, maybe not.

The wet blades kept slashing flesh. Another minute's worth of growling and two agonizing sobs later, we'd run out of enemies. We, however, were still very much around.

Taali—that was her name—began looting the corpses. The Elven auto translate offered a prompt: *Ta* meant *a fox,* while *Ali* stood for *a shadow.* A Shadow Fox.

Apparently, I shouldn't have wasted my time waiting for signs of appreciation. "You're welcome," I mumbled and began dressing. The rustle behind my back stopped and I could barely hear her guilty voice.

"Thanks..."

I turned round and gave her an encouraging smile. "Not bad for a train. What was it, a pull gone wrong?"

Taali stood there looking over me as if wondering whether I was worth continuing the conversation. She swung her bangs again, squinted at the sun and lowered herself into the meditation position. Finally, she condescended, "Yeah, kind of. Pulled a couple too many."

"What's the point? Virtually no experience, is there? They're small fry for you."

Taali cringed. She didn't seem to be too forthcoming. Still, eventually gratitude got the best of her. She took the gnoll's bracelet out of her bag and showed it to me.

"Do you farm them?" I asked. "Are they for sale?"

A tear glistened in the corner of her eye. Biting her lip, she nodded and looked away. I just didn't get it. She got sadder with every question. Better leg it, if I didn't want to get stuck here for the next thirty minutes serving as a shoulder to cry on.

I crouched over my gnolls and picked up my loot. The gnoll worker dropped a couple coppers and a pretty blue stone.

"Sorry," I couldn't help asking. "One last question. Any idea what this is?"

She barely glanced at it. "A laurite. A rare drop. In a shop they'll give you three silver for it."

"And if I offer it to other players?"

"Could be four. Could be more. Those who level jewelry, they buy them sometimes."

Then she lost all interest in me and stared ahead, meditating, as she waited for hits and mana to restore. The girl could use a bit of cheering up. I fumbled with the stone and handed it to Taali. "A present. Take it. From a surviving partner in combat."

She looked up at me, surprised, and shook her head with apparent regret. "No, thanks. You keep it."

"Just take it. It's my second one today," I lied.

I forced the stone into her narrow hand and smiled. "I'm off to town, then. Good luck and good hunting!"

The girl gave me a shy smile. "Thanks."

"Come on, Rover. Great deeds await us!"

Chapter Six

After a few more minutes of leisurely walking along a well-trodden path, I reached the edge of the forest with a view of the town wall. Here, Rover and I had to part ways. I was running a high chance of walking into a guards patrol, and Elven warriors wouldn't appreciate a zombie visitor. I had to tread carefully in my dealings with the city.

Higher-level Necs normally had a special spell to put the raised undead to rest. I was forced to utter the trigger word, "*Begone!*" With a guttural groan, the zombie fell apart. Its translucent soul flitted up to the skies while the earth swallowed the remains of its flesh. RIP, dude.

The small area in front of the town gate bustled with people. Players and NPCs—that is, AI-controlled characters—buzzed in and out of vendors' stores, either getting rid of petty loot or stocking up on basics. Others searched for hunting parties to join, while even more were busy striking deals in the safety of a popular public place.

I wasn't in a hurry, though. The vendors weren't interested in offering a fair price, exploiting the gamers' penchant for a quick sell. Not that I had something to worry about, not with my few pelts and petty gnoll loot. Still, it wouldn't hurt to investigate. I networked with the vendors a bit, memorizing a price or two to compare them later to those in town.

Ten guards stood watch by the gate, mainly level 100, plus a sergeant and a mage, both 130.

I respectfully spoke to the mage, "Would you be ever so kind, Sir, to direct me somewhere where I could spend the night without too much strain on my wallet?

He looked me over with his typical customs officer's eye and laughed. "Won't do your wallet any good, straining. It shouldn't even try to cough if you ask me. Past the gate, turn left and keep walking until you come to the market square. Ask for the Three Little Pigs Inn. Their prices are set to suit any wallet.

I froze, thunderstruck. The mage guffawed. "Love to see this sort of reaction from your kind. The inn belongs to the Olders clan. Was started by one of the Immortals. Get off then, I've got work to do. And keep an eye on your wallet. It may be thin but our local guys aren't squeamish."

I nodded and followed his instructions. Leaving the thick tunnel of the gate tower behind, I turned left. The lower city didn't resemble the Elven architecture of online fantasy pics. A normal medieval hole in the wall, some of it dusty, some clean. Could be cleaner, actually. Closer to the city center, a few celestial blue spires showed in the haze. There, a magic beacon glinted next to the iridescent bubbles of dome shields. All the sightseeing had to be done there: the palace buildings, the arsenal, guilds, banks: whatever captured the game designers' fancy and whatever wealthy players could afford to invest into pricey Sector A lands. Whenever I needed a break from gnolls, I could always go there for a peek.

I found a small shop that traded in everything that moved. Their prices indeed were five percent higher than those behind the city limits. Now I was nine silver richer. The coins bore a profile of a stern-looking Elf against the backdrop of the rising—or, alternatively, setting—sun. Add to them two handfuls of coppers I'd farmed earlier, total count 260. Their current rates were 1:100 silver to copper and 1:10 gold to silver. In total, I had one gold, one silver and sixty copper.

On top of that, I could sell a dozen bracelets for a couple dozen copper apiece. Virtual gold converted to real-life US dollar at 10:1. So all of today's loot wouldn't buy me a beer in the real world. Not good.

My eye caught on a shop sign which featured, besides various blades and armor, also a few octagonal Soul Stones. That's funny. I pushed the heavy door and walked in. A scarred beast of an Elf glanced over me, his heavy eyes deceptively indifferent.

"We don't buy trophies," he murmured and continued polishing an equally beastly broadsword.

"I wouldn't dream of insulting you with any such offer, Sir Gunnar," I said in my best deferential voice. "As I walked past your shop, I noticed the picture of some excellent stones. I have a funny feeling I've seen them somewhere before. Could you be ever so kind to tell me what they are?"

Gunnar cringed, exposing an excellent pair of fangs. Did he have an orc or two in his family tree?

"Keep going, stranger. These stones don't drop from rabbits nor are they sold at jewelers'. You don't look as if you can afford rabbit crap."

That hurt. Really. I undid my bag strings and dug in for a handful of stones. "How's this for crap?"

His face froze. In one smooth swift motion, he stole past me and barred the door. Then he turned round and laid his heavy hand on my shoulder. I braced myself for more trouble.

"Welcome, brother."

Quest completion alert! You've completed a secret quest: Dark Brotherhood.

Reward: 1 gold

Your relationship with the Dark Alliance has improved!

Your relationship with Gunnar has improved!

Congratulations! You've received Achievement: The First in Town. You've become the first person in this town who has completed the quest: Dark Brotherhood.

Reward: +100 to Fame

Fame points are extremely valuable. Famous characters can access unique quests, develop rare abilities or acquire secret knowledge.

See Wiki for more details.

New quest alert! Dark Brotherhood II.

Quest type: secret, rare

Find the Fallen One's secret supporters in the cities of the Lands of Light. Every new worshipper will double your reward.

Would you like to accept the quest?

Good. Time to breathe a sigh of relief. That guy Gunnar looked scarier than he really was. And I got a ton of goodies to boot. Accept: *Yes.* No question about it.

The unexpected piece of gold doubled my property. My inner greedy pig, still mourning the loss of the laurite, purred as it bit the coin to make sure it was real.

And I couldn't even have hoped for Fame points. Normally, to get them, you had to either engage in some back-breaking farming, earning weird achievements like Rat Catcher that you got for every ten thousand rats trapped. Alternatively, you could get them for some truly rare, if not unique, achievements in a particular location or city, if not in the whole world. Without Fame points, you couldn't even dream of having access to the elite game content open only to the Top 5% of all players.

In the meantime, Gunnar busied himself laying a small table groaning with liquor and cold cuts that filled the shop with the smells of ham and herbs. My stomach rumbled prompting a new system message:

Warning! You're hungry and thirsty. Your body can't regenerate Life points or mana any longer. You need to eat and drink ASAP!

The Elf guffawed. "You must be starving, brother. Do me the honor. Here in this rathole of Light one has nobody to share a drink with."

He proved to be a convivial type. He drank and chatted non-stop, mixing city gossip with his own elaborate war stories. He asked me to come again soon promising all sorts of discounts for his Dark brother. When I asked him for some Necro gear, he gave me a skeptical look and shook his head.

"I'm dealing mainly in heavy steel armor. Chainmail is the limit. But you casters, you don't even wear leather, only rag shit. Same with weapons. A shield, a long sword, a mace—all this I can get you. Had you been a Death Knight, we'd have equipped you like you wouldn't believe it. It wouldn't cost you that much, either. I've got some interesting things here."

To prove his point, he jumped from the table and disappeared into a store room. He came out almost straight away with a weird-looking bone staff, all carved and plated with gold and silver—or it could have been solid gold, I wouldn't know. Gunnar pressed some knob causing the top of the staff to explode in a dazzle of black flame. It flared out and swallowed all the light around it creating a dim hemisphere a couple feet in diameter.

I peered at the object:

Staff of Dark Flame
Item Class: Rare
Effect 1: +5 to Intellect, +3 to Strength, +3 to Constitution
Effect 2: +3 to the raised creature's level when hand-held.
Effect 3: The raised creature deals +10% fire damage.
Effect 4: Each of the raised creature's attacks has 2% chance to ignite the target, adding 210 points Damage.

What a beauty. Wish I had two of them. Actually, if you had indeed had two, would their effects add up?

"Oh wow. How much?"

Gunnar darkened. "If it wasn't for class restrictions, it would cost at least five or six hundred. But right now who would need it in this fucking hole? It's yours for a hundred. Really," he got so worked up he knocked down a wine glass and didn't even notice it, "in the Dark Lands, you'll sell it for a couple grand."

I shook my head, disappointed, and hurled my flat wallet onto the table. Dammit. A Nec would kill for a staff like that while a Death Knight wouldn't even know what to do with it. A Knight's pet is too weak, so raising it even ten levels wouldn't make much difference. And the Knight would be stupid to use up one hand holding it instead of holding a shield or a two-handed sword. What a shame.

Overall, we'd enjoyed each other's company and parted almost as friends. I double-checked my directions for the Three Little Pigs and, swaying, continued on my way. It was getting dark and I really had to find somewhere to spend the night.

The inn wasn't difficult to find. You couldn't miss the enormous sign with three dancing characters looking happy as pigs in shit.

The door opened into a brightly-lit main room. Large and clean, it was crowded with tables and what looked like quite comfortable seats. About forty people—groups and singles—were busy chewing, drinking, talking and laughing. And there was enough space left for three times as many patrons.

No one paid much attention to me, even though my shabby appearance stood out in this roomful of high-level players. I approached the bar and addressed the imposing innkeeper,

"Good evening, Sir. I was wondering if I could rent a room for the night."

He cast me an ironic glance and went on polishing a beer mug, waiting for me to go on.

I raised an eyebrow. "Is there a problem?"

The innkeeper mimicked my expression making my heart twitch with jealousy. "Aren't you going to ask me for a job? Dishwashing, wood chopping?"

"I don't think so... Sir. You can always hire a Chinese android to do your chores. They will wash your dishes for a night, chop your wood for a week or stab a dummy with a wooden sword for a month. Doesn't interest me in the slightest. I'd rather pay you."

The innkeeper chuckled, pleased with the answer. "That's the way to do it. Don't take offense, kid. We get all sorts here," he waved his hand in the air, "Santa's little helpers... They'll slop around with the dishcloth until they learn that this type of quest—full immersion, mind you—only ends after sunset, so they vanish before you even catch their name."

"In all honesty, Sir, I'm often too lazy to take my coffee cup to the sink. Not that I'm proud of it but just to give you some idea of my opinion of that sort of quest, if you know what I mean."

"Absolutely. I've got just the room for you. Plain but clean. Perfect for a night or to drop one's bag in. One gold per night. With all respect, can't afford to let it any cheaper."

I shook my head in disbelief. He didn't want much, did he?

Seeing I was on the fence, the host stepped up on his persuasion skills. "Dinner's on the house. Plain but filling. You've never tasted beer like we have."

All right, all right, he won. I produced my gold piece and slammed it on the bar.

In return, I received a smallish key and some advice. "Room ten. Second floor. No going upstairs. Floors three and four don't like being disturbed. In case you don't know, The Pigs are owned by the Olders. The digitized clan, like most of our customers. So show some understanding. They don't play: they live here. Go sit at the table. Dinner's in a minute."

Great timing. I nodded my complete understanding and took a place at an empty table.

A couple minutes later, a cute waitress brought me a beer and a bowl of pickles. I wasn't hungry at all after Gunnar's exercise in hospitality, but when they brought in a plateful of fried potatoes... seriously, I just love the virtual world for being able to stuff oneself silly without gaining an ounce. It wasn't your junk French fries from the corner joint but true-to-God potatoes fried in plenty of fat in a heavy iron skillet with generous amounts of chopped pork and onions... For the next fifteen minutes, I was absent from both realities.

I was sitting there, happily stuffed, and finishing my second beer when the door opened letting in a strange couple. The man, tall and burly, bristling with weapons and armor, stomped in with a slim Elfa in his wake. She scampered along, clinging to the man's hand.

Replying to the patrons' greetings as he walked, the man brought the Elfa to the large gong in the center of the room. He reached for the mallet and offered it to the girl, smiling. As he nodded, she squeezed her eyes shut and hit the gong with all her negligible might. *BAAAANG!*

The sound still echoed in the corners when the patrons jumped up, applauding. The locals seemed all to know what was going on. Only a couple of strangers like myself stared around with confused smiles.

The man raised his hand asking for silence. "My friends. As you have all gathered, we have a newcomer. Let's be grateful to the perma effect for our second lives and for this adorable young lady."

The audience cheered and raised their mugs. The burly man went on, "Just think I was leaving through the West Gate yesterday morning and who do I see but this lovely newblette. Sitting there hugging bunnies she was, feeding 'em daisies."

The room burst into healthy laughter. The girl blushed and attempted to hide behind the man's wide back. Two brutal-looking female warriors, all leather and blades, started elbowing their way toward her from the back tables. They fussed around the girl, whispering, stroking and soothing.

"So! Last night I was coming back from war, same road, same gate. And there she was, the poor wretch, still level one, chasing butterflies. Really funny was the way she ran, sort of waddling, like a duck with both legs broken. All right, I thought. This morning I'm out again farming. And this character here is curled up by the wall sleeping. I couldn't take it any longer. I woke her up and spoke to her. Checked her for all the signs. She's perma all right. She's one of us now. What's your name—Lana? Or do you prefer Lanileth? Mind saying a few words about yourself?"

The girl faltered for a moment. Then she plucked up courage and spoke softly.

"My name's Lana. I'm eighteen. Cerebral palsy since birth. When my parents learned that I wouldn't walk, they gave me up to an institution and legally disowned me. When I turned eighteen, I was supposed to get social housing. But the new law had changed it to a monetary compensation. Which stretches nowhere. I had some friends who promised to help me. They took the money and disappeared. I... I was reading the handicapped persons' forum looking for some painless ways to end my life. And I found this perma thread there instead. I asked a few questions, the forum members suggested a few names and addresses. I went to some underground perma parlor. They gave me some papers to sign. I gave them the rest of the money. So here I am..."

The girl gave the room a timid smile. The burly warrior patted her shoulder, removed his gold-gleaming bracelet and slid it onto the girl's wrist.

Immediately the bracelet shrank to fit, as if it had always belonged to her.

"A gift. Otherwise it might take you some time to buy anything if you limit your leveling skills to bunny-hugging."

The audience clamored their approval. A line of givers formed, giving the girl a thin purple-bladed dagger, a stack of gold pieces; someone placed a pair of earrings on the table in front of her, then a ring, and yet another ring, glistening with a strange-looking gem.

I had nothing to give her but I got an idea. I walked out the door and came back in a minute with a bunch of little plain blue flowers that grew along the fence. They pleased the Elfa a lot. She blushed and hid her face in the flowers, apparently unaccustomed to human attention.

My knees gave way as a heavy hand slapped my shoulder. The burly man, already nursing a beer mug, gave me a wide smile. "Well done. I'm sure she'll appreciate that. Here, we're forgetting that girls want flowers, not cold steel."

Now was a chance to talk to a local. A *digitized* local.

"I'm afraid that's all I have," I nodded at my table. "Fancy another beer?"

He looked me over. "Well, if you're serious..."

He slouched in his seat, made a complex sign to the bar tender and turned to me. "What's that about?"

"It's my first day in the game. Just curious."

"So why are you sitting in a bar instead of hunting? Any idea what kind of folk we have here?"

I nodded. "Personally, I've got *nowhere* to hurry to. Got loads of time. Enough to do everything."

The warrior grinned. "Going perma?"

"Yeah. Unforeseen health problems. But provided it all works out, it could even be for the better. I seem to like it here."

"Well, whatever you say," the man echoed.

"What's gonna happen to the girl now? Are you accepting her into the clan?"

"Which clan?"

"The," I tried to remember, 'the Olders."

The man snorted. "Who told you I'm one of them?"

Shit. I'd completely forgotten that default settings showed nothing but a player's name.

I opened the menu and ticked a few boxes. Now if you concentrated while looking at a player, a prompt popped up over their head,

Eric. Level 109. Veterans.

Veterans had to be his clan name.

"I'm sorry," I said. "It's just that the innkeeper said that everything here belongs to the Olders. And I haven't had much chance to adjust the system settings yet."

"Never mind," Eric said amiably. "You're right about the old farts. They own quite a lot here. In any case, they prefer to stay in their clan castles or in their mansions within the gold line. You won't see them in a bar. They have their own watering holes. Fucking sharks. You see, it's all those old boys, some successful businessmen, a few millionaires even.

They all decided to start a new life. They shit money. They transfer some of it to AlterWorld and use it to buy and sell. And build. Actually, they've been quite useful with their money-making mentality. They can't help it. They've set up a proper bank as an alternative to the game one. A post office, texting services..."

My ear caught the familiar word, "Texting? You mean, texting the real world? From a real cell phone? How d'you do it?"

"How d'you think? Elementary. You PM a player positioning as Text—that's his nickname. In the message, you put the phone number and the text. And transfer him a gold piece. He sends your message to the number provided. It's not just one player, of course. It's a whole business."

The mind boggles. Weren't these guys great. But a gold piece... Was it the only price tag they had?

Eric watched my discouraged face. "Too pricey for you still?"

"Not exactly. The price is probably right. But I've just paid the only piece of gold I've farmed for a room. I've got another one that came with a quest I didn't ask for. But I'd rather keep it for a rainy day. You can't expect this sort of luck too often."

"Was it a girl you wanted to text?"

"No. Mother. She's worried sick, you know. For our parents we never grow. And she can't work out all this game shit."

Eric fell silent for a moment. "Go ahead, type it. I've got a subscription. You pay fifty gold a month and can text a novel if you want."

"Thanks, dude," I dictated a quick message saying that everything was fine, that I had it all worked out and lived in a good hotel. My headaches were gone and my appetite was back.

On hearing that last bit, Eric smiled but sort of sadly. "Just like back home. My mom was the same. I was an active-duty officer, six foot four, and she was checking if I was wearing warm underpants and whether I'd packed her homemade meatballs."

Seeing him overtaken by gloom, I promptly changed the subject. "This clan of yours, what's it about?"

Eric cheered up a bit. "Combat vets. Mainly the two Chechen wars, the second Georgian campaign and the Far East conflict. But we also have a few military advisors, foreign intelligence people, special forces, and even a few handicapped Afghan vets. No internal shit—no police or anti-riot men. They have a clan of their own. There's some sort of cold war going on between us. So you see, it's not much we can do with this chick. But we need to find her a place and something to do before she gets into trouble. Things aren't as easy as they seem here. We're now talking about building a nursery to train new players for the clan. We're short on healers and buffers. Normally we only get true blue warriors, if you know what I mean."

Honestly, I was quite surprised. I didn't expect to find so many professional military in the game.

Eric gave me a crooked grin. "I can't tell you how many of us are here. It's classified. Let's put it this way, it's a three-figure number. And as for why we're here... D'you know how I used the bathroom after the second Georgian campaign? You pull your pants down and clamp the drip. Then you unstick the plastic container from your hip, pour its contents down the toilet and stick it back on again. A frag in my stomach, half the bladder down the drain. Shit happens."

He paused. "Some motherfuckers made billions in army supplies. Those in the arms industry got their cut, too. And those on top helped them carve up the budget. And all the while young lost-eyed kids kept fertilizing the ground in strange lands with their blood. That's the way it goes..."

He turned to me. "D'you see that guy over there flirting with girls—blond hair, blue eyes? If you met him in the real world, you'd have had nightmares for a week. He spent twenty minutes keeping the enemy away from his APC, not letting them get close enough to finish off his guys. He was so burned that dogs pissed themselves with fear when they saw him. Do we still sound too many to you? Each of them here is a bodiless, soulless stump..."

He was right. Shit happened. But I had another question to ask him, too. "I've noticed a funny thing here. Whoever I speak to, they're all Russian. Your clan, too. Where are all the foreigners?"

"Oh, dude. You sure you read the Terms and Conditions? Or did you just tick the box? Relax. No one does. I didn't. I had it explained to me, too. The game localizes users using their IP addresses, their interface language, their address and credit card issuer. They know who we are and where we are from. So they throw us all into one language cluster using an algorithm that only the admins know. This is mainly a Russian-speaking zone. We have some Eastern European players, a handful of unidentified immigrants, but not many, just within statistical error."

"Wait a bit. And what happens if some Frenchie wants to play for the High Elves? What's he gonna do?"

"P-lease. AlterWorld is quarter of the size of the globe. Plenty of Cities of Light to go around. I have a funny feeling the developers split us up for a reason. Once we sorted out our internal differences, we might start a new world war. Now that's some serious money—real money. Today's billions are peanuts in comparison."

I gave it some thought. Actually, he could be right.

Overall, our conversation proved quite productive. As night approached, I walked upstairs, slightly swaying. I sleepily looked over the clean and comfortable little room, pulled off my clothes and shut out, ending my first day in the new world.

* * *

Strictly confidential

Experiment Log 425 of the Globe 4 classified facility.

Subject: male, 35 year old, healthy. Digitized in the virtual world New Amazons Build 0.827.

The player 'went perma' after 70 hours of full immersion. Further consecutive disconnection of the Internet, the game client and the FIVR capsule did not affect the digitized character.

All attempts to log into the same account resulted in a brief message:

Connection error. Player already in game.

On the fifth day after going digital, the player reached level 12. But none of his achievements were logged into the server database. Manual changes to the database, including account removal, did not affect the digitized subject. This allows us to conclude that the perma effect creates an independent copy of a game character not covered by the game world's database. All our attempts to directly manipulate the player have failed. The only possibility to do so is by indirectly controlling him via the game world and other characters.

Chapter Seven

I lounged in bed enjoying that blissful weekend feeling. No alarm clocks, no hasty breakfast before rushing off to work alongside equally sleepy and grumpy—never knew why—fellow citizens.

Birds' songs poured in through the open window. The heavy door all but blocked out the ground-floor sounds: quiet voices and the rattling of plates. Someone burst out in cheerful laughter. The smell of fried bacon tickled my nostrils. I stretched with a happy smile—my joints made no cracking or clicking—and sat up in one smooth motion, enjoying the sensation of a perfectly healthy body. The thought of its potential use intoxicated me. Enough larking about. Time to kill some gnolls. They had to be missing me.

Before I left I decided to spend my last gold piece on another night. The innkeeper scooped the coin off the bar. "What time should I expect you?"

"Not before nighttime, I suppose. Time to let some gnolls' blood."

He nodded his understanding. "Wait a sec. I'll arrange for some sandwiches."

Shit. I kept forgetting to eat. This wasn't real life where you could skip a meal. Here, once you're hungry, you'd better quit whatever you're doing double quick before you're flat out of mana.

"Thank you, Sir. I completely forgot."

The innkeeper gave me a knowing smile, like, he'd been young too once.

The red-faced waitress rushed in from the kitchen and handed me a sizable packet and a still warm flask. I looked inside.

Three Little Pigs Sandwich, courtesy of chef.
Amt: 5.
  Use: +3 to Strength, +3 to Constitution for 2 hrs.

Strong Herbal Tea
Use: Speeds up mana regeneration 3% for 2 hrs.

Surprised, I looked up at the innkeeper. "Are you sure? This stuff sure costs more than the gold piece I gave you for the room."

He gave me a wink, grinning. "On the house, kid. Eric gave me a whisper about you last night. You're one of the locals, almost. It's all right, really. Just enjoy your food."

I thanked him again, wistfully packed up the delicious-smelling goodies and headed for the door.

On my way to the Gnoll Hill I checked my friend list. Cryl was offline. But the sad Taali girl was there. I sent her a toothy smiley, just to cheer her up. A couple minutes later I received a cheeky winking face. My mood upped a few degrees. Life was moving on.

There it was, the hill from yesterday. Still lots of people but nothing like last night. I wasn't going to join a group, not quite yet. I wanted to play solo for a while to explore my char's potential.

I raised a rather average zombie, attracting a few curious glances in the process. It wasn't often they saw a Necro right here in the heart of the Lands of Light. I placed the remaining Soul Stone in a separate pocket in case I had to raise the pet again right in the heat of battle.

And then we got cooking.

Four hours and two stupid deaths later, I was almost level nine. Two gold pieces clinked in my wallet, plus about six hundred copper. Luckily, virtual money didn't weigh much: a thousand pieces equaled two and a half pounds. Twice I'd been to town to get rid of my hefty nickel-and-dime loot. I had about forty bracelets and the same amount of Soul Stones. I kept leveling slowly but surely, the few deaths resulting mainly from a couple of unlucky pulls. Gnolls had a large aggro zone what with their constant scurrying about, messengers running to and fro. Turned out it wasn't a good place for an easy hunt.

I wasn't bored, running an angler's adrenaline rush as I scooped the loot out of bodies. I spent meditation breaks scrolling through the location chat. Somebody was still looking for a Red Bear, offering first three and later ten gold for the creature's whereabouts. A quest pet, apparently. Petty peddlers squabbled among themselves buying and selling stuff. Bracelets were in constant demand so I could have done a bit of haggling if I wanted to. Plenty of buyers around.

Having restored mana to full, I rose, mechanically dusting my pants. I had to get myself some clothes, really, walking around in a basic free kit like a green newb. And the cloak... better not say anything about it. I just hoped that Taali had chosen a different leveling location.

I noticed a ranger player appearing from the nearby woods, his health flashing an orange alarm. He took a dozen paces, turned toward the trees and shot a few arrows at a yet unseen target. His gear was quite impressive, his armor gleaming with complex traceries, his rings glistening with gems. Even the arrows he shot left strange purple residue in the air.

I peered at him. *Karish. Level 38.*

A big fish, too big for this location. Who was he firing off at?

Then I saw it. Red Bear himself, as large as life and twice as ugly. About six foot eight shoulder height, he was studded with arrows like a pin cushion and was also twice as scary for it. His frantic eyes sparkled yellow, each the size of a saucer. The beast bared his teeth, each a good dagger long.

The ranger lunged forward, shortening the distance between them. The bear was having a hard time. He had barely 10% life left.

As the fighters approached, I looked around for a place as far from the bear as possible. One swing of his paw, and I could do another corpse run.

The archer stopped within ten paces from me. He turned round and grabbed his bow. Twang, twang, twang. The bear's life bar shrunk to the size of a hair. He was toast.

But the bear still had enough in him to surprise us. He reared up, knocked an arrow aside in full flight and bellowed. Not just any old bellow, either:

You hear the wild roar of a primeval beast!
You're petrified! Your body is paralyzed with fear!

Jesus. Just then my pet remembered his default owner-protection settings, grumbled and lunged toward the bear. Where did he think he was going?

Veins bulged on the motionless raider's neck as he struggled against the invisible chains. The bear limped toward the man and in one powerful jolt pulled him under himself. I could hear the smacking of heavy paws. A few seconds later, everything was over. A small grave appeared where the archer had died.

The bear turned to my zombie pet who had during all that time pounded the beast's wide back. Absolutely pointless. The level gap was too big. The zombie either missed or couldn't pierce the armor resulting in zero damage hits. When the paralysis finally ended, I stirred, racking my brains for a solution. The pet was little help, I could see that. He could only defer the monster two seconds max. And if I cast the DoT or the Deadman's Hand? He was almost sure to resist both. The only thing that might work was Life Absorption. It had always worked, ignoring the target's resistance to magic. How much life could the bear have left? One or two percent at most. Definitely not a hundred. I couldn't escape so I could just as well try it.

I selected the bear as target and activated the spell.

Red Bear has sustained 14 points Damage!

You've received 14 points Life! 90/90
The zombie gnoll has been clawed! Damage sustained: 190 points!
The zombie gnoll tried to punch Red Bear but missed!
Red Bear has sustained 15 points Damage!
You've received 15pt Life! 90/90
A critical hit received! Red Bear has clawed the zombie gnoll resulting in 390 points Damage!
The zombie gnoll is dead!

The bear hobbled toward me. Pointless running: even though he could barely move his legs, each step was so wide he'd catch up with me in no time. And he also had that bellowing skill. He'd just paralyze me and kill me. Oh shit. He was rearing up.

The bear stood up glaring at me with hatred.

Red Bear has sustained 13 points Damage!
You've received 13 points Life! 90/90.

The beast opened his jaws wide and bellowed just as I finished casting the spell again.

You hear the wild roar of a primeval beast! You're petrified! Your body is paralyzed with fear!

You've dealt a critical hit! Red Bear has sustained 28 points Damage!
You've received 28 points Life! 90/90.
Red Bear is dead!
You've received Experience!
Congratulations! You've reached level 9!

Racial bonus: +1 to Intellect!

Class bonus: +1 to Intellect, +1 to Spirit!

5 Characteristic points available! You now have 20 Characteristic points!

Congratulations! You've received achievement: Goliath!

You've killed a creature 10 levels higher than you!

You've been awarded +100 points Fame!

Congratulations! You've received achievement: Colossus!

You've killed a creature 20 levels higher than you!

You've been awarded +500 points Fame!

I just stood there frozen, my mouth gaping in a silent whoopee, my dropped jaw fully describing my feelings. What a coincidence. Un-freakin'-believable. Had the archer stayed alive, I'd have dealt a certain amount of damage but gotten no experience at all. More than that: had the ranger been bound to this location, then he'd have received all of the experience even in death. But the archer must have either arrived from afar or teleported to the city and hadn't yet bound to the location. Enter me. His damage list was now empty. God only knows where he'd respawn now. Having said that, hardly any class allowed you to wrestle down a bear while there was at least one percent life in him. No steel or magic would have made a dent in him. What incredible, enormous luck.

The paralysis released me. Rubber-legged, I hobbled over to the beast. I reached out to touch his powerful frame and sank to the ground in awe. The Soul Stone. I clenched it and peered at the properties:

A Soul Stone. Contains the soul of level 36 Red Bear. Use the Summoning the Undead spell to raise it.

Not yet realizing the full scope of my luck, I moved the rest of the loot into my bag. Besides the Stone, I also had Red Bear's Heart and two vials of Bear's Blood. I'd have to look into them later.

I sat down on the ground, dumbfounded, rolling the little rock in my hand admiring the play of light on its facets. Wonder if I could use it? Apparently, the mana level required for summoning depended on the player's level and not on that of the summoned creature's. I didn't see any problems in that respect.

I could only explain what happened next by the catatonic state I was still in. You wouldn't expect me to admit I acted like an idiot, right? Why, oh why did I try to cast that summoning spell?

The earth bulged. The enormous bulk of a zombie bear crawled out of the depth. Summon my aunt! How did you go about burying him back in the ground? Why on earth had I had to summon him?

I heard stifled cries behind me. A group of three minor Elves stood behind my back.

"What... what's that?" a level five female warrior pointed a trembling finger at the beast's bulk.

"That," I said bitterly, "is my pet. Model *My Brain Hurts*, version *I'll Rip Your Head Off.* Cute, isn't he? Just don't disturb him, he's easily excited. Aren't you, Hummungus?"

Chapter Eight

I didn't need to ask myself what to do next. Teddy was my ticket to level 30 and beyond. Ideally, of course, I had first to get to level 10 and choose specialization. Then I had to spend some quality time rearranging my characteristics and choosing the right spells. Only then could I pack my lunch box and walk out one fine morning, prepared for a long and rugged marathon.

But what was done was done. Even though it complicated my task, it was no reason to regret it. Now I had to concentrate and brace myself before I screwed it up and lost the pet.

I reached for the flask and took a large swig of tea. I swished it around my mouth enjoying the taste. Then I packed the flask back and slapped the bear's side, cold and resonant like a drum.

"So, Hummungus? Ready? Off we go!"

And off we went. The bear wasted gnolls in two hits, three max. It took them about seven minutes to respawn—pointless waiting—so we kept on moving down an ever-narrowing spiral with the dungeon entrance as its center.

Very soon I realized I couldn't collect all the loot. Another fifteen minutes, and I'd start losing speed, what with my strength and all, and in another twenty, I'd shudder to a halt like a brick-loaded strongbox.

I emptied my bag onto the ground, putting aside the more valuable items. Soul Stones, bracelets, an odd piece of jewelry, the Bear's loot and the food. That was it. The rest I left lying on the ground: some shabby clothing, bits of ore, a few rusty weapons and other such trash loot. After that, I organized the looting process: down to pick up a few coppers, in they go, clinking, into the wallet, one second to rummage through the rest and leave the trash on the ground. Very soon I looked like a trawler pulling in netfuls of fish. Behind my back, youngsters were quarreling over my cast-offs like a flock of seagulls. About a dozen of them followed in my tracks picking up everything that lay in temptation's way. Soon they self-organized and formed a waiting line; they even agreed on their share of the drop before the gnolls were even killed, estimating their chances of a fat loot.

In a few more minutes, the bells finally jingled.

Congratulations! You've reached level 10!

Warning! This is the first key level. You aren't immune to other players' attacks any more. Proceed with caution!

When killed by an NPC, you'll lose 15% of the experience gained at the current level.

You will receive 1 Talent point per each level. See Wiki for more details.

Choosing specialization and distributing my points in the heat of the fight wasn't a good idea. Better not rush it. Once done, I couldn't undo it. In any case, it was Teddy who did all the fighting as I barely had time to cast an occasional spell.

Within ten more minutes, the bells jingled again. Level 11.

The spiral kept shrinking as we approached the fence blocking the entrance to the caves. We had to fight our way in, for two reasons. First, the surface mobs were limited to level 10 which prevented me from using Hummungus' full potential. Secondly, I was a bit concerned about the archer's reaction when he returned to pick up his stuff. He could be quite upset to see my pet—so upset in fact that he could pepper me with arrows simply to make himself feel better.

Two warriors guarded the gate, backed up by a shaman covered with dangling charms. This was getting interesting. I hadn't come across any gnoll warriors earlier. They had all been gatherers, messengers and other such small fry. Not that it made any difference to the zombie bear. The warriors lasted about ten seconds. The shaman managed to cast three freezing spells, very spectacular but utterly useless. Talking about a bear in a china shop. Ready or not, here I come, you can't hide.

I turned to my *remora* crowd. "Listen guys, I'm going down the caves now. I might be down there for quite a bit and I'll be way too busy to cover you or accompany you back. You'd better go back now before the gnolls respawn."

Most of them saw my point and hurried back along the by now footworn path. All but one small level-nine rogue. I didn't know him.

He answered my surprised stare with panache. "I don't think they'll notice me. I've got stealth all maxed out. If I croak, no hard feelings, man. But at least I'll get all the spare loot for myself."

He grinned as he activated stealth and turned into a translucent, blurred figure. At five paces, he'd be totally invisible. Okay, then. I'd have done the same. Freebies are sweet.

Then I noticed a long row of cages along the fence's far edge. Several dozen, by the looks of it. Locked inside were emaciated prisoners—mainly Dark Elves although I noticed a couple of other-race captives, too.

I walked towards the closest cage, curious. A haughty Drow glanced at me out of the corner of his eye before focusing again in front of him.

"Dear Sir," I spoke. "Is there anything I could help you with?"

The Elf barely deigned to turn his head. I opened the pet control interface and chose the *Speak!* command. The bear reared up and growled. It wasn't the Wild Roar ability, of course, as the zombie hadn't preserved it; but the sight of a fifteen-foot growling behemoth impressed the Elf enough. He nodded at the heavy lock of his cage door.

"My name is Inerion. My group was out farming in the nearby woods when gnolls lured us into a trap. Their shamans put some sleeping weed blossoms into the water upstream from where we filled our flasks. When we came to, we were here already. If you get hold of the key, I'll reward your service well. If you fail, then just kill me here and now. I don't want to be slaughtered like a sheep and sacrificed to their Beast God. I have a few gold pieces. You can have them for the trouble."

New quest available! Freedom Ain't Free.

Go down Gnolls' Dungeons and find the key from the cage.

Reward: experience and improved relationship with the Drow and Dark Alliance.

Alternative quest available! Coup de Grace.

Help the Dark One to end his own life, saving his soul from Beast God.

Reward: some gold.

The Elf looked past me with an expression of eternal sadness. Captured characters would undoubtedly undergo some changes, but their AI controller was bound to remember everything. I didn't think many players had ever bothered to look for the key. Most likely, they'd stormed the cages and killed off the prisoners for an armful of easy gold. Never mind. I had with me there a short-leashed wonder waffle to do just that. Together we could go through that cave with a fine-tooth comb and get him that key of theirs.

I actually walked from one cage to the next, getting the same quest everywhere. In the last one languished a slim, scarlet-haired Drow maiden, beautiful in a haughty and indifferent way. A thin carved collar flashed crimson on her neck. I offered my help to her, too.

Slowly, she shook her head. "I thank you, young warlock. I am not going anywhere without my warriors."

New quest available! Free the Drow Princess I!

The Cutthroats' leader can't leave her men imprisoned. Dead or alive, famous warriors always come back together. Or they don't come back at all. You must free all the captured Elves.

Reward: Access to the Quest Free the Drow Princess II.

A cutthroats' Princess? Apparently, I was into some serious people. I ran my eyes over the line of caged Drow. Inerion, level 94. Lauinel, level 101. Akhsan, level 98. Princess Ruata, level 161. What had I gotten myself into? How had my gnolls managed to put these aces behind bars? Was this cave really as low-level as I thought? Let's just hope I was dealing with nothing more serious than goblin magic or game developers' sick sense of humor.

I accepted the quest and nodded my agreement with the Drow maiden's conditions. An emaciated face, thin wrists, a blue vein pulsating on her neck. How long had they been here?

I dropped my bag and knelt, feeling inside for a sandwich. Then I turned to a silent rogue nearby.

"You think you could spare some food and drink?"

He nodded.

"You mind sharing it between the Drow, please? I'll make it up to you."

The kid nodded again and reached into his bag without saying a word. He seemed all right. I had to add him to my friend list. That would make him my second rogue friend.

The Princess pressed a clenched fist to her chest (and a wonderful chest it was, I had to admit) and gave me a slight bow. "Thank you, my High brother. I shall never forget it."

Quest alert! Free the Drow Princess I quest is now unique!
Reward: Unknown.

I mirrored her gesture. For a second, I stared deep into her eyes, my gaze cementing my promise. Then I turned around and walked towards the cave's entrance without looking back.

The cave wasn't pitch black but rather semi-dark. Colonies of some fluffy moss clung to its walls and emitted a purple light, lending the place the likeness of an acid club.

Normally, the first few dozen feet are safe in any location. This is where teams meet before the raid and this is where they stack up the killed monsters in order to clear the way. There you could often see a player in his underpants about to start looking for his grave somewhere in the depths of the tunnels.

Right now the safe spot was deserted. Or so I thought. Then I heard a fearful *hick!* I turned my head, trying to locate the source of the sound, then slapped my bear's iron ass to push him aside. In a niche behind him sat Taali, crouched in a heap.

"Gotcha!" I offered her a hand but the girl got stuck so deep in the crack that it took me some brute force to drag her out. "How did you manage to get in there?"

"How do you think?" she glared at the bear. "You've got your hippo to thank for that. He's sort of bigger than you think."

Okay, okay. I glanced at her stats. She was 14 already, leveling slowly but surely. Actually, considering the time she spent online, she could've done better.

"How's farming? How're mobs?"

"Actually, I only pull them from the edge. I manage to do about a dozen before they respawn. Gnoll warriors mainly, levels 9 to 11. You can get a few casters here, like shamans, healers and summoners, but then it's more difficult."

The girl fell silent and circled the bear with mistrust, studying whichever parts of him she could peek into. My pet shifted from foot to foot, red-eyed, not detecting any aggression toward either him or his master, his non-retractable claws screeching on the stone.

"Is it all yours? Wow. Where from? Is it my imagination or it used to be a Red Bear in its past life?"

"I still can't believe it myself. Don't even ask me to do the same again. It was a bit like jumping into a glass of water—you can do this sort of thing but once."

Taali shook her head. "Holy cow."

"You could say that. Well, I'm off then."

I crossed my fingers, praying the girl wouldn't ask me to join their group. Not that I'm greedy or anything. Far from it. But this was a single ticket. True, Teddy could get us both beyond level 30. But it would take twice as long—no sleep, no logout. Could take a day or two. Tired, we'd most likely start making mistakes and flunk after ten hours or so. No amount of thanks and eyelash-fluttering could convince me to do it.

Taali proved quick on the uptake. "All right, sir. Off you go. By the way, from what I've heard, Gnoll King drops some crazy paladin gear," the girl glanced at me meaningfully.

I breathed a sigh of relief and saluted her. "Yes, ma'am. I got the message."

She laughed and poked me in the shoulder. "Go rattle your sword for a bit. Make sure you stay in one piece. There's only so much you can loot."

Who was it who said that women prefer men with potential?

I waved her good-bye and stepped inside the cave. Taali had already mopped up the first few rooms. I peeped into the next one. A couple of gnoll warriors guarded the entrance and the exit. A few patrols were cruising the room in chaotic and unpredictable trajectories. In the back, a master gnoll was fidgeting over some ancient-looking machine. Level 14, he was the highest of all present, surrounded by a handful of apprentices. In total, just a snack for my pet. Let the show begin!

I didn't care much about a nice clean pull. Teddy had no problems handling a train. I simply selected the warrior closest to me as target and said, "Attack!"

With a growl, the bear charged.

After two minutes of animal noises, metal clanging and paws slapping flesh, the first room was gnoll-free. I glanced up at my experience bar. The fight had added twenty-four percent, not bad at all. I went through the bodies picking out the most valuable spoils. I wasn't sure whether to take Soul Stones or not but decided for it. You never knew when you might die, and that way I always had some high-level items. I was happy to see some quest bracelets—not just gray ones as earlier on the surface, but also a couple black ones. If I wasn't mistaken, they went for a good fifty copper.

I stopped for a moment checking the master gnoll. Among other trash, he dropped a heavy bunch of lockpicks. I fingered them, thinking, and turned around looking for my rogue friend. I couldn't see the little thief but the disappearing objects I'd discarded gave his location away.

"Hey, dude. Mind showing up for a bit?"

The rogue unstealthed and looked up at me, curious. He couldn't do much else, actually. He was kneeling with the end of his bag between his teeth where I'd just smoked four of the warriors, scooping in the battle booty.

I laughed. I couldn't help it. "Boy, you're a scream. What's your name? Bug? Suits you, sort of. If you think you're a super thief, here're some trade tools for you."

I flung him the lockpicks. The kid grabbed and inspected them.

"Zool! And I'm not a thief but a super spy. I'd love to level all stealth skills and become No 1 Spy."

"You go for it, dude. A spy will never want for work," I tried to conceal the skepticism in my voice. "If you don't mind me asking, why is your char the size of a garden gnome? Where have you seen a High Elf two feet tall?"

"I've just told you. Spies may need to crawl into places, especially hiding places. It's perfect."

"It is indeed," I had to agree. "Go ahead and hide, then. We're off. Hummungus, heel!"

After twenty more minutes, the kid realized that his eyes were bigger than his belly.

"Overload," he said wistfully. "Two more items, and I won't be able to move. Stealth speed is half the standard as it is. I might go to town and flog it all. Thanks, dude. Good luck and good hunting!"

I waved him away without looking up from a freshly-made map. This was another problem with my unplanned marathon, the fact that I hadn't even got myself a caves plan so now I was groping my way through like a newborn kitten. All that time, we'd been taking the corridors to our right, inspecting the rooms one by one as we approached the central hall and the stairs down to the second level.

It still took me and Hummungus another half-hour to get to the central altar. By then, I was level 14 going on 15. When I'd reached level 14 a few rooms back, a few new system messages had popped up.

Congratulations! You've received Achievement: Impervious.

You've stayed alive for five subsequent levels!

Reward: +100 to Fame

A few seconds later, another message blinked on,

Server alert! Server update 2144:

We have introduced a new measure aiming to restrict a summoned creature's level regardless of the player's class. A summoned creature's level is now limited to that of a summoner +30%. In case of summoning a higher creature, its level will be automatically lowered to comply with the above formula.

This measure does not apply to item and buff bonuses.

E.g.: Necromancer, level 10, has a Soul Stone level 20. Item bonuses +2 to level. You can raise a level 15 pet.

Oh. AI was quick on the uptake. Apparently, they kept a firm eye on this achievement to make sure no one could abuse bugs for leveling.

After a few more seconds, Admin PM'd me with a message that made me chuckle.

Dear Player,

You have recently helped us to detect certain gaming scenarios which could potentially disrupt the game's balance.

As a thank-you gesture on our part, please accept this Sky Stone. It can be attached to any cloth or armor item as any other gem. It also has 10 characteristic points for you to add to the parameters of your choice.

Thank you for your cooperation.

We remind you that per Section 14.7 of EULA, Administration has the right to review all game logs, including the combat and social chats.

Oh well. Big brother is watching you. At least they gave me a carrot, not a stick. I studied the stone. It resembled a large multifaceted ruby the size of a dollar. I got an eyeful, then shoved it deep into my bag. Later. Now I needed to do some leveling while I was still fresh, had plenty of food and was out of mobs' way. Time to move it.

Chapter Nine

The altar melee was a piece of cake. With the regularity of a grinder, my pet kept working on whatever gnolls happened to be around. At a certain point, his health dropped to 90% only to restore gradually back to his signature 100%. The Head Shaman, the local mini boss, cast a bit of rather useless magic, clouding my bear in blue smoke and piercing him with bolts of purple lightning. The fire show came to an abrupt end when Teddy finished with the last defender and turned his attention to the shaman himself. After a dozen hits, another level 17 corpse lay sprawled on the floor.

Ding! 15! Six levels in an hour and a half. Awesome. I frisked the corpses piled about and bent over the shaman, curious. A heavy bronze key and a little silver ring. I thought first that it was the quest key which opened one of the cages. It wasn't. Apparently, it opened the squeaky door that led to the dungeon's second level. The ring was a different story.

Lore Ring
Item Class: Uncommon
Durability: 20/20
Effect: +3 to Intellect

Nice. I tried it on, and the mana bar jumped up thirty percent. I glanced at the clock. Only three minutes left until the mobs respawned. I gave it some thought and decided to stay for a new mop-up. I had to admit I liked the ring so much I could use another dozen.

I jumped up onto the altar and froze in the lotus pose, watching the show. Teddy won again, 9:0.

The loot surprised me. No key this time. Either it didn't drop twice or it was rare loot to begin with. In the latter case, the key could be of some value so I could try to get some money back for it.

The ring I did get, albeit different.

Gold sapphire ring
Item class: Common
Durability: 20/20
Effect: none. Just a pretty trinket.

I raised the ring up to my eyes. Nice one. I threw it into my bag adding it to a handful of other jewelry. I could sell it or give it to the girls I'd met—their numbers steadily growing, luckily for me as I was already itching for it. Especially because most females here looked like Barbies on steroids, covered with token amounts of lace, transparent silk and some jewelry. The sight of slim Elven maidens doing their corpse runs like some bikini beach joggers, was too much for any red-blooded male. Damn those art designers. A plague on both their houses.

The sex question was more than resolvable here. You could give in to temptation in your own house or in somebody else's with the hostess' consent. Brothels were another answer to it. All in all, sexual activities in virtual reality were more than popular. Before the arrival of the FIVR, a quarter of all Internet traffic had been porn. Now imagine, instead of two-dimensional pics and dubious-quality videos, the ability to experience a more than real gratification with the most beautiful of all Internet girls. This was one of the cornerstones of the FIVR success. Sex, entertainment and adrenaline, multiplied by one's superiority complex, all in one unique product. Mind boggling.

I shouldn't have thought about girls. I shook my head dispersing the unwanted images and had another swig of herbal tea sending my thanks to the Three Little Pigs' innkeeper. Then I turned the key in the heavy carved door. A wide staircase led down, lined with smoky torches.

"Hummungus, come, pup. Be quiet."

History repeated itself. Here, mobs were juicier, level 18 and above, growing stronger as we approached the third underground floor. After half an hour, I received a new message.

Congratulations! You've received Achievement: Immortal.
You've stayed alive for ten subsequent levels!
Reward: +500 to Fame

Fame Alert!
Your Fame has exceeded 1000 points!
You've reached Fame level 1: "People are talking about you".
Friendly faction vendors might surprise you with lower prices. You will also gain access to some secret quests.

Not bad at all. My joy was slightly spoiled by the fact that all these achievements were cheats, to a point. Had it not been for my free Teddy ticket, I'd still be a nonentity. I made myself a solemn promise not to think too much of myself and to generally keep a low profile.

After a few more minutes, the already level-19 me fought my way to a wide corridor leading to the floor's main hall. There I could fully appreciate the developers' sick sense of humor. The staircase down to the third floor was right opposite the gnolls' barracks. Whether it was AI trying to be funny or this was the basic layout, I didn't know; all I could see was that they were falling in on the drill ground in front of the barracks. A dozen and a half warriors, all my level, plus a level-22 Gnoll Chief and the floor's mini boss, a level 25 Gnoll General.

The biggest problem was, they stood shoulder to shoulder. Any party that fought its way down here would have to deal with the entire gang. There simply was no other way. It didn't feel good. Seventeen mobs against a pet, however tough, and I couldn't even interfere for fear of pulling aggro onto myself. My current level was purely nominal: all my skills remained level 5. I was a walking bag with lots of available characteristic points and talents. I still had to get my three talent points from Grym for level 10. And I still had to choose specialization in order to unblock new skill tree branches. My last levels had brought me nine more points which I didn't really want to invest even if I had somewhere in which to invest them. I needed to get a bit of sleep first and think clearly. In other words, my pet was the only real force that counted. I was little more than a walking talking makiwara.

I stepped a safe distance back, blessed my pet and, choosing the General as target, pressed 'Attack'. The Gnoll Overseer would be next. I wanted to minimize my pet's exposure to the strongest opponents.

Even when still alive, Teddy hadn't been known for good self-preservation skills. He lunged at the opponent with all the enthusiasm of reckless courage. Immediately his life bar began to shrink. It took Hummungus twenty seconds and 15% hits to finally put the General to rest. The Chief took slightly less. And still the gnolls were too many. Way too many. They surrounded Teddy and started pounding his sides and back, nailing him with crits. Soon he had ten opponents and barely half life left. After another minute of melee, the ratio became seven to forty. Three to thirty. Two. One. Done. I breathed a sigh of relief. Good boy!

I came over to the bloodied beast and patted his chewed ears. "Way to go, Hummungus. You made your daddy proud."

I let Teddy regenerate. We had another three or four minutes before the gnolls respawned. He needed a bit of rest, and it wasn't a problem to mop up the hall again. The mobs would respawn one by one, in the reverse order of their death. Teddy risked virtually nothing against singles.

I checked the corpses again collecting the booty. About a gold piece's worth of cash, half a dozen bracelets and a couple Soul Stones. Loot was getting more interesting here, with a variety of steel weapons, armor and chainmail. All had decent defense parameters albeit without any extras. Unfortunately, I had to leave it all lying on the ground: my modest strength didn't allow me to lug around hefty objects. As Murphy's law would have it, I might not be capable of even lifting some of the more promising loot ahead.

Talking of the devil. The Gnoll General dropped a sheer treasure: a massive key, a red bracelet of the type I hadn't seen before, and a pair of heavy chainmail gauntlets. I ran a check:

Red Bracelet. Serves to identify gnoll elite.
Item class: Common
Durability: 25/25
Weight: 0.24 lb.
Effect: +5 to Armor, +1 to Strength

Excellent. I slid the bracelet onto my wrist. If I got another one, I'd wear it on my other arm for some added strength and a bit of armor. Waste not, want not. No point in selling it even, at least until I found an adequate substitute. I weighed the gauntlets in my hand.

Chainmail Gauntlets. Crafter unknown.
Item Class: Uncommon
Durability: 45/45
Weight: 3.3 lb.
Effect: +12 to Armor, +3 to Strength

Great item. Had to be worth at least ten or twelve gold. In the bag it went. Good job Necros couldn't wear heavy armor, otherwise I'd have to choose whether to sell or keep them.

My inner greedy pig stirred happily. Things were looking up. The questions of finding a roof over my head and some daily bread in the shape of a potful of meat and potatoes had ceased to hang over me like some sword of Damocles. Now everything I earned on top I could invest in gear and character growth. Good job, too, considering I'd spent my first day busting my ass, and all I had to show for it had been barely enough for a bed and a meal.

"What the &ç@$!" yelled the gnoll who'd respawned first, only an arm's length from me. His heavy saber swooshed over my head. I ducked behind the bear's back just in time.

The warrior tried to get to me again. I barely avoided a stab to the face. The pet stepped in and pulled aggro onto himself with a couple of expert hits.

Whew. I crawled into a relatively safe corner, waited five seconds and began draining the mob's life. So stupid of me. I'd nearly got myself killed, too busy examining the trophies.

By the end of the melee, I calmed down a bit and made a mental note to be more careful in the future. I ended up with level 20 and a lovely pair of hammered steel greaves, with +15 to armor and +4 to strength modifier. Looked like the General only dropped heavy armor. Not my thing. Worth picking up, anyway, even if only to sell it. Pointless hanging about much longer. I still had the dungeon's lower floor to do. Both loot and experience were better there.

I allowed the pet a few minutes to regen and walked down the stairs. Here, the rooms didn't resemble dungeons any more. It looked more like a second-rate mansion house. A few bits of furniture stood against the tapestry-lined walls lit by large bowls of burning oil. Who'd have thought the place was that serious. Here, the gnoll warriors were replaced by guards, far more dangerous. Mainly I came across groups of three: two guards plus either a sergeant or a caster. The mobs' levels were predictably higher. The night was going to be anything but relaxed, our little outing quickly turning into an obstacle race. The bear was still capable of handling the trio without much trouble albeit losing one-third life. I really needed to know how to restore his health. Or rather, I was sure that Necros of my level had to have it somewhere but I stuck to my resolution not to fiddle with the stats during the marathon.

Really, would I hole up in some dark corner and, brain-dead with fighting, try to solve single-handedly such crucial problems? Not a good idea. A mistake could cost me dearly. So I had to weasel our way out.

Bit by bit I managed to use the Deadman's Hand to control one of the guards. In the meantime, Teddy dealt with one or two gnolls depending on how clean the pull was. Then he finished off the one I controlled. A quick meditation, and we moved another hundred feet, heading for the throne hall which housed the juiciest monsters and the sweetest loot. I was also quite worried about the absence of quest keys for the Drow cages. I had to keep going if only to locate the place or the mob who dropped them.

In another hour and a half, I did level 24 and received another achievement, for staying alive for fifteen subsequent levels. Another thousand Fame points into the kitty.

Then, quite unpredictably, a new message popped up:

Congratulations! You've received Achievement: The Untouchable.
Your enemies have failed to deal you damage for 5 subsequent levels!
Reward: +500 to Fame

Apparently, I'd done good. I hadn't made a single mistake. Luck had a lot to do with it, of course. Only they seemed to be sort of generous with their Fame points. If it continued like that, I was going to walk out of the dungeons to a red carpet reception.

On we went. Corridors, rooms, halls, gnolls, gnolls and more gnolls. I was already sick to death of their dog chops. Was it my imagination or were they really emitting that canine stench?

My eyes ached from the torch flames. Patches of light danced amid shadows and wisps of smoke that clung to the ceiling. My fatigue started to show. I found a safe room, parked Teddy and lay flat for ten minutes or so, relaxing with my eyes shut. Gradually, I felt better. I munched on a totally yummy sandwich washing it down with sweet tea, eternally grateful for the buffs. Teddy refused the food point blank but sniffed the tea with interest. Some funny zombies around...

Then I checked my bag to see if I could get rid of a thing or two. The last couple of items had sent me into overload. Seven thousand copper were weighing me down but it would be stupid to leave them, right? Luckily, the third-floor mobs dropped silver. On the bottom of the bag, I discovered a whole mine of Soul Stones. I chose ten or so of the stronger ones and destroyed the rest which gave me a small bag of magic dust—a crafting ingredient meant for alchemists, blacksmiths and the like. That seemed like changing one bunch of trash for another, but it would be a shame to leave it, wouldn't it?

By then, the pet had regenerated. I didn't feel that bad, either. Time to go.

As it turned out, our safe room was only a few steps away from the throne hall, in some sort of auxiliary corridor. I had a good look around. A long room, brightly lit, with pairs of brutal-looking guards frozen statue-like by the columns that supported the vaulted ceiling. The throne stood against the far wall. On it sat the Gnoll King surrounded by his entourage. They weren't packed too close together. From where I stood I could just about pull two monsters at a time.

So we got the show going. Between the two of us, we smoked three pairs of gnolls in less than five minutes. I kept casting Deadman's Hand, controlling one of the guards as Teddy dealt with his partner. My pet killed a mob in thirty seconds, and all that time I kept my target nailed to the ground as it cursed and tried to squirm itself free from the invisible bonds.

Then we advanced a little to take over the mopped-up space. One last effort. We only had the King, the Priest and two of the officers left.

The officers looked top class. Up to their balls in armor, with double swords on their backs, these level 28 beasts could put up a serious fight. And still I thought they wouldn't be a problem as long as I saved my pet enough life, for we didn't have enough time to meditate. And we still had the dungeon boss to take care of.

I started the fight using the same tried and tested scheme by controlling the officer next to me. The mob struggled, helpless, and groaned as he drew his two swords. The second guard swung round and dashed for us. The King and the Priest remained seated, childishly ignoring the danger. This, of course, was only gaming convention. Gnolls' aggro zone didn't exceed seven or eight paces. Once outside it, you could dance and bare your ass in full view of the monster. Having said that, the higher your opponent's level, the more aggressive he became. Some mobs were so amazingly hostile they could sense an enemy miles away, sometimes from the other end of their location.

The officers proved stronger than their lower-ranked buddies. They had more life and showered us with hits. Still, the eight-level difference was nothing to sniff at. After another minute plus a bag of nerves and twenty percent off the pet's life, two more corpses were added to the hall's interior design.

We took a short break to regen and decide on our tactics. I had no idea about the King's abilities. No good taking the risk pulling aggro onto myself.

Should I freeze the Priest so that the pet could attack the King? No good. The Priest was a caster himself. Even tied to a spot, he'd make mincemeat of me. So all I could do, really, was set Teddy on them, then play it by ear.

I selected the Priest as target. His being a mage left him with less life. Also, I hoped that I just might disrupt his concentration and stop a couple spells. Just to make life a bit harder for him.

Teddy, attack! The moment he crossed the aggro zone's invisible boundary, the King cast some ability that blew away a third of Teddy's life. Immediately, the King started reciting a long spell while the Priest pierced Teddy with a lightning bolt. The pet pounded him back. Twice the Priest failed to cast a new spell until finally he managed to send two curses, one after the other.

Then it was my turn to open my eyes wide. The King summoned his pet, a zombie gnoll. Was he a Necro too? Or rather, judging by his heavy armor and the abilities he had, he had to be a Death Knight. I highlighted the zombie. Level 20, too low for a Nec.

The King cast another curse and reached for his two-handed sword. For another fifteen seconds the fight could go either way. Then the Priest finally collapsed and we were on the rise. Teddy still had 40% life left when I joined in, casting one Life Absorption after another. Another minute of vigorous fencing, and the hall fell silent.

The first couple of guards respawned about a hundred feet away from us. Still, we were relatively safe for a while. The pet needed time to regen, so I was going to do the next round on my own, mopping up the five mobs by the throne. The hall was big and crowded enough for us to pull a guard or two when we needed, as long as we kept an eye on the ticking clock.

I crawled out of my corner and, stepping cautiously over the corpses, came up to the pet. He only had about 10% life left and looked it, too. I smoothed out his disheveled fur.

"Go take some rest, Ted. Well done."

I could use a break, too. My nerves were in shatters. Heaving a sigh of relief, I slumped onto the throne. Comfortable enough. Would be nice to haul it back to my Three Little Pigs room.

"Great job, dude," a voice said right over my ear.

I jumped. Bug's tiny outline appeared out of thin air.

"You asshole!"

He gave me a happy grin.

"You've nearly scared the pants off me," I continued. "Where've you been, you son of a midget?"

Bug sat down comfortably onto the slain King's corpse. "Been to town, sold up, raised sixteen gold, by the way. I can give you half if you want. It's only fair. Thought I'd go back. You think I didn't see you were permanently online? Got some grub on the go in case you're interested."

So! The kid was smart, organized and quick to deliver. Cautious, too. And quite prepared to go half in the hope of more profits. Slick operator.

"How did you get here through all the doors?" I asked him.

Bug produced the bunch of lockpicks and clanged them in the air. "Took me half an hour to open the one on the first floor. The mechanism wasn't too difficult but honestly, I've never really bothered with the skill. The second one I must have gone through right after you. It stood open and all the barracks were empty. But I think I took a wrong turn, so at stealth speed it took me an hour to get out. When I came here you were up to your eyeballs in gnolls. I decided not to distract you."

"You did right," I said as I kept replaying one particular thought in my mind. "You can keep the gold. I didn't want it to begin with. I have another offer for you. How would you like to earn a bit of money working as a wardrobe?"

"What do you mean?"

"Look. I fully intend to stay here for a while. There'll be loads of loot. If you took a dozen pieces of armor and the same in cold steel, that's it, you're in overload. We'll do it differently. We'll put you behind the throne, in this archway here. Then we'll be loading you with everything the gnolls drop. It doesn't matter if you can't move. What's important is that your bag can accommodate anything—this throne if necessary, as long as you don't exceed the 100 slots limit. Is that what your bag is—basic for 100 slots? So we'll stuff it solid. Otherwise, what's the point of going virtual?"

The kid still wasn't getting it. Had I overestimated his talents? "And how do you want me to lug this throne back?"

"Easy. You'll get a free ride to your spawn point. All you need to do is wait for the mobs to respawn. Then you remove stealth and off home you go. Three hours later, you go to the cemetery to find your grave. It'll be there for a week before it finally decays. In the meantime, you take the items to the store bit by bit. We'll go fifty-fifty, what d'ya think?"

Instead of replying, Bug rose and stood in the archway trying to impersonate a wardrobe. He spread his arms wide as if opening the imaginary doors, then opened his mouth—apparently, signifying the top shelf—and mumbled,

"All set. Load me up!"

Chapter Ten

Once Bug was ready, I rushed to the fallen officers before they decayed, unwilling to lose the trophies I was due. They dropped some cool armor plates, greaves and pauldrons—no extra characteristics, but with decent defense parameters up to level 20. Good tank gear. It had to cost something even if I just took it to some store or other. The Priest made my day: he dropped the first quest key with a complex multitoothed barb and a digital rune. Wonder if it was the Dwarves' work? It didn't look like something made by hyena men. Their paws weren't up to it. Overall, the Priest proved a walking stash. Eight silver pieces, a red bracelet, a Soul Stone, the key and an interesting belt decorated with plates:

> *Steel Gratitude Belt*
> *Item Class: Rare*
> *Durability: 55/65*
> *Weight: 5 lbs.*
> *Effect 1: +16 to Armor, +5 to Strength*
> *Effect 2: When healing allies, may give a 5% chance of doubling the spell power without additional mana expenditure.*

I had a funny feeling I knew who'd be happy to wear it. Looked like Taali had been wrong and paladin-type loot could drop off Priests and not just

Shamans. As for the King, he was as Dark as they made 'em.

I sloshed across the pools of blood toward the remaining monster. Let's see. A gold piece and a half. A bracelet. Another key—the rune was different this time. And most interestingly, a heavy forged breastplate.

Gnoll King's Breastplate
Item class: Rare
Effect 1: +30 to Armor, +5 to Intellect, +1 to Strength, +1 to Constitution.
Effect 2: The raised creature has a 30% chance of keeping one of its special skills.
Class restrictions: Only Death Knight

So that's why the place wasn't crowded. Apparently, the dungeon boss only dropped Death Knight stuff. Which was of no good here in the Lands of Light. Had the dungeon belonged to the opposite faction, it would have been packed solid. I'd have to store my loot in the bank until I had a chance to come across some Dark vendors. Provided they didn't smoke me on the spot.

The bear bellowed. I jumped up and looked at the throne. There, respawning was in full swing. With a hoarse growl, the two officers reappeared first, followed by the Priest. The pet had no qualms about repaying his second chance at life. The brief fight was followed by a ringing silence as we waited, wary, for the King to reappear. One minute, two, three. That was funny. He should have respawned by now.

I quickly crossed the room and frisked the bodies, stumbling under the weight of an officer's double sword. The priest didn't let me down. He respawned with full pockets: some cash, a bracelet, a key and a crudely made ring with a simple +15 to life effect. Still no King. I just presumed that bosses couldn't respawn as often as regular mobs. Very well. We could wait till next round. If he still hadn't turned up, we'd have to pull some guards from the hall's farthest corner.

Staggering under my overflowing bag, I walked to the archway where I'd left the stealthed Bug. I tapped a finger on the wall,

"Knock, knock, open up!"

I could hear some heavy wheezing, swearing and the sound of metal clanging against metal. "Are you making yourself a nest? Come on now, off with your stealth and on with your trading mode. I've got some stuff to give you."

Finally, Bug came into view, all ruffled, poking the wall with his lockpicks.

"What have you got in there? A peep show? Why did you make that hole in the wall?"

"This ain't no hole. That's a lock in the door. A secret door!"

"No way!" I crouched and peered into the dark.

It was a lock all right. The whole niche, concealed within the archway, was actually a door.

"How cool is that? You think you can open it?"

Bug gave a tired shrug. "Who knows. It looks like some special kind of lock. I think I'll alt-tub now to a closed clan forum I know. I'll do a bit of search there about this little door and how to open it."

"So you're not in FIVR, then? Are you in 3D?"

"Exactly. Already since morning. I've maxed out the time limit."

"I see. What's that forum you're talking about? How did you get access? You don't belong to a clan, do you? Or do you have another character?"

Bug winced, apparently not too forthcoming. "They're tough. No, I don't have another char. I only have this one. As for the access... I did tell you I wanted to be a super spy, didn't I? Well, that's how I got the access."

He gave me a wink and sent me a sales invitation. I dumped all the regular steel into an opened window.

"Think you could change some copper for gold?" I asked. "You're not going anywhere, anyway. And I honestly can't stand straight any more."

"Be my guest," he mumbled, his attention focused on something else.

I added seven thousand copper and peered at Bug's frozen absent stare. I tapped a finger on his forehead. "Anybody home? You owe me seven gold. Go ahead, shoot it. And take the stuff, quickly, before the mobs respawn."

Things were falling into a pattern. We kept killing gnolls, to mixed results. Some spawns brought no trophies at all, just a couple bracelets and a piece of armor. Once the fight was over, I collected another helping of stuff and passed it over to Bug who regaled me with the latest four-letter news about the game developers and their doors and locks. I'd grin, crawl back onto the throne and lower my lids to meditate. I was exhausted.

The King reappeared only after an hour. The timing was really bad. I had just turned my attention to the Priest when the dungeon boss arrived with two guards in tow. Not good, considering my fear reflexes had somewhat atrophied while I'd been ordering my pet around from the comfort of the throne, only raising my backside to cast a sluggish spell. Now I had to face the boss himself.

I tumbled to the ground, harvesting a couple of hits from the guards. Then I jumped to my feet and backed up casting Deadman's Hand, trying to bring the aggros under my control. Finally, one of them froze. Teddy had finished with the Priest and turned to the King. Make it quick, boy. My Life flashed orange by the time I managed to restrain one of the guards. Even though I'd have loved to restore whatever hits I had left, I had to switch target to the first mob and freeze him again. Stay where you are, you son of a bitch.

I kept switching from one target to the next, deterring the gnolls while the bear finished the King off and joined in the fun. The rest was history.

Whew. That was close. But I had something to show for it: a mountain of corpses and my almost-level 27. Among the more interesting loot I counted a couple of keys and some good greaves dropped from the King.

Gnoll King's Greaves
Item class: Rare
Effect 1: +22 to Armor, +50 to Life, +3 to Strength, +3 to Constitution

Effect 2: Increases the chances of dropping Soul Stones 6%.

Class restrictions: Only Death Knight

Excellent.

Then I heard a happy yell from inside the niche. "Got it!"

Something clinked. A stealthless Bug pushed the secret door open with a flourish. That's my boy. I thought he wouldn't make it.

The new room was dark, the only feeble light coming from a glowing pictogram on the stone floor.

I peeked inside but didn't discover anything worth our interest, apart from the crimson reflections licking the walls and ceiling. "What's that, the gates of hell?"

Bug took it personally. "What hell are you talking about, boss? This is a portal. It'll take you right up to the first floor into the room closest to the entrance. You can go visit your Elfa girlfriend if you wish. When I went past her, she was still busy slaughtering gnolls by the dozen."

"Yeah, right," I chuckled. "And spend another hour and a half getting back down here. It's cool, anyway. How did you manage to open it?"

Bug hesitated. "Er, this clan portal, they have a cool piece of software, a lockpick tutorial. So I fiddled with it for a bit. They actually say it takes on average three hours to work it out."

"Dude, you're awesome."

I slapped his shoulder and climbed the throne which already felt like part of me. We had another hour to wait for the King to respawn so we could just as well make ourselves comfortable.

Time kept going. After a few more fights, I collected a full set of keys and got to level 29. I received another Achievement, for staying alive for twenty subsequent levels, and Fame Level 2: "People know your name". But this kind of fame came with strings attached. On one hand, this was virtual reality where aggro mobs only understood brute strength. But on the other, I was no TV star and didn't enjoy the audience's attention. Never mind. Plenty of time to look into what they'd said.

It was time for the King to respawn again. Seeing that Bug didn't look particularly happy, I sent him an invitation to join the group.

"Come on, click *Yes*. I'll take you on for this round. You can do with some leveling up."

Judging by his eager acceptance, he had to be sitting bolt upright by his computer staring at the XP bar and anticipating an experience downpour. And we got cooking.

The mobs' next respawn went without a glitch. I was finishing off the King when Taali's message dropped into my inbox.

U there? Help!!!!!

Oh. Awful timing. I glanced around, made sure I was safe and typed away,

Whassup? Where are u?

A long pause was followed by a brief answer,

3PK at gnolls level 1.

The bear killed the King. I stuffed the loot into the bag as fast I could and turned to Bug. "Gotta dash. There's an Elfa I know being killed by some PKs. You just keep going as we planned. I'll keep you posted. If push comes to shove, remove stealth and go straight to the cemetery. See you in town. OK?"

"No problem," Bug raised a clenched fist. "Make 'em eat dirt."

I nodded and walked past him through the portal. The last thing I heard was Bug's indignant squeak when the bear squeezed itself past him into the archway.

For a second, I lost all sight and orientation. Then we found ourselves in the purple-moss room. Two level-11 gnoll warriors lunged at us, growling. Barely a mouthful for my Teddy.

I squinted at the map trying to work out the exit location. I made two hurried steps toward the archway and examined the corridor behind it. Three caster Elves stood with their backs to me. In front of them rotated a translucent spawn sphere. Then it stopped and jingled down in a cascade of broken fragments. Taali stood in its place, surrounded by a couple dozen of her little graves. She was having a hard time of it.

The Elves loved it. One of them quickly paralyzed the girl while the two others began hurling fireballs as her body jerked with electric charges. That hurt a lot. Bastards.

"Hummungus—attack!"

The Elves jumped, squeaking with surprise. They had a point: the first thing they saw was the bulk of a bear charging at them. Teddy hadn't had enough regen time after his last King job, therefore he looked slightly out of shape, read: spine-tinglingly scary. His torn bloodied hide was covered in burns and stabbed wounds. Forcing his large body through the corridor, Teddy looked a bit like a subway train speeding down a tunnel.

Bang! A heavy paw slapped one of the scumbags. Either with surprise or in pain, he slumped to the floor. The remaining two backed away while the bear finished off the unlucky one in a few saucy smacks. Level 20. For Taali it was way too much to handle; for Teddy, a minor distraction.

You have killed a player of the Faction of Light!

You relationship with the Dark Alliance has improved!

You have 1 point on your PK counter! In case of your death at the hands of another player, you have 1% chance of dropping an item.

You have fewer PK points than the killed player (1<72) which makes him a legitimate target. You receive 1 point off your PK counter.

Not good. I still had Bug in my group. He didn't need all those faction games. I opened the menu and deleted him from the group. A few seconds later, my PK counter dinged twice, only to drop back to zero. None of the bastards had gotten away. They'd all died there and then.

I came to the girl. She sat on the floor with her face in her hands, crying softly.

"Stop it. It's okay. The cavalry's here, the bad guys are punished. Good has triumphed all around," I gingerly stroked her bare shoulder. "Come on, get up now. You need to put something on before you catch a cold," I kept blabbing unconsciously, trying to attract her attention.

Taali raised her tearful face and looked up at me. I quickly unlaced the bag and produced the belt I'd set aside for her. "Here, look. Exactly what you ordered. Perfect for a paladin."

Unsure, the girl took the present and peered at its characteristics. A faint smile crossed her face. Relieved, I hurried on, "I also have a ring for you, a nice one, no extras but really pretty. I need to find it in my bag first. It's a real mess—my bag, I mean. Get up now."

Mechanically, the girl stood up. Still sniveling, she walked around the cave stopping by the empty graves and touching them one by one. They all disappeared. She finally found the very first grave that contained her clothes and began to pull on armor.

"What happened?" I couldn't hold my curiosity any longer.

"Jerks," she said.

She put her clothes back on, tried on the belt in front of an imaginary mirror and gave me a happy smile. Nothing like a new trinket to make a girl happy. She crouched next to me.

"I was fighting when those jerks entered the cave. When they saw me they didn't even bother to wait till I was finished with the monster. They just paralyzed and attacked me. To add insult to injury, the gnoll nearly killed me. Then they beat me up and took all the money..." the girl gave me a meaningful look.

Hey, I wasn't that stupid. I frisked the bodies. One had nearly seventy gold on him; the others, a couple silver. And a personal badge each. In the meantime, Taali went on.

"And I, in my eternal wisdom, had set up my spawn point right here. It seemed safe enough, no need to go far in case you get killed. So thirty seconds later, I respawn and these jerks are still here laughing, discussing the state of my undress, offering to dance with me, like, on mutual consent. I punched one and kicked the other in the balls. Apparently, they didn't like it so they killed me again. After that, I couldn't do a thing: I'd respawn, they'd paralyze me and kill me again."

Okay. I made a mental note to hide my resurrection point away from prying eyes and potential problems. "Did you have much money?"

"Nearly fifty. All I earned today."

"Here, take it."

I counted fifty coins and gave them to the girl. She grabbed the gold and hurriedly poured it down her bag. Then she froze and raised her guilty eyes to me. "Please don't think I'm some kind of skinflint. I just need this money really badly," her voice weakened with every word until she sulked again, crouching in a heap on the floor staring into space.

That wasn't right. I sat opposite her and took her narrow hands in mine. "Taali. Are we friends or not?"

She shrugged weakly.

"Has something happened? Why are you constantly tearful? You tell me. I can understand. I'm condemned, too. I have an inoperable brain tumor. Don't you see I'm stuck here all the time? Don't you see I'm trying for perma mode?"

Her eyes grew wider. "Are you?"

I curled my lips. I couldn't take it any longer. "You want a doctor's statement?"

Taali shrunk back. "I'm sorry. Actually, I'm Tania."

"I'm Max."

She nodded, sniffled and reeled off. "You want to know what happened? I'll tell you. We were two sisters. Both beautiful, both happy, both dedicated athletes. Tania was the big sister. She was nineteen and the younger, sixteen... So one day the little sister was walking home from her athletics practice. A big black car stops nearby. Two big guys drag her inside. The rest you can guess. When they dumped her by the roadside in the morning they left her for dead. Only she wasn't."

As Taali spoke, her face grew hard. Her clenched hands turned white. "Some good Samaritans found the girl and brought her to the hospital. Then the police investigator arrived. She was very sympathetic with my sister at first. But apparently, the police found some eyewitnesses who identified the car and the guys. Which was a problem. One guy turned out to be third deputy to some local statesman or other. The other happened to belong to a very rich and well-connected tribe in one of those corrupted Caucasian republics. This cute and cuddly police officer became a vicious Gestapo bitch overnight. She demanded more medical checks. She questioned the girl about every detail of that night. Asked her if it felt good. Wondered if she could have provoked the 'boys' herself. My sister couldn't sleep after her visits, waking up screaming every half-hour. And so it went on, day after day, interrogation after interrogation. Then the bitch said she'd have to have a talk with my sister's teachers and classmates to find out more about her moral standing. Said she'd have to tell them all about that night, all the details. My sister came back home that day, locked herself in the bathroom and slit her wrists. The case was closed. The bad guys walk free. The police bitch swapped her two-year-old Beamer X7 for a brand new luxury version X8. Now the big sister spends all her time off work in the FIVR. She hopes to raise enough money to buy a gun. And she will. Even if it takes a whole year. That's it, basically."

I fell silent for a while. "You sure you won't miss?"

Taali smiled bitterly. "I've got bronze in the regional biathlon championship, in case you're interested."

I paused. Then I raised my head to the ceiling, "AI, you think you can hear me? Just for your information. If anyone learns what we've been talking about, this girl won't survive the night. So please don't grass her up. You'll kill her if you do."

The girl gave me a puzzled look. "You think?"

"Could be. AI is our god. He's omnipresent and omniscient. You never know whether he hears you or not."

I scrambled back to my feet. "As for your story... I understand. I'll see if I can help you. Just please don't jump the gun, literally. You'll only give yourself away and won't avenge your sis."

"You really approve?"

"Well. I'm double dead, if you know what I mean. I can go out in the street and shoot whoever I want. I won't live less because of it—I'm gonna die in a week or two, anyway. On the other hand, I'm in a game and I'd love to stay here for good. Also, the rules are different here. These guys," I gestured at the three Elven graves, "they hurt you and were punished. Instantly. They were hurt too. They lost their money and gained a few enemies. And no amount of statesmen's mandates can help them. That's fair. I like it. So I'd do the same if I were you."

At that moment, the three Elves crashed back in, albeit barebellied. Talk of the devil. Seriously, had they made a decent comeback, we'd have probably given them the chance to pick up their stuff. Instead, the kids were craving revenge. Without saying a word, they cast paralysis on both of us and showered us with fire arrows and fire balls.

The kids didn't seem to have learned their lesson. With a roar, Hummungus charged. Stripped of their stuff, the Elves lasted exactly half the time. My PK counter didn't grow: the kids had attacked us first turning the kill into defense and bringing me three more personal badges.

I spat on the floor. "What a bunch of jokers."

"Prats," Taali corrected me. Seeing my puzzled look, she explained, "They are *Pratz*, a PK clan. They have their own castle in the neutral lands. Most of them perma players. A nice collection of scumbags. Officially the clan's name is *Bratz* but everybody calls them *Pratz*. I think they'll call in reinforcements. We'd better move it."

"Affirmative."

I PM'd Bug telling him I wasn't coming back and that he should stick to our plan. Then I glanced at the girl. "It's probably better if I take you to town. Before you get into more trouble."

She raised her eyebrows. Then, for the first time since I'd known her, she beamed. "Go ahead then, my little Necro. Guide me."

Chapter Eleven

After the dungeons' dim light, the soft glow of the setting sun blinded me. As I blinked it away, the Pratz jammed my message box with threats. Thanks a bunch, kids. You've saved me the trouble of marking your names. I blacklisted the eager boy scouts in a specially created folder: now the game interface would highlight their names in red to warn about potential danger.

The Drow Princess—you couldn't confuse her operatic voice with anyone else's—cried out from where the cages stood. Her white fingers clutched the cage bars. I followed her gaze. A High Elf was walking along the cages finishing off the prisoners one by one. Three bodies already lay on the filthy floor when the player approached his next victim, shaking his bloodied sword clean. What did he think he was doing?

"Wait here, I'll be right back," I said to Taali and ran, adding under my breath, "Hummungus, keep an eye on her!"

I made it in the nick of time. I grabbed the Elf's sword hand and jerked him round to face me. "Wait. Why are you doing this?"

The Elf looked me up and down, assessing my shabby garb, then freed his hand in one smooth motion.

His strength parameter had to be much higher than mine. Which made sense: not only was he a warrior, but he was also up to his balls in most amazing gear. His matching armor had to have cost him a fortune; his sword gleamed purple, its blade entwined with runes. He had to either be a donator or belong to some top clan which helped equip their members. He was five levels below me but it didn't seem to bother him much.

"Fuck off! It's my quest. I get one gold per head and faction relationship improvement. There's nothing for you to catch here. They only respawn once every twenty-four hours. I've been genociding them for three days now."

"I have a quest with them, too. Since this morning."

The warrior smirked. "That's your problem, dude." He shrugged and turned away, raising his sword.

Dickhead. I grabbed his shoulder again. "Wait."

He frowned, threat in his glare.

Hurriedly I counted off the coins. Easy come, easy go, whatever. Trust me to take it from some scumbag only to give to another.

"Here," I handed him the money. "Seventeen cages. Seventeen gold. That'll break you even. No touching the prisoners now."

Quest completion alert! You've completed a secret quest: A Friend in Need.

Donate the lion's share of your property to help those in trouble.

Reward: A Smile of Fortune. Luck will follow you around for one full week. It will increase your crit chances, send you rare loot and do various other things associated with good luck and Gods' assistance.

The Elf took the money and thoughtfully weighed it in his hand, casting appraising glances at me. Finally, he came to a decision and dumped the money into his bag.

"Well, if you're so rich and desperate to keep them alive, you'd better come up with thirty more gold and I'll think about it. Happy with that? If you aren't, do yourself a favor and fuck off."

He was enjoying it, staring at me with a smirk as he stood there rocking from foot to foot. He tapped his sword against an armored leg, its blade sending sunspots into my eyes.

Apparently, by paying him off I came across as weak and eager. My tatty looks and the absence of a clan badge plus the ease with which I'd parted with the money made the guy think he was in luck for a loaded wuss.

I scowled. "Listen you, shit for brains. You've got your money, now piss off. If you don't, there're always other ways."

He just laughed. "There are indeed."

He buried one steel boot toe in my stomach sending me flying a dozen feet.

You've been attacked by another player! Self-defense doesn't affect the PK counter!

Good news, yeah. Twenty percent life vanished into thin air. It hurt, and it was wrong. Especially as it wasn't some clever combat trick but a regular kick. It smelled of real trouble.

From the cages, the bear bellowed and went for him. The Elf didn't budge. He pursed his thin angry lips and threw the heavy shield onto one arm.

The bear rammed him but the player deflected the blow with his shield and stayed on his feet. Immediately he parried with the sword, knocking off 5% hits in one lunge. Jesus. That way he'd smoke Teddy as well. I started casting everything I had as fast as I could, all my arsenal. DoT, DoT, Deadman's Hand, Life Absorption, Life again, and again. Taali came running. She tried to heal the bear not knowing that ordinary cleric healing spells didn't work for a zombie. Seeing this, the girl grabbed her sword and attacked the Elf from behind. Was she really crazy or just a good friend who'd take your side without first finding out who was right and who was wrong?

We did get the better of him in the end. He was tough as nails, no doubt about that. Donators were tops. By the end, I had no mana left; even Teddy looked much worse for wear, his life hovering at 25%. As the warrior died, he gave me a memorizing glare full of promise.

You have killed a player of the Faction of Light!
You relationship with the Dark Alliance has improved!
The killed player has 12 points on his PK counter!

A cautious bastard. He chose his victims well. I was lucky I'd made thirty levels in two days. I'd been immune to PK until earlier that morning, and already had had three fights. If I'd taken my time leveling like everybody else, my PK counter would have kept growing with every skirmish.

Very well, mister donator, let's have a look at your assets. Four to one that you drop something worth our while.

I walked over to his grave and touched it. Gold clinked as I became about sixty coins richer. Forty gold net gain. Being a PK definitely paid, no wonder young players couldn't help it. He dropped no clothes, unfortunately, only a name badge.

I received a PM. *You're toast.*

He didn't mince words, did he? Looked like I got myself a stubborn and dangerous enemy. I knew I shouldn't have provoked him but leaving his threats without an answer really wasn't kosher. So I trolled him a little:

Awesome sword, THNX. Perfect for me.

He responded with a cluster of F-words. I made a mental note of his ability to lose his cool. Then I blacklisted him. His name was Tavor. I was going to remember that.

Taali came up to me, looking concerned. "What's going on here?"

"Nothing, really. Just a lowlife who saw I had money and wanted to relieve me of it."

"That's not good. Did you see his clan badge? Forest Cats. A big rich clan with a very bad name. Normally no one would mess with them. Problems are guaranteed."

I thought about it. She was right. Not good. But did I think I could've done it differently if I could replay the whole thing? Probably not. I just couldn't see a kiss-and-make-up scenario there.

"One problem at a time," I said. "He didn't notice you at first and then he only saw your back. I don't think he had time to ID you. And don't worry about me. I level up while you sleep," I repeated an old joke.

Still concerned, she shook her head. "Let's leg it, then. It's getting hotter by the minute. First the Pratz and now the Cats."

"Wait up. I'll just close the quest."

I walked to the cages already ravaged by Tavor. There, the Elves' motionless bodies lay in blackening pools of blood. That really wasn't right. Taali's soundless steps echoed from behind me. She stopped by my side, silent. Then she took my hand and looked up into my face.

"You all right?"

"Yeah. Just sorry for them. I told them I'd come back and save them."

Her eyebrows jerked up. "Sorry for whom? They're just digit codes. Part of the program, that's all."

I swung round and locked her eyes with mine. "What am I gonna be, then, once I turn perma—a digit code? Is that what you think? So that anyone can swat me like a fly? And how about those thousands already in the game? Are *they* just values in the server's binary code?"

Taali didn't answer, dumbfounded. "I... I really don't know," she whispered.

She turned to the bodies. Her eyes were different now. Then she crouched, slid her hand between the bars and covered a dead warrior's face with the end of his cape. "That's better. That's... right."

I nodded and hugged her waist. The girl didn't draw back. In fact, she cuddled up closer.

Quest completion alert: Last Honors. Quest completed!

Pay funeral honors to dead heroes, whether friends or foes. One day someone might pause over your grave remembering the brave warrior's resting place.

Reward I: Doubles the time your grave stays at the cemetery before it decays.

Reward II: Your tombstone changes from granite to marble.

Taali shuddered. Apparently, I wasn't the only one who completed the quest.

"Congrats."

"Likewise,' the girl nodded. "I love white marble."

I never felt comfortable about this kind of quest. I had a funny feeling AI generated them on the run, just by watching and evaluating our actions. Then it would either reward or punish them guided by his own particular brand of logic. Wonder if it was possible—just as a social experiment—to place a hundred million people in a virtual world, then use the stick-and-carrot policy to train them to conform to a particular society model? It sounded absurd. Or was it?

I opened the bag and scooped out a couple dozen identical keys. Matching the key runes against each cage, I walked along freeing the prisoners one by one. As each Drow lowered his or her head in gratitude, I received more quest-completing messages:

Quest completion alert: Freedom Ain't Free. Quest completed!
Reward: Experience
Your relationship with the Dark Alliance has improved!
Your relationship with the Drow race has improved!

The diplomacy bar showed that my relationship with both had shifted from hatred to dislike. That way it would soon go up to neutral, making it possible for me to trade with the disciples of the Fallen One or even dare out on an occasional visit to their cities.

The bells dinged after I freed the first couple dozen of them.

Congratulations! You've reached level 30!
Racial bonus: +1 to Intellect
Class bonus: +1 to Intellect, +1 to Spirit
5 Characteristic points available! You now have 125 Characteristic points!

So! There I was, a gift-wrapped enigma, formally level 30, looking like a level-zero noob in his start-up garb. Specialization not chosen, characteristics and Talent points same as they were at level 5. A blank canvas. Never mind. Teddy's potential would last me another five or six levels. Soon it was time to end this hectic marathon. Then we could take a break, maybe even have a whole day off. We'd see the city, have a quality meal in the Three Little Pigs, and then we'd start pondering over choosing skills and distributing the points.

As I was thinking, another message popped up.

Congratulations! You've received Achievement: Slow on the Draw!
You've made Top 100 of the players who haven't chosen Specialization by level 30.
Reward: +1500 to Fame

Very nice. Slow on the draw! Talking about lame fame. The fact that we were at least a hundred had to be good news, I suppose. A hundred slowmoes, so to say.

Finally I'd freed all the surviving Elves and got to the end of the line, approaching the Dark Princess. Her face was as passionless as ever. I showed her the key and nodded at the massive lock. The Princess lowered her eyelids slightly. You were welcome to understand it whichever way. I shrugged and turned the key in the rusty lock, then forced the screeching door open.

Quest completion alert: Free the Drow Princess I. Quest completed!
Reward: access to unique quest Free the Drow Princess II.

The Elven Princess stepped out gracefully. She pressed one hand to her heart and lowered her head in gratitude.

"I thank you, my High brother. My warriors are now free; the shame of captivity won't befall the House of Night. I didn't ask you to help me, but you freed me nevertheless. So please accept the Drow Princess' gratitude."

Looking me in the eye, the Princess lay her hands on my shoulders and, rising on tiptoes, gave me an indifferent kiss. Her lips were warm, soft and supple. She had a heady smell of wild strawberries.

Buff alert! You've received a lifetime buff: the Mark of the House of Night.

Effect: Drow's Friend. Your relationship with Dark Elves has improved to amicable.

For a brief moment, I lost myself in her black eyes. Then I pulled myself together and bowed low. "I appreciate the honor, Madam."

A sniff came from behind my back. I turned around. Taali was trying to look the other way but her nostrils flared. Binary codes no more, heh?

The Princess pressed my hand with her slim fingers, reminding me of her presence. "I will need your help, friend. Are you prepared?"

"Always prepared," I muttered, pulling my hand free. All women were the same. You offered them a hand and they took an arm. That's the power of love for you.

The Princess pointed at the carved collar still hugging her neck. "No idea how these hyenas managed to lay their hands on a rare artifact like this. There're not many Magic Negators of this level around, and we do know where most of them are. I have a funny feeling the Gnoll King was only instrumental in a bigger game by the Houses of Fire and the Moon. But it's of no consequence to you. Just help me remove it. Get the crystal key from the King."

New unique quest available! Free the Drow Princess II.

The Princess' powerful abilities are neutralized by the Magic Negator. Go down the sinister Gnoll Dungeon, reach the palace and find the key!

Reward: Unknown

Oh well. Who was I to say no to unique quests?

"I will help you, Princess. But can you give me a clue what it looks like? The King and I, we're bosom buddies. Seen him five times or so today. I'm sure he won't say no," I attempted a Clint Eastwood grin.

Her eyes smiled. "It's a red crystal with the same carving as the collar."

The Princess leaned closer, showing it to me. She smelled so good that my head went round. She pushed a lock of hair to the other shoulder and bent her head, exposing a chiseled neck burdened by the unwanted accessory. My heart missed a couple beats. I shook my head to concentrate on the business at hand and forced my eyes away from her velvet skin, her tantalizing cleavage and a pulse beating over her collarbone.

I peered at the pattern snaking along the collar. I could have sworn I'd seen it somewhere before. I frowned, trying to remember. My loot. I'd been in a hurry to go and help Taali so I'd stuffed the last batch into my bag without having a good look. I vaguely remembered seeing something similar in there.

I dropped the bag on the ground and dug into it. There. Could it be the crystal? By then, ordinary keys had stopped dropping and I'd already collected a full set. Then after a chain of nearly-empty respawns, the King had dropped that squiggly thing. Apparently, that didn't happen every day.

I picked up the crystal and handed it to the Princess. "Is that it?"

For a moment, she lost her natural cool. She grabbed the key and touched the Negator with it. The collar clicked and opened.

She beamed. A smooth gesture, a few singsong words—and her clothes fluttered, the fabric regaining its pristine whiteness and order. After that, she broke into a dozen hasty spells casting group buffs, healing the wounded and sending astral messengers. Her appearance had changed—now she looked like the Royal she was.

Finally, the Princess turned to me. "I do appreciate what you have done for me and my warriors. You can count on our gratitude when you too need help. Please accept this artifact as a reward for your courage and chivalry. I ask you but one thing: do not ever leave it in greedy hands. This collar can bring about a lot of misery with an ill will and a bit of imagination."

Quest completion alert: Free the Drow Princess II. Quest completed!

Reward I: The one-time right to summon the warriors of the House of Night. To receive help, ask any Drow to put you in contact with a House representative.

Reward II: Magic Negator and Crystal Key.

The Princess nodded me goodbye and activated the portal. One by one, her men entered the radiant archway. She left last, leaving me with a heady forest scent and a strange yearning.

"Impressive," Taali remarked. Was she jealous or something?

"Yeah," I mumbled and packed the new gizmo with the rest of them. About time I started thinking of raising my Strength parameter. I could also use a new bag for two or three hundred slots. "Come on, then. Look up. I have a funny feeling the Pratz cavalry will be here any minute. And I owe them for six graves. My Inbox is chock full of their filth.

"So is mine," the girl nodded. "Judging by how fast they come, the little jerks sit it out somewhere waiting for help to arrive."

"That's possible. Come on, Hummungus. Left-right, left-right!"

Chapter Twelve

We walked out of the gnoll dungeon and headed toward the city. The gnoll workers that had only yesterday seemed so tough and dangerous kept lunging at us from everywhere, only to face Teddy the Bodyguard. The enormous level gap didn't leave the suckers half a chance. Groups of low-level players watched us walk past, although admittedly Hummungus was the center of their attention. I didn't mind. On the contrary, I made sure to showcase him at his best, making him bellow and lunge as I played with "Attack!" and "Off!" We even did our good deed for the day by tearing apart an impressive train that some over-eager ranger had dragged to his group. Taali gave everyone a quick heal, handed out some buffs and off we went.

As we walked, she demanded to know every detail of the Drow quest. She'd probably decided to do it herself. She looked really funny when she asked, stern-eyed, if a Drow leader absolutely had to be a woman or whether a male prince or knight could also be accepted? I had to put on a serious face and tell her that indeed a knight was okay, why not. On a white charger, yeah right. She was still a child. Shame I couldn't give her the keys which turned out to be non-transferrable.

When we were a few hundred feet away from the city, I slowed down. The forest ended there. "That's it, Taali. I'm afraid I can't go any further. The guards will start aggroing Teddy. I'm too close already. I've seen a couple of patrols here before."

"Never mind. Thanks for your help. For everything..." she paused.

"Stop it, will ya? You think I'd leave a girl in trouble? I'd kick any amount of ass for a friend."

She raised her head and looked me in the eye. "A friend?"

I took her slim hands in mine. "Whassup? Sure we're friends. Why would you doubt that? Is it because of that Drow chick?"

"It's the way you looked at her."

"Oh. How can I explain," I hesitated. "Body chemistry, you know? Game designer magic plus pheromones in combination with abstinence, a new fitter me and tons of naked bods walking around."

I didn't think she understood all of it but her face lit up. Much better. I hated to see her sad as a panda without bamboo. "Could I ask a favor of you? I'm like a walking Fort Knox at the moment, lugging around over a hundred gold. You think you could pop it into the bank for me? I can't go to town myself, you see."

Taali gave me a serious look as if searching for an answer to some unasked question. Then she nodded. "Thanks."

"What for?"

"For trusting me. Come on, where's your money? I really need some cash to get that Versace robe."

She could still joke, which was a good sign. At least I hoped she joked. I handed her the money and nodded at the looming tower tops. "Off you go, then."

She wasn't in a hurry to leave, though. Devils danced in her eyes. "Did you say abstinence?"

She stepped toward me and gave me a firm kiss—artless but passionate and uncompromising as youth itself. Then she swung round, her mane of hair lashing the air, and strode toward the city.

I shook my head, flabbergasted. What kind of day was this? The amount of adventures, conflicts, emotions and beautiful women had exceeded the yearly real-world quota. I liked it.

Finally I pulled myself together and took the familiar trail back into the woods toward Grym's cave. I had barely fifty paces left to cover when I heard Hummungus' fierce roar behind my back, followed by a scream.

"Die, you spawn of the Dark!"

I turned around just in time to see my pet being attacked by two of the city guards. A bit further, a mage was whispering something into a radiant crystal. A patrol. Talking of the devil.

Probably, the best thing would be to smoke the pet myself and make an inconspicuous exit. But either my affection for Teddy or the mob-respawning, bear-bellowing instinct that I'd acquired in the last twenty-four hours got the better of me. Both, most likely. The guards weren't much to write home about, both level twenty-five. The mage was level thirty. The further away from the city one went, the weaker patrols became: not so much combat force as a rapid report system. But I had a bad feeling about the mage, apparently on a hotline to somewhere.

You've received experience!

Warning! You've killed a guard of the City of Light! The Sun King doesn't approve of those who kill his subjects!

Your relationship with the Dark Alliance has improved!

Your relationship with the Alliance of Light has deteriorated!

Bad, too bad. I remembered reading that it was never a good idea to attack allied NPCs. Reputation could plummet and it could take you a lot of time and drudgery to restore it. Actually, I could understand the Admins. I'd had some experience with certain servers where the players butchered quest characters and bankers, even slaughtering entire trading towns. I'd once watched the server's top clan raze a biggish city. This, of course, tended to ruin the gaming experience and could potentially alienate the average player. This I knew but I couldn't do much about it now. The second guard died, too. The remaining mage wisely chose an escape route. He cast a slowing spell over my pet and, while Teddy tried to kick away some roots entangling his legs, he popped a portal open and disappeared in a blue haze.

Not good. You didn't have to be a mind reader to know that the place would soon be crawling with guards.

I frisked the corpses. Nothing special, just some silver and a few gamers' badges. Now I had to get to the cave double quick. The passage was too narrow for Teddy: he was bound to get stuck halfway through, but as long as no one could see him from the outside, it had to do. A couple steps down was good enough.

This time the cave was brightly lit, just for a change. A dozen makeshift candles oozed wax. Grym the Hermit in rolled-up sleeves was busy pounding some pungent ingredient in a mortar. When I stumbled down the steps into the cave, he glanced over at me but continued with his work. Then his eyebrows rose. He set aside his bowl filled with some shimmering powder and walked over to me.

"You're surely full of surprises, young warlock. You've gained strength fast. Probably a bit too fast. In the Dark Lands you'd still be a green newb, but here, right under the High Ones' nose..." Grym shook his head in disbelief.

I had too little time for subtleties so I grabbed the bull by the horns. "Thank you, Sir Hermit. Would you be willing to teach me something new?"

Grym nodded and made a magician-like gesture. "Absolutely. You're long overdue your reward."

Congratulations! You've received 3 Talent points!
You have 23 Talent points available!

Excellent. We'd sorted out all the old odds and sods. Time to look forward to new heights.

Grym put an end to my reverie. "Have you managed to demonstrate your loyalty to the Fallen One?"

Jeez, what did he want from me? It's not as if he'd given me any tips, was it? What was I supposed to do, spit on the altar in an Elven temple? Maybe hand out some anti-Elf leaflets printed by the Darks' underground? Or even fly the Fallen One's colors in the dark of the night from the watchtower's spire? Having said that...

I started rummaging through my bag, found what I was looking for and brought a jingling bundle of the players' badges to Grym's eyes. "Will these do?"

The old goblin studied the offering. Then he grinned and nodded. "Excellent. You'll get a gold piece for each High scumbag you've offed. I'd rather you brought me their ears but the badges will do nicely. If ever you come across more of such loot, remember old Grym."

Quest completion alert: Demonstrate your loyalty to the Fallen One II. Quest completed!
Reward: Gold

Grym rummaged through the folds of his robe and produced seven coins. I liked this job. Wonder what he'd give me for the guards' badges? I slapped my pockets and produced my remaining booty. The hermit started and leaned forward. His face sharpened, vulture-like. He examined every badge, stroking and bringing them close to his nose. Then he nodded, satisfied, and emitted a hoarse laugh.

"You've made my day, young warlock. Old Grym hasn't seen this kind of loot for a long, long time. What can I give you in return?"

I paused for a moment, thinking. Another handful of gold wouldn't help me much. Asking for some unique gear was rather stupid. Having said that...

"I'd like you to answer a question."

Grym looked interested. "Oh, really? Spit it out, then."

"I'd like to know how I could find the Dark Guild of the City of Light. I've been meaning to have a talk with their master. He might have some secret quests for me. Or he could share some ancient lore to help me on my chosen path..."

The goblin saddened, shaking his head. "The Dark Guild's secrets are too much for a newb to bear. Go and find yourself some easier quests first, and one day we might come back to this conversation."

New Quest alert! Knowledge Breeds Sadness!

Keep Grym and his cave a secret for a minimum of ten days.

Reward: Access to quest: Knowledge Breeds Sadness II!

I nodded, accepting the quest. What a pain. They seemed to arrange quests in stages. You'd be old by the time you got to the bottom of it all.

"I'll be back in ten days," I said by way of goodbye and headed for the exit. I didn't want to wait till he blew me out like the first time. Teddy was still stuck in the corridor and I didn't want to be smashed in mid-air against his fangs.

"Go," the hermit heaved a sigh. Was it my imagination or had I gleaned some compassion in his voice?

Teddy was waiting for me, doglike. I patted his neck and walked up the gnarled steps out into the fresh night air. Where to now? Back to the caves? Level 1 and 2 mobs were all highlighted in gray now—they wouldn't bring any loot or experience. Level 3 gnolls were mainly green: I got the loot but virtually no XP. The Throne Room mobs' names were highlighted in blue, which meant that they were slightly below me. And still, in another hour or two I'd have nothing left to farm there, with the exception of the King. It would take too long. I needed to find a new hunting ground. But not now, in the middle of the night. Should I maybe curl up under some tree or other and have a nap until sunrise?

I walked along, musing, when the flapping of wings added to the night forest sounds. A large gryphon crashed onto the trail in full flight and hissed at Hummungus. I stopped dead in my tracks. A Lieutenant of the Royal Guard jumped off the gryphon's back. I tried to leg it. Too late. The Lieutenant uttered a short spell, pinning my feet to the ground. Teddy lunged to my defense. The Lieutenant waved his hatchet in the air, and the bear cartwheeled back, his life halved. Another assault sent Teddy flying like a lapdog, his life blinking in the red zone. And still he wobbled back toward the Elf. I hurried to open the pet control panel and pressed 'Off.'. Immediately I noticed a rabbit nearby, selected it as target and ordered Teddy to attack it. The chase could take him away from the guard while I would try to talk my way out of it somehow.

But what was that? Had Teddy just ignored my commands? Head shaking, one wet eye glancing at me, the bear kept advancing toward the guard who was watching the beast with a lazy curiosity. Then the Lieutenant whispered a spell and flung a drop of fire from his hand. The flames consumed Teddy. The pet's status icon closed and disappeared.

No! Something got into my eye so I could barely see the Elf raise his staff sending a wide beam of light up into the sky. Like a beacon, it attracted another dozen gryphons which descended onto the narrow trail like a murder of crows. Strong gauntleted hands grabbed me. A voice thundered over my ear,

"Laith the Warlock, you're under arrest for worshipping the Fallen One, for summoning the beings of the Dark, for Elves-targeted assaults and for the murder of City of Light guards."

Chapter Thirteen

The courtroom was imposing. Massive columns supported the gloomy relief ceiling. A small platform in the middle was supposed to hold the accused and his guards. Above it loomed a monumental podium for the judge who doubled as a prosecutor.

There I was now, shuffling my feet, boxed in by several burly warriors. From time to time I glanced up at the judge or peered at the pictures covering the walls and ceiling. The prosecutor pontificated, reciting my crimes. He couldn't go on forever though because time was money, and games no exception. He couldn't risk losing the audience's interest in the magnificent setting and the case itself. The judge paused and reached for a new scroll of parchment, about to summon up.

"On the strength of the evidence and considering these are first-time offences, we condemn Laith the Warlock on multiple counts to ten days' imprisonment. The accused will be denied any magic skills or contacts with the outside for the duration of the sentence. On the expiry of the imprisonment, all charges will be waived and reputation partially restored."

The judge stopped and gave me a meaningful look from above his parchment. Couldn't they just execute me or something? Chop my head off, then next thing I knew I'd be back at my spawn point, fresh as a daisy. But now they'd lock me up in some dungeon or other and I'd be stuck there for ten days like a giraffe in a zoo.

The judge studied my sour expression and raised a finger to the ceiling.

"But under the edict of the Highest Sun King, a first time offender accused of abusing his magic skills may be pardoned."

I pricked up my ears. This had to be their version of good cop and bad cop. Now they were going to recruit me as a canary.

I wasn't too far wrong.

"For this, the accused has to report to the authorities the names of those who trained him in the art of dark magic, as well as those who knew about his activities but failed to report them."

I'd had a funny feeling he'd say that. So that was the good cop speaking. And what did the bad one have to offer? I just hoped it wouldn't come to torture. Whoever heard of a gamer being tortured in full immersion for his own money? Having said that, Grym the Hermit had expected something of the kind, judging by the anguish in his voice. He'd probably been imagining himself tied to a stake. Don't you worry, old man, I'm not going to sell you down the river. It's not my sort of thing. Also, judging by the way their useless law was worded, I was supposed to rat on everyone: Taali, Bug, Cryl, whoever. And that was a totally different kettle of fish.

The judge gave me an expectant look. I shook my head. Not terribly upset, he went on.

"The accused can also be eligible for parole if he agrees to pay a fine of twenty gold pieces for every day of unexpired term. Do you wish to pay two hundred gold to the City treasury? In that case, you'll be provided bank access. You have five minutes to make a decision."

Bank access wouldn't help. In actual fact, my combined capital had already reached a hundred and ten gold. Plus tons of salable stuff, like the bracelets and the King's loot. But I'd given the money to Taali, and no one would allow me to go around flogging my stuff. I checked my friend list. Taali was asleep, but Bug was still up and about. I PM'd him.

"Hi. Where are you?"

"Admiring the cemetery. Waiting for my grave to appear."

"I see. You wouldn't happen to have a couple hundred gold for a day or two? I'm in a bit of a jam."

"I'm afraid I don't, chief. Got a fiver in the bank. And about twenty on my corpse. Plus the loot—I dunno how much but I could always arrange a quick sale. Not two hundred, but it'll be something. My corpse will be here in an hour and a half, plus I'll need some time to flog the stuff. Will that do?"

"It's all right, bro. Time is a bit of an issue. Never mind. Thanks anyway. I might be AFK for a while. Just put my cut aside. I'll find you."

"Got it. Is it serious?"

"Not really. Just one of those things. NPC problems. Leave it. Over and out."

"Take care, dude."

That was it. Looked like I'd have to do time. I shook my head to the judge's quizzical stare. He shrugged: *as you wish.* Then he set the scroll of parchment aside, rose and banged his gavel on the desk.

"The sentence is effective immediately."

The platform where I stood turned out to be a teleport pad. For a brief moment, a blue light enveloped us, followed by a boom. Suddenly we were standing on an identical platform inside a building made of thick slabs of stone.

The mage on duty took my paperwork from the guards, glanced over them and nodded.

"Welcome to Gray Bastion. This will be your home for the next ten days. In accordance with the sentence, you'll be denied magic skills for the duration of your incarceration."

He gave a wink to someone behind my back. A steel collar snapped shut around my neck.

"This is a basic Magic Negator. You'll be able to remove it when you're ready to leave the building. Please make sure you don't do anything stupid. Then you won't regret the time of your stay in the Bastion. Now will you please surrender any weapons, scrolls, battle artifacts and any potions you might have. You will be returned them once your sentence is completed. Do not try to cheat. If any illegal objects are found on you once you've cleared the security gate, they will be confiscated in favor of the City."

"What a bunch of jerks," I mumbled rummaging through my bag. My neck hurt as my new piece of jewelry kept shrinking. A normal player would either log out for the duration of his imprisonment or simply find the wretched twenty bucks to pay the fine. Only I had nowhere to turn...

After checking in whatever blade weapons they'd found on me, they pushed me toward a shimmery arch. I cleared it without a hitch, apparently putting the anxious guards at ease. I was an Elf killer, what do you want. Then they walked me along many corridors until finally we came to a massive steel door. The guard fiddled with the lock, swung the door open and pushed me down a long passage lined with bars. I didn't have a chance to see it in much detail before a monster charged at me.

Hell Hound, level 150, the helpful interface prompted. I shrunk. My back hit the door so hard I very nearly forced it open. A taut chain clanged, stopping the monster just a few feet away from me. It was spitting drool, glaring at me, its powerful front legs clawing the air.

The door behind me squeaked open. A grinning guard inspected me, then added, disappointed, "Dry as a bone. Was it so hard to shit yourself? Now I've lost a gold piece."

"Dumbass," I managed.

The guard guffawed and waved to someone at the far end of the corridor, "Pull your doggie back, will ya?"

A winch screeched. The chain pulled taut again, dragging the hound back into the depths of the dungeon. The creature struggled, hissing, sending sparks and bits of stone fly from where its claws struck the floor tiles.

One touch of those claws, and you were back to square one, a.k.a. your spawn point. Now that's a thought. I stepped forward, but a gauntleted hand jerked me back.

"Don't even think about it... the Immortal One. You're not the first smartass here. The doggie has been trained to pace its eating habits. It'll start by chopping off an arm or a leg, then leave you as is to wait for the cleric's morning rounds. No one's gonna let you die on us. Don't even try."

He led me down the now hound-free corridor toward one of the cells and pushed the bars open.

"In with you! And make sure you stay away from the door. The doggie can reach in quite far."

Good advice. I drew a mental line a few feet away from the door. Then I looked around. Not bad at all. The cell was dry, with a decent bunk bed, a mattress and a quite thick blanket. A pitcher of water and a piss pot with a lid. In an Egyptian hotel this would pass for a star and a half. Never mind. Good enough.

"When's meal time?" I asked the guard busy with the bars.

"Twice a day. Gruel and water. You won't gain much weight, that's for sure. But if you ask nicely, we might get something sorted out for you from the inn next door. You need to order big portions though. Three quarters won't go past the guards room, if you know what I mean."

"I'll remember that. Right, chief. Time to lock up. I need to get some sleep."

Finally, the endlessly frantic day was over. I was all tuckered out. I dropped the bag onto the floor, pulled off my sandals, bracelets and shirt, splashed some water onto myself and fell asleep the moment my head touched the mattress. It felt like a king's featherbed.

Chapter Fourteen

My second morning in my new world. Gorgeous turquoise skies, fat fluffy clouds and rusty bars blocking them out from poor old me. Crickets chirping, birds singing, the hound clanging its chain in the corridor. A world of contrasts.

Wonder if I had already gone perma? Or was I still just a visitor? According to Eric, there was a way to check your status somehow. Stupid of me not to have done it when I still could.

Should I get up or should I maybe have a sleep in? Apparently, I had nowhere to hurry to, but a bite to eat wouldn't go amiss. I still had some of Bug's crackers in my bag. I guessed I could always finish those.

My parents had firmly instilled in me their no-eating-in-bed philosophy so if I wanted breakfast, I had to get up. I washed my face with whatever water I had left, donned my shirt and gave a pensive look at the chamber pot, whatever it was supposed to signify. Players had no calls of nature, that little I knew. But how about NPCs? Or digitized permas? I really should have done some research on the place I wished to emigrate to.

The crackers went down with enthusiasm. Having finished my scratch breakfast, I hit the bed again and made myself comfortable on top of the blanket. I checked the chat and the inbox and tried sending a few messages. No way. Everything was blocked. I went into settings and after some fiddling around, got access to the Wiki. Thank God for that. Having said that, why shouldn't it work—it was part of the in-game service, after all. And now was just the right moment to sit down and finally study everything from cover to cover. Great stuff.

First things first. Time to choose class and distribute talent points. This was what we had:

Class: basic, Warlock
Level: 30

Strength: 10
Intellect: 72 (mana=720)
Agility: 0
Spirit: 37
Constitution: 14 (hits=140)

125 Characteristic points and 23 Talent points available.

Excellent. A caster worth his salt was obliged to have superior intellect and spirit numbers. Choosing High Elf with his racial bonus was already bringing its first rewards: his "plus 1 to Intellect" had already earned me 30 extra points, almost half of all my mana.

Choosing a class was pretty straightforward. A Warlock could only specialize as a Necro or a Death Knight. Just in case, I decided to look into it deeper to be sure I hadn't missed some detail or other. So I got stuck in the Wiki until lunch time. I could hear them heave off the hound's chain, bring in breakfast and change the water in the pitcher. All the time I just sat there, going through dozens of open Wiki pages, guides and character calculators. As I did so, a *plan* started to form.

My initial choice, Necro was more or less clear. An ideal choice, really. Its limitations: fabric armor and not enough hits. Also, his class-specific items with intellect and summoning bonuses were expensive and highly sought-after.

And as for the Knight... Being a hybrid class—a cross between warrior and Necro—he was initially weak and hard to level up. Which made sense, really: imagine a caster who'd spent ten levels doing pure magic, and then he was told: *you're a warrior now, here's your sword and heavy armor, time to do some tanking.* At that point, his pet's and necro branches would slow down, blocking access to new spells right until level 30. Instead, he had two warrior branches and a debuff branch while his class bonus switched to strength and constitution.

And despite it all, Knight was one of the hardest chars to level. You really struggled to go up, using every Talent point the moment you earned it. The first 100 levels, Knight kept gaining momentum until finally his spells and skills hit the critical mass threshold, turning him into a very dangerous opponent indeed. Which was why normally Knight was either a high-DPS tank or a group debuffer so valuable in raids. I hadn't seen any mentions of pet-controlling Knights. Which got me thinking...

Why weren't there any Knights leveled up as Necros with maxed-out summoning branches? I could see three reasons for that.

One was narrow-mindedness. If you wanted a Dark pet controller or a zombie master, then you went for a Nec. If you wanted a warrior with some magic skills and if you hated the powers of Light but still wanted to be a paladin—choose Death Knight and level him up to tank.

Second. In between levels 10 and 30, Knight absolutely had to spend all his Talent points. That's why by the time the summoning branch opened again at level 30, there was no way he could catch up with Necro as far as raised pets' levels were concerned. And if you still decided to go for it, you stopped developing as a warrior but remained a lousy pet controller for a very long while.

The Admins tried to fight that balance discrepancy the best they could. There were lots of Knight-restricted items available with Intellect and summoning bonuses. And still every new level widened the gap between Nec's and Knight's pets.

Finally, Intellect had its problems, too. A hybrid tank had enough item and initial bonuses to invest his class bonus and precious characteristic points into strength and constitution.

None of those three made any difference to me, literally pushing me into taking Death Knight.

I played with the calculator and items database, cladding the resulting char into various gear and picking the stuff with pet bonuses. I had to admit, I loved the end result.

Based on my current situation, I drafted a level 200 character. I distributed his talents and points, chose the right epic items for him and checked the outcome.

My jaw dropped. I'd created a unique char with plenty of life, enough strength to wear heavy gear, several yummy class abilities and some uber items with top intellect and summoning parameters a Necro could only dream of. In total, this behemoth of a Death Knight could raise a pet a good ten or even twenty percent higher than a Nec. No matter how hard I tried, I couldn't come up with a similar combination for Necromancer.

Phew. Time to take a break and let the information settle in. I shook my head, closing all the opened windows and forcing myself to focus on the outside world. The sun was already high and warming my cell quite nicely. Time flies when you're having fun. I poked at the cold gruel in a bowl, cringed and pushed it away. No way I was going to eat that. It wasn't the third world, after all.

The chain clanged. I looked up to where the hound stood in the corridor studying my bowl and sniffing the air.

"You don't mean you would eat *this*, do you?" I asked, incredulous.

The hound didn't answer, its eyes fixed firmly on the bowl. I shrugged and pushed it toward the monster. The creature stopped it with a deft paw, sniffed it and sneezed, just like any dog. Then it gave me a look of silent indignation and shoved the bowl back to me.

"Well, I'm sorry. I warned you. I suppose, you'd rather have some steak, would you?"

Was it my imagination or did the thing really nod its agreement?

I made a helpless gesture. "With all the abundance of choice, steak is something I haven't got. Sorry, babe."

The hound heaved a sigh and walked past. Did they starve it or something?

After a couple hours, a squeaky cart arrived with our dinner. A sergeant started to distribute the meals from cell to cell.

"Listen, chief," I called out to him. "How about some human food? Even rats won't eat what I've got."

"Absolutely," the man brightened up. "Know the rules?"

"Sure. Three servings for you, one for me," I paused and glanced in the direction of the chained hound. "Actually, make it two. A steak, some decent bread and some veg, whatever they have. A big steak, rare. And something to drink."

"Alcohol's not allowed," the sergeant stopped me. "I could get you some herbal tea. It's good," he added.

"Will do. How much?"

"A silver piece per serving plus an extra one for a complimentary pitcher of beer for the guards. Six silver in total."

"There you go, smooth talker. Wait. Here's the same for tomorrow's breakfast."

I did a quick bit of math and realized I'd be out of pocket in six days flat. Never mind. I'd have to go on a diet starting tomorrow. One meal a day should be plenty.

He was back with my order double quick: I've known restaurants with slacker service. The chain clanged again as they dragged the hound into a far corner. The guard hurried to carry a large trayful of food into my cell and rushed off, apparently not trusting his messmates.

The chained thing was back just as fast, sniffing the meat in the air. I took one look into its hungry eyes. Good job I ordered some extra to avoid its drooling gaze.

I picked an enormous steak, just gold and brown on the outside, and hurled it at the dog. Teeth clattered. I heard happy chewing in the dark.

"That's it, babe. Off you go. Let me eat my share in peace."

The hound gave me a meaningful stare. *Thank you, the Dark One,* resounded in my brain. I started and spilled my tea. It couldn't be telepathy, surely? Jeez. Mutants everywhere.

I was having my late dinner mulling over the info I'd gathered. The more I thought about it, the more I liked the idea of a pet-controlling Knight. I just couldn't find fault in my logic. But if so, how was I the first to come up with the idea? Or could it be because no one before me had hit the lucky combination of a Warlock of Light having a free ride to level 30? Never mind. Someone always had to be the first, so why not me?

I put down the pitcher of herbal tea—quite decent, I had to give them that—and opened the character menu.

You've chosen specialization: Death Knight.

You can use any kind of armor, shields and weapons.

Skill Tree available: Strength

Skill Tree available: Weakness
Skill Tree available: Fury
You've reached level 30! Summoning Skill Tree is now unlocked!
You've reached level 30! Blood Skill Tree is now unlocked!
You've reached level 30! Death Skill Tree is now unlocked!

Strength skill tree was all about using various weapons, aggro hits, combos and such.

Weakness skill tree: various parameter-lowering debuffs, both single and group ones.

Fury skill tree: mainly personal buffs, including attack speed buffs, impact buffs and such.

Summoning skill tree. My main area of interest, it was virtually identical to that of Necromancer.

Ditto for Blood and Death ones, albeit they were lagging 20 levels behind Necro's. Nothing you could do about that. You couldn't beat Nec at his own game. But even so, my recent Hummungus experience had shown that a high-level pet could easily power-level his own controller.

Very well. I turned to characteristics. My lack of Strength was becoming somewhat of an issue. The 10 points I had were an insult: just three or four armor plate items could send me into overload. I had to have Strength at 40, at least—50 would be even better. One way would be to bluntly invest a few points in it. But then I would be no different from any other Knight and all my meticulous point-saving would have gone down the drain. Logically, if both constitution and the class bonus kept growing, then all I needed to do was wait another thirty levels or so for the misbalance to rectify itself. By the time I was level 100, Strength would naturally reach level 80 and that was where I wanted it to be. I wasn't going to do much blade-rattling, anyway.

All this meant I had to take a different route— which promised considerably more pain in the back but offered the best returns once I reached top levels. I wasn't going to invest anything in Strength, although I might buy a few rings with a Strength modifier. God knows I needed them.

Now, Constitution. On one hand, it was almost a carbon copy of Strength. On the other, though, the more hits you had, the higher were your chances of survival in battle. The misbalance was obvious: at level 30, my 140 Life could last me three hits, four max. I gagged my screaming inner greedy pig and invested 25 points in Constitution.

Agility. If I was meant to be a bull in a china shop, so be it. The most useless parameter at this stage, it didn't deserve a single point.

Last but by no means least: Intellect and Spirit. I poured everything I had left into them, two to one. Now my character panel looked like this:

Class: Death Knight
Level: 30
Strength: 10
Intellect: 139 (mana=1390)
Agility: Spirit: 70
Constitution: 39 (hits=390)

Much better now. Phew. Enough for today. Lights-out time. Tomorrow we'd see.

I spent the next morning lounging in bed. The blissful weekend feeling was back. Nowhere to hurry to, no business scheduled and a nice big breakfast to look forward to. The closest thing to a pleasure cruise. Talk of the devil, I heard chow coming.

The chain clanged. The bars slammed. A trayful of food on the stool by my bed started wafting its flavors. The guard didn't look very happy when he heard that there wouldn't be another order until tomorrow morning. The bastards were spoiled rotten. Soon they wouldn't fit through the door frame.

The hungry-eyed hound made her appearance just as I lifted the lid off a fragrant roast.

"Listen sweet, if I indulge you now, what are you going to do in a week's time when I'm not here anymore?"

Food! echoed in my head.

"You've got a cheek, you," I chuckled. "Think you could learn some manners first?"

Food! Me! Hungry!

What would you do about it? "There, take it. It could have been my dinner, mind you. You think you could show me some secret way out, by way of gratitude? Once free, I could get you a whole deer, what would you say to that?"

A wave of ruefulness flooded my brain—vague images of an endless plateau covered in folds of solidified lava.

"Is that your home? Sorry, babe. Didn't mean to rake that up."

Mechanically I reached out and scratched the hound behind the ear just as I'd do with any other dog. The fact dawned on us both at once and we both froze, scared of upsetting the fragile balance. Then the monster tilted her head. The armor plates covering her neck parted exposing her anthracite hair.

"Want me to scratch you some more?"

Gingerly I fluffed up the scruff of her neck praying that it wasn't the last time I'd seen my hand. The hound growled like an oil generator. My head was flooded with images of a warm nest full of blind pups and the enormous dog mother licking clean the still-soft joints of their future armor.

"Feels good, eh?" I almost envied the beast.

I indulged her for a while, then nudged her head away. "Enough. Let me have some breakfast too. Pick up your steak now before the ants have it."

After a hearty meal, I got some quality shopping time in spending my Talent points.

First, I took Life Absorption, Deadman's Hand and DoT and upgraded them one level. Laughably little, just enough for a level-10 Necro. Still, I had to concentrate on the pet. He was my main weapon. I switched to the Summoning branch and spent three points on increasing the summoned creature's level. You only had that opportunity once every ten levels, so it was better to use it when one could. Now the summoned pet would be three levels higher by default.

Next. A heal for my zombie. This was something I really needed. Now the raid team was complete: I was three points poorer but at least I had a tank and a healer. Cast time was too long, almost three seconds, and only restored 170 hit points, but I wasn't a healer any way you looked at it. Then I spent three more precious points on passive skills.

Intellectual: The summoned creature receives 5%*3=15% of the killed creatures' experience.

Vampire: The pet receives back 1%*3=3% of the damage dealt as restored life points.

Lich: The pet has a 0.1%*3=0.3% chance of receiving one of the killed creature's special attacks or skills.

I had a funny feeling I'd jumped the gun. It was probably a better idea to take those skills after level 100 when I didn't have to change the pet every five minutes because of the level gap. But I loved the process of improving my mini tank so much I couldn't help making him as tough as I could.

Next, I moved on to buffs:

Fire Shield. Deals 7 points fire damage per each hit received.

Agony Armor: Raises the summoned creature's armor level 80 points.

Zombie's strength: Raises the summoned creature's strength 30 points.

Bigfoot: Raises the summoned creature's life 300 points.

Finally, as a caster, I had to splurge on a few mandatory spells:

Reincarnation point: Allows one to set up a resurrection point in any location in the world.

Teleport: a slow (7 sec cast time) spell sending one to his reincarnation point.

Sending you there alive, mind you, all your stuff included. And once I reached level 50, I could have an improved teleport for the whole group, counting pets.

That was it. I'd spent it all and now was a full-fledged level 30. Still, on the outside my char remained a mystery. At first sight, you could take him for a warrior which should discourage those wary of challenging heavily armored targets. Once they saw my pet or my own magic skills, they'd take me for a Death Knight, and rightly so. But if they decided to select my pet as target, his level reading would come as a nasty shock. To surprise the enemy is to defeat him, whoever said that.

Closer to lights-out after their miserable excuse for dinner, I decided to inspect my bag. I poured its entire contents onto the floor and started sorting all the stuff into separate piles. I reminded myself of Robinson Crusoe surveying his salvaged treasures.

I made an inventory of the bracelets.

Gray: 66

Black: 41

Red: 85

Almost twenty gold, not bad at all. I wondered about the dungeon exchange rate of bracelets to French fries. I had to ask the sergeant if he was willing to barter. Life wasn't much fun on an empty stomach.

Pieces of armor, 4
Class Restrictions: Death Knight

I had gotten them off the King and it looked like I could use them soon. It wasn't as if I was going to sleep in full armor, but I might dress up a bit before checking out.

Soul Stones: 114. I had so many because at a certain point I'd forgotten to dump the low-level ones. I divided them into two piles: one for those level 26 and over, and the other for the lower stuff. The latter I'd have to pulverize and research the market.

Gimme!

I started. The hound stared at me through the rusting bars.

Gimme!

"Give you what? I'm all out of steak, babe. Next delivery tomorrow morning."

The hound waggled her head. I could see the beast was tense and ready to fight. Whatever had come over her?

Stone!

As if she would know what to do with it. Oh well, it wasn't as if they were in short supply. I chose one of the worse ones and pushed it towards the hound. The creature sniffed it and flicked it away with an angry paw.

More!

"Hey, send it back my way, will ya? Waste not, want not."

I chose the worst of the best stones and pushed it toward the creature. She tossed it away the same way as before.

More!

My inner greedy pig raised his ugly head. I shook myself free from his grasp and picked the best stone I had which contained the soul of the level-29 Gnoll Priest.

"There. Please give it back to me if you can't use it."

Cringing, the hound sniffed the rock for a while. Her glare switched to the remaining stones. Finally, convinced that this was the best I could offer, she leaned over the poor gnoll's final refuge and sucked in the air in a very peculiar way. A light wisp of mist reached from the stone to the hound. The stone lost its shimmer. Curious, I looked at its properties.

Empty Soul Stone. Ready to take a restless soul.

Help me, the Dark One!

"What kind of help do you want, babe? I'm not giving you any more stones."

The hound looked up into my eyes flooding me with a tidal wave of déjà vu. The already familiar basalt plateau, studded with smoke pillars, ran with rivulets of liquid fire. I saw a powerful pack of hell hounds, led by my steak lover. A small image of herself appeared, struggling free out of a summoning pentagram. A heavy chain around her neck. A bastion encircled in a ring of powerful spells. A freedom lost. A wild, overwhelming surge of despair.

New quest alert! Unique quest available: Hell's Temptation!

Help Hell Hound to gain her freedom! The Gray Bastion is safely concealed from other reality planes. Even in death, Hell Hound can't go back to Inferno. Place her soul in a Soul Stone and deliver it to a Dark Altar of your choice.
Reward: Unknown

So! *Accept,* what else. One question remained, though. "How do we cram your soul into the stone?"

The hound answered with the emotional equivalent of a knock on my forehead. *Kill me.*

"What? What with, may I ask? I've got no weapons. And I've got this wretched Negator on my neck."

Remove it.

"Pardon me?"

Same emotion, doubled. I felt my forehead itch.
The key!

"Which key, you numbskull?"

The master key. From a top level Negator, the hound pointed her nose at the crystal key from the Drow collar lying in the heap of unsorted trash.

Could it be that... because if it could, then I was a dork to end all dorks. Slowly I brought the key to my collar, afraid of scaring away my luck. It clicked. Yes! I was a regular dumbass. Any inferno mutt was apparently smarter than myself. What's that grin on her face, was she reading my thoughts or something? I gave the hound a look of suspicion, but all she did was shift her paws, impatient.

"Oh well. Thanks for the tip. But even so, babe, you're level one hundred freakin' fifty. All the mana in the world won't be enough to polish *you* off."

The hound gave a mental face palm. Then she shook her head parting the armor plates that covered the back of her neck. She sat back like a dog about to scratch its ear, protracted her pale blue claws and slit her own throat open. A thick jet of blood hit the wall. The mutt lay on the floor watching the dark pool grow around her. Her life bar began shrinking. You couldn't really commit suicide in a game by slitting your own veins. Any blood loss would only cause life to shrink deep into the red zone. After that, it would restore gradually—so in any case, you'd need a *coup de grace*. There were other ways to end your own life, though. You could always drown yourself or jump off a cliff. Whatever.

In less than a minute, the blood flow almost stopped. The hound had five percent life left at most.

Do it.

I began reciting Life Absorption, over and over again. Although the spell was advertised as foolproof, I kept running into resists. When the mutt's life bar had shrunk to a hair, she sent me one last message,

Thank you.

You've received experience!
Congratulations! You've reached level 31!

Racial bonus: +1 to Intellect
Class bonus: +1 to Strength, +1 to Constitution
5 Characteristic points available! You now have 5 Characteristic points!
1 Talent point available!

Almost straight away, another chain of messages ran across the screen. Thirty two. Weren't they generous. Having said that, you had to be an optimist to celebrate your luck behind bars.

I didn't get any Fame points this time— apparently, because of the Hound being a quest monster.

A stone glowed in the pool of blood on the floor. I peered into it.

Soul Stone. Contains the soul of a level-150 Hell Hound. Use Summoning the Undead spell to raise the monster.

Oh, no. Did I say Hell's Temptation?

Chapter Fifteen

The next morning was hectic. Guards, investigators and officers of all ranks ran up and down the corridors questioning everyone. I just kept shrugging, showing them my empty hands and pointing at the collar around my neck. In any case, didn't they see the hound was all of 120 levels out of my league? The interrogators scratched their heads and moved on.

The hound's corpse and blood had disappeared a few minutes after it had died. I had swung the chain as far along the corridor as I could. The two smaller Soul Stones lay abandoned on the floor for another hour. No one but me could pick them up, apart from an NPC like the hound herself. But in her absence, all dropped items had a limited life. Game developers didn't want their world to be cluttered with trash. Besides, you never knew whose hands the item may end up in.

So technically, the guards had nothing to confront me with, apart from the fact that my level had soared overnight. But I was prepared to feed them a story about some particularly complex meditational quest. They were welcome to prove it wrong if they thought they could.

All night I had been fighting off a desire to use the teleporter and leg it. Then reason took over. If I jumped the jail, I had to leave town, and it was something I wasn't prepared to do. I had only just made myself a few friends and began learning the lay of the land. I'd been lucky enough to come by a few quests and a place to stay. I really didn't feel like giving it all up in order to run to either the neutral lands or the Drow's' territories. So I'd made a conscious decision to do my term and go out with a clean reputation. I had used the master key to lock my collar and crashed out. In the morning, all hell broke loose.

They delivered my prepaid breakfast only in the evening, apologetic about the unprecedented concentration of top brass per square foot. By then, the place was back to its normal quiet, disturbed only by the shuffling of a guard who'd replaced the runaway bitch. The Hell Hound. Another headache, as if I didn't have them enough already. On one hand, the raised pup could be my free ticket to level 50 and beyond, regardless of the summon limits. On the other, I had a quest, an unknown reward and my own word. Which word? Who had I given it to—a binary combination? To AI? Or ultimately, had I given it to myself? Nothing but questions.

Days dragged by. I loafed around. The guards only showed up during the daytime and slept it off in the guardroom at night. That gave me a bit of time to play around with the settings. I removed the Negator, summoned a low-level pet and fitted it with all the buffs I could think of. This was an entertaining but rather unproductive way of reminding myself I was still a Necro. At least I got rid of a few rats scurrying about.

In the evening of day five I was scrolling through the Wiki, bored and listless, when an admin message popped up.

You've received a personal money transfer: 3000 gold.

A note has been added:

Hi, son, how are you? Love, Mom.

Oh. I sat up in bed. The quick note felt like the first letter from home for a rookie. From home... from my mom. For a brief second, I couldn't fight the desire to go back. My eyes searched for the log out button. Stop now. Get a grip.

I checked my available funds. 3002 gold, 4 silver and 31 copper. Well done, mom. I had indeed asked her to send me a hundred bucks, and do it on the tenth day of full immersion. She'd done it on the seventh. Couldn't wait. Mothers! Now we were rocking.

I stood up, walked to the bars and called out to the bored guard.

"Listen, chief. I'd like to pay up and get out. Think you could get hold of some top brass?"

The guard gave a lazy yawn and didn't budge. "Inspector has already drunk his nightly shot of Dwarven Extra Dry. He'll be heading home in a minute. Pointless looking for him now. You'll have to wait till tomorrow, dude."

"Hey, did you hear me?" Anxiety took over me. The freedom, so close only a moment ago, had flapped its wings departing in a direction unknown.

I produced a heavy gold piece and tapped it against the bars. "If you make it quick, you won't regret it. You can tell Inspector he won't be out of pocket, either."

The coin disappeared into the folds of his uniform. The guard hurried out. About ten minutes later, I'd already started losing my patience when an unhappy inspector made his appearance.

"You'd better have a damn good reason to impose on my personal time," he said meaningfully, rubbing finger and thumb together.

I flashed the gold coin but the inspector didn't bite. Behind his back, the guard signaled me with his open paw, apparently signifying the size of the baksheesh. Those game developers were barking mad. Having said that, it could be a clever way to remove superfluous funds from circulation. I just loved the way they did business. All you needed to do was draw some pictures of virtual gold and sell it to the players for hard cash, then prevent the inflation by charging the in-game currency for various services and consumables. If a player paid vendors just one gold a day, multiplied by forty million players, the company would rake in a hundred twenty million bucks a month. In reality though, the amount of money changing hands had to be a hundredfold more. Selling game gold wasn't a problem: the problem was acquiring considerable amounts of it as the Administration limited hard cash deposits to ten grand a month. If they didn't, the first relocated billion would be enough to crash the world economy. Having said that, an interested millionaire would always find common ground with the game owners— this was business and not a charity bazaar. All they'd do, they'd charge him for a palatial residence complete with vestal virgins, but he'd still have to queue for his cash with the rest of us. The best the

Admins could do for the likes of him was to offer them a more agreeable exchange rate.

To cut a long story short, I had to pay him off. The Inspector graciously accepted my fiver, then charged me another hundred for the rest of my term. After yet another half-hour of red tape, I stepped onto the gray teleport pad.

"Till next time," the mage on duty smirked before activating the portal.

My feet jerked slightly with the impact. I found myself on a grassless spot about twenty paces from the city's north gate. I knew the place well. This was where I'd first entered the city. The sun was setting over the bustling crowd of players who'd just come home from work or school and jumped into their FIVR capsules. The night gaming session had begun.

I hurled two copper to a vendor and got myself a large frothy mug of beer. The drink had a pleasantly chilled straight-from-the-fridge taste. No idea if it was done by magic or as part of the game reality.

Freedom! I stepped aside and sat down on the grass. Blowing the froth off the beer, I longed for a handful or salted peanuts, but I was too comfortable to get up and walk around searching for them. Life was good as it was.

I emptied the mug in two hearty gulps and stretched out, basking in the evening sun. A shadow blocked it out. I opened my eyes: Eric.

He grinned, plopped down next to me and elbowed my ribs. "Long time no see! Where've you been, dude? I was already thinking you snuffed it a bit earlier than planned. Either that, or your plans to go perma didn't work out."

I sat up. "In your dreams. I was doing time, that's all."

"Whatcha mean?"

"Nothing really. Just some cops banged me up. Like, I'm a nasty Necro, so the guards started aggroing my pet and we had to smoke them double quick. Plus a few other things, enough for a short stretch. Then the cavalry arrived, well, they got me. I'll never forgive them my pet. Too good for words, he was."

I threw my hands in the air showing how much I missed him. Still, deep inside I was celebrating. The sight of a dumbfounded Eric was just too funny.

"You don't mean it."

"I damn well do. Only been out for ten minutes."

"You're too much, dude."

"You bet. You should stick with me if you want a nice cozy cell."

He guffawed.

"Listen, Eric. I've been meaning to ask you. Is there a way to find out whether I'm perma or not yet?"

He tensed, suddenly serious. "You mean you don't know yet? How long have you been in full immersion now?"

"Seven days non-stop."

He phewed. "Let's have a look. Close your eyes."

I did.

"Can you tell me where the sun is?"

I concentrated. The warm sunrays seeped through my eyelids and warmed my right check. I pointed without even thinking.

"Good. What else do you feel?"

"Hmm, let me think. There's a breeze in my face. A fly is crawling up my arm," I said, waving it off.

"Can you smell anything?"

"I can smell dung. And food. Flowers. I can also smell beer on myself and sweat on you."

"I didn't get the chance to remove my armor today," Eric murmured, embarrassed. "Let's try one other thing," he rattled through his bag. "Where's it now... ah, here, take it," he handed me a heavy piece of steel. "Tell me all you can about it."

I commented as I studied it. "It's either a knife or a dagger. Sorry, don't know much about them. It's old. The handle is leather, well worn. The blade is dull and rusty in places. It smells of rotten leather, and also of earth and steel. Very old, I'd say. The rust is flaking off."

Eric chuckled and took the thing away from me. "You can open your eyes. Well, congrats, dude. You're one of us now. Full immersion or not, a normal player wouldn't have noticed half of the stuff you've just told me. They call it virtual reality, but it's still a fake. But it's your home now. That's why you experience it full scale."

I looked at him, still unbelieving. "You think? Doesn't sound very convincing to me."

He smiled. "Okay. Let's do another check. But this one will depend on how long you've been in perma mode. Where's south east?"

I pointed without even thinking.

"How did you know?"

"Well, we've got the compass, haven't we?"

"Are you sure?"

I glanced over the interface and saw that the compass was gone. What the hell? How did I know, then?

Eric was having the time of his life watching me. "No one knows how it happens. The digitized players start losing the interface. Or rather, its functions turn into their own skills. The compass is one of the first to go. All the location maps get imprinted in your mind—that includes places where you haven't yet been to. By the way, you have camera eye now. Remember the last monster you killed? Can you list the objects he dropped?"

"Not a monster," I corrected him. "It was a guard. Two silver, nine copper and a badge."

I froze. I couldn't believe it. I really did remember.

"You see?" he said. "It means you were already digital when you did it. You have computer memory now. All you need is to open the logs and you'll remember it straight away. Cool, eh? Now the big check. Press the logout."

I felt uncomfortable. I'd press it, and it would throw me out. My dream life would turn out to be just that, a dream.

"Don't be a chicken, dude. Coming under fire feels much worse, I tell you. And still people do it. Go ahead and press it."

I pressed. Then I pressed again, and again. I froze for a second. Then I yelled in a George-Michael-ish falsetto,

"Freedom! Freedom! Freedom! You've gotta give for what you take!"

I jumped to my feet and did a bit of a song and dance. The bustling crowd turned their heads to look at me. Eric watched my dervish act with a smile. Then he gave me a bear hug.

"Congrats, dude. You've fooled the Grim Reaper. That's official. You back to the Three Little Pigs with me? This calls for a celebration."

"Sure I am. The memories of your chef's roast kept me going in the slammer. But first of all I've got to get to the bank and the post office."

"They're on the way. Which bank do you want? The AlterWorld or the Olders'?"

"They have their own bank?"

"They have lots of things."

I gave it a thought. "What's the difference?"

"The difference is, the Olders have a lower interest rate. They've also introduced lots of third party services like mailing, and better deposit and withdrawal options for perma players. Even special credit rates."

"Sounds good. Can I get a mortgage?"

"Don't laugh. You won't live in and out of hotels forever. One day you'll want a place of your own."

"Fair enough. Let's go see the Olders', then."

A ranger Elf came flying past us. I had a funny feeling I'd seen the guy before. As I frowned trying to fix the face to a place, he yelled, "Ten gold pieces to anyone with Red Bear's coordinates!"

But of course. This was the dork who'd given me Teddy on a silver platter.

Having said that... "Eric, any idea why they're all so obsessed about that bear?"

He cringed and waved the question away. "Don't even remind me. I've wasted a month of my life on that wretched thing. I'd spent two weeks farming him all over the location. Finally, some freakin' noob sighted him and thought of nothing better than to post it in the chat. Before I got there, the place was so packed the poor Teddy got buried under all the wannabes. For the next two weeks I used to sit by the town gate, just like that ranger over there, promising a king's ransom to anyone who'd direct me to the Red Bear. Finally, I got a tipoff, but when I got to him, there were four more dudes there already chasing him. I freaked out and added 4 kills to my PK counter. Piece of cake—I was already level 80 by then. Then I smoked the bear, and what do you think it dropped? A heart. Not a single vial of blood. It happens quite often. Sometimes you get none, other times you get two. After that, I just gave up. I'm not going to spend another month chasing him around the location."

As he spoke, I impatiently shifted from one foot to the other. "And? What's all this about his heart and blood? Come on, tell me."

Eric looked up at me, surprised. "Hey, keep your hair on. It's a quest. What else do you think it is? One of the best mounts around. The Royal Alchemist has a stuffed Red Bear and wants to try his animation potion on him. But he needs two more ingredients: the bear's heart and blood. If you give them to him, he can animate the bear and give him to you for a riding mount. Better than a horse. The Bear's weak at first, but that's not what matters. First, he can fight together with his master. And second, the bear receives some of your experience on top of his own. It's up to you how much you allow him to have. I think it's up to 10% or so. The Bear levels up really well, so the sooner you have him the more impressive the result. It can make a good top tank or alternatively, a cross between a mount and a truck. Too cool for words. Just don't hold your breath, dude. Have a look at me first. A whole *month* I've been after him."

Eric shrugged and turned away. I kept staring at him, my mind replaying what he'd just said. Did he mean you could revive the bear? Hummungus, pup! Daddy's coming!

Chapter Sixteen

When the initial stupor had passed, I grabbed Eric's sleeve and dragged him away from the main road. I dropped my bag on the ground and squatted, rummaging through its capacious inventory. Eric shifted his feet nearby, clueless as to what was causing the delay. Finally I found what I was looking for. I looked up at Eric and handed him one of the two vials containing Red Bear's blood.

"Take it. It's yours now. Just a trinket to celebrate my success."

Unsure, Eric reached out and squinted at the vial, moving his lips, as he read the item's ID. Then he jerked his hand away. "Any idea how much this costs? Judging by your newb kit, it's not as if you shit gold."

"I've got two gold, to be precise. The rest I had to splurge on takeaways. Jail food nearly killed my palate."

"You could sell the vial for a couple grand. Three, even. In gold." I could see he was dying to accept the gift but his honesty was getting the better of him.

My inner greedy pig, who had only a moment ago been hopping up and down celebrating my freedom and the unexpected financial windfall, squeaked and dropped senseless with shock.

That was serious money. Had I known it, I'd have thought twice before giving the vial away. But claiming it back would mean a total loss of face.

Besides, I liked this honest, cheerful and straightforward tower of a grunt.

I grinned, "Oh, whatever. You only live once. Take it. I'll distract my inner greedy pig before he throws a fit."

Eric managed a shy smile and accepted the vial. "I'll be damned, dude. You won't believe how much time I've spent chasing after him. The bear is one hell of a mount. I'll do some work on him and he'll be slaying dragons. I owe you. Don't say anything. You're a Necro, aren't you? We'll have to check the bank. I'm sure they have something for you."

"I'm actually a Death Knight," I corrected, pointing his sense of gratitude in the right direction. "I specialize in pet summoning."

Overjoyed, Eric slammed my shoulder. My health bar quivered. A few guards exchanged worried looks as they passed by, tightening their grip on the weapons.

"Quiet, you ox. People have been killed with a lighter touch," I rubbed my aching shoulder.

He just grinned nonsensically, pressing the vial to his chest. "Come along, then. I'll take you to the bank, pick up the heart, then I'll go pay the alchemist a visit. My guys will freak out when they see me coming on the bear's back."

"Hold your horses, will you? I'm coming along. I want me a bear, too."

"Do you? Have you got another bear kit?"

I gave him a wink. Eric was brimming with emotion.

"Dude, you're awesome. Shame I can't refer you to our clan. You need to have combat experience to join. You haven't been in action, have you?"

"I did service, sure," I hurried to explain. "Air defense. Shoot'em down, sort'em out on the ground. But I wasn't in action, no. Probably for the better."

Eric nodded. "Most likely. But if we decide to start a nursery, I'll give you a reference and an invitation. You'll be a standby guy. Think you'll join?"

I shrugged. "We'll see. Thanks, anyway."

In the bank, everything went hunky dory. As a perma player, I was eligible for a low-rate bank account, providing my digitized status was confirmed by another perma with a solid track record. Eric fit the role fine. Among other freebies, they gave me a thirty days free texting number. All the messages arriving at the number were forwarded to my inbox. I could also use it for sending outgoing messages, but I couldn't do it myself, only through an operator. The plan was so good I signed up for automatic renewal: retaining contact with the outer world was worth the fifty gold it cost me.

I tested it on the spot, sending my Mom a quick and rambling message reproaching her for sending me too much money too soon, then thanking her all the same. Then I slapped my forehead and sent her another one in all-caps:

MOM! I WON'T DIE! I'VE MADE IT! YOU CAN TURN THE CAPSULE OFF NOW! I'M IN PERMA MODE!!!

I felt a bit uneasy typing the last sentence, but I'd been convinced by both Eric and my failure to log out.

I thought about their Internet services. It wasn't real Internet, of course—more like a paid database for perma players. You sent your search request to the operator who looked it up and sent you the most relevant search result. Twenty gold per request. A bit pricey for me at the moment, but it might come in handy at a later date.

The Olders seemed to have made it big. They basically controlled the service market. Need someone to look after your grave in the real world? Or a lawyer to take care of your offline property? Hire a nanny or a house help for your surviving family, buy whatever you fancied, check on your wife to make sure she hadn't stranded in your absence—easy.

So, for a nominal sum, you could subscribe to two news feeds: one that covered the virtual and the other the real world. The moment I heard about them, I had them both hooked up to my account. I also ordered a couple of books and subscribed to new offers from some of my favorite authors. I was shaking in anticipation of the moment when I hit my bed in the Three Little Pigs, pressing the full screen button and opening the latest bestseller sequel.

Finally, they offered me a choice of ID rings for instant account access. Every ring was personal, bound on equip, with various extras to choose from.

"This is our local handwork," the clerk's voice rang with pride as he handed me the silver ring with a +5 Strength modifier.

Regular players received a plain copper ring with no extras. Only permas were eligible for silver ones. I tried not to think who you had to be to get a gold one. Eric didn't wear his ring in public. Either he belonged to that choice category, or simply didn't want to publicize his perma status.

Problems were waiting at the bank's exit. I was still studying my new ring and only stopped when my head rammed a chainmail shirt. I raised my head. Tavor, the greedy Elf, was squinting at me. I didn't like what I read in his face. During my five days in the slammer, he'd kept leveling and was now 37. He didn't waste his time, did he? Having said that, his money and items could buy him any level he wanted.

Tavor grabbed my shoulder. "So, Drow savior? Fancy seeing you here. Mind following me to the arena? I've got something you might like... not."

I tried to shake his hand off but couldn't. The difference in our strength parameters was quite amazing. I should probably invest more into strength: you never knew when a perma like myself might need it.

Besides, Tavor wasn't alone. Three of his fellow clan members surrounded us and pushed us away from the bank doors. Their actions were quick and smooth—they must have done it a thousand times before. No idea how it all would have ended, had Eric not come out to join us.

"Hey! What's going on here? Get your hands off him, quick."

He rammed through their barrier and shoved the Forest Cats aside. Tavor gave him a moody look studying his level and the Veterans' clan badge.

"Sorry, dude. I'm afraid it's none of your business. The kid owes me. You don't want to interfere."

I struggled myself free. "I owe you nothing. You attacked me first. Then you fucked off and now you're the man? When you've got your hoods with you? Whassup, dude? Can't you manage it on your own?"

Tavor spat at my feet ignoring my challenge. The ring around me drew tighter.

Eric splayed his elbows, pushing my assailants aside. "He's my friend. Enough now. Are you fucking mad, settling your accounts in town? One drop of blood and the place will be crawling with guards. Give it a rest."

Tavor squinted at us, weighing up his chances, then apparently decided not to push his luck. His glance happened upon my ring.

"A perma, are we? Well, well, well. You know what? You're toast."

He turned away and called out to his henchmen, "Come on, guys. He's not going anywhere."

Eric stared after them. "You're good at making enemies, bud. What you really need is to join a clan. A strong one. Lone permas are in for a lot of trouble."

"Problem?"

"You could say so," he mumbled. "Just something people say about them. All of them, not just the Cats, you understand. Keep your eyes peeled now. Watch your back. Practice some invisibility spells. I also suggest you get Crystal Vision and keep it on you at all times. It'll allow you to see stealthers.

Never create resurrection points in deserted areas: they might track you down and run you through your own personal hell, a death a minute for a week. They have special guys with unlimited PK counters who do just that. By unspoken agreement, permas are supposed to be immune from this kind of treatment, but... You know what I mean. Don't flash your ring in town. Your status is nobody's business. By the way, why didn't you just call the guards? While you're in town, no one can hurt you."

"Yeah. Stupid of me."

"You've got to get savvy now. For you it's not a game anymore. Trust me, this place isn't as cute and cuddly as it may look."

I nodded absent-mindedly. Then a thought crossed my mind. "Is it," I snapped my fingers, searching for the right word, "all this Wild West, is it really necessary? Even the Olders, what do they get out of this pissing contest with these thugs?"

Eric walked and dragged me along, explaining as he went. "All these old-age citizens, all the crafters, bankers and pacifists—normally, they just don't want to go beyond level 10 so they can preserve their startup immunity. So not every noob is a newbie, if you know what I mean. Some of them take a different route. They pay to be power-leveled. After two months, they are level 200-plus and all done up in so much epic gear you'd need a raid party to get one up on them. I may be exaggerating a bit, but not much."

We stopped by an affluent alchemy shop. Eric froze for a bit, checking the map. Then he pointed confidently, "This one. We'll go in together, I'll close the quest, you accept it right after me and close it, too."

Once inside, I was instantly distracted by the shop's contents. Before, I just couldn't afford to use any of those potions so now I eagerly studied their choice and prices. They had some classics: life and mana elixirs which worked over a period of time, allowing you to use them in battle but not giving you any considerable leveling advantage.

I picked up a Minor Health Potion. A tiny vial contained barely a mouthful of bright red liquid. It cost one gold piece. You squeezed it in your hand, and the stopper came out on its own. It started working thirty seconds after being swallowed, restoring up to 40 points health over a period of 10 ticks 5 seconds each, followed by a 3-minute cooldown during which you couldn't use it again. The idea was to minimize the time wasted on mana and hits regen while complicating protracted combat, allowing for easier soloing to those classes traditionally weak in solo leveling. Plus it helped relieve players of their money, no question about that.

The shop also had all sorts of potions: various armor and attack speed buffs as well as those increasing strength, agility, intellect and crit probability. Plus Eye of a Cat, Fish Breath and Crystal Vision as well as tons of other things.

Next to them stood a small collection of attack elixirs: poisons, acids and Molotov cocktails. Launching them was just like hurling gold at a target. An expensive exercise.

Safely tucked behind the shop owner's back, a protective magic field glittered over a special display. I studied its contents and phewed. For five hundred gold, those little vials raised any basic characteristic 1 point. Cooldown: twenty-four hours. Max cap: 200 extra points. For two thousand gold, you could get yourself an extra Talent point. Cooldown: five days. Cap: fifty points. Oh well. Tough toys for tough boys, and prices to match.

Then I heard a bear bellowing outside, followed by Eric's shrieks of delight. My heart shrunk and fluttered in my chest. Hummungus, sweet old Ted! I hurriedly approached the owner.

"Is it true, Sir, that you're looking for some rare elixir ingredients?"

The Elf owner, a picturesque type with bleak expressionless eyes, nodded gravely. "I am. I'm quite prepared to pay for any internal organs of rare beings."

New quest alert! The alchemist shop owner spends a lot of time looking for new magic formulas. For that purpose, he eagerly buys body parts from monsters level 100 and beyond.

Reward: Gold or Unknown Elixir.

Pardon me? I did accept the quest, no question about that. But where's my Teddy?

I felt a bit nervous. "Excuse me? Are you looking for something in particular?"

The owner didn't play hard to get. "Sure. There are a few things I'd buy from you right now. Or if money isn't what you're after, I could offer a swap for the resulting monster."

New quest alert! Bring the alchemist the heart and some blood of Red Bear, indigenous to the City of Light area.
Reward: Money or a unique mount.

Phew. Relieved, I dug into my bag for the quest objects. "I think I just happen to have what you're looking for."

The alchemist, wonderfully impassive, only wished to know what kind of reward I preferred. For a brief moment, he disappeared into a side room. When he came out, he placed on the counter a bone whistle on a leather strap.

Summoning Whistle. Binds when picked up. Summons a unique mount: Red Bear.

I grabbed the precious object and brought it to my lips. The alchemist recoiled, shielding himself with his hands. "Please don't! Not in my shop!"

Oops. That was a bit stupid. I mumbled my thanks and rushed out. Once in the street, I gave the whistle an almighty blow.

"WRRRGHRRRAAAAH!"

"Hummungus!"

Congratulations! This is your first riding mount. Would you like to rename Red Bear?

Yes!

A system window popped up displaying the mount's name. I deleted it and entered a new one:

Hummungus!

Chapter Seventeen

Teddy was good: tall, strong and perfectly alive. His old zombie incarnation was not a patch on this one. I patted his hairy head and, unable to control myself, gave him a peck on his wonderfully moist nose.

"Man, I missed you. We'll be together a long time now."

"Just look at them," a sarcastic voice said behind me.

I turned round—and shrunk back with a yelp. At about an arm's length from me, Eric sat astride his own bear. The creature was done up in gray and green camo patterns and bore the befitting name: LAV. From what I remembered from my army days, it stood for Light Armored Vehicle. On one side it carried the Vet Clan's logo: a shield with a star, enwreathed by an olive branch and a St. George's ribbon. On the other side was the bear's registration number 171, drawn in white paint by a rather unsteady hand.

"What on earth have you done with it?"

Eric sat up. "Cool, eh? I'm sure you haven't checked his settings yet. You can edit his appearance to your heart's content—within certain limits, of course."

I shook my head.

"Looks like AI's idea of limits offers a lot of room for interpretation. What's with the registration number?"

Eric rubbed his beast's muscly side with a look of nostalgia. "It was my lucky LAV, that one. Two years I drove it. In the end, it got scorched in Tskhinvali during the Second Georgian campaign. All my guys survived, though. So it's my lucky number. Come along, then. We need to get some grub. My stomach thinks my throat's been cut."

My bear was well-appointed with a quality bridle and saddle. He wasn't hard to mount but very comfortable to ride. I told Hummungus to follow Eric and dug deep into his settings.

Riding Mount: Hummungus (Red Bear)
Level: 1
Strength: 30
Constitution: 30
Attack: 10-20
Speed: 3 mph
Rider: 1
Weight-carrying capacity: 0
Special abilities: none

For your information: A mount can participate in combat alongside his owner. A mount can follow the same key commands as a summoned creature, plus special path commands. In case of death, a mount loses all of its current level experience and remains unsummonable for the next twenty-four hours.

Nothing difficult. I had to keep him safe: his respawning, albeit delayed, was already good news. I opened his appearance settings. Aha. That's where Eric let his fantasy run wild. It did cost him, though.

Twenty gold for changing the pet's color plus another ten for each logo added. You could also upload your own patterns to change the bear's skin. Should I too go for camo? Or maybe, white with a blue stripe? And blues'n'twos on top, yeah right. In the end, I decided against trying the beast's patience. I was quite happy with the way it looked for the time being. Still, I had a funny feeling that the local mounts held quite a few surprises in store for me, including Barbie-Doll pink lions and fluffy rhinestone-studded ponies.

With a beep, the PM icon flashed. Again. And again. What's all the rush? I opened my inbox and my jaw dropped. That Elven chick, Taali, could cuss when she wanted to! I didn't even know you could convey the simple question, *Where have you been all this time?*, in as many F-words.

I chuckled and shot off a reply, inviting her to dinner at the Three Little Pigs and promising to explain everything there. She didn't answer. Could she be angry with me? Never mind. This could actually make a good acid test for our friendship. If she did come to the Pigs that night, prepared to listen to me and accept the truth—great stuff, we were still friends. If she didn't... well, then she was just another whacky gaming chick. In which case it wasn't meant to happen, as simple as that.

While I was at it, I checked my friend list. Both my rogue friends, Bug and Cryl, were online. I invited them to the Three Little Pigs, too. Bug replied straight away,

OK. Will pick up cash from the bank on my way.

Good kid. I'd have to look at the results of our Wardrobe op. If it worked, I'd better keep in touch with him. I had a funny feeling you couldn't very easily survive here on your own.

Cryl didn't answer, even though the green light of his online status kept glowing. Wonder if he'd blacklisted me by mistake? Pressed the wrong button? I'd love to cross paths with him again somewhere, he was too funny to lose contact with.

We arrived at the inn to numerous sighs of delight. Eric must have PM'd all his friends, impatient to impress them. They met us by the inn's gates. A small crowd gathered around LAV, studying and touching the patient phlegmatic creature. They preferred to give mine a wide berth, though. Hummungus cast warning glances at the strangers and bared his teeth, growling when someone came too close. The two Red Bear clones definitely didn't share the same character.

We could let them go for the time being until the next ride but Eric asked me to leave Hummungus near the inn for a bit of atmosphere. He sat his own beast by the opposite wall. Together, they made a fine pair of doorway statues, enormous and threatening.

I was already inside and walking across the hall nodding to a few players that looked familiar when Taali PM'd me saying the bears wouldn't let her in.

I waved to the instantly-wary Eric and walked out. The furious girl was keeping a safe distance from the doorway. I could see Bug hurrying toward us at the end of the street.

"Off, Hummungus. They are friends," I patted the bear's neck and walked over to Taali raising my hands in a mock gesture of surrender. I leaned over her, giving her time to decide whether she wanted me to kiss her or not. At first, she recoiled, her hands pushing at my chest. She paused and looked up into my eyes. Shaking her gorgeous mane of hair with determination, she grasped my neck. Her lips, hot and impatient, clung to mine. What a girl.

I heard a sarcastic applause behind my back. It was Eric, just making sure his new friend hadn't gotten into more trouble.

"Ah. So this is the girl who stuck by you through thick and thin when you were banged up? Pretty lady."

"Banged up?" Taali tensed. "What's he talking about?"

"Never mind," I shrugged. "I'll tell you later. Wait a bit, here's the rogue coming, he's invited too. Good guy, Bug's the name. We have a reason to celebrate."

She gave me a puzzled look. Had she thought I'd invited her to a candlelit date? I had to be losing my grip. I'd focused too much on my own problems just lately.

I touched her hand. "I'll explain it all to you in a moment," I whispered. "Just wait a bit. Everything happened too quickly, that's all. I'm sure you'll understand."

Taali squeezed my hand and nodded. "Okay. I was worried, you know. You told me you were going perma. I just thought you hadn't... or couldn't..." she sniffled.

"Hush, baby. The worst is already past."

She raised a puzzled eyebrow. I gave her a wink.

When Bug came closer, the alert bear needed a new dose of calming down. It wasn't a good idea to unsettle him any further and upset the passersby, so I gave him another pat behind the ear before clicking the *Dismiss mount*. The bear vanished into thin air. Excellent. With a regular horse, you'd have to clean him after every race, brush him, give him food and drink, check his hooves every five minutes. And this was more like calling for a cab: you just summoned him whenever you needed a ride, then folded him back into an artifact.

Taali only shook her head, watching. "You're a Necro, right? Hummungus used to be your zombie. And now he's more like a lapdog, all alive and obedient."

"That's where you got it wrong. I'm not a Necro, I'm a Knight. And as you can see, my Teddy is more than alive. Come on now, in you go. I think Eric's got a table waiting for us."

He had indeed. Eric had staked us a good table in the middle of the room and was now busy dictating his order to the waitress, waving his hands like an angler boasting the size of his catch. Looked like we were in for at least a roasted pig. He met my eyes and glanced toward the gong. How could I forget. My hand on Taali's elbow gently directed her toward the table.

"Go sit yourself down," I whispered. "I won't be a minute."

I walked out into the center of the room and picked up the heavy mallet. Conversations died down. The other players turned in my direction. I took a swing and hit the gong, filling the room with its vibrations.

Everyone jumped up from their seats, catcalling and clapping their hands. Someone whistled. It felt as if I'd just drawn a line under my past life and turned a new page. This was my new life now.

"The first round's on me. This is to living!"

I didn't get any gifts—apparently, I didn't look enough like a scared level 1 Elven maid to prompt a baby shower of sympathy. Which was good because I wouldn't have known how to accept it from so many strangers. Everyone was happy for me and drank to my future fortune. Which, for me, was more than enough.

Just as I was taking my seat at the table, Eric—who looked embarrassed for some reason—slammed the oak table top with a heavy triangular shield. He'd already grilled me on our way there, demanding to know my future character configuration. Now he seemed to have come up with a welcome gift. But why was he blushing like a schoolgirl?

"A gift. Specially for you. Hang on a bit, don't try it on yet. Let me explain first. There's a location, called Hatred Fortress. A real-life castle, I tell you, filled with very humanoid aggros. Not easy for a solo player, but quite doable for a full 100+ group. Mobs guard the walls in threes, usually two archers and a shield bearer who holds two shields covering them. Serious tanks love his left-handed shield—it's a rare drop, especially appreciated by Death Knights. Quit grinning, this isn't it."

He looked at my disheartened face and laughed. "This is its twin brother. A right-hand shield: extremely rare and just as useless. Useless for almost everybody but you. Those who've chosen a one-handed sword can't use it because then they can't use their sword hand. And those who've chosen to be ambidextrous, only do it because they want to use two swords. In other words, an object of unique parameters and equally useless. Enjoy."

I had a closer look at it.

Jangur's Battle Shield
Item Class: Rare
Slot: Right Hand
Effect: +20 to Strength, +20 to Constitution, +55 to Armor
Fences the caster off with a protective shield absorbing 500 points damage.
Cooldown: 5 min

Oh. My inner greedy pig clutched his heart and slid down the wall. As for me, I was nearing nirvana. This was my sort of thing. These were the kind of bells and whistles that came with unconventional leveling. A unique antique object, as useless as a handleless suitcase: too heavy to carry and too good to scrap. How many treats like this were stashed away in high-level players' rooms and cookie boxes? I wanted it all, in triplicate.

"Thanks, dude," I managed. "You couldn't have done better if you tried. You know my leveling pattern now. So if you come across something in the same league, just let me know. No more gifts, please. I'll be happy to pay what they cost."

I patted the shield one last time and forced it down the bag. This was one of the things I liked here: even now that I was perma-stuck, the world around had preserved certain virtual qualities. For instance, my bag was spacious enough to fit three dozen footsoldier's shields and the same number of spears. I preferred not to dig too deep into physics and wrote it down as local spatial magic. Easier that way. Could well be magic—who was I to tell?

Bug waved to me to attract my attention, then glanced around meaningfully: *was it all right to speak openly there?* I nodded.

The kid stood up and reported, "I took all the trash to a shop, got fifteen gold for it in total. Then I auctioned the more interesting ones. They weren't too special so they went off for a couple gold each, but it's still sixty-three gold plus fifteen, that's seventy-eight gold, nothing to sniff at. Half of it is yours, as agreed."

The sales mode window blinked open. Bug dropped off the money and PM'd me a detailed sales report. Excellent job. The kid was already level 16—not bad at all. His class wasn't easy to level: you needed patience and a good knowledgeable group. In gratitude, I sent him all my gray and black bracelets—over a hundred in total. This extra dozen gold didn't make much difference to me but it could help him rise another couple levels.

Bug didn't play hard to get. He thanked me calmly, accepting the gift.

Taali hadn't wasted her time, either, and had already made level 25. Ah, dammit, this wasn't the day to skimp. About ninety red bracelets landed in her bag. She was more express in her gratitude, earning me another kiss.

After that, we just relaxed and had a good time. A new future, excellent food, a few trusty friends and your girl sitting next to you—what else do you need to enjoy a night out? I took a moment to send my compliments to the innkeeper and inquire about a room. No problem, apparently, even though he strongly recommended I moved to the third floor. My new perma status demanded the keeping up of appearances. The inn's second floor was reserved for regular players who either wanted to stay overnight or sought some entertainment. It wasn't a proper place for a perma player to stay. I didn't insist. The new life had gone to my head and the money was burning a hole in my pocket. This was how I got myself a new monthly expense of two hundred gold.

We whooped it up until late at night. Bug was the first to bail out. Eric looked us over with an all-knowing stare and drifted off. The sad Taali thawed out a bit and even dragged me out for a dance a couple times to some artless tune from three local musicians who showed up later that night.

Finally, when the inn was almost deserted and she couldn't dance any more, she sat opposite me and buried her chin in her hand, staring at me with those moist, shiny, tipsy eyes. Then she leaned toward my ear and whispered,

"If you just wait a bit... I need to relogin. I still have two hours of full immersion on my limit left. You could show me your stamp collection."

Hips swaying, she headed for the ladies' room.

We walked upstairs together.

Chapter Eighteen

I'd had a lovely sleep. A clock somewhere in my peripheral vision showed a few minutes past nine. The PM icon flashed soundlessly: last night, I'd turned off all the audio settings. Sometimes I felt like a cyborg stuffed with implants. There I was, alive in a living world, but surrounded with pop-up windows of system messages, chat boxes and hits/mana bars. It would be a good idea to ask Eric about his experiences. An old-time perma, he must have a much deeper fusion rate.

I'd woken up perfectly alone. Taali had logged out a long time ago. Logical, really: no reason why she should spend the night in a capsule, and a 3D one at that.

I checked my inbox and saw her message. Oh well. I was accused of taking advantage of an intoxicated girl, followed by a vague promise of more of the same tonight. Women and their logic!

Next in the inbox were my two newsfeeds I'd subscribed to. Shame the third-floor apartments didn't come with room service. Would be great to order a coffee and some sandwiches to go with my morning read. Now I'd have to go and take a table downstairs. Only the fourth floor rooms came with chambermaids summoned by a bell. They were for high middle class—not the stinking rich who had their own mansions, towers or even castles, but for those who could afford to part with five hundred gold a month—a sum to be reckoned with, whether here or in the real world.

I pulled on my seedy newb rags. About time I got rid of them. Today had to be the day. As I walked downstairs, the kitchen regaled my nostrils with the delights of fried bacon. I couldn't resist it much longer and ordered a big fried breakfast upstairs in my room. It wasn't as if it could clog my arteries any more, was it?

The waitress promptly brought in a plateful of fried eggs, tomatoes, onions and crunchy wafer-thin slices of bacon. Plus some cheese on toast served with butter roses, a pot of jam and a large mug of steaming coffee. All included, just like in Benidorm. Spending money started to feel good.

Now I could finally have a good look around my new room. Last night I was too busy with other things. The room was twice the size of the one I'd had before. The large king size bed had already passed the stress test with flying colors. Also in the room were a desk, two chairs, a recliner, a carved wardrobe and a massive chest. Heavy curtains covered the tall wide window. Excellent. Still I wouldn't mind having a peek at the fourth-floor rooms, just to know what to aim for.

Once I'd satisfied my first hunger, I sat back with the ever-hot coffee mug and opened the newsfeed. First I checked the real-world headlines for what I wanted to know most:

The Easy Lease Company has been reported to have trebled their FIVR capsules lease deposits. It claims that over 16% of all capsules rented within the past year have been returned in non-operable condition. The most common faults include reflashed memory, tampered chips and hacked monitoring hardware.

The RusStats' records for the last six months have shown suicide rates in Russia to have dropped 21%.

Wages in all sectors related to development and promotion of new virtual worlds have reached a new record high. However, the industry experiences a severe shortage of qualified professionals at all levels.

Russia's three biggest companies specializing in virtual worlds tailor-made to private order have announced their being unable to accept new orders for the next two years. Despite the recent soar in prices, demand still far outpaces supply in this particular sector of the gaming industry.

A new high tech facility growing artificial intelligence crystals has been finally launched in Malaysia. This is hoped to decrease the deficit of AI crystals on the world market. The construction of the second phase of the project is said to be progressing ahead of schedule.

The tragic accident a week ago when the militant faction of the Femen radical group had detonated both of the Padishah virtual world's data centers caused our readers to commiserate deeply with the families of over a thousand perma players who inhabited the Padishah world together with over eight hundred thousand regular players. Yesterday, the backup database was finally installed on the game's new servers. Much to everyone's relief, the digitized individuals proved safe and sound and had *even achieved a certain progress in the game. They expressed their surprise at the absence of regular players during the past week. The government is yet to comment on this remarkable event.*

I closed the inbox and leaned back in awe. Just think what opportunities this could breed... prospects of immortality, even? And what if I got fed up with it all? Was there a way to finish my life permanently, so to speak? Because if there wasn't, fifty percent of AlterWorld's population in another thousand years or so could consist of half-witted level-100500 Dark Overlords? Oh well...

I copied the last news bit and forwarded it to Eric. Let him give it some thought. Doubtlessly, the powers that be had long been in the know. They must have already stripped down and reassembled hundreds of virtual guinea-pig worlds, improving living conditions in our overpopulated prisons in the process. I'd love to know what had happened to those half-baked worlds floating in the middle of virtual nowhere with their digitized jailbird inhabitants. A terrible thing, come to think of it. You create a virtual version of hell, fill it with undesirables, then pull the plug on the server. Would it mean eternal hell? Or did an unplugged virtual world gradually decompose? One day we might know all the answers...

Not good. That called for some quality comfort eating. I topped a slice of toast with generous layers of butter and jam. How's that for a calorie bomb? As I crunched on it, I opened the gaming newsfeed.

Top European clan the Prophets have successfully completed their three-day raid on the Fear Plane. The total value of the auctioned loot exceeds one million gold.

Nagafen slain! For the fifth time in the history of the virtual world, this powerful dragon was killed by players of the United Asian Alliance. They then proceeded to discover Nagafen's precious egg in the dragon's nest. The raid's main question remains, which one of the Allied castles will be marked by the Black Guard's winged presence?

Many of our readers expressed their surprise when the Golden B Amero clan had their patrimonial Gold Bastion listed for sale the other day. Bidding completed yesterday at the record price of seven million gold. The same day, the clan leader explained their reasons for selling the place in an open forum. According to him, guild rangers had discovered a new Colossus-class castle in the frontier lands. The proceeds from selling Gold Bastion will go on the new castle activation, as well as paying virtual property taxes and buying up the adjacent lands.

This is Russian cluster news. It's been eight days since the Fathers began holding the entrance to the Valley of Gloom. The notorious dark clan block other players' passage to the location. The analysts suggest the discovery of a new dungeon behind the clan's actions. As you probably know, every newly discovered location acquires a unique 50% bonus to experience and loot for the whole of two weeks.

The legendary Pain Blade has been seen in possession of Les Miserables clan leader. This is the second known specimen of its kind in our sector. It's *not quite clear how Les Miserables came by the artifact considering that the Blood Lord's Dungeon has never been completed once in the last month, and the vampire boss himself has never been slain.*

We congratulate Yanir, combat leader of the Dark Side clan, on reaching level 240. Way to go, Yanir!

On a lighter note. A level 1 newbie has been sighted in the tutorial zone of the Korean sector. Apparently, the beginning player has spent the last three weeks assaulting a training dummy with a bokken sword. Someone needs to tell him that his feats won't affect his characteristics until he leaves the T-zone.

Whew. That was me done newswise. Just by reading it, my new world had expanded from the size of a small medieval town to the more customary size of a planet. Time to move it, anyway. As a friend of mine used to say, the smaller the distance between your ass and the couch, the less money will fit through it. So up with my ass and off we go.

First thing I popped in at Gunnar's, the vendor of all things brutal, and made him happy by finally purchasing the long-desired Staff of Dark Flame. Much to my chagrin, he didn't happen to have any more yummies. That is, he had loads of cool stuff but all of it was quite commonplace—and not at all cheap.

I also visited the tailor recommended by the innkeeper. Thank God I didn't need to explain to him my need for new underpants, a T-shirt and a pair of socks. Game developers seemed to understand that wearing a steel cuirass or mithril boots on one's bare body in full immersion was not a gamer's idea of fun. So they came up with this interesting feature when you could wear two or three items per each clothing slot, but only one of them would bring bonuses and the others, marked as optional, would serve purely utilitarian functions.

Having finished with the undies, I also bought quite cheaply a few pairs of decent pants plus a couple of shirts and a lightweight suede jacket. Just for those days when I didn't feel like walking around like an armored wardrobe. I changed straight away and immediately felt a different person, way up the social ladder: not a bum any more but a noble adventurer. All I needed now was a new pair of shoes which didn't take much time in acquiring, either.

Closer to lunchtime, I popped in at the jeweler's on my way back to my room. He wanted twelve gold for the rings I had in mind: those with +5 to either Strength, Intellect or Stamina. The jeweler wasn't too forthcoming with discounts. Either he was a stingy old sort or he was paying me back for my neutral stance in the city.

After a hearty lunch, I took a strategic position in the recliner and laid out my trophies on the table. They started to take the shape of a nice raid kit. The Staff of Dark Flame and the shield ruled it. I decided to decorate the shield with the Sky Stone—the Admins' gift—for the extra +10 to Intellect.

Now I finally had time to inspect the Gnoll King loot. I reached to the bottom of my bag:

Gnoll King Charm

Item class: Rare

Effect 1: +3% to magic resistance

Effect 2: Pain Mirror. Gives a 3 to 100 probability of reflecting the damage dealt to you toward the attacker.

Effect 3: Servitude Mirror. Gives a 3 to 100 probability of reflecting the damage dealt to you toward your summoned creature.

Class Restrictions: Only Death Knight

I especially liked the charm's dual purpose, in both raid and PK kits.

As for jewelry, I still needed eight rings. Yes, eight, as AlterWorld's inhabitants didn't wear rings on their thumbs. There was another cool thing about it, too. You could replace earrings with a second charm: good news for most male inhabitants who weren't looking forward to sporting some fancy palm-size half-pounders like Dragon Earrings and the like. We had none of those medieval sailors among us who used to stick a gold earring in their ear hoping for a decent burial.

Finally, bracelets. I had to admit I'd overgrown the +1 to Strength ones I'd farmed from the gnolls.

Having said that, why hadn't I thought about the auctions? They should have a massive choice— granted, it was limited to only City of Light players, but they counted tens of thousands. Now. Where's that search panel?

I opened the sales interface.

Items available: 141.901

Oops. A bit over the top. I limited my search to "*Buy Now!*" items. I had no time for bidding gamble.

Items available: 103.811

That's better. I limited my search to items between 10 and 2000 gold.

Items available: 28.514

Right. This was something I could work with. Any other way I could trim it down further? After a thought, I limited the search to Death Knight items.

Items available: 354

That was it. I decided to weed it down even further. Show objects: gauntlets.

Items available: 16

Good. Now I could examine each lot personally. No hurry.

They had some interesting stuff there. Nothing too uber: most of the unique, rare and epic items were soulbound by definition. Those that weren't, cost a fortune and even then you had to put your name on a waiting list. This world had far more millionaires than available epics.

My problem was also in my particular leveling pattern. Most of the stuff here was meant for a classic semi-tank. Finally, I found something worth my while:

Gauntlets of the Soul Catcher
Item class: Rare
Effect 1: +34 to Armor, +11 to Intellect, +11 to Spirit, +11 to Constitution
Effect 2: Increases chances of dropping Soul Stones 7%.
Class restrictions: Death Knight
Price: 650 gold

That was just too good. And too expensive. I had to decide how much I could afford to splurge. I had, in total, just under 2700 in gold. I had to set aside five hundred at least as a reserve fund, to pay the rent and for emergencies. Ideally, I'd have to aim for ten times as much, twenty even. Just in case my grave somehow decayed with all my stuff in it: what was I supposed to do at level 100 in my underpants? I had to set aside another thousand for any unmissables—plenty of them around when you needed to have available cash there and then. Okay. I had twelve hundred to play with.

Having decided on the tactics, I still had to consider my strategy. Was it better to invest into mid-range items like that King loot? It sure would last me another thirty levels. Or should I aim for some choice top items like those gauntlets that would serve me indefinitely?

Finally, I decided not to bother with the mid-range. It was better to buy a few top things I really liked. For the rest, I'd have to make do with inexpensive gear, replacing it gradually with rare and unique items.

I pressed *Buy*. Immediately, messages started popping up, confirming the bank transfer. I ignored them and opened my bag, impatient. Oh, the beauty of teleporting. I couldn't take my eyes off the opalescent black armor. On one hand, sixty-five bucks for a collectable is nothing to sniff at. But on the other... If any of these things—like these gauntlets, for instance, with their intellect and spirit bonuses, damage absorption and rare items search— if any of them were available in real life, how many hundreds of millions would they cost? And in any case, was this world any different for me from the real one? The quick answer was: no, it wasn't.

I decided to look for some shoes.

Items available: 22

I looked through them. Nothing I really liked. How about a helmet?

Items available: 26

The first one definitely was meant for some tank, not for me. But the next one... was I having delusions of grandeur?

Crown of the Overlord
Item class: Unique
Effect 1: no extra characteristics
Effect 2: When worn, adds +3 to a summoned creature's level
Effect 3: Renders all the undead such as skeletons, zombies, spirits, etc. neutral and unable to

attack first. Halves their aggro radius in case of the wearer's attack.
    Class restrictions: Death Knight, Necromancer
    Price: 1450 gold

Now that was the closest thing to a cheat. The item had been listed thirty minutes ago. It would be gone any moment. Every fiber of my gaming addict's being could sense the crown's concealed potential. I could only explain its moderate price by its class restriction, especially here in the heart of the Lands of Light. Dammit. This buy could crush all my financial schedule. Or could I maybe write it off under Emergencies? My inner greedy pig nodded enthusiastically. Could it be that my portable mini vermin was prepared to part with gold? Well, then I simply had to have it.

The next moment, the crown took pride of place on the table. It looked the part. With something like this, I could rule the world. Joke.

I had six hundred left on my balance. Time to switch to economy mode and check out jewelry. Should I look at craft items first? Why not. It couldn't be that expensive.

I sorted the items by price and parameters. This looked like a curiously interesting object:

Distraction Ring
    Item class: Craft, Uncommon
    Effect 1: +1 to Armor, +1 to Strength, +1 to Agility, +1 to Intellect, +1 to Spirit, +1 to Constitution
    Effect 2: +1% to all types of magic resistance
    Class restrictions: none

Price: 14 gold

The offer had a note from the owner.

My wholesale leveling of jewelry allows me to sell most items at cost price. PM me if you're looking for something in particular.

That was pretty logical. Those players who leveled craft skills were obliged to produce hundreds and thousands of items. What were they supposed to do with them if the market was oversaturated and you didn't have a hope in hell of getting a fair price from a shop? So everyone was trying to at least get their money back.

After some thought, I ordered eight of them. For that money, a very decent offer indeed. Then I opened the vendor's selling list. There they were, just as I thought: Distraction Bracelets, identical to the rings, only belonging in a different slot. They cost a gold more. I picked up a couple, then started looking for a charm. Having said that, the vendor had had enough from me. I opened other people's lists and stopped my choice at an unimpressive Knowledge Charm: +3 to both Spirit and Intellect. Cheap and cheerful.

I filled the rest of the slots with inexpensive and unimpressive items. I'd have to replace them all gradually at a later date. At the moment, I was dangerously close to a financial collapse.

Having said that, the idea of choosing myself a profession had lingered. It was no good throwing punches around for a living. I needed something more pacifist, something that would bring in money as well as self-enlightenment. I gave it a minute's thought and remembered a few recent scenes: the exorbitant potion prices and the shop owner's transfixed stare when I'd offered him some magic dust. I looked it up in the Wiki. So, I was right—the dust made the basic magic ingredient in most elixirs. And I was basically a walking factory of the above which made my offers very interesting. Naturally, I couldn't dream of competing with clan crafters with their hundreds of hired workers. But their produce hit the open market but rarely: crafters mainly only catered to their own clan's consumption. I dreaded to even contemplate the costs of a top clan's one-day raid.

The Wiki didn't have much on Alchemy—just a dozen pages filled with basic descriptions and primitive recipes. Unwilling to fall into the same trap that the developers had laid for newbs, I signed up for a complete manual. In less than a minute, it arrived in my inbox—a two-hundred page behemoth of an e-book. Apparently, the request was common enough to justify an automated mailing response. The size of the manual humbled me, but no one said it was going to be easy. Which was good news, really. It meant that a man of intelligence could always make a few bucks doing it and not get bored in the process.

I glanced at the table buried under heaps of armor. I just had to try all that stuff on. I changed into thicker clothes, ticked them off as optional and put on all the items one by one. I literally felt stronger. The life/mana bar went through the roof.

Someone knocked. The door swung ajar, letting in Taali. I turned to face her. She froze for a second.

"Holy cow. If this isn't Dark Lord! You think I could try on the crown?"

Chapter Nineteen

The next morning was busy. Taali and Bug were supposed to be coming at ten o'clock and I had lots of things to do before then. We planned our first mission—two days into the woods. Our agenda: farming, profession leveling and fine-tuning our teamwork. The other two had agreed unreservedly. With the weekend coming, they had plenty of spare time for a quality outing that promised decent dividends of both experience and mana.

Despite the fact that Taali had left rather early, I hadn't gotten much sleep the night before. I'd been studying professional manuals. That's *manuals*, in the plural, as I'd soon realized that alchemy had to be leveled alongside the flaying and herbal skills. Otherwise I'd have to rush to the auctions every time I needed some ingredient or other, which would cause my production costs to soar. So I'd ordered two more manuals and a detailed farming map of the area, then spent the rest of the night going through them.

In the morning, I had a quick bite to eat and started doing my Master Guilds rounds. I first went to the Alchemy Guild to get my apprenticeship status. Now I was free to level it up to 50 after which I was supposed to go back, this time to pay some solid gold for being promoted to journeyman.

You had to pay your way through the professional stages, seven of them in total. But at least my choice of professions was only limited by the size of my wallet and the amount of hours in a day. Talking about my wallet. I still had to splurge thirty gold on a basic alchemy kit that included some scales, metering spoons, measuring tubes, and a few basic recipes. I also had to buy another hundred vials for the duration of the raid. Good job you could stock them up twenty per slot, otherwise I had no idea how I'd have packed it all up.

Next, I visited the Herbalists and the Rangers Guilds: the latter, to study flaying and buy a skinning knife. I didn't actually need to hold it in my hand as long as I had it on the inventory list. That was almost it. One practice left to do. I searched the city map for the Happy Palate restaurant. According to the guide book, its owner accepted all and sundry for apprenticeships. The book was right: soon I acquired a fourth profession plus a set of spices and recipes in the vein of Spiced Wolf, Fox Relish and Smoked Bear. Almost everyone here had leveled cooking at some point, at least its first free stage. Which made sense: it would be stupid to starve to death next to a freshly killed rabbit. And once you reached the Famed Master stage, it opened your way to some very interesting recipes.

My inner greedy pig was past all hope by then. He even managed an occasional half-hearted nod when I was reading through the list of dishes available for skill points 450 and above.

As in:

Smoked Dragon Fillet
Level required: 100

Use: Restores 990 Health and 990 Mana over 25 sec. Must remain seated while eating. The character becomes well fed and gains 20 points both Strength and Constitution.

Apart from its apparent gourmet value, the freebies that came with the dish were motivation enough for any player to level cooking.

By ten in the morning, everyone was present and correct. Even Taali chose not to play the spoiled diva and logged in two minutes before time. Remembering our past experiences and the older players' advice, we set up our resurrection point right in the inn's courtyard.

Taali and I managed to do it ourselves; then I had to change Bug's bind point, too, as the kid knew no magic. To do that, we accepted him into our group, after which I selected him as target and cast the spell. Immediately a system message popped up,

Player Bug has agreed to the changes made to his resurrection point.

That was it. We headed for the gates, then toward the woods and further on, directly east, for about four and a half miles. When the town wall disappeared from view, I stopped the group and summoned the pet. Despite my level 32, the biggest stone I had was only 28: the one I'd gotten from the Gnoll Priest all those days ago. Never mind. Soon we were going to fix it.

My heart sank when I cast the summoning spell. This had to be my first field test with my custom-picked skills and gear.

The earth bulged. A zombie gnoll crawled out of a black mole hole. He was 30—not a wonder waffle, but not so bad at all. A regular Death Knight without all those skills and gear would have raised a level 20 pet, 24 at most. I done good, especially considering I only had two top items.

I started adding buffs to him: Fire Shield, Agony Armor, Strength of the Undead, Bigfoot. Their little icons appeared under the zombie's life bar. When you concentrated on any of them, a prompt popped up:

Strength of the Undead. Adds +30 Strength to the summoned creature. Time remaining: 59:31... 30... 29...

The timer kept ticking down. Knowing that it wasn't possible to keep an eye on the boxes in the heat of battle, I set up an audio alarm. Then I configured the quick access panel to farm mode. Stun. DoT. That was it. Time to get going. Or get riding. With that thought, I summoned Hummungus. His current speed was quite low so the others didn't have to run after him. But his presence added extra weight to the group and might discourage an occasional PK. I climbed aboard him and off we went.

I'd only basked in the comfort of Hummungus' saddle a hundred paces before my first find crossed our path. A lit-up contour of a small yellow flower blinked blue in the grass on my mini map. I bent out of the saddle to pick it, then studied it before shoving it in my bag:

Congratulations! You've found a Sunleaf flower!
Your herbal skill has improved! Current level: 1

Now we were cooking! Still, my initial joy quickly turned to impatience when I spent the next ten minutes constantly scrambling in and out of the saddle. Finally I gave up and ordered Teddy to follow me as I walked ahead picking new herbs here and there.

After an hour and a half of leisurely walking, we arrived at the spot the guidebook recommended. We'd already left Green Woods behind with their cute sub-level 10 creatures. Then we'd crossed Thick Woods with their occasional aggros, none over level 20. Finally, we fought our way through Sleeping Woods. Three times we had to protect Bug from various local monsters who thought him an easy prey. Of the three of us, Bug with his level 17 was the smallest, while the local wolves and bears could be anything up to level 25 and didn't wait for an invitation to aggro you back.

Now we'd reached the clearing that formally divided the Sleeping from the Wild Woods. Our collective reason decided it was best for us to split up, at least at first.

Taali and I were going to pull our beasts from the Wild Woods while Bug would go solo and do the same from the Sleeping Woods, then kill his prey not far from us. Taali would then heal him and buff him up while I would send Teddy to help him, making sure my mount wouldn't get more than 50% hits or strip Bug of his experience. That way we could avoid the level gap penalty while giving Bug a decent chance to level up a bit. True that it complicated both mine and Taali's existences, but the pure fun of it and a chance to get ourselves a good friend outweighed the cons.

"Where shall we set up camp?" She looked just too cute with those flowers entwining her helmet. The flowers had been my idea. I'd noticed the joy in her face when I'd bent down to pick the Sunleaf, quickly replaced by disappointment when I stuffed it into my bag.

Setting up camp was one of the great scout skills. I'd decided against leveling it, knowing that Taali had chosen it for herself. The skill had lots of bonuses. The first levels allowed you to choose a flat place and start a fire which you could then use for cooking and lighting and which also had a small life and mana regen bonus. Once you reached higher levels, you could make a stockade, a fire circle, a wickyup and a hut. It was definitely worth leveling once I was back to town, as I really shouldn't rely on Taali always being around.

I had a look around searching for a place that had good visibility and pulling properties and allowed for a bountiful hunt in the absence of other prospectors. Finally I pointed at a clearing some fifty feet away. "That's a good place, my lady."

Taali smiled and turned on her femme fatale look. Head up high, hips swaying, she walked over to the chosen point and began setting up camp. What a child she was, really.

I turned to Bug, "Any questions? Got everything prepared?"

"Always prepared," he answered sarcastically. "Three hundred throwing knives, four hundred bandages. Beverages, two full stacks."

"What have you got there?" I asked.

"Twenty flasks of ginger beer and the same of tea."

"Excellent. We should renew buffs first, then we can start. Let's go to the camp. She must have everything ready by now."

Just as we approached the fire, a message popped up,

Warning! You have entered a camp set up by Taali.

Status: free access

Within six paces from the fire, mana and life regen grows 1 point per second.

Warning! The camp does not protect you from aggressive creatures!

I nodded my gratitude to her. "Rebuff!"

Taali cast life- and armor-improving blessing spells over the two of us, then raised Bug's and her own Strength. That was logical. I didn't need a strength buff as I was too busy to fight, anyway. In the meantime, I renewed the zombie's bonuses. Hummungus hung about nearby, looking hurt. He really needed some freebies, too.

"Taali? You think you could cast something nice over my bear? I know you can't do it for the zombie."

She shrugged and exploded in a string of spells. A bunch of colored icons appeared on Teddy's panel. "Sixty mana," she said.

I nodded. "I see it. Come on, Bug. You start. We'll keep an eye on you for the first couple of pulls."

He picked up a throwing knife and bolted into the woods. Ten seconds later, we heard an angry growl. Bug ran out onto the road first, followed by a Grizzled Wolf.

I just shook my head. The Wolf was level 24, a bit too much for Bug. The kid reached the camp and turned round, meeting the beast with a blade in each hand. I waited a few seconds and told Teddy to attack.

What with his level 1, Hummungus was too young to tank properly. The best he could do was stay out of trouble and nibble at the wolf's side. Bug didn't hold well at all. His health kept dropping, so that soon Taali had to start healing him. After a moment's thought, I decided to cast a DoT. And again. Between Teddy and my DoTs, they stripped the beast of 30 or 40% life. Bug did the rest. The wolf met a sad end. But in the future, sending Bug solo wouldn't be any good. I had to come up with alternatives.

"Right, dude," I said to him. "I think we overdid it a bit. It's a bit early for you maybe, you can't really stand against them on your own. And if we get busy with our own mobs, then sooner or later we'll get distracted and get you killed."

Bug lowered his eyelids in agreement. Even though we'd already showered him with experience, he wouldn't last long without our support.

"You think you'll come into some cool abilities in the next level or two?" I asked.

Bug perked up a bit. "I think so. I get a bleed combo at level 18, and then a crippling hit with a 13% attack delay at 19."

"Okay. Let's do it this way. For the next hour, we'll work entirely for you. We'll be healing you and taking care of 50% of your mobs' life. Until you do 19. Then we fall back on our old plan. Forget the bandages. We'll do it as fast as we can. Ready?"

It worked. He did the two levels in forty minutes—even faster than we thought. I had to admit I'd overdone it a couple times, accidentally stripping him of his experience. Not overdone it, even. When I'd seen that things were under control, I got cheeky and spent the time leveling alchemy, only pausing to cast another DoT and tell Teddy to attack.

In less than two hours of our journey, my herbal skill had reached 32 as I'd harvested an impressive bunch of various plants, flowers and roots. I checked the available recipes. Apparently, I could now make a vial of Minor Life Elixir and also Agility Elixir. The latter I couldn't care less about, but I was sure Taali and Bug would be happy to use it. In any case, leveling my profession was all that mattered to me at the time.

I reached into my bag for my traveling alchemy kit. I placed two life roots into a measuring tube and added the tiniest metering spoon of magic dust. Then I placed the resulting vial into a special slot in the Transmutation Box and closed the lid. A red light flashed underneath it.

You've failed to make the potion! Try again!
The following ingredients are ruined:
Life Root, 1
A small pinch of magic dust, 1

Oh, well. I raised my head to make sure everything was under control and added the missing ingredients again. The lid flashed green.

Success! You've created a vial of Minor Life Potion!
You've reached level 1 in Profession: Alchemy.

I lovingly took out the vial. For some reason, things you make with your own hands make you feel better, which is a fact exploited by numerous brands selling you lopsided DIY furniture kits more suitable for dwarves that for human use. Ah, forget it.

By the time Bug screamed "Yes! Nineteen!" I'd already used up all the herbs I had, raising the skill to 23.

I proudly pointed at where three dozen tiny bottles were lined up by the fire. "Welcome to Dr. Death Knight's clinic," I said, filling my quick access slots with vials. Others followed suit, snapping up the rest.

A few minutes later, I gingerly stepped onto the moss of the Sleeping Woods. The first to meet me was the SUV-sized hulk of a grizzly bear. A couple levels higher than myself, he was perfect for a test pull.

I cast a DoT with a snare. The creature bellowed, causing wood rot to cascade below. I shook my head, stunned by his voice. Was it his skill or the developers' sick sense of humor again? Was there a way to put the sound down here? I bolted. A flower of Purple Cineraria flashed under some fir tree or other. I tried to memorize the place to be able to come back to it at a later date.

Both Hummungus and the zombie stood by the fire as I'd told them to. You couldn't get further than fifty paces away from your pets. If you did, the mount would revert back to his artifact and the zombie could follow one of two scenarios. He would either crumble to dust in the absence of his owner's control or turn into an uncontrollable aggro. If some Necro left behind a high-level creature like that in a newb location, it could keep devastating the area for a long time until finally killed by a stronger player. And as it didn't offer any loot or experience, few would bother laying an unleashed mob like that to rest.

I turned to the pet. "Attack!" Then I slowly moved to face the grizzly bear.

Now we had to wait a few seconds as agreed. No one wanted to pull aggro to him or herself. Finally, Taali swung her sword entering the scene. The tip of her blade drew some kind of pictogram on the beast's side. With a guttural shriek, she hit the creature with her shield, finishing her act. The battle chat started flashing messages.

Failure! Taali's sword has dealt a powerful blow, but the Grizzly is still resisting her attack!

Which was when I joined the fun. I first sent Teddy to attack him. Then I cast a DoT with a snare, and another one, ending by casting two heals over my zombie. Somewhere in the wings, I heard Bug's cry for help.

I turned round. The kid was pulling two wolves from the woods. Too early. He should have sat out our first pull and watch us handle it. I switched the target and cast Deadman's Hand over one of the wolves, adding a DoT for good measure. Once the spell wore off, he'd start aggroing me, and then we'd see. Was I a semi-tank, after all? By then the grizzly and Taali were at 30%. On my command, she broke off the fight to heal Bug and herself. The zombie was still holding while Hummungus kept nibbling at the grizzly's back. I cast a DoT over each of the three mobs and renewed Deadman's Hand on the wolf. Taali rejoined us as I cast several Life Absorptions. Too much for the grizzly who promptly collapsed, bellowing. Keeping an eye on Bug, we finished off the remaining wolf while the kid terminated his, too.

Phew. That wasn't too difficult. Good team work, without walking a tightrope. We could do it. We'd had a stress test instead of the easy one we'd expected, that was all.

"Regen," I said. They sat down for a mana-restoring meditation while I quickly rushed to get a plant I'd discovered earlier, picking up another Sunleaf on my way. My herbal skill happily jumped up another point.

I looted the corpses. The wolf dropped a couple of chunks of meat while my newly-acquired flaying skill gave me an Eye of a Wolf. It didn't cost much but could be used for Night Vision Elixir. Waste not, want not.

The grizzly dropped nothing but a hefty handful of copper. True, farming Soul Stones solo was much easier than as part of a group. Each group member lessened my chances. With two of us, Soul Stones dropped half as often—even less when Bug joined us. In theory, you weren't supposed to notice it that much because logically, a group had to kill more mobs than a solo player. But in reality, the stronger the group, the more ambitious its goals and the higher the monsters the players target. That raised both loot and adrenalin but dramatically lowered the group's kill chances. I didn't even want to calculate the chances to get a Stone off a raid boss attacked by a group of two hundred players. Such chances had to be too depressing to bother.

"I'm ready," the girl reported.

"I'm off, then?" Bug shuffled from foot to foot, impatient.

"Go ahead, then. Scream if you need help. Use your bandages and elixirs. I'll be going, too."

The hunt started to fall into a pattern. After another twenty minutes, Hummungus had finally reached a new level.

Congratulations! Your riding mount Hummungus has reached a new level!
Hummungus' current level: 2
4 Characteristic points available!

Excellent. The night before, I'd had Teddy's leveling all worked out. I was going to increase his damage, and as soon as Hummungus started to pull aggro to himself, I'd start working on his hits. And the next day I planned to invest in his speed a little. Until now, it all had been going to plan. I opened Teddy's menu with a steady hand and raised his Strength four points.

In yet another twenty minutes, a celestial glow embraced Taali and almost immediately, Bug.

"Ding!" they shouted.

A quarter of an hour later, it was my turn to celebrate. Level 33, finally.

Chapter Twenty

The sky glowed crimson. The majestic fir tops had already swallowed the sun when we took stock of the day's exhausting work.

Our results were nothing to sniff at. I'd done 39, Taali 35, and Bug had very nearly hit 30. He needed another ten mobs to do so, but by then we were on our last legs. It had to wait till tomorrow. Nine hours of non-stop farming and about twenty close shaves. One of them had proven too close for Bug who'd had to walk back to us all the way from the city. If he hadn't splurged his own gold piece for a speed buff as he cleared the city gates, he'd still be trying to catch up with us. And then there was that wretched PK.

By that time, Bug had already joined our group, causing the Soul Stone loot to shrink into insignificance—one every fifteen minutes if we were lucky. I opened the Wiki to look for whatever was causing such a discrepancy. Apparently, apart from the party size penalty, we also had suffered a huge level gap. This was done to discourage the more clever players who might want to hire an assistant a hundred levels higher than themselves hoping he'd pull their chestnuts out of the fire for them. In theory, they still had a good chance of decent loot this way, but realistically it approached the same chances as hitting a rigged casino jackpot.

Don't get me wrong: I wasn't complaining. Experience kept coming, loot kept dropping, and I'd already made a nice little pile of high-level stones. My zombie gnoll had already bitten the dust, replaced by a level-36 zombie wolf. Bug kept pulling all sorts of little critters from the woods nearby. He waited till he got close enough to me and whispered,

"There's somebody around. Either stealthed or invisible. I have this Piercing Vision ability. If the guy gets too close or his skill is too low, I can see him.

"Who?" I mouthed soundlessly as I cast another DoT over a Mad Fox he'd fetched me.

He shrugged. "No idea. I've only seen his blurred outline a couple times but I wasn't fast enough to target him. Some PK sniffing around, I think."

After the battle I stopped Bug before he dashed off to get another monster. "Coffee break. Everyone, come and sit over here."

I waited for my friends to get seated. "Taali, we have a strong suspicion that there may be a PK prowling around. I suggest we go into paranoia mode. No taking risks. Make sure your hits don't drop too low. Start healing at fifty percent, not thirty. Everybody, keep mana over fifty, too. Bug, you stay within our sight, don't wander off, just keep pulling monsters from the edge, okay? If he doesn't show up in thirty minutes, we'll consider it a false alarm and stop for a smoke break."

The PK attacked us after ten minutes. Bug had just come back with an enormous patriarch wolf when the undergrowth parted, letting out a coal-black level 44 werewolf. He charged toward us. The creature just couldn't be local. According to the guidebook, they only inhabited the Cursed Woods which were coming next. No way it could have started aggroing us from that distance. Someone had to have set him on us.

You've been attacked by another player! Self-defense doesn't affect the PK counter!

The earth bulged around my pet. Powerful growths entangled the zombie's feet rooting him to the spot. That gave me some idea of what our attacker could be. I selected the werewolf as target and started casting Deadman's Hand, time after time, trying to control him.

"The PK is a Druid," I shouted. "Fifty to a hundred feet at three o'clock. He's controlling the werewolf. Bug, get up there and try to break his spells. Taali, make sure we don't die."

Finally, my third spell went through. The beast raged a few paces away, unable to move. I still couldn't see the Druid even though the same strong roots had already pinned down Hummungus and Taali. A stealthed Bug, like some mad tortoise, scurried toward the suspect enemy location. In the meantime, we had to finish off the werewolf while we still could if we didn't want to lose both our lives and experience. I cast a couple DoTs, renewing my control over him, when the air around me flashed with enemy spells. The Druid had already immobilized whoever he could and was now deciding on who to get rid of first. His choice fell on me as the one with two pets and the highest level. Who was he, attacking a group of three so brazenly?

Angry Earth! Tree roots come to life and entangle your feet, immobilizing you and dealing 110 points damage.

Beehive! A swarm of wild bees attacks you dealing 60 points damage.

Stings sent an agonizing rush through my body. Hey, that hurt. Apparently, the Beehive spell was also a DoT which went off every six seconds, annoying me no end on top of dealing damage.

I started healing, casting Life Absorption over the poor werewolf. His hits kept dropping. Sometimes the stinging bees prevented me from finishing a spell. The Druid sent another DoT my way, adding his own weak but frequent hits. Finally, the Gnoll King's Charm kicked in:

Pain Mirror is activated! The enemy spell Moonlight has been reflected toward the attacker.

Take that, you bastard!

Ouch. The werewolf broke the spell, covering the distance between us in one mighty leap and sinking his teeth into my belly, stripping me of 20% health in under ten seconds. The freakin' Druid just didn't know when to stop, did he? I kept casting Deadman's Hand as I crawled away from the immobilized werewolf. My life flashed in the red zone. It looked like I was a goner.

Taali saved me by spending on me her daily allowance of Holy Hands skill. Tada! The Druid had to be absolutely furious.

"I got him," Bug yelled.

Apparently, he'd managed to steal toward the Druid who was cloaking behind the stones, then hit him with a bleed combo to his back. The bastard had chosen a great vantage point: he'd peek out for a moment to select a target, then cast a series of spells.

Finally, the wolf collapsed. My four-legged friends rushed toward him but I selected the Druid as target and yelled "Attack!" Let's see how his magic helps him against three hand-to-hand fighters. That's provided we slowed him down first before he ran off, what with his druidic speed buffs and all. I cast a DoT with a snare, then another one, three times in total. His PK gear had to have some great resists until finally, my last DoT got to him.

The Druid crawled out onto the road, apparently with the intention of legging it. Hummungus had already frozen, paralyzed; now the pet stopped moving, too. Only Bug kept perforating the son of a bitch with his blades.

The Druid's life had shrunk into the red zone. He used a quick spell for a short teleport, reappearing a good fifty feet away from us. Immediately, he began casting a long spell. Judging by the familiar visual, it had to be a teleport to a bind point. I pulled some more life off him waiting for Bug to arrive. He hit the Druid with another combo, blood splattering everywhere. But the PK was in luck. He finished casting the spell and disappeared with a pop.

"He's gone to die, the bastard," I managed. "I got two DoTs on him."

Bug nodded. "I gave him a 140 bleed combo in the end. I don't think he can heal."

Warning! You've killed a player of the Faction of Light!
Your relationship with the Dark Alliance has improved!
The killed player has 271 points on his PK counter.

What a shame he was gone. With numbers like these, he was bound to drop a few quality items. He'd had some nice gear.

Oh, no. That was the werewolf again. He somehow managed to break free and sunk his teeth into my flesh. But now there were three of us plus two pets, however little mana we had left between us. So we survived. Luck had a lot to do with it, and we'd been lucky twice: the second time was when the creature's corpse dropped a level 44 stone. The werewolf had been great, but I chose not to change horses in midstream and stored the stone away till a later date.

Thus we kept leveling for another hour in moderate paranoia mode: we didn't let mana and hits drop below 40%, all the time waiting for the Druid to come back with a (literally) vengeance. But apparently, he had easier targets to pursue. That's the summary of our busy day.

Closer to the evening, Bug left me his share of the loot to sell and logged out right there by the campfire. Taali put on a brave face intending to go back to the Little Pigs with me, but soon the exhaustion took the better of her. We sat by the fire for a bit until she started to nod off and I had to force her to log out and get some sleep.

This was how I found myself alone in the night woods, taking in its sounds and the heady pine scent. Then I activated the teleporter and ended up back at the inn. Great invention.

The next day was a bit like the first one. When I reached the camp site, Taali and Bug were already in the game, half-heartedly discussing some hot new movie. Five minutes after initial hugs and kisses plus a rebuff, we were already wasting yet another bear. My zombie wolf had already risen to level 46—and added his share of fun. Buffed to its ears, it tore apart whatever the puffing and panting Bug could drag his way. The kid stopped fighting and just kept running around in widening circles bringing us mob after mob.

We did a level each within an hour, with the exception of Bug and Hummungus who'd done two. The bear's potential began to show. He seemed to be conscientiously working off the 10% experience I'd lavished on him. I'd have given him fifty, had it been technically possible, but even so, at level 12 with almost 80 Strength, he occasionally managed to pull aggro to himself. He received one special skill point for every five levels. The choice of skills made my eyes goggle. It allowed you to create your own unique combination. After some thought, I decided to concentrate on combat skills first: the weapons and the armor. Armor, yes. Apparently, nothing prevented you from cladding your mount in steel, giving him fangs of mithril and claws of moon alloy, then finishing the design off with silver spikes all over his body. I'd already seen a shop that offered just that.

All the items Bug had farmed in the Wild Woods were highlighted in blue. Too low for me. We smoked mobs faster than he could pull them. So we decided to move deeper, closing in on the Cursed Woods where, according to the guide, we could have plenty of level 40-50 mobs and some decent loot.

We got there quickly. The Wild Woods couldn't stop us any more. Yet another clearing revealed a wall of dark gnarled trees overgrown with bright green moss. We set up camp and followed the already-tested scheme, acting cautiously at first, studying our new opponents to see where we were compared to them. Gradually, we began working faster with more confidence. From time to time, I'd swap places with Bug and circle the gloomy trees looking for new herbs and mobs to pull. Three times I was grateful for having popped into the Herbalists Guild that morning to get my journeyman status. Although my pocket sensed the loss of fifty gold, the growing skill warmed my heart and filled my bag with new finds.

That day, we had to farm until we dropped. The two others had to go back to work the next morning and didn't want to lose the opportunity to exchange their time for the hard currency of fun and experience. We'd done a lot, considering we'd started two hours earlier and didn't stop until the stars had come out. Had it not been for Hummungus' Mule skill, we'd have had to leave the loot on the ground. I'd first discovered it when he was level 15 and (greed getting the best of me) just had to improve it once he'd reached 20. It allowed us to load him fifteen pounds for each Strength point—almost a quarter of a ton in total. Clenching my teeth, I also invested a few precious points into his speed: at two Characteristic points per mile, it was prohibitively expensive.

Personally, I'd reached 45 and done another 1/3. Now in case of my death I wouldn't be thrown back to 44. The other two were catching up with me slowly but surely: even though they'd been lower initially, Teddy kept pulling some of my experience to himself.

Taali had reached level 41 and Bug, 39. We were weary but eternally pleased. This was a perfect day for a great team like ours. Virtually no mistakes: the group had fallen into step, like cogs in a well-tuned machine. No PK was throwing any wrenches in the works that day, either.

Taali didn't let me off easily. She'd saved three hours in full immersion and she now expected me to work it off in kind. And this girl had some fantasy. Not that I would object. An amazing lover plus my new body, young and untiring. An eternal youth. An eternal bliss.

I made Monday my day off: to have some rest and maybe do a bit of crafting. I still had a quest to close, too. I kept Grym firmly in mind—he owed me one for my not having grassed him up to the Elven cops.

I spent Monday morning in bed. I sent Mom my daily message and on second thoughts MMSed her a screenshot of yesterday's party. Our group, arms around each other, stood over the two dead wild pigs we'd killed at the end of the show. My cute little beasties hovered in the background. A sight for sore eyes.

The waitresses knew me by then and happily obliged by bringing breakfast to my room. I checked the last two days' worth of news. Both worlds were boiling with the realization of the fact that perma players had become independent from the real world. The newsfeed illustrated it well.

The real world news:

The New York police have apprehended a serial killer who's digitized over eighty people by luring them into his own virtual world—a makeshift version of the Inquisitor software. As the police attempted to gain entry to his servers in the basement of his house, they accidentally set off a security device causing a powerful electromagnetic impulse to destroy all of the data storage media inside. No backup databases were found. The fate of the digitized persons is yet unknown. One can only hypothesize on the horrors they may have to face.

A human rights activist demands a total ban on developing new virtual worlds with violence levels over 30.

Brazil's biggest jujitsu school has announced their intention to alternate real and virtual classes. Their experience shows that virtual practice is just as effective in creating new brain pathways and reinforcing muscle memory. And unlike real-life practice, virtual classes prevent students from making mistakes which has proven to be three times more effective than traditional training.

A senator from Arizona has proposed a law that would allow the digitalization of the country's prison inmates. That would help to solve the problem of overcrowded prisons as well as eliminate violence among prisoners. The project has already passed a preliminary hearing. Our experts believe it might be approved very shortly.

The virtual newsfeed was just as eye-opening.

Missing: Mr. Guinnari, a level-203 mage, digital since 203X, member of OlderBank, Drowville, Management Board, honorary member of the Olders' Guild. Mr. Guinnari went missing five days ago when he stopped answering all incoming messages.

The Free Prospectors Association seeks volunteers to join them on their upcoming expedition into the Forgotten Lands. Requirements: level 100 and above, with high scout skills. The expedition aims to release an updated composite map of the new territories. The coordinates of all class A and B objects will then be auctioned, and all expedition members will receive a percentage of sales.

After their recent successful raid on the Seventh Heaven, the Steel Warriors Clan has reported finding a scroll containing a yet unknown cleric spell, dropped from one of the Wardens of Heaven. Its contents and characteristics are kept secret.

Fuckyall, the Russian cluster's strongest Paladin who pledged his allegiance to the Goddess of Heaven, has completed a unique six-month quest he received from the Fairest One's personal messenger. As a reward, he received an artifact containing a raid teleporter to an unknown location.

Oh well. The feeds didn't seem to be bursting with good news.

Anyway. It was time for me to go and see a Goblin I'd once known. I got into my armor, summoned Hummungus and headed for the East Gate surrounded by envious stares.

After five minutes' ride on the unhurried mount's back, I arrived at the hermit's cave. Gosh, it had been a while...

The cave entrance popped open, letting out a player in a newb's loincloth. Another masochist. The player stared at the bear, incredulous, before noticing me in a Dark Lord's full gear.

I nodded. "Welcome, Dark brother."

"Eh... the Fallen One?"

So! I'd been confused for Grym before, but not for a deity. Then again, probably it wouldn't be a good idea to annoy the local pantheon by petty identity theft. I shook my head.

"I'm just a player like you. I came here two weeks ago, just like you have now. So it's all in your hands. It won't be easy but you can do it. See you!"

I slapped his shoulder and ducked to enter the dark passageway. The Staff of Dark Flame automatically swallowed the light inside, plunging the cave into darkness. Old Grym was in. He studied me, his tired eyes squinting. Then he shook his head.

"You've grown much stronger, young knight. I start to believe that the Fallen One is kind to you."

I shrugged. "Any help is appreciated. I don't think you're aware that I've been arrested by the King's men and spent some time in the Bastion. I bailed myself out a few days ago. I promised you to keep this cave a secret. So I didn't tell them about it. Could you tell me now where I could find the Dark Guild?"

He sighed. He looked old and frail now. His eyes glinted as he hurried to turn away from the light. "I can. Now I can."

Quest completion alert: Knowledge Breeds Sadness. Quest completed!

Reward: access to unique quest Knowledge Breeds Sadness II.

Grym sank onto a wooden bench. "The Dark Guild's secret is that there's no Dark Guild any more. Whether through treason or by accident, but the Light Lord's servants discovered us. Under the city, there's a whole network of catacombs. There, in one of the caves, used to be the Dark Altar—the heart of our Temple. There weren't many Dark disciples in the city. When the High warriors flooded the catacombs, we were doomed. The novices held the passages while the Masters' Circle was preparing for the last rites."

He paused and went on, "The spell a disciple casts after death is much stronger that the one he can cast while still alive. They managed to break a tunnel through to the lower planes to summon help. But the cooldown was so massive that the Circle collapsed, killing most of them, and the Altar exploded into thousands of fragments. The monsters of the Dark lost control and killed all living beings within their reach. Even the Light Lord's servants were finally forced to retreat. They sealed the catacombs entrance up so that no one could enter them till the end of time. I was the only survivor, stripped of most magic powers by the titanic surge of necro energy. Still, I managed to escape through a secret passage. Alone. This is the sad story of our Guild, young Knight..."

I just sat there, puzzled. What now, then? Apparently, there was no Guild any more. Neither Guild Master nor Altar. Where was I supposed to get class quests? How could I do what the Hell Hound had asked me to?

"Isn't there anything at all we can do?" I asked.

Old Grym raised his head and looked me straight in the eye, "There might be. There's always a way."

I perked up. That was it. The second part of my quest. "I am ready, Hermit."

Grym solemnly nodded. "I didn't for one moment doubt you. The secret passage still exists. You can use it to go down the caves, reach the Temple and find an Altar fragment. For if you have a part, however little, filled with Dark power, you can then use it to restore any of our destroyed Dark temples in this world. Unfortunately, there're many more of them than I'd wish to admit."

New quest alert! Unique quest available: Knowledge Breeds Sadness II.

The Forces of Light failed to destroy the Dark Altar with cleansing rites. Overflowing with uncontrolled power, the stone exploded. But the power of its fragments is massive. Go down into the catacombs and obtain an Altar fragment.

Reward: Access to unique quest Knowledge Breeds Sadness III: Temple Restoration.

I accepted. Still, I had a lot of questions left for him. "How do you expect me to go through the catacombs if even the Guild Master failed to do so?"

"Do not worry. Darkness plays fair. It gives everyone a chance, whether you're a green newb or a legendary hero. Darkness offers everyone the opportunity to show their true colors. Only once, mind you. You don't get a second chance."

"Okay. Where's that secret passage?"

Grym chuckled. "Don't worry. You won't have to travel far."

He raised his hand, motioning part of the wall to disappear. A heavy door stood behind the fake stonework illusion. I walked over to it and pressed my hand to the door.

Warning! You're about to enter a personal quest dungeon: City Catacombs.

Difficulty level: Nightmare (monsters' level exceeds yours by 10 to 20)

Tries allowed: 1

Duration of stay: unlimited

Number of players: 1

Would you like to go in? You have 1 try left!

No. Not now. I wasn't ready yet. I shrunk, eyeing the door with suspicion. "Tomorrow," I nodded to the hermit. "I'm coming back tomorrow. I need to get ready."

Walking up the stairs, I kept repeating under my breath, "I need to get myself well and truly ready."

Chapter Twenty-One

I wasn't going to change my plans because of that quest I'd gotten myself into. On the contrary: now I really needed some quality time off. The quest was nothing to sniff at and the rewards could be worth their weight in gold.

I spent the next morning doing some crafting. My alchemy had been stuck at 50 points since our last farming session, so now I was forced to go to the Guild to upgrade my status. I also bought another hundred empty vials and some new recipes. My two days' worth of farming now allowed me to put my vast collection of ingredients to good use.

The money situation just didn't want to look up. I had less than three hundred left in my account. I hadn't had any interesting loot over the last few days—the beasties had mainly dropped pelts and alchemy ingredients. This was compensated by excellent experience, but it also meant I had to address my finances. Overall, we'd farmed about two hundred gold, but then we had to share it between the three of us which made the results less than impressive.

By the evening, I'd filled a hundred twenty vials with various potions. After some thought, I auctioned all the Minor Life elixirs, leaving only two for myself: a medium vial of life and the same of mana. Both healed you 100 points, not bad at all. I'd also added a few more exotic bottles to my collection, like True Vision, Invisibility Vial and Fear Potion. The latter duplicated a useful new spell I'd learned last night. A very clever bit of magic. It allowed you to frighten the target so much that it bolted away and kept running for ten to fifteen seconds, scared witless. The effect stopped once you dealt damage to the target. It was a competent use of control spells like these that decided a player's efficiency. Stuns, roots, blinds, fears—these were things that nearly always meant the difference between a victory and a defeat.

I put the remaining Talent points to good use, too. I raised the summoned creature's level, fine-tuned my buffs, Life Absorption and DoTs, then got myself a new poison-based one. I distributed the Characteristic points between Intellect and Spirit 3 to 1. That was it, no spare points left. As far as skills were concerned, I was all maxed out.

I spent the evening with Taali. We went for a walk around the city, stopping occasionally in a café or two. We listened to a nice band, followed by a performance from a truly talented singer. All of them were just other players enjoying themselves in the role of a minstrel. Later that night, two fire mages offered an impressive firework display in the city's main square. Altogether, it had been a great day.

The next morning I donned full combat gear and headed for the city gate hoping to buy myself a couple of nice fat buffs. After some wait, a high-level cleric arrived and, sitting down on the parapet, posted his price list in the chat. I hurried to pay him for the most expensive hit buff he had: a four-hour +110 Life. He charged me twenty gold, the bastard, plus I needed a piece of malachite to make the spell work. At least he added the free gift of a +90 Armor buff. In total, counting the shield I'd gotten from Eric, good old me was worth over 2000 Life. Not easy to smoke; my Life Absorptions could give one bad indigestion. Finally, I ran across a Conjuror and got myself a 30-min mana regen bonus. Now I could go back to the cave.

The hermit studied me without saying a word. Finally, he nodded his approval and waved his hand in the air, removing the spell. The passage opened. I stepped in.

"Good luck," the weak voice croaked behind my back.

The door slammed shut. The bars clanged. It didn't look as if I'd be able to go back to reclaim my corpse. Either I'd walk out of here on my own two feet, or I'd be doomed to spend the rest of eternity on the graveyard bench with all the other disrobed losers.

A steep rough passage had been cut in the limestone. A set of two torches had been mounted on the wall every dozen feet or so, allowing me to see my way. I concentrated on their flames, triggering a pop-up:

Torches of True Flame. No stealth or invisibility spells can hide one from the light of Primary Fire.

Yeah, right. Apparently, AI wanted me to fight in the open. I couldn't just steal my way to the altar. The torches would make super artifacts. I tried to pull one off its mountings. As if. My inner greedy pig heaved a sigh of disappointment. Okay, time was money. The buffs weren't going to last forever.

I reached into a pocket where I'd stored the Soul Stones I'd so lovingly selected last night. My private elite. One level 50 and two 49.

I recited the summoning spell. Alert and long-limbed, Plague Panther arose from the stone fragments. She'd been a pain to capture, using at least three skills to fight us.

When the dust had settled, I noticed a new message in the system chat.

Activation alert! Gnoll King's Breastplate has activated its magic effect! The summoned creature has preserved the Bleeding Wound ability giving 5% probability of delivering the attacked creature a blood wound and dealing 140 points damage over 10 sec.

Excellent. My heart missed a beat as I checked the panther's level—51. Now we were cooking. I switched to the alternate spell layout and buffed her up a bit. After a short regen stop, I summoned Hummungus who filled the narrow cave passage. All ready. Time to do it.

The passage led to an enormous hall, its fallen columns teeming with imps. Well, well, well. Zombies I'd expected. But these were hell monsters. Then again, who said it was going to be easy?

The imps—the same level as the panther—whizzed across the room. You needed good spatial thinking if you wanted to pull only one mob and not a dozen out of the air packed with monsters. I watched them for a while before casting a DoT with a snare over one of them. The imp dived to the floor and hedgehopped to me. The panther intercepted him halfway, then Hummungus joined in. I waited a few seconds before casting a couple more DoTs. Then I got closer, exposing myself to his hits, redirecting some of the damage to myself. I shouldn't have any regen problems; plus it was time I started using the shield's effects to help absorb the indecent amount of hits. No need to get my pets exposed if I was entitled to 500 damage off each pull.

The melee lasted another minute. Finally, the imp shrieked and collapsed. One done, a thousand to go.

I did a quick status check. Mana loss 20%, Health on full, the panther down 30%, Teddy fit as a fiddle. Not bad. Looked like I could manage two mobs, if necessary. Immediately I reminded myself not to get too greedy. Wouldn't be a good idea to attempt a fresh monster with mana under 50%. Better safe than sorry: the dungeon was a one-off thing.

I looted the imp's corpse. Holy cow. I could use a couple of those. Seven silver and a Soul Stone. My inner greedy pig was drooling over himself as he estimated the number of monsters, multiplied it by seven and calculated the difficulty factor equation. Myself, I was more than happy with the Soul Stone, a great replacement to the one I'd just used.

As I later found out, hell creatures' souls were quite loose in their bodies, dropping Soul Stones twice as often. Still, at first I didn't know what to think about their abundance.

The first hall had taken me almost thirty minutes. The mobs were too difficult for solo pulling. At least they didn't respawn. Once I mopped up the room, I walked around the perimeter creating a map and checking the room for any buried treasures. Herbal skill kept clicking as I picked some mushrooms and a handful of glowing moss and transferred them to my bag.

And what would that be? A clay-sealed niche glittered silver in the corner. I slammed it with a gauntleted fist. The clay cracked, letting silver coins trickle onto the floor.

Congratulations! You've discovered a treasure!

Your Piercing Vision ability has improved! Current level: 1

This is a passive ability that demands no activation or training. You should spend some time visiting the locations abandoned by humans and searching for hidden treasures.

Great timing. I scooped up the silver. Thirty coins felt heavy in my purse. Off we go, then!

Two and a half hours later, I was sitting next to a long passage. At its other end stood the floor boss. My shield and staff lay on the dusty floor next to me. I lowered my eyelids to keep an eye on the monster while I enjoyed the cold beer and sandwiches, courtesy of the Three Little Pigs' chef. The floor hadn't cost me much blood. I'd done my best to spare Teddy and the panther which even managed to steal the fire imp's Ignition ability.

Then the Lich skill got activated, adding more smoldering corpses to the dungeon's interior. In all honesty, I hadn't been sure if accepting it was the right thing to do. By now, I'd done 1.5 levels as opposed to Teddy's two. And still I was angry. I stroked my precious pocket with a level 52 stone, the one which now held the soul of a Succubus. My heart craved revenge. The hellish thing had kept casting Magic Nullifier, stripping both me and the panther of our precious buffs. I'd really had to watch my back for the last hour of combat. I was so upset I even improved the Bone Shield to absorb 130 points damage. Not much—a hit or two max—but it's that couple of hits that very often makes the difference between life and death. Also, I liked this kind of buffer, enabling me to receive part of the damage in exchange for some mana I could use on shield regen.

There was another good thing about it. While I tried to use magic under the mobs' pressure, I inadvertently improved the passive concentration skill. It allowed me to resume a spell broken off by a hit without losing concentration: no need to start casting it all over again. Which was when I discovered another mega bonus my leveling pattern offered. Pure mages didn't really get a chance to level this particular skill. They simply couldn't be exposed to hits: it was a sign of certain death for them. That's why any hand-to-hand fighter who got close enough could make mincemeat out of a mage before the latter could finish the spell. Which was exactly why mages had so many control spells to keep their distance in battle.

As for me, I could have afforded to tank, all the while leveling up that truly life-saving skill. Looking into the future, I could see an amazing top character: an impervious caster armored to his ears, with an equally impervious concentration. Love it.

I turned my attention to the floor boss. She was beautiful in the Lilim way, a cross between a demon and a human, a whip in each hand. What I didn't like was her level. 55. In theory, it had to be the ceiling for this particular dungeon. Who would the next floor boss be, then? And could anyone tell me how many more floors I was yet to do?

The boss was alone. Without much thinking, I sent the panther to meet her: I was too wary of some vicious ability in the vein of the Gnoll King's daily Deadly Touch to attack her myself.

Whips cracked. The panther's blood and tufts of hair flew everywhere. I cast a bunch of DoTs and sent Teddy toward her. But Lilim was full of surprises. She uttered a short songlike spell, and the bear swayed in a trance. For combat purposes, he was now little less than useless.

Enchantment! Hummungus has fallen for Lilim's charms! He is temporarily unable to control himself and follow your orders!

You Succubus bitch. I stepped in, redirecting some of the damage to myself as I tried to draw out the fight, allowing Teddy and the DoTs enough time to work. I pulled out at 60%, renewed the spells and gave the bear a quick heal. Teddy came round and was about to jump into action when he froze again like a tit in a trance. Oh—I just hoped I had enough mana left. That's the triumph of intellect for you: I took a swig of hits/mana elixir, my second one in that fight, renewed the shield and stepped back in. Rinse and repeat.

Bang! Lilim collapsed. The dungeon's walls shuddered, its ceiling crumbling, sand flying everywhere. The torches flared up twice as bright. The floor was cleansed.

Only then did I notice a short pedestal and a tiny stone on it, glinting black. I picked it up.

Tiny Fragment of the Dark Altar
Item class: Rare
Suitable for improving other items
Requires level 50
Effect 1: 10% bonus to all Dark spells (Blood, Death, Hatred, Shamanism, etc.)
Effect 2: 10% resistance to all spells of Light

Aha. This wasn't the quest object yet, but a hefty freebie nevertheless. I crouched over Lilim's body. Ten gold coins clinked. My hand grabbed the whip.

Whip of Constraint
Item class: Rare
Weapon type: one-handed
Damage 31-48, Speed 2.1, Durability 180\180
Effect: Gives 9% chance of getting control over the victim and paralyzing it for 1.5 sec

That was It. A stun puncher on speed. Bug would absolutely love it. But I had to agree with my inner greedy pig in that we couldn't afford giving freebies just at the moment. Most likely, I'd have to auction it.

After a quick regen, we walked down the stairs to the second floor. Same stones. Same glowing torches cast shadows on the sooty ceiling.

In the very first hall I walked into a huge slug, its insides bulging under the translucent skin. A loathsome creature, too big for a monster. I really, really didn't like it. But I had no choice. There was no way I could bypass it. Banzai!

Teddy made a dart for it, his teeth sinking into the soft flesh. The creature squealed. My mana bar shrank.

Warning! The slug has used Mana Absorption skill to strip you of some of your mana!

I knew it. I knew it couldn't be as easy as it looked. I had to smoke the bastard quickly before it drained me dry. I reached for more elixirs.

But the monster was full of sick surprises. With every 10% Life lost, it produced two level 40 maggots. Every thirty seconds it emitted a blood-curdling squeak. I had to send my pets to fight the maggots while I had to cast Life Absorption over the slug double quick. That was the only way I could deal some fast-working damage.

That had been close. But at least now that we knew the monster's tactics, we could come up with some quality countermeasures.

Er... had I just done 47? I hadn't even noticed which particular pair of maggots had earned me a new level. Having said that, Hummungus didn't seem to have risen in level for a while. I opened the menu. WTF? The pet's level had frozen at 23. His experience bar was maxed out. Why wasn't he growing? I opened the Wiki. After two minutes' search, it became abundantly clear. A combat mount's level couldn't exceed half of that of the player. Shame. Still, it made sense. The comments advised not to get too hung up on numbers. The most important thing was that a combat-leveled mount could pull the aggro from a pet onto himself. So his level didn't really matter as long as it worked well in the end result. True, where would I have been without my Teddy? I wouldn't have even smoked the first dungeon boss, that's for sure.

I distributed the characteristic points based on the fight results. Every spare point had to go into Intellect. You could never have too much mana. I also maxed out Life Absorption. I definitely lacked kill speed, which could be quite dangerous as the slug had just shown me. I frisked the corpses. Twenty maggots gave me three handfuls of gold, a dozen vials of craft slime and eight low-level Soul Stones. I hoped the floor wasn't going to be all like that. My inner greedy pig got restless, seeing top Soul Stones slipping through his grabby fingers.

I spoke too soon. Four hours later, I was sitting near the floor boss enjoying a well-deserved rest and a snack. I still hadn't farmed a single decent stone, but at least my bag was bulging with five pounds of magic dust. The slugs had been a pain. I'd finished the floor by long dangerous bouts of fighting interspersed with even longer butt-hurting episodes of mana regen. Slugs kept siphoning my mana, so by the end of every fight it hovered dangerously close to zero.

Then I saw the Slug Queen spread all across the hall right in front of me. An enormous belly bulged out of its weak little frame topped by a tiny head. I didn't like any of it. Including the monster's name.

Never mind. Fortune favors the brave. Come to Daddy, you slimy bitch. Hummungus—attack!

Grrhhrw! Bang!

His first bite ripped the Slug Queen's ripe belly apart, letting out a crawling mass of maggots. Jeez, how many of them were there? Forty at least.

I targeted one and recoiled in dismay. Level 40? That was the end of it. Were those game developers completely bonkers or something? This was way too much even for a fully equipped group.

I didn't give up, though. Mechanically, I tried to do crowd control, backing as I immobilized the mobs. Thank God their speed wasn't up to much but neither was mine: this was a closed space after all and not a battlefield. Consulting the map so as not to let them corner me, I kept backing up, controlling those who tried to stick their necks out. My two pets were still busy in the first hall.

A message popped up reporting experience received. One maggot less. As if that would change anything. I switched my attention to their new leader trying to slow him down. Excuse me? Why was he 39 now? I clicked on a few others, but all the maggots seemed to have lost a level. Another experience message—it had to be Teddy, he must have wasted his opponent. All the maggots became 38. I got it! The more of them there were, the stronger they became. If we killed another dozen, we'd make mincemeat out of the rest. Come on, Teddy. Come on, everyone!

Hopeful and encouraged, I decided to fight my way back to join the pets. They were sure to need my help and guidance. The maggots lined up along the corridors, each of them trying to kick or even poison me as I ran past them.

I met my pets halfway. The panther was doing her best—probably, due to her Vampire ability. Teddy wasn't faring so well. By the time I called him off, his life was flashing in the red zone. I shielded him from the mobs, gave myself a heal as I finished off another maggot, then healed the bear. Crowd control. Experience. And some more. Come on, Ted. Your turn to help the panther.

The dungeon shuddered. The torches flared up. Holy cow, we'd done it. Plus, all three of us had done another level in the last thirty minutes. I didn't even mention my 49, not when the panther had managed to skip to 52. If the results of this melee were to be believed, we'd even grown stronger. I invested some more into the Bone Shield which could now absorb 260 damage. It looked like I was going to love it.

The maggots weren't that poor. Each dropped a gold piece. I stuffed the forty gold into my bag and walked over to the Queen who had died at the death of her last offspring. Any loot? A vial, glowing bright through the piles of slime.

Mystic Skill Essence
Item class: Epic

Contains a random skill. In order to learn the skill, drink the contents of the vial.

Oh, cool. Never heard about anything like that. I sat down for a regen and opened the auction panel. They didn't have anything of the kind listed. I checked their sales history. A couple weeks earlier, a similar vial had been sold for twenty-six grand. Admittedly, it had dropped from a hundred-plus monster and had all the necessary screenshots and paperwork. I wondered how much mine would cost without either? Would anyone believe my word? Should I sell it or should I try it myself? Jesus. Hell's Temptation, part two.

By the staircase down to the third and last (hopefully) floor, I saw a modest pedestal. On it lay a black fragment. I picked it up.

Small Fragment of the Dark Altar
Item class: Rare
Can be used to make a Minor Travel Altar
Requires level 50
Effect 1: 20% bonus to all Dark spells (Blood, Death, Hatred, Shamanism, etc.)
Effect 2: 20% resistance to all spells of Light

Yess! I could use that. Only how was I supposed to make the altar? And where could I buy the recipe? Questions and more questions. In any case, an interesting little stone. It definitely had potential, so in the bag it went.

The next floor was hard. All the monsters there were level 55—the limit. On top of that, they were all different. Hell hounds, desolators, demons, destroyers, abyss creatures... you name it. Every time I had to brace myself, preparing for new surprises. The mobs' skills were unknown and their tactics, unpredictable.

I was sitting on the floor, completely run down, leaning against the panther's icy side and staring at the familiar archway leading to the floor boss. I'd almost finished in there. But how could I fight on without Teddy? Yes, you heard it right. Hummungus had heroically thrown in the towel. My (admittedly short-sighted) leveling him for strength had finally backfired. For one brief moment he'd pulled the aggro to himself, and that was enough for the Lord of the Abyss. Now Ted was out of circulation for the next twenty-four hours. Awful timing.

Anyway! Time to close this circus show. It had been nine hours chopping monsters non-stop. I renewed all the buffs, activated the shields and boosted up mana.

Fragments of broken stone crunched underfoot. Trying to step noiselessly, I walked to the passageway and peeked in. And there they were. Aquilum, the Dark Guild magister, and his entire Masters' Circle. All present and correct, guarding two more pedestals—or rather, the fragments resting on them. Aquilum the High Lich and eight Master Liches.

I slumped against the wall. That was it. That was the end. Apparently, the surge of necro energy was too powerful for those Dark guys to die their own death. Magic had summoned them as its servants. Or could it be the obligatory end of the game for the likes of myself? I really didn't know. I didn't want to try.

The choice of the undead for the final battle had to be an unpleasant surprise for anyone about to finish the dungeon. To spend all day fighting beasts of inferno only to end up facing a totally unknown and unexpected enemy.

Three Master Liches defended the first Altar fragment. The second one was about sixty feet deeper down the corridor, past six more Liches and the High One. The Masters were level 55. Aquilum, in disrespect for the dungeon rules, was 60. What was I supposed to do with them all?

I couldn't get to the second picket without fighting through the first one. And I had nothing to do it with, even if Teddy had still been here with me. With my level 52, there was no way I could fix three 55 mobs. Freakin' zombies. Wait a sec. Had I said zombies? I pulled the crown off my head and reread its properties.

Renders all the undead such as skeletons, zombies, spirits, etc. neutral and unable to attack first. Halves their aggro radius in case of the wearer's attack.

Still not quite knowing what I was doing, I somehow sensed this was the only possible way, no other options available. I slammed the crown back onto my head and stubbornly walked toward the first block. The Liches' gazes followed me. The creatures didn't move, though. I gave them the widest berth possible as I walked behind their backs and stealthily reached for the stone. Even if they were going to smoke me, I'd have the stone first.

Squeezing my eyes shut, I clenched it, quite logically expecting a hit. Shoulders hunched, I waited for about half a minute. Then I stood up and breathed out.

I examined my booty.

Fragment of the Dark Altar
Item class: Rare
You can use this item to restore the destroyed Dark Temple Altar.
Requires level 50

A message popped up.

Quest completion alert: Knowledge Breeds Sadness II. Quest completed!
Reward: access to unique quest Knowledge Breeds Sadness III: Temple Restoration

Another one:

New quest alert! Unique quest available: Knowledge Breeds Sadness III: Temple Restoration

It's been many hundreds of years that the Lands of Light had no Dark Temples left. All of them, including the First Temple, had been desecrated and destroyed. Use this fragment to restore any one of the deserted Temples!
Reward: secret

Accept. No question about it. I still had that Hell Hound quest to take care of. But why would they need the second stone, then? Why seven liches guarding it?

I gingerly squeezed into the guarded circle and walked over to the pedestal to read the fine script.

> *Large Fragment of the Dark Altar*
> *Item class: Epic*
> *You will need this stone to restore the destroyed First Temple Altar!*
> *Requires level 50*

> *New quest alert! Secret unique quest available: Knowledge Breeds Sadness IV: The First Temple Restoration*
> *For years, the Large Fragment of the Dark Altar has been soaking in necro emanations. Use it to restore the mythical First Temple, destroyed by the Alliance of Light some five hundred years ago.*
> *Reward: secret*

Aha. Curiouser and curiouser. *Accept,* definitely.

I reached out and picked up the fragment.

> *Warning! You already possess a Dark Altar fragment! Dark energy concentration is approaching critical levels! If you pick up another fragment, the possibility of ripping the world apart approaches 100%, resulting in a new outbreak of the Darkness! Leave one of the stones on its pedestal!*

Yes, yes, I got it. As if I didn't know about the A-bomb and stuff. Plutonium 239 had a critical mass of twenty pounds or something. Here it probably was something along the same lines. I tiptoed to the first pedestal and gingerly placed the first fragment onto it. Then I came back and packed the Big Fragment into my bag. I looked around to make sure I hadn't forgotten anything. I hadn't. Time to teleport.

A hand touched my shoulder. I froze and squinted at a Lich's mummified fingers. Slowly, I turned around. Empty eye sockets glared at me. The sockets of the Aquilum the High Lich.

"You must destroy it."

The voice was wispy but somehow it tore through your brain. I winced with pain. "Destroy what?"

The Lich's withered skull turned toward the first fragment I'd left on the pedestal.

"The stone. Its magic won't let us go. There's enough of it here to last another several thousand years. If you remove at least some of it, we'll be able to retire to the afterlife.

"How do you expect me to do that? I wouldn't know where to start. You need that second-floor slug up there for that sort of job."

"I'll show you."

"We'll show you," The Liches repeated in unison, circling me.

Aquilum laid his bony hand on my head.

Congratulations! You've learned the out-of-class spell: Astral Mana Dispersal.
Cast time: random

Mana expenditure: 100 points per sec

Every five seconds, the spell absorbs target's mana. The amount of absorbed mana doubles with every tick. The first tick absorbs 1 mana pt., the second, 2, the third, 4, etc.

Warning! If you receive damage or run out of mana, the spell will be broken off. This is a High Circle spell: even your Concentration skill won't be able to help you.

Warning! All High Circle spells have the highest aggro generation. Your chosen opponent will select you as a target.

Holy cow. I shook my head, disbelieving. I wasn't quite sure how I could use this wonder freakin' waffle, but thanks anyway. Still, I had a problem.

"Thank you, Magister," I said. "But I'm afraid, I only have enough mana left for the first twenty seconds of the spell. That's four ticks. Minus the stone's twenty mana—provided the magic works on it."

"Don't worry. Just start. We'll give you all the mana you need. The stone is protected against us. We can't harm it, anyway."

I shrugged. No harm in trying. I moved the shimmering icon to the control panel and activated the spell.

The earth shattered. The walls shook, sending rivulets of stone fragments from the ceiling. A black twister began to form before me. The targeted stone covered with a fine web of black lightning. Impressive. It did give the caster away, though. No way anyone could miss a display so spectacular.

The Liches closed in with a singsong whine. My mana bar stopped dropping and began creeping back. The fragment was now visibly shrinking. One of the Liches collapsed, emptied. But the undead was still alive, if you'll excuse the pun. Another minute. The stone had shrunk to half its original size. But now only two of us remained standing—myself and Aquilum. Tick. Tick. Tick.

The mana flow stopped. I held the spell for another twenty seconds and collapsed, pinned to the ground by an invisible load. My head span.

Quest failure alert! You've failed the unique quest: Knowledge Breeds Sadness III: Temple Restoration.

Before I could tell them where to stuff it, another message popped up.

Warning! Casting the Great Spell results in a magic cooldown. You won't be able to use magic for the next 5 min. You won't be able to cast this spell again for the duration of 24 hrs.

Bastards. Couldn't they have told me earlier? Not that I was in a hurry, anyway. I turned to the Liches. One by one, they noiselessly rose, gave me a silent bow and disappeared in flashes of black light.

Aquilum turned his frightening frame to me. "Thank you, Dark brother. Is there anything I can do for you?"

As I sought for an answer, my inner greedy pig perked up and began jotting down a quick wish list.

"Think fast," the Magister said. "I only have a few seconds left in this world. My magic powers have been depleted by the rite. All I can give you is information."

"The First Temple. Do you know where I can find it?" I blurted out.

Aquilum nodded, showing me I'd asked him the right thing. "The Dead Lands. The Valley of Fear. You'll make it. The crown will help you, and so will the altar fragment. Fare thee well! We will not see each other again in this world."

In this world? Did he say *this world*? As if we could get to the other one.

Or could we?

Chapter Twenty-Two

The eternal void swallowed the Liches. I stood alone in the enormous dungeon. Grunting like an old man, I scraped myself off the floor, brushed off the little stones biting into my hands and had a good look around. It wasn't often you found yourself in such a large, deserted and perfectly safe space. If I could talk Grym into giving me the keys or if I could find another entrance, this could be a perfect secret camp site.

I walked over to the pedestal. The fragment still lay on it, dull and lonesome, decimated in size. Sorry, dude. It's not easy to say "no" to nine Liches. I peered into the stone.

Medium Fragment of the Dark Altar
Item class: Rare
Can be used to make a Big Raid Altar
Requires level 50

Effect 1: 25% bonus to all Dark spells (Blood, Death, Hatred, Shamanism, etc.)
Effect 2: 25% resistance to all spells of Light

Yes! I cautiously reached out and picked it up. It worked. Excellent. I was sure I could use it at some point. Not the next day or even the day after, but I knew it would come in very handy.

I wasn't in a hurry any more, so I decided to explore the catacombs. It took me three hours to get into all the nooks and crannies and tap all the walls, and then to break open all the chests, jugs and boxes I'd discovered. I found four money stashes, a basket with a decent choice of elixirs and any amount of vegetable matter like mushrooms, moss, mold and some pale-looking herbs. My herbal skill had hit the 150 points limit long ago. If I wanted to level it further, I had to go back to the guild masters for my craftsman status.

That was it. I could go home. I walked back up to the first level and knocked on the door. As if! I tapped a fancy rhythm to let Grym know it was me and not some intruding monster. Still he didn't open. Apparently, this place had only two exits: either by teleporter or feet first.

I turned around and walked back thinking how on earth I'd gotten myself into this mess. I could probably invest one of the still-available talent points into a group teleport. That way I could take the panther back with me. Still, I already knew it wasn't very clever, arriving in the city with a zombie in tow. Once bitten, twice shy. It was a crying shame to leave kitty in the catacombs but there was no other option, really.

My absent-mindedness nearly cost me. Deep in thought, I stumbled on something and went flying across the hard floor. In an attempt to stay on my feet, I grabbed the first thing that was within my reach—a torch, but I only succeeded in pulling it out of its mounting. Clutching it, I collapsed in a heap on the floor. My health bar shrank back, but I couldn't care less. I was holding the torch. *The Torch*!

Torch of True Flame
Item class: Unique
No stealth or invisibility spells can hide one from
the light of Primary Fire.
Item type: Independent. Does not disappear
when deleted from the inventory. Can be activated via
the artifact menu.

Great. I could use it. I opened the settings. Brightness, color of flame, flame on/off. Exactly what I needed. I shoved the expired torch into my bag. Waste not, want not.

I spent the next hour giving the dungeon another search, trying everything that appeared to be bolted down. As a result, I became the proud owner of two more torches and a large shield that I at first had taken for some ornament on the wall. The shield's parameters looked like a mixed blessing:

Ogre's Siege Shield
Item class: Unique
Requires level 50
Effect 1: 370 to Armor
Effect 2: halves the player's speed

It fit into my bag sending me into overload. Now I was heavy and slow enough even without being equipped with that Ogre's armored wardrobe. It was definitely time to go. I patted the panther's neck, silently wishing her to avoid disembodiment but instead, turn into the dungeon's new legend: a new aggro monster. Then I activated the portal.

It opened with a quiet pop, leaving me standing in the Three Little Pigs courtyard. A player jumped out of my way, cussing good-naturedly under his breath. I smiled and took in the city's night breeze carrying the fragrance of roasting meat. My feet heavy and tired, I slouched to the front door.

As I crossed the hall, I exchanged a few words with some of the regulars and was about to go upstairs to my room when Eric waved to me from his corner table. I was always happy to see him. He had this talent of making everybody around him feel good.

He wasn't alone. A man was sitting to his left, his expression serious, his eyes cold and attentive. The fancy cordwain armor and double blades glowing by his sides betrayed his class. A rogue. I looked up his level. 160. Holy shit.

To Eric's right sat another character—and he definitely didn't belong there. A plump little man with balding temples squinted at me shortsightedly. He was wearing a pair of plain pants, a shirt and a business jacket, wherever he'd got that from. He must have had them made to measure. A classic office rat if I'd ever seen one. Level 9. So! He probably had his reasons not to exceed it. A crafter? Or a moneybag?

Eric rose and gave me a bear hug. "Come sit here, dude. Gents, this is Laith, a.k.a. Max, known for his equal doses of luck and masochism." He pointed at the rogue, "And this is Dan from our Branch of Light. He's our top cloak and dagger."

The rogue reached out an unhurried hand. "You talk too much," he said to Eric. "How many times do I have to tell you that?"

Yeah. Some sort of secret-freakin'-agent character. These guys were taking the real-life stuff a bit too far for my liking. They probably couldn't help it, being in the military and all that. On second thoughts, they could be right.

Eric ignored the comment and introduced the second man. "This is our dear Mr. Simonov. He is our bookkeeper, one of a kind. His dangerous profession left him with no option. It was either doing time or going digital. Mr. Simonov wasn't into games then. He set all the settings to default 5, then added his real name and appearance. And off he went. Good job we noticed him in time. If we hadn't, God knows what would've happened to him. So please meet the North Castle treasurer.

The bookkeeper rose in his seat and offered me his hand. "Pleased to meet you, Sir."

I nodded. "The North Castle? How about the South one?"

Eric gave me a happy grin. "Count on it. We have a South one and an East one. We don't have a West one, though. Not yet. But with any luck..."

The rogue frowned, "Eric."

"Please. As if our enemies don't know how many castles we have."

"This is classified information. The castles aren't the problem. Your unprofessional attitude is."

Eric shrugged him away. Which probably wasn't such a good thing. This devil-may-care poise of his could well be the reason behind his low clan rank.

"Sit down, I tell you," Eric bellowed at me. "They're bringing the grub now. We've only just arrived. Why are you wobbling about like a wet noodle?"

I couldn't help smiling at the picture. "I'm dead, man. Been farming for fourteen hours flat. Mopping up a dungeon. Only teleported here a minute ago, loaded like a Pakistani donkey. My mount was supposed to bring another half a ton. But he's gone to the Rainbow Bridge now. Guess, he needed a break from me."

"You eager beaver," Eric grinned. "Very well, then. Surprise me. You were full of surprises in the past."

For a moment, I hesitated whether I should disclose my finds. Still, I trusted Eric. Besides, it probably wasn't a bad idea to raise my weight in his clanmates' eyes. They looked like the right kind of crowd. I'd better stick around.

I took out the whip and handed it to Eric. Uninterested, he passed it over to the rogue.

"A decent toy. Not bad for a mid-level," he commented. "Might go for a hundred fifty gold."

Hm. I'd hoped it would bring more. I pushed the whip to the edge of the table and groaned with the effort as I took out the shield. It must have weighed half a ton. Eric's eyebrows rose.

"Holy shit. Are they cutting up a cruiser somewhere? Is that where you got yourself this whack of armor plate?"

The rogue only shook his head. "First time I see anything like it. Mr. Simonov?"

The treasurer readjusted his non-existing eyeglasses. He looked at the shield scratching his head. "Could be a hundred. Or a thousand. A very peculiar object. Might prove perfect for some specialist job or an unorthodox leveling pattern. I should auction it with the highest reserve until it finds its buyer. Unless he needs some money fast. In that case we could buy it for potential long-term speculation. But in that case, I'm not going to offer the real price. He needs to understand that."

I nodded. This was sound advice, worth disclosing my loot. Eric looked at the other two, pride in his glare: *didn't I say he was full of surprises?* I reached into my bag. He stared at me, puzzled. "What else have you got there?"

I pulled out a torch and pressed the mental *On* button. It could be my imagination but all the other lamps in the hall seemed to have flickered and dimmed.

The rogue perked up and leaned close to read the stats. Then he drew toward me. "How many have you got?"

I tilted my head. "This is classified information."

Eric guffawed and slapped my shoulder so hard that I received an attack message.

The rogue was hard to shake off. "I'll give you a grand each," he glanced at the treasurer who slowly nodded his agreement. Apparently, they did have the money.

I was a bit taken aback but the rogue kept applying pressure. "This is a good honest-to-God price. Torches aren't common loot but frequent enough to have a stable price. You're not going to use them, are you? What would you do with them?"

I tried to come up with an answer but he didn't want to wait. "You see? You don't even know. We do. We can use them for lots of things. To illuminate the main corridor, for one thing. And the treasury corridor, and the conference hall. You get the picture. The True Vision spell is no good against a high-level rogue. I have the skill I can see them with, but I can't be everywhere, can I? All these spies and thieves are the bane of my life. If he doesn't pilfer everything he sees, he'd hide in stealth under the conference table and in under twenty-four hours collect all the confidential information he can sell. Some of us just can't hold their tongues, can they?" he gave Eric a meaningful look.

Finally, he laid his trump card. "We can be grateful. Which is a lot. Believe me."

I nodded to show I understood what he'd said. And still, I forced myself to decline the offer. "Sorry. I really can't think straight at the moment. Too tired, I suppose. I'll think about it tomorrow, okay? No offense."

He nodded. "Well done. You've ticked the right box. Had you said 'yes', I'd have been quite happy knowing I'd browbeaten you into it. But I don't think I'd have trusted you with anything serious."

I breathed a sigh of relief. I really didn't want to have any problems with this crowd. So I reached into the bag again and froze, grinning at Eric.

He leaned forward. "Don't fuck around. What else have you got?"

I produced the vial.

The rogue slumped back in his chair and raised his hands. "I give up. I don't care what else you might have there. I'll pay you fifteen grand for the whole lot."

Mr. Simonov studied me with interest. "Excuse me, Sir? You have any idea what you've got there? Even real-world money won't buy you this kind of mob droppings. Any top clan buys them like hot cakes. They always need them to level their leading raid tanks or damage dealers."

Eric was fingering the vial. "Who dropped it?"

"A floor boss in a unique personal dungeon I've been to. A level 55 slug, this big."

"Done any screen shots?"

"No. Stupid of me."

"Check the log files provided they're still available, and save them. They might come in handy when you want to sell it."

The rogue raised his hand, attracting our attention. "Would be nice if you gave us first option before you auction them. You wouldn't regret it."

I nodded my understanding.

He paused, thinking. "The day after tomorrow we're having an open house day. Come see us at the Castle. It doesn't happen very often. In fact, it's only the second time we're having it."

"Beg your pardon," Eric butted in. "I was going to invite him myself."

I didn't want them to argue. "I'd love to come. May I bring a date?"

"Suit yourself. Eleven o'clock there'll be a group teleport from the Three Little Pigs. Don't be late, you two: the Castle is about an hour on foot. Make sure you've got all your combat gear with you. There'll be tons of competitions. You just might need it."

"Will do. Now where's that waitress of yours? I'm hungry as a bear."

I stuffed all the goodies back into the bag and found a moment to take it upstairs to my room. As I changed, I got an incoming message from Taali. She'd just logged in. She had missed me. She said she couldn't wait to show me a particular fragment from the Kamasutra: page thirty-four, second paragraph from the top. Probably, I should have a light meal, after all.

An idea struck me. I paused for a second and reached inside my bag for the umpteenth time that day. Then I went back downstairs and had a talk with the bartender. A fistful of gold changed hands.

Not a minute too soon. In a whirlwind of jewelry and minimal clothing, Taali burst into the hall leaving dumbstruck patrons in her wake, the heels of her suede boots clattering victoriously.

We had it all: a good meal, light wine and some pretty intimate dancing. Finally the girl gave me a meaningful look and retired to the ladies' room. I got the message. I said my goodbyes and smiled at my friends' simple jokes involving men's marital duties as I waited for her to come out. Then I scooped the girl into my arms and took her upstairs to enthusiastic applause behind my back. She hid her flushed face in my jacket.

When we reached my room, I set her back on her feet and pushed the door open.

She gasped, wide-eyed. "What's all that?"

The Torches of True Flame cast red, green and blue hues across the darkened room. Flowers littered the bed and the room's floor. A large sea shell on the table crooned a sad song.

I put on the air of a travel guide and began pointing at my exhibits. "To your right, the Torches of True Flame. You should have seen that secret-service guy, he was chomping at the bit to get them. To your left, Romance Aura #5: a collection of wild flowers made to my own recipe. Finally, the Singing Shell from the Sirens' Island. You probably know that male sirens are absolutely brainless. So these shells learned to copy the female mating song to lure stupid human males into offering them some fish and fruit. Apparently, the sirens' mating song affects our subconscious in the most mysterious way stimulating sexual pleasure."

Her eyes glinted. Her nostrils flared, a sharp tongue licking the red lips. In a smooth elusive motion that only a woman can master, her dress slid down to her feet. She stepped over the silk heap.

Now it was my turn to gasp. Two masterfully tattooed roses entangled her body in a desperate combat, their buds opening and shutting down, thin shoots spiraling up to hug each other and part again. Pitiless thorns pierced the fragile leaves.

"What's all that?"

"This is a vibe tattoo. It copies the host's mood. There's only one artist in the whole city who does it. By appointment only."

"And what mood would this flower battle signify?"

Her eyes glinted again. She stepped close and whispered in my ear, "You're about to find out."

I had a long lazy morning to compensate for my night's exertions. Taali had left very early and I couldn't sleep afterward. The shell had kept crooning its sad song until I had finally thought of offering it a few pieces of fruit from the bowl. Taali wouldn't be back until later in the evening. I had no desire to go farming again. This felt like a good day to give myself a break. I had to look into my current affairs and maybe potter around the auction house a bit before sorting through all the goodies I'd amassed. Finally, I could just laze about with a book.

They sent me up some breakfast. Bliss. What could be better than the smell of fresh coffee in the morning?—only a cigarette. Unfortunately, the game was fighting tooth and claw for more audience and the 'no smoking' tag granted it the precious 12+ status. Good job their alcohol lobby had managed to sink a similar liquor ban allowing the likes of myself access to an occasional beer.

Having finished my breakfast, I opened the auction house. All the elixirs had sold, adding to my healthy balance. I followed the ex-bookkeeper's advice and put up the shield for a grand gold. Let it hang there and wait for its chance. Then I sorted through the herbs, turning whatever I could into elixirs and making a list of missing recipes to buy. When my alchemy skill finally hit the limit, I pushed the Transformation Box away. Tired. 'Nuff workin'.

I changed into some plain city gear and consulted the inn keeper about some places to see. Then off I trotted for a walk. Freedom.

First thing I paid two gold for entering the city zoo. Normally it was one gold, but that day they had a unique guest exhibit, the Bone Dragon—an enormous beast caught about a month earlier in the Dead Lands that was now touring all the big city zoos.

The zoo boasted quite a selection of animals. I'd expected to see the usual varieties and was impressed by their choice of infernal and lower-plane creatures. Every cage had a sign telling you everything about each monster's usual habitat and skills—a true bestiary of sorts. I was eternally grateful for my new absolute memory as I studied sign after sign, comparing and analyzing them. Dome shields rose over some of the cages protecting visitors from the animals' magic or mental attacks. The shields were powered by massive artifacts coupled with an accumulating crystal: the same type of protection the locals used widely for fortification purposes. The better-off castles installed similar magic umbrellas, large enough to cover the entire premises. Those not so rich made do with protecting key areas such as gates, towers, dungeons and the like.

Walking leisurely, I finally reached the main attraction. The dragon was overpowering. His massive bone frame stood four stories tall, filled with billowing darkness glinting gold. Utterly beautiful.

His heavy head turned toward me, reacting to that last thought. The green searchlights of his eyes stared at me. The powerful surge of emotion pinned me to the ground. A mixture of irony, contempt, eternal angst and finally, surprise.

Dark One? resounded in my head.

"Well, hello to you too. Stop yelling, will ya? My head's gonna burst in a minute."

The dragon eased the pressure.

"What are you doing here?" I asked.

Been unlucky enough to be born here. Won't be staying for much longer, I'm afraid. We're not popular with the locals.

Another wave of hopeless angst flooded over me. People around me started to disperse, apparently feeling the same.

"Anything I can do for you?"

He replied with a mixture of skepticism and just a dash of gratitude. His eyes pointed at the massive cage made of some arcane metal and at the powerful dome powered by three artifacts, the crystals inside them enormous. *You're too weak and young, Elf.*

I sent him a mental image of myself, taken when I was holding the Astral Mana Dispersal spell.

The Dragon was suitably impressed. *It could help, you know. Provided you could hold it for a good dozen ticks. And provided you were afforded that time.*

Shame. Such a handsome creature. And so doleful... broke my heart, really. Leaving him there felt like pulling tails off puppies.

"Sorry, Mister Dragon, Sir. That's all I've got, I'm afraid."

The Dragon appreciated my honesty. *Don't worry. I can end my existence any time I want. I can always descend to the Fallen One's chambers on the lower planes. Which is a shame, really. It has taken me centuries to build up my current strength. In any case, time isn't so important for us. There's another thing that keeps me here. My nest. Once every ten years we lay an egg and share our magic supply with the growing chick. I've already missed three hatches, hoping to accumulate enough strength to grow a Phantom Dragon. Two even. I've laid two eggs—two potential Phantoms of power untold. And when I was circling the sky singing my song of triumph, I let my guard down and flew straight through a portal that opened in front of my nose. You can see where it took me.*

I nodded. That had been a clever trick, whoever had done it. I needed to give those portals a good think. The inklings of an idea began to form in my head.

In the meantime, the Dragon lunged toward me. The mage responsible for the artifacts jumped up.

Help me, O Dark One! I have no hope of getting out of here. But my nest is hidden well, and few can break the egg shells. The chicks have enough of their own mana to last another couple months. After that, they're done.

New quest alert! Grief of a Dragon
Without access to life-giving energy, Bone Dragon's unique batch of eggs is dying in the remote

and perilous Dead Lands. Share your Strength with them to prevent the rare creatures from extinction.

I accepted. The Dead Lands. Sounded like it could be on my way, anyway. Everything looked as if I was in for a long journey. The Dragon looked at me, hope in his eyes. What else did he want? Hadn't I just accepted the quest?

I'm afraid of even asking you...

"What is it?"

I wonder if you could find enough energy to help the chicks hatch?

"How much mana does it take?"

Not much. About a thousand from your current stores. More would be better. Each.

I choked. Not much! I'd grow old brooding the wretched things.

New quest alert! Grief of a Dragon II

Send enough of your Strength to Phantom Dragons to allow them to break free.

Reward: Unknown.

Hm. *Accept*, no question about it. But I really couldn't promise anything.

Sensing my indecision, the Dragon hurried to add, *I'll bestow my aura imprint on you. It'll help you cross the Dead Lands and enter the Valley of Fear. It's inhabited mainly by the undead. In the center of the Valley there's an abandoned Castle. The nest is on top of the North Tower.*

"Wait a sec. A temple—is there a temple there?"

You bet there is. It's enormous. But it's dead like everything else around it.

"Oh."

You think you can help me?

"I'll do what I can."

Very well, then. Catch!

Inside his skeletal frame, darkness swirled, boiling, bringing golden sparks to the surface, then consolidating them into the shape of a gold spear. It pierced the power shield pinning me with the Dragon's aura. Alarms wailed. Teleports popped open, letting out guards, mages and paladins. The Dragon curled up and shoved his head under his wing. Not he looked totally harmless. Time to leg it.

The moment I was out of the warriors' sight, I activated the portal and teleported back to the inn. Whew. Looked like I'd got out safely. A lunch was called for. I'd have to think about this strange stroke of luck over the meal.

I got a message from Taali as I ate. Apparently, she'd managed to finish early at work so now, she said, she was completely at my disposal. Literally.

I shook my head free of all clever thoughts, switching to date mode. So much for my plans for the day. I hadn't even started with my sightseeing.

Taali had changed yesterday's dress for another revealing Elven attire. My life! Should we go straight back to my room? No, not if she had anything to do with it. My appreciation wasn't enough: her getup demanded some quality exposure. So we went for a walk.

First thing, we visited the Stele of Lovers. A fragment of a stone wall, tall as you like, was said to have been left from the ancient temple of Lada—the Slavic goddess of love and beauty. As tradition demanded, we had to splurge on a pot of indelible paint and the services of a steeplejack kid who climbed up the wall to immortalize our combined initials in stone. The cost depended on the brightness of the paint, the height at which *Laith + Taali* had to be displayed, and the size of the lettering. Taali tried not to laugh as she watched me decide on the price of this token of our romance. I paid ten gold to the business owner, inconspicuously shoving another one in the kid's open hand, which had the effect of enlarging the words twice the size. The business owner frowned, uncomprehending, while Taali cast proud glances at the bystanders.

After that, we went for a ride on a unicorn. Contrary to the legend, you didn't have to be a virgin to tame one. Also, this one had an unnatural penchant for sugar: for one or two lumps he allowed me to stroke his horn which, also according to legend, guaranteed you endless prowess in bed. It was Taali who brought me a handful of sugar lumps—not in the way of a subtle message, I hope.

Afterward we went to the Artists Quarter. Taali rejected the offer of a full-sized nude statue of herself. Instead, I happily paid for her portrait in oils—a wonderful work and very quickly done, God bless virtuality. By then, we were fed up with walking, so we teleported to the inn where we went up to my room to hang the picture on the wall.

For some reason, Taali decided she had to choose the right place. She climbed on a chair and leaned against the wall hugging the heavy portrait. I was faced with the strong curve of her bare back covered with the tattooed flowers rustling in the wind. Unable to help myself, I laid my hands on her waist. The flowers shifted, restless. Taali froze. My hands moved up and forward, gradually disappearing under the silk of her dress. The flowers raged, lifelike, beginning their combat.

The picture, you said? I did hang it the following morning.

Chapter Twenty-Three

One thing I liked in Taali was her punctuality. Dressed to the nines, ten minutes to eleven next morning she was trying to force the door into my room. Did I say punctuality? More like lack of consideration, really. We went downstairs and joined a small crowd of other people waiting to be teleported to the Vets' Castle.

A teleport popped open letting out a Vet mage.

He looked over the crowd. "I'm not going to bother with a temporary portal. Too much hassle for what it costs. I think I'll use group teleports. It'll take us three trips to 'port all of you. Come on now, join in the first group."

He sent out the first five invitations, including Taali and myself. Then he cast the teleport spell.

Warning! Portal spell activated. Destination point: Sunrise Zone, East Castle. Press Confirm to teleport. 10... 9... 8...

I confirmed. The next moment we found ourselves in a small hall, its walls lined with numerous gun ports. The rough stonework, dented and molten in many places, bore the signs of constant repairs.

We were greeted by a sergeant on duty in full armor, his weapons glinting, his glare professionally stern. He checked his guest list and waved to someone, causing a heavily wrought portcullis to inch up. Below it lay the castle rooms.

Smiling, the sergeant apologized for the delay. "Welcome to East Castle. You are now in the Portal Hall. It's the only place where you can set up a bind point. But I shouldn't do it if I were you, not without clearing it with internal security first."

Very well. We walked through a short passageway and under an arch which opened into an inner court. There, a girl about twelve years old curtsied, handing us each five little ribboned medals.

"These are 'likes'," she answered our silent question. "If you see something or someone you really like, you can give them one. The persons who have the most at the end will win one of our prizes."

Her smile and her childish spontaneity pared to the quick. Without thinking, I hung a medal around her neck. Laughing, Taali did the same.

Before we could step aside, we heard Eric's deep voice nearby. "Hello, O Dark One! And his lady! Where have I been all this time that I missed this gorgeous girl? At least I deserve a kiss, I suppose."

Grinning at his own joke, he pretended he wanted to hug her. Taali laughed, fighting off his advances.

I took on the role of a jealous admirer, "Get lost or I'll turn you into a toad!" The girl fled his arms and hid behind my back, laughing.

A child's laughter echoed under the arch. We turned around simultaneously.

"Amazing, isn't it?" Eric whispered. "A child in this virtual world. A real child, I mean. A perma."

That was it. That's what I couldn't quite place here. AlterWorld was virtually devoid of children. Sure enough, this wasn't a good place for little 'uns. Besides, you just couldn't separate preteen girls from their bodylicious avatars or cute anime-style pics. Boys did the same, too. Why would they choose a spotty wuss as their new embodiment? Actually, this was how you could tell a teen player: by his overstuffed beefcake body.

"No? How old is she?"

"Twelve. But she was one of the first to go perma two years ago. Her dad was a colleague of ours, a special-ops guy, a good one, too, always out on missions, mainly in some hot equatorial places. Left the girl with her mother which apparently wasn't a good thing. She was a real piece of work, her mother, spent all her time in beauty salons, never had time for her little girl. When her dad learned that she'd been perma-stuck, he spent three days making withdrawals, cashing in and selling up. Then he went after her. He's one of those who founded our clan, by the way. He has the rank of Captain now.

"But the girl? Don't you understand she'll always stay a child?"

Eric stole a look around to make sure no one was listening. Then he leaned close as if to share a secret... and yelled triumphantly, "In your dreams!"

We backed up. Eric guffawed, pleased with the effect, then lowered his voice and added seriously, "She *is* growing, believe it or not. She's half a head taller now than she was a year ago. We just don't know what to think."

I fell speechless. That was too much. I had to sit down and try to digest the news.

"Our analysts claim it depends on one's mindset. If you think young and move about a lot, your body may begin to rejuvenate. If you feel tired and depressed, your skin will sag and you may start growing gray hair and wrinkles."

I shook my head. "It's crazy."

"But it's true," Eric said. "Take our Mr. Simonov. He's lost forty pounds—also in a year."

We walked in silence for a while, trying to absorb the news, finally arriving at some stalls and rows of restaurant tables. A large banner flapped in the wind. It read:

Cooking Contest! Likes are welcome!

Eric rubbed his hands in anticipation. "This is my favorite stall. I didn't eat anything last night to save some extra space. Come on, quickly!"

We dived deep into the cloud of mouth-watering smells. Eric dropped his cape onto a table, picked up a large tray and bored into the crowd. I looked at Taali. Together we walked toward the first stall.

Holy cow. Talking about localization. The Russian salad. My favorite, generously spooned into large bowls brimming with mayo and diced chicken, just the way I liked it. Noticing my eager eyes, Taali held me an empty tray.

I smiled to the woman behind the stall. "Can I have some Russian salad, please?" I pointed at the bowl. "Actually, make it as much as you can."

She laughed good-heartedly, then pulled out the biggest bowl she had and filled it to the brim with the long-forgotten treat.

"I'm temporarily AFK," I dropped over my shoulder to Taali. Grasping the bowl, I hurried back to our table and tucked in.

That was too good. When Taali finally came, she had a trayful of yet more salad and two glasses of a bright yellow sparkling drink.

The girl looked upset. "She won't tell me the recipe," she moped as she held out one of the glasses of what tasted like Fanta.

"Why should she?" Eric reappeared. "They say it's a contest, but here everyone is trying to come up with something they can make money with. Didn't you hear about that guy who sent AI a request to generate a potato-based crispy savory snack? He even added a file containing its smell and taste—pulled it out of our database. You can get everything online these days—from the smell of donkey dung to the taste of monkey puzzle tree shavings."

"And?" I managed through the salad.

"That was it. AI gave him a complete formula. The guy took some sneezewort shoots and a few leaves of kangaroo paws, plus a few other odds and sods. Chopped them up, sprinkled something on top and deep fried the whole lot. Got potato chips as we know them. The guy invested everything he had in it. He paid the generation fees and secured the rights to the unique recipe—which probably cost him ten times more. But he wanted to have the monopoly. To play it safe, he also patented his recipe as +10% to maximum taste. A food and drinks monopoly isn't cheap. But the product had a truly universal appeal, an ideal mass market. Virtually every inn and restaurant had to buy his recipe. Now you can crunch on your favorite flavor as you play, and the guy has retired on the income to his Alpine chalet. See how it works?"

I nodded. "Wow. Wonder if I could do something like that?"

Eric lovingly eyed his fat slice of rye bread topped with yellow butter and generously sprinkled with rough salt. He bit into it with relish. "You're not the only one. If the truth were known, there's just too much money around. Have you heard about the profession of digital interior designer? It's currently one of the hottest jobs in the real world. Have you any idea how long it takes to create interiors for a fifty-bedroom castle? It's more than a year's work. I suggest you check out the digital furniture auction. You might lose all interest in farming and wish you could become a virtual cabinet maker, turning designer chairs for the get-rich-quick crowd."

I couldn't believe my ears. I'd never looked at gaming that way. Actually, I should stop calling it gaming. This wasn't a game anymore. This was the world I shared with dozens, if not hundreds of thousands of other perma players. And that was today—but how many of us would be there tomorrow? Also, this world was young, too young, its biggest goldmines still untouched—undiscovered, even. Speaking about which, I seemed to have the makings of an idea...

In the meantime, Eric was devouring whatever was piled up on his tray: a plateful of Siberian dumplings followed by a dish of blinis and caviar, then a shot of vodka chased down with some pickles.

I couldn't help it. I handed the woman cook a like and was rewarded with another bowlful of the salad which I necked under Taali's amused stare.

Taali had preserved her own likes and even acquired some more. Some sleazy type—an Elf, by the looks of him—hung a medal around her neck and bowed, muttering something about her ethereal beauty. I sensed the hair rise on the nape of my neck as I eyed her wussy admirer. The realization took me unawares. Was I really jealous? Sensing the change in atmosphere, Taali grasped my shoulder, coldly thanked the Elf and pulled me away from the scene.

Eric was waiting, ready to tow us to the next venue: a pet beauty contest. Everyone could enroll their mounts and familiars or whatever else they had managed to summon.

"Watch my LAV," Eric pointed a proud finger at his bear, all kitted out in camo and armor. Then he noticed three likes hanging off the beast's ear. "I can't believe it. We're popular!"

Taali and I looked at each other and gave the bear a like each. Eric was ecstatic.

"Come on now, won't you summon yours? Your bear and mine are made for each other. You never know, they might even make us some baby LAVs," he chuckled.

"Does that mean yours is female?" I teased him. "Because Hummungus is a hundred percent male. No, I don't think they're in the same league. LAV is just too gorgeous. So you two are welcome to your fifteen minutes of fame."

Pleased with the praise, Eric didn't insist. I stepped aside and quickly sorted through my Soul Stones. You wanted a pet? You'd get to see one, now.

A maggot would be out of place here. What about a demon? Might do. A Hell Hound? Could work, especially if I put it next to all those lapdogs. Ah. The Succubus. A demoness in scanty clothing, curvaceous and horny—literally. The stone was level 53, a bit of a shame to waste it. But if the truth were known, I had too many of them. I clenched the stone and cast the summoning spell.

The earth parted. Infernal flames glowed in the void. The smell of sulfur hung in the air. The crowd shrank. Well, death flatters no one. She must have been quite a looker when still alive. Even now her darkened skin and black lips afforded her a certain charm. To top it all, she was level 56, no less. Wish I could have this kind of luck in raids.

Eric clapped his hands with enthusiasm. "Awesome! We have virtually no Necs here in the Branch of Light. A couple of newb masochists, that's it. Let the guys get an eyeful of a real demoness. I don't think many have seen them before. Over fifty percent of the Castle's population are civilians. Fighters' relatives, crafters, bankers, analysts and other embroiderers of the truth."

Indeed, we seemed to be gathering quite a crowd. Next to all the cute and cuddly gryphons and unicorns my infernal creature looked a sight. Attracted by the turmoil, a squad of guards elbowed their way toward us. Assuring that order was maintained, they saluted and disappeared for duty elsewhere.

"Eric? What's next on the agenda?"

He paused, thinking. "The guided tour around the castle, but I'd better take you on one myself now. That way you'll see more without all the hustle."

Of course I knew they were out to impress us. So I was quite prepared for some quality showing off on their part, especially as it comes naturally to military types. That's their forte and always has been. And still they managed to surprise me. Amaze me, even.

The Arsenal was jam packed with weapons. No idea who they were meant for, as every player had their own unique kit anyway. To my blatant question, Eric mumbled something about cluster wars, total mobilizations and squirreling some away for a rainy day. Ordnance was stacked up along the walls: hundreds of bunches of arrows, darts and crossbow bolts. In the alchemy stores, thousands of vials lined hundreds of long shelves, arranged by their type and level, making me feel utterly inadequate.

Trumpets blared outside. Eric perked up. "They're signaling the guest tournament. Are you in?"

That sounded interesting. An extra fighting practice never hurt. And this was a tournament with all that crowd watching you, your date among them... I found it both flattering and motivating. I wasn't worried about making a complete fool of myself: my character was strong and original enough and my gear was good.

"What are the rules? Prizes?"

"What do you think?" Eric looked offended. "This is all official. We've got AI's confirmation and paid all the dues. The victory brings you real fame points. Only the guests can participate. The clan warriors will have their star turn at the end, out of the competition. There're four groups: one for levels 10 to 33, another up to 66, the third group is for those up to 100 and the last group for those above. You're 52 now, aren't you? Not high enough, I'm afraid. We've way too many guests this time, probably four hundred in total, and I'm sure quite a few are at the top of your group. Still, there's no harm in trying. The fights take place in the arena. They don't affect your PK counter so it's all good healthy fun, really. There'll be betting there so you can back yourself if you wish to."

I looked at Taali. Eric noticed our exchange and hurried to add fuel to the fire. "On top of the main prize of five hundred gold, the winner will have the right to choose the Tournament Queen. Her portrait will be hung in the hall of fame until next year. Actually, there will be four winners and four respective Queens, one in each group, but I still think it's cool."

I sensed the girl's hand squeeze mine. She didn't say anything, I knew she wouldn't. But I understood well enough. Which eighteen-year-old girl didn't dream of being chosen tournament queen in a real medieval castle by a real champion knight? Regardless of the fact that his name was the opposite of Ivanhoe. Death Knight or not, who cares?

I nodded. I'd made up my mind. I might even enjoy it. "I'm in. Show me where to sign my name on the dotted line... in blood."

Eric dragged me to the main arena, delirious with the opportunity to root for one of his own team. The closest thing to participating, I suppose. The rosy-cheeked Taali trailed along. When I reached a bit of an open space, I sent the demoness a command to rejoin us. I hoped she wouldn't get lost. The entire distance was no more than a hundred feet as the crow flies.

The demoness came running. She resembled a Christmas tree covered with likes, flowers and ribbons of every color.

"So!" Eric and I said in unison.

Apparently, the guests loved the tame inferno creature. We removed and counted the medals: thirty-two in total. But we left her the flowers and ribbons which hopefully made her look innocuous enough.

I got my number and was waiting for the draw to start. In the meantime, Eric was lecturing me on the tournament rules.

"You can't use scrolls, elixirs or other people's buffs. There's a ten grand limit on gear. If you die in the arena, you'll respawn right here. Don't worry, we won't send you all the way to your bind point. Judging by the amount of applications, the winner will have to have five fights. I don't know if you aim for victory but I'm pretty sure you'll get to the quarter finals. There're many strong fighters here today. Some of the favorites are a paladin, a rogue and a warrior, all levels 63 to 66. Would be great if they knocked each other out as soon as possible.

Finally they announced the first pairs. The fighting happened in two arenas at once so we didn't have to wait long. I was lucky with my first opponent, a level 39 enchanter. No idea what had prompted him to participate, but an easy win was always welcome. I decided not to show all my aces prematurely and stashed away all the gear with summon bonuses. The demoness promptly dropped six levels. Then I reached for the primitive sword and shield that the management furnished the fighters with.

"Eric? How's the betting going?"

"It's not. No one's betting on you."

Shame. But I wasn't counting on it, anyway.

We entered the arena. The ref cast a Magic Nullifier and started the timer. We were given one minute of rebuffing and meditation which I used to cast a few buffs over the demoness. The enchanter, on the contrary, was trying too hard, casting all sorts of magic right until the time ran out. I had a funny feeling it wasn't going to help him. I unleashed my cutie.

It was all over in 26 seconds. I hadn't expected him to last that long. In the end, I had to root him to the ground.

Congratulations! You've won 1/16 of the East Castle Guest Tournament!

50 points Fame received!

Aha. Now I could see the logic behind all those low-level entries. The applicants hoped to do a round or two and get their share of freebie fame points.

Eric had definitely warmed to his role as my second. He fanned me with a towel and even tried to massage my shoulders through the steel breastplate. Taali joined the audience on a bench, but I could clearly see her excited face. Could I have thought just a month ago that I would take part in a knights' tournament—my friend spurting out last-minute fighting instructions, my lady fidgeting in her seat clasping her hands in agitation? Never in your life. A month ago I could only think about pain, medication and my looming death. Regardless of how this virtual saga would affect my second life, I knew I wasn't going to complain or regret my decision.

The second fight was equally easy. All the more reason to act it out, wearing a struggling expression, brandishing my sword without really hitting very much, casting DoTs and generally enjoying myself. The level 50 cleric had lasted all of six minutes, having restored his health 100% four times in that period. But still, a healer is no killer; he didn't have a chance against me, especially considering his hard-to-level pattern of a group and raid cleric.

Congratulations! You've won 1/8 of the East Castle Guest Tournament!
100 points Fame received!

Before engaging in that second fight, I had asked Eric about my betting chances. This time there had been a few bets placed.

"Four to one on," he'd said.

"Which means? If I bet four hundred and I win, I get five hundred back, is that right?"

"Precisely."

I'd given it a thought and decided to wage every available penny I had. I just couldn't see how I could lose to the healer.

"Here," I said, "I've got eight hundred gold. Can you place a bet for me, please? An extra two hundred never hurt."

He studied me. "You sure?"

"Absolutely."

"Then I might do the same. Don't let us down, bud."

Now that I'd won, he slapped my shoulders, overjoyed, while I tried to avoid his fists from denting my armor.

"Easy money, bud. Five hundred, that's a windfall. Way to go! Who's next?"

He spoke too soon. The theory of chance put me up against one of the favorites: a level 63 warrior in expensive gear. A sword in each hand, he was a perfect damage dealer. And now, judging by his PvP armor, he was prepared to take on another player. Engaging him in close combat wasn't a good idea. I only needed to know who he thought me to be. If he believed me to be a knight, then he had to have plenty of armor and hit buffs. But if he had taken me for a mage, he had to wear some magic-resisting gear. Me, on the contrary, I was wearing my full combat kit I could use to face any emergency.

"What are the stakes?"

"Seven to one on."

I didn't need to ask more. "Bet two hundred for me. In the worst-case scenario I get to keep it."

Eric scratched his mop of hair. "Okay, you've talked me into it. I'll stake five hundred on you, too. Make sure you don't go down."

When I stepped out into the arena, I had an eerie feeling of déjà vu. It had all happened before. Either I used to be a gladiator in my past life or it was a flashback from a recently seen movie. The sun stood high at its zenith—no good trying to manipulate my opponent to face it. The stands hummed, discussing the just-finished fight in the second arena. Taali sat there, pale, anxious and close-lipped. A fellow paladin, she understood my chances well.

The warrior was good. The judges lingered, discussing some problems with the cost of his gear. Finally, the warrior got fed up. He pulled off a few rings and threw them to his partner. I tensed up, challenged by his defiant confidence. Just you wait, pompous bastard.

"One minute to go," the ref announced.

The warrior didn't move. I, on the contrary, had to work fast. I used the first thirty seconds to cast every buff I could think of over the demoness. Then I got both my shields out and slumped into the arena for a meditation blitz hoping for at least a hundred extra mana. As I warmed my backside in the hot sand, I summoned Teddy. The warrior's eyes squinted to a slit. You didn't expect that, did you?

The bell rang. The warrior charged. Jumping up, I sent both my pets to intercept him while I cast Deadman's Hand hoping to keep him at some distance. Ignoring my pets, he covered fifty feet in two seconds. No way we could stop him. Showered with double-handed hits, I cast the spell three more times. At least the shields absorbed them allowing me to stay concentrated. Seven seconds, minus both shields. The bastard had already dealt me 800 damage. Either he'd figured me out or he was a natural DpS.

Finally, my fourth spell got to him. I ran aside, trying to increase the distance, then cast three more DoTs. Only two worked. My inner clock was pushing me against time to renew the spells. If I failed, I might not get a second chance. The warrior was handling the demoness well, but his choice of speed weapons had played a trick on him. The Fire Shield only dealt 7 points damage, but it did so in response to every hit from that tireless DD.

I cast Deadman's Hand three times—finishing the last one as I faced the lunging warrior, my pets pounding his back. I'd done it. Now he was rooted to the ground in the center of the arena. My reaction times halved. I cast three heals over Teddy before turning back to the warrior. Three DoTs. Deadman's Hand. The warrior was at 40%, my mana at 30%. I didn't want to use Life Absorption: it wouldn't be too productive at the current mana-to-damage ratio. I had to play for time. I healed the demoness again and cast some more DoTs. Now I was almost empty. I had to use mana to immobilize the warrior. He at 10, the demoness at 10, mana at 0. Teddy was fit and healthy. The warrior shouldn't have ignored him, but ignore him he did. I exposed myself, engaging in close combat. That did the trick. Fed up with banging his head against a fire wall, the warrior was tempted with an easy win. He went for me.

Then I knew. I knew why he'd done so. His eyes glinted red. I heard a growl. Ability: Berserk. His blades glittered with Friend of Fire. His armor glowed crimson: Mars' Hand.

The stands gasped. Eric bellowed, drowning out the noise, "Don't push it! Get back!"

I'd have loved to have gotten back, but one of his combos had paralyzed me for three seconds. I writhed, showered with blows, until I could finally move and duck aside. In a matter of seconds, my hits were in the red zone. The guy was a freakin' killer. Another shield buff. Five minutes down already. With what meager magic I'd saved, I renewed Deadman's Hand. It went through, luckily. The demoness' life started blinking. But it looked like the warrior had lost his abilities and hit a cooldown, losing the last drops of his life. Done.

Congratulations! You've won 1/4 of the East Castle Guest Tournament!
200 points Fame received!

Eric erupted in a volcano of praise. "Max, you're too much, man. Three and a half grand! Plus the five hundred before that! You're my lucky charm!"

Was I really? I suppose so. I stood there, numb with triumph. Had I known the warrior's full potential, I'd have never bet on myself in a thousand years. But here I was, fourteen hundred richer. You couldn't complain, really. Plus the experience earned, priceless in itself.

I collapsed onto the bench Eric had helpfully pushed toward me. Time to regen before the semi.

Chapter Twenty-Four

There I sat, restoring mana and calming my nerves. Eric fussed about, desperate to please me, offering me a drink of water one moment, a cookie the next. Fed up with him flickering in front of me, I asked him to go and check the draw results. I was loosening up now. The inner greedy pig was busy uploading a long shopping list in my brain. The gold windfall was already burning a hole in my pocket.

Eric returned quicker than I'd expected with good news. Firstly, we'd been granted a twenty minutes' break before the semi. Not only for our sake, but also for the audience's who were tired, too. The stands filled in anticipation of the best fights. Secondly, I was going to fight a 59 wizard. Tough enough, but better than the other options: the 63 paladin or the 66 top rogue. Would be great if those two annihilated each other in the process.

"What are the stakes like?" I asked Eric. No point letting the money lie idle. It needed to grow. The first million was the hardest. After that it apparently got easier.

"Three to one."

"Excellent. Every little bit helps."

"It's three to one on *you*, bud."

I stared at him. "Pardon me? The wizard is seven levels above me. Why would anyone bet on me?"

Eric shrugged, reluctant to explain the obvious. "For the same reason as you don't seem to doubt your victory. They weren't born yesterday, either. He's not just any old wizard, but a raid nuker, leveled to deal maximum damage in minimum time. His DpS is at least three times yours. But..." he fell silent.

"But what?"

"I think you know it yourself. You just haven't realized it yet, have you? Deep inside, you're calm because you know you can do him."

I had to admit he was right. "I think I can. I can compensate his damage with my combined stats. Plus I have Life Absorption. And I also have two pets. If they end up in a clinch, he'll be finished in fifteen seconds."

Eric nodded. "Exactly. If you only had one pet, two out of three he would've done you. But he won't find it easy trying to control two beasts and kill you at the same time. He might be lucky, of course. His spells might work the first time round dealing lots of crits. It can happen, within statistical error. So three to one is very good."

Behind him, Taali voiced her frustration. "So are you two going to elect the Tournament Queen or are you in it for the money?"

If she wanted to shame Eric, she chose the wrong person. He wasn't the blushing type. "One can have it both ways, can't he, babe? Your knight in shining armor here has already brought me four grand gold and made two more for himself. Oh. Sorry, bud. Hope I haven't said too much."

I shook my head, "It's okay. We haven't reached the family budget stage yet. So I don't squirrel any loose cash away, if that's what you mean." I turned to Taali. "We've made a few bets here, pretty risky ones though. But this fight is as good as fixed. I should stake a few if I were you. It's entirely up to you, of course. It has to be your decision and your responsibility."

"Yes, I heard what you two were saying," she answered. "I suppose I could try. I have eleven hundred gold. That's all I've managed to put aside this month. Where should I take it?"

Her words made me physically sick. If the girl blew all her money now, I'd be the one to blame, no matter what I'd just said. I'd have to compensate her losses. Too late, anyway. I shouldn't have suggested it to begin with. No good deed goes unpunished.

Eric scooped our savings—over seven grand in total—and took it to the bookies. Five minutes later, he came back happy, rubbing his hands. "Guys, you won't believe it. The tournament has attracted two out-of-town bookies. They too accept bets on the outcome, with much better rates. What they offer is almost two to one. In other words, we might end up with ten grand if Max doesn't let us down. I might need some strength elixir to lug all the gold away."

I didn't like it. "What if they make off with the cash?"

"They can't. All financial professions are licensed. To put your foot in the door, you need to either pay a non-returnable entry fee to AlterWorld Bank or fork out for the insurance. It costs a fortune but then all liability payments are guaranteed. Cheer up, bud!"

As he spoke, Dan came to greet us, looking preoccupied.

"There's the cloak and dagger coming," Eric waved to his rogue friend. "Come sit with us."

Dan didn't share his excitement. "Happy now?"

"Sure."

"Placed your bets for the next fight? How much?"

I tensed up. "Everything we had."

Dan turned to Taali. She nodded her decision to double up.

Eric frowned. "I did bet quite a bit, too. Why? Have you nosed something out?"

"You can kiss your money goodbye, folks. This is a stitch-up for gullible little boys," he looked at Taali and added, "and girls."

Taali gasped and covered her mouth. Eric jumped up. "Don't drag it out, man. What is it you think you know?"

"How much life do you think this wizard has?"

I gave it some thought. "A thousand? Fifteen hundred?" I met his ironic stare. "Let's make it two. Where would he get more? Even I don't have two, with all my shields and stuff."

"Five and a half thousand! A thousand of his own and three more from gear. Plus a personal buff and Eternal Maggot shield charm."

We fell silent.

Dan went on, "This wizard has been working with those out-of-town bookies for a while. But it's the first time they decided to try and fleece us. I'm now looking into how they managed to obtain the invitations."

Eric struggled to think. "Shit. How did they manage to pass gear restrictions?"

"Easy. The charm is four grand. But the rest of his hit gear is crafted. Top stuff but quite cheap. He has more than enough mana. Considering his stats, he'll have plenty of time to rip an opponent apart, caster or no caster."

"Max, no worry," Eric tensed. "You'll do him standing on your head, bud. What's your gear cost? Send me a viewing permission, will ya?"

Warning! Eric wants to view your equipment parameters. Allow: Yes/No.

I pressed *Yes* as I answered his question. "Should be about two and a half grand. I've no idea how the judges have valued it, though."

"Almost five grand," Dan said. "The judges use their own worldwide database to evaluate all stuff at its current retail price: gifts, special offers, everything."

Eric finished examining my gear and scratched his absent stubble. "Your jewelry is trash, pardon my French. I'm off to the bank now. Will see a few guys I know on the way. I think we'll be able to pool together a few Rings of Magic Life. They should fit the ten grand limit. And they'll raise your mana and hits a thousand percent. It ain't over till it's over."

He started for the exit when Dan stopped him. "Wait up. I'm not done yet. A little birdie told me that this wizard is leveled as a fire mage. All his top spells are fire-based. His previous history shows his preferred pattern: controlling the target, then scorching it this way or other. To which I think we have an answer."

He turned to me and held out his open palm. Two gold rings glistened with heavy rubies. I opened the parameters.

Ring of Fierce Flames
Item class: Rare
Effect: 45% resistance to fire
Requires level 50

"Take it. Just don't forget to give it back to me after the fight. Now you have over 100% resist. It doesn't mean you'll be able to ignore his spells. But you won't be so easy to smoke, either."

I slid the rings on my fingers. They felt uncomfortable. I'd never liked large signet rings. Then I asked the question that worried me most. "Why are you helping us?"

He laughed. "Let's just say I like you. Besides, I want to show you that our clan can appreciate its friends."

"I can appreciate that, too. Although I have a funny feeling you have a double agenda here somewhere."

Dan laughed even louder. "You nailed it. I have quite a few, if you know what I mean. But you probably already realize that."

I paused, trying to second-guess his motives and brainstorming a few versions. "Could be several things. Could be that you're trying to protect the clan's assets. Or preventing potential fraudsters from infiltrating your territory. Finally, there could be something in it for you, too."

For a brief moment his face froze, devoid of all emotion. The mask of the cheerful rogue came off, replaced by his real expression, that of a Stalinist NKVD officer. Then he brought his emotions back under control and demonstratively applauded me. "You're not stupid, you. No need to remind you that talk is cheap and..."

"And silence is golden," we all answered.

The rogue chuckled, convinced. "Eric. The same applies to you. It's your money at stake, too—literally. But I'm not going to interfere. It might scare them off. So you're welcome to your little party. Lots of people betting at the moment so they're in it for a good couple hundred grand. It's a big loss for them but they can handle it. So I don't think they'll quit, not until the tournament is over. Max will be in the final against the 66 thief who will mince the paladin in the semi. So I just hope he'll be in for a nasty surprise. You got your torches?"

I nodded.

"I'm counting on you. They need to learn a few things so we'll teach them a lesson. The clan bet some serious money on the last fight. They can't refuse it: we can be quite persuasive when we want to. I'll see you during the break. Get ready now. You have five minutes left."

I watched his back as he walked off. "He's too much. First he brings us up shit creek without a puddle, then he generously saves us and lectures us like children, and now we're playing by his rules, up to our ears in some dirty scheme of his."

"Please don't," Eric said. "He's not so bad. Talking about children... he has three of his own out in the real world. He was in that personnel carrier when it drove straight over a landmine. Dan got thrown out of the hatch. It's a miracle how he survived. Broke every bone in his body, including his spine... imagine how it feels for a red-blooded male to be left paralyzed with a beautiful young wife and three preschool kids. So he went perma. Didn't have a pot to piss in. He made it all by himself. He can support his family now."

"And what about the beautiful wife? Sorry, I don't mean anything. Just that... they're in different worlds now."

Taali tensed up. Apparently, my question touched her to the quick.

"Difficult to believe, but they're just fine. At least on the surface they are. She manages to find a few minutes every night to meet him in the FIVR. Sundays are their family days when his kids take over the castle. He and his wife, they're just waiting for the kids to grow up and leave home. Then she'll move over here permanently. You call it a strange relationship? I'd say, it's no more strange than the family of a sailor. Or a trucker. At least here they can see each other every day."

We fell silent, thinking. Going perma had turned our lives ass over tit, creating the most weird combinations and relationships. Taali and myself were a prime example... I stole a glance at her. She sat there biting her lip and staring vacantly in front of herself. What was she thinking about? What was she up to?

The bell. I stirred, clearing my head and concentrating on the fight. I took another step, and there I was back in the arena. The breeze played with the wizard's robes opposite, sending grains of sand flying in the air. The man stared at me with a sarcastic smile. Planning to surprise me, eh? That we were yet to see.

The stands were brimming with people now. The clan's lounge didn't stay empty, either: I could make out Dan in the company of other officers. Did this mean that the top brass were all in the know, or were we striking gold for one of them in particular?

The bell. Rebuff. I boosted the demoness' life and strength and left the rest till later. I had to go easy on mana. Then I summoned Hummungus and sat down to meditate.

The demoness squinted her black eyes at the sun while the bear fidgeted, leaving deep ruts in the sand. Impatient beasties. They were going to love the crunchy wizard guy.

The bell. I jumped up. After a standard textbook opening, I sent in the pets. The wizzy responded with an equally textbook sequence. One root followed another until my pets froze in the middle of the arena, pinned to the ground. Oh well, that was what wizards generally did. Immobilizing the two pets was one thing, but keeping them immobilized was quite another. After a brief and random interval, both would escape, and then the wizard would have to break whatever spell he was casting, switch target and try to catch them again. Giving me a welcome break so I could concentrate on him.

At least that was how I thought it would be.

I cast a DoT and started another, tense with foreboding. It was taking him too long to cast. I was in for some sick surprise.

A meteor flashed across the sky, its gleaming drop of fire hitting the ground right at my feet. *Bang!* The earth shattered. Both my magic shields dissolved without a trace. My health shrank 30%. Holy cow, I thought I had that fire resist of theirs? Provided what had hit me *was* fire, of course.

The wizzy began casting more magic. My new absolute memory recognized the colorful play of light as another meteor spell. I hurried to cast Life Absorption, but all it did was siphon hits off his outer shield. No way I could disrupt his concentration. With another bang, my health bar dropped into the orange zone. At least some of the damage had missed me but I had a funny feeling it wouldn't help me much.

Finally, Teddy broke free, covering the distance to the wizard in a few powerful leaps. He was already ripping the wizzy's shield apart when a new spark glistened in my opponent's hands. I barely noticed his smirk as I hurried to bring my hits up into the yellow zone, restoring about 30% life. It wasn't fair. Fortune shouldn't be so one-sided!

The skies flashed with another tracer. *Bang!*

Servitude Mirror effect activated. The damage dealt to you has been reflected toward your summoned creature.

Lady Luck, I was wrong. Thanks! Furious, the wizzy began casting a new spell when Teddy and myself finally broke through his fifteen-hundred-gold shield. His blood flew everywhere. Enraged, the demoness broke free, too, forcing the wizzy to drop his spell.

Then he surprised me. He cast a Random Portal, a quick spell which allowed you to evade an attack. Only workable within the limits of the arena, it was still enough to help him retreat. He went flying about twenty feet, unable to begin a new spell. My beasties went for him. Another teleport, this time to the far end of the arena, was some three seconds' run for my pets. He sent two fire bolts my way and teleported again. We started playing chase: a fire bolt, a teleport, then another, all over again.

His tactics were quite original. All those aerobatics had equaled our DpS. In theory, whoever had the most mana could now win. If I lost mine, I would be dead within a couple of minutes, unable to restore life. Actually, I shouldn't have blamed the rings. Now that I had enough stats, Lady Luck seemed to become more balanced. I kept resisting every third spell and avoiding quite a bit of damage. My two beasties kept getting to him so by the time both of us ran out of mana, he only had half life left.

By then, I was already empty. My casting looked more like hand-waving. Mentally, I was apologizing to everyone who was about to lose their money.

The stands shook with the fury of all those who'd counted on a quick 30 or 50% to their money. Now their stakes were about to give up the ghost.

The wizard pirouetted once more and froze. But unlike him, I still had my guns about me. In a spray of blood, my pets had finally sunk their teeth into sweet magic flesh. The wizard raised his hands in the air. Was he going to surrender? If he was a perma or playing in full immersion, then it could hurt, of course. Not much—a bit like being attacked by a swarm of mosquitoes on a summer night. Not that it mattered. The rules didn't provide for surrendering in the arena. My shark-tooth pups were welcome to him. Like myself when nervous, I too started eating all sorts of junk.

Congratulations! You've won the semi-final of the East Castle Guest Tournament!
400 points Fame received!

I left the arena to the audience's uproar for the third time that day. I was all done in—a slack mass of burned-out nerves. Wonder if in the virtual world your digital nerve cells could regenerate?

I turned and walked into Taali's hands. A very excited Eric was prancing around us. "Dude, we did it!"

Yeah, right. He'd been a big help. But I was too tired to protest, so I just nodded to him, smiling. After all, I'd just earned myself a grand, another six hundred for my girl and two grand for my friend. Plus I'd saved a whole lot of strangers' money.

Talk about the devil. Dan didn't fail to show up. I just hoped he wouldn't ask for a confidential report in triplicate.

He was in a good mood. "Way to go," he slapped my shoulder. "He had a trick or two up his sleeve. All those teleports and the opening sequence, all those meteors—it's not the school of Fire, but an Air and Earth combo. When I saw the third one coming, I thought that was the end of you. Great job, seriously. Now you have fifteen minutes. You can listen to me as you rest. The rogue did the paladin in. His technique is as blunt as a crowbar. Stealth behind your back followed by a killing combo. Sprint, stealth. He's leveled for arena practice. Must be planning to become a PK or a mercenary, one of the two. You're a baby against him. But for every cunning stunt there's a stunni-"

Grinning, Eric breathed in, about to add something definitely not for ladies' ears. Dan planted his elbow in his ribs, causing my friend to burst out coughing.

Then he turned back to me. "What do you know about combat tactics? Tell me."

I shrugged and gave his words some thought. "I allow him to stealth past me, then take out the Torch. It allows me to see the target. Then I kill him."

Eric grunted, impressed by my brevity. "Well, right. Don't forget to control him. He knows you will, so he's wearing the right gear. You need some different control spells that won't allow him to break free and hide in stealth."

"Did I say otherwise? You have something to offer?"

He nodded and reached into his bag producing a pair of enormous, weird-shaped steel gauntlets. He pressed a clasp or something which rattled, releasing silvery blades.

Winnypore's Moon Blades

Item class: Rare
Weapon type: for combat mount only
Damage 46-58, Speed 2.4, Durability 190/220.
Effect: Gives a 11% chance to blind target with moonlight, paralyzing it for 1.6 sec.

Awesome. Teddy would love them. I would love them myself if I could afford them.

"Aha. Claws of Winnie the Pooh," Eric butted in. Then he added, seeing our confusion, "That's what we call them here. They look the part, don't you think?"

Dan produced a handful of rings and poured them into my open hand. "These will bring you up to the limit. Winnie's Claws are four grand. The rings are rather simple, seventy hits and about fifty gold each. But you'll have eight of them. They just might save your skin, if necessary. Oh, and can I have my Fire Rings back, please?"

Oh. I'd hoped he wouldn't remember them. Never mind. My inner greedy pig wept as I exchanged the rings.

The sight of my agony made Dan laugh. "I promise you that if you win the final, I won't ask for this stuff back. Whatever you have is yours. Wait a sec. I got a message."

His eyes clouded as he switched to his inbox. "I see. Bets are six to one against you. Don't put too much pressure on our broker. If you want to bet, go to the other two."

The more you have, the more you want. I had three grand, Taali only two. And this seemed to be a safe thing. We could be missing out on a whole lot of cash. It was sink or swim.

I turned to Dan. "I don't suppose you could lend me some money for half an hour?"

He gave me an appraising look. I hated to be indebted to him of all people, but we were already up to our ears in his little schemes so the least we could do was put the situation to good use.

"Very well," he finally said. "I have some idea of how much you've bet. I'll send word to Mr. Simonov and he'll double it. Good enough?"

"Perfect. Thanks!"

"It'll all come good," he said slowly, making it clear it was no free ride.

Taali gave me a frightened look as if saying, *are you sure we have to do it*? I lay a soothing hand on her knee: *cheer up, babe; we'll make it.*

Dan jumped to his feet. In a typically digital gesture, he squinted his eyes at the virtual clock. "That's it. You've got five minutes. Better get ready."

I knew what he meant. I summoned Teddy and showed him his new outfit. He even seemed to stand taller when he clicked the blades in an out a few times sending sparks flying over the paving stones. I leaned back against his warm side and closed my eyes. Hummungus froze as if afraid of disturbing his master. Was it my imagination or was he really changing? Growing more, er, alive? Showing some glimpses of emotion? Or was I going off my trolley?

Eric next to me sniffed, shifting from one foot to the other. Taali cuddled up to me, hugging my arm. So calm and secure...

The bell. Taali started. Eric slapped my shoulder. I got back to my feet and gingerly retrieved my arm. It was time.

Again—the arena, the golden sand. My opponent, calm and confident. I lowered my head ever so slightly, greeting him. The rogue mirrored my actions. I seemed to like him. How weird. This wasn't a snobbish schmuck like that wizard. I paused for a second and did something against all logic. I PM'd him.

PM. Some unhealthy activity here today. I shouldn't bet on your winning. Bad idea.

The next second, I received his reply.

TY. Already know. Not the 1st time. Seen them around. Never bet where they operate ;-)

I seemed to be lucky when it came to rogues. Having said that, I hadn't seen Cryl for a while. I wondered if he was stuck in jail like I had been, nailed for stealing something he shouldn't have to.

The bell. Rebuff. Time to give it all. I had enough mana to handle him. Now I had to keep him in my sights and hopefully not die too early.

Bell. No more bets. The stealthed rogue disappeared from sight. I took five steps forward, exposing my back and inviting him to use my negligence. Would be good to catch him between my pets and the edge of the arena. My brain pulsated in unison with the countdown. It was time.

I attached the staff to my belt and clutched the torch. Activation: max. The rogue backed off, exposed by the rays of True Flame. So he'd seen one of them before? Well, tough.

I turned to my beasties. "Attack!"

The rogue unstealthed, darted to one side to avoid the lit-up area and disappeared again. Oh well, time to do a bit of running. The arena was rather small, about fifty feet in diameter at most. I zigzagged across it, but he was nowhere to be seen, the bastard. I did it again. This time I saw him, trying to squeeze his way along the barrier. I bolted for him. Attack! He tried to duck this way and that, saw it was no good and went for me. My pets intercepted him halfway. I promptly cast Deadman's Hand, but still the rogue made it through to me. We engaged in close combat. Not all of his combos worked face to face: most of the best ones were of either the backstab or vault kinds. But it was no picnic, I tell you. He showered me with blocks of rapid shallow hits interspersed with powerful bleed combos. I was still trying to control him, but he was too fast. My magic shield collapsed. Too bad. Bone Shield went out with a flash. Numerous flesh wounds hurt, disrupting my concentration. In a flash of light, I used the Moon Blades to paralyze him. Ducking aside, I cast Life Absorption, but the rogue was already going for me, dripping blood from my beasts' attacks. I bolted again, trying to keep my distance, but the rogue was faster. Even under pressure from Hummungus and the demoness, he caught up with me in under five seconds. His armor was covered in blood, his health shrunk to 50%. He was no tank at all. He couldn't be, what with his meager armor and hits, his stealth and magic-resistant armor.

I stood there taking his hits, casting an occasional Life Absorption. I lasted about fifteen seconds purely on my armor and stuff until paralyzation kicked back in, sending the rogue's life into the orange zone. His speed dropped. Time to play tag again. I made him chase me around for another half-minute while my pets finished the job. At the last moment, I turned round and activated the last Life Absorption. I thought it would be fair. He deserved being killed by his adversary and not some wretched zombie.

I won.

Congratulations! You've just won the East Castle Guest Tournament!

1000 points Fame received!

Fame Alert!

Your Fame has exceeded 7000 points!

You've reached Fame level 3: Everybody knows you.

Friendly faction vendors might surprise you with lower prices. You will also gain access to some secret quests. Local dignitaries may invite you to their official functions.

The stands were raging, people throwing down likes and ribbons into the arena. Gold glittered in the sand. Did they have a special collection boy or was I supposed to crawl on all fours picking up their offerings? I bowed slightly to the audience and walked over to the exit—not mine but the one where Dan had just reappeared, smiling. I came over to him. He gave me a bear hug; we slapped each other's shoulders causing the stands to scream with delight again.

"Everything OK?" I asked.

"Great. Everything went without a hitch."

I shook his hand one last time and hurried to where my friends were jumping with impatience. I glimpsed a magic bubble cover the finance sector as Dan and three of his high-level clan members hurried toward it, about to seize the winnings. How much could it be?

I hugged Taali and kissed her. Total strangers applauded me and I accepted their praise. Then I peeled off my armor and basked my tired body in the breeze. Taali suggested I wash my face; she brought a pitcher and poured some fresh water onto my head and shoulders. Life was good.

A couple minutes later, Eric came back running—he'd been checking our winnings. He was beaming, which told me he'd been paid in full.

"The two have been skimmed for every penny. Here's your cut," he announced.

He handed me thirty four thousand gold. Not bad. I very nearly went into weight overload. This was serious money gamewise. My inner greedy pig was beating his head against the wall, ecstatic.

"And that's for you," Eric handed Taali her share. Twenty-two grand. She cried softly. I stroked her thick hair and whispered in her ear, soothing her.

She looked up at me, tearful. "I'm scared."

"Of what? No one can take it from you. There won't be any problems. Besides, it's not that much money, after all. A couple grand USD, big deal."

"I didn't mean that. I have some more money saved back in real life, too. Now I have enough to buy a gun. But I'm scared..."

"Normal," I said. "If you were calm and cheerful, now that wouldn't be normal. You sure you don't want to give this whole revenge thing a miss? Alternatively, you could hire someone. Find a junkie in need of a fix and pay him to plant a rusty nail into the client's liver."

"No. I must do it myself. It's personal."

I could understand her. Logically, it made sense. If someone killed your sister, whether directly or not, you had every right to smoke the motherfucker and he had to be grateful it was only him and not his entire family up to his cousins twice removed. But Taali wasn't the type. She'd get burned even as she bought the weapon. All those Internet hired killer ads and guns-and-drugs forums were 99% police joints to trap naive wusses. Even I was totally inadequate when it came to advice giving. Besides, I now lived in a different world.

"Taali, we just won't be able to pull it off. You'll get into trouble before anything else. Shall we leave it to the pros? Eric here spent half his life in the army. I'm sure he has all the right contacts and skills. And he's digital—he has no reason to rat on you."

She paused. Then she breathed what sounded like a sigh of relief. "Okay. As you say. I'm an idiot, I know. So stupid of me to even think about it. And now I've dragged you into it, too."

"Relax. We're not in the system, not yet. The local moneybags may well be, for succession purposes. Good for them. To all intents and purposes, the criminal law doesn't apply to us."

"To us?" she said. "To you, Max. You're local. I still live in real life."

"Oh, right. I keep forgetting. But do you understand that sooner or later they'll single you out? What you gonna do once you smoke them?"

"There's only one place where I could be happy," she said. "Here. And they can't really get to me here. I'll have to go perma."

I paused remembering a poet's words. *You're responsible for what you have tamed.* I couldn't say whether it was love but we felt good together. We walked the same road, and I wouldn't mind our journey to be long enough. I leaned toward her and kissed her.

"Very well, babe. You know where you can stay at first if you want to. There's your portrait in the room already, anyway. And I might give you a tip about how to rig a capsule and meet my mom in the process."

Chapter Twenty-Five

I patiently waited for Taali to wipe away her tears and only then waved to Eric. He stood a short way off, shifting from one foot to the other, unwilling to be in the way of our whispered secrets. He might look like a gorilla on steroids but he had a lot of tact. Great guy. I poked his shoulder with a fist and whispered, unable to contain myself, "Thanks, bro."

Eric looked perplexed. "What for?"

"For everything. What would you say to us meeting in the Three Little Pigs, say, tomorrow night? We have reason to celebrate."

"Why not?"

"Excellent. There's another thing we'll have to discuss. Taali here plans to go perma. But before she can do that, she has to pay off a few debts in real life."

"You need money, then? I've been meaning to buy a few things but they can wait, I suppose. How much do you need?"

"Thanks a lot, but that's not what I meant. These aren't the kind of debts you pay in gold. This kind of stuff you pay in lead."

Eric wrinkled his forehead. His eyebrows rose. He looked at Taali. With a sniffle, the girl nodded.

Eric shook his head in disbelief. "Can you ever do anything normal? You can't just sit quiet, can you? Shit. I hope it's not contagious. Never mind. We'll talk about it tomorrow. There's our cloak and dagger coming to see you again. He can't live without you these days."

Dan looked pleased with himself. He strode toward us, confident and straight-backed, like a baron crossing his castle courtyard. Then he turned to a good-looking woman nearby, pointing at his non-existent wrist watch and waving an open hand in the air. Apparently, he wasn't going to stay with us for long.

He gave me a firm handshake and gallantly bowed his head to Taali. "Great job. It went like clockwork. Those two are stripped to their underpants. Shame we won't see them again. So, Mister Robin Hood and his merry men, are you happy with the pickings?"

I lowered my eyes playing the poor penniless Jew. The show didn't fool him. Even my inner greedy pig didn't know the state of my finances as well as that guy did.

He smiled knowingly and shook his head. "Both you and your bear can keep the gear as promised. As a sign of our appreciation. I've got something else for you, too."

He held out a recognizable ring engraved with the Vets' crest. I peered at its characteristics.

Personal ring bearing the Clan's logo and an inscription: Clan Friend.

Eric's eyes widened. Apparently, they didn't offer this sort of thing lightly.

Dan read the silent question in my eyes. "I told you we could appreciate a good turn. Now we can return the favor. When you need help, just show this to a Vet. They might not move mountains but they'll do what they can. This isn't so much to thank you for what you've done but rather as a gesture of goodwill and our request to count you among our friends."

He didn't make it easy, did he? Could it be that he knew about the Temple? Or maybe a high-level Dark One disguised as a High Elf was valuable enough in itself? Not being able to divine his hidden agenda made me angry. I couldn't ask him directly: he'd just pretend to take offense with my questioning the sincerity of their offer. But in any case, I had better give them something back. That was one way to feel less obliged.

I reached into my bag and produced the torches. "Thanks a lot, man. I mean it. Please accept these from me," I handed him both torches. "I hate being in debt."

"What debts are you talking about?" he shrugged. "But we really appreciate these torches. Your fight has shown us all their multifunctional potential."

On hearing his last words, my inner greedy pig clutched his heart and slid down the wall in despair. I had to remind him about the heap of gold the two of us had amassed today. With Dan's help, mind you.

One question kept bugging me. "The bookies won't string themselves up, I hope? Did they lose a lot?"

He laughed. "It's a high risk business. We made them hit their operating limit of one million.

They should be thankful. In real life, they might not have left in one piece."

A hundred grand USD, not bad at all. No wonder Dan was beaming like a cat that got the cream. "Just to bring it into prospective, how much does your castle cost?"

He gave it some thought. "There isn't a fixed price. It all depends on how badly the parties want the deal to go through. About four million, I'd say, or possibly five. It also depends on its condition. And on how well it's stocked with structures and artifacts. Only we don't really want to sell it, even if we were offered six million for it," he grinned. "Very well, then. I'm off to enjoy the big day. My wife and kids have come to see me. Come around later if you want to meet them. Make sure you stay for the banquet and the dance."

He turned around to go, but then slapped himself on the forehead and turned back to me. "Oh, Max, you'll have to hang around for a while. The constable of the castle will be having an awards ceremony in the arena in half an hour."

I nodded. Awards are sacred. Presently, a young boy—one of the junior cadets, according to Eric—came running with an armful of likes and ribbons from the audience. He slammed a small jingling purse on top of the heap and reported,

"Cadet Invincible2022, delivering sixty-eight likes, untold ribbons and ninety-two gold on quartermaster's orders, Sir!"

Eric saluted him. "Thank you, cadet. Dismissed."

"Proud to serve the clan, Sir!"

The youth about-turned sharply, marched three smart steps and then darted away.

"Some discipline you've got here."

Eric grinned. "Don't fool yourself. The cadets, yes, they're tested for stability and discipline. So they fag about for a month until they're promoted and officially join our ranks. Then it gets much more relaxed, as you can see."

We spent the next half hour adorning my pets with likes and ribbons—a pointless but funny activity. Finally, the trumpets blew a clarion, inviting the audience back to the stands and the winners to the arena. They fiddled with the settings turning the sand red, color-matching the setting sun.

The constable Major Medved was large and awesome. A paladin nearing level 200, he stood head and shoulders above me and was twice as broad. A magnificent cape hugged his frame—red velvet embroidered with gold. I wondered if all this color-coordinating was the cause of our waiting till sunset. The four winners next to him looked like preteen truants in the principal's office. Only the level-130 Barbarian who'd won the top division might have been a reluctant match but even he, despite his height, paled into insignificance next to the Major.

The constable bellowed, "Natinel, level 32 Ranger, who in honest combat has proven his right to the Champion's Bracelet, accept your prize!"

The stands cheered, the plaudits enthusiastic even if not too numerous. The ranger stepped out and accepted the engraved bracelet and a purse with a hundred gold.

"Do you know of a lady you would like to proclaim Tournament Queen?"

The ranger's voice came out squeaky and childish. "I do! It's Lena from freshman year."

The Constable drowned his laughter in a coughing fit. The stands screamed with delight. This time their applause was longer. It took Major Medved some time to bring the crowd under control.

"Unfortunately, the lady has to be present at the castle. I suggest you bring her along to the next tournament."

The Constable turned to me. "Laith, level 52 Death Knight, accompanied by a bear and a demoness. Today you have shown a strong fighting spirit and excellent combat training as you kept defeating the strongest of your opponents. Wear this well-deserved bracelet with pride. We'll be happy to see you here next year."

The stalls clapped their hands in unison. Only fair, really: I'd provided a lot of the show that day, and quite a few of them had made a nice profit or at least hadn't lost their gold. As a welcome addition, a heavy purse dropped into my bag.

"Sir Laith! Do you know of a lady you would like to proclaim Tournament Queen?"

"Yes, Sir Constable," I answered in the same key, getting into the medieval spirit. "Lady Taali has captured my heart. Truly she is the Tournament Beauty Queen!"

"So be it!"

The trumpets resounded. The arena gate swung open, letting in Taali in a long cream-colored robe, riding a white unicorn. She looked stunning like some princess in exile. Eric, proud and magnanimous, was leading the unicorn by the reins. When had they managed to arrange all that?

The unicorn approached. Taali jumped off into my arms. The stands whistled, envying us, as the Constable concealed a smile behind his mustache.

Finally he raised his hand, ordering silence. "Truly Lady Taali deserves the title of Tournament Queen! Your portrait will be the centerpiece of our Hall of Fame. Please accept this modest prize!"

He walked down his platform and handed the girl a custom-made platinum tiara. Taali blushed, eyes glistening. Her chest heaved, betraying her excitement.

Later, we didn't remember much of the remaining ceremony. We just stood there holding hands and whispering. Ditto for the banquet and the dance.

And later that night... later I envied my own luck. Now I knew the best way to a woman's heart. You needed to become her knight, to win a tournament and publicly announce her the Beauty Queen. All men are welcome to this page from my book.

In the morning, as I sat in my easy chair with a cup of hot coffee in my lap, I sensed again the void in the local worldbuilding. Anything for a cigarette. Suddenly I flashed back to the thought that had hit me as I'd gobbled that Russian salad. I needed to get a recipe for cigarettes. Unique, preferably. Naturally, you couldn't solve this kind of problem straight out, but if I'd learned one thing in life it was that every problem had multiple solutions. I had money now, so I could afford to toy around with the idea. I ordered the smell and taste files and chose classic Marlboro as a prototype. I thought a bit more and pulled out its complete specifications. Length, color, dryness, burn rate and a dozen more production standards.

Right, let's try and see. I dug into the menu and found the recipe generation application form. Oh well. Ten gold for each attempt. Not too expensive, but still. I started filling out the form.

Incense sticks for temple rites. Dry mixture. Color: yellow brown. Chopped to specification and wrapped in white paper. One end is filled with fiber to 1/4 of the length of the stick. When lit up, smolders for 8 min filling the room with fragrant smoke.

I uploaded the smell and taste samples from the file. That seemed to be it. I crossed my fingers and pressed *Submit.*

AI didn't think long. In less than a minute, I received his reply:

Warning! It seems that your recipe will result in creating an item which is identical with certain prohibited items.

Item name: Cigarette, 91% match
Item name: Cigar, 86% match
Item name: Tobacco, 79% match
We advise that you can't create a new item with more than 50% match.
Change the item's ingredients and try again.

Aha. So that's how it worked, then. And if I deleted the filter? I changed the recipe and submitted it again. Same result, only the cigar and cigarette's percentages had swapped places. Oh well. Apparently, I couldn't create the recipe from scratch. I had to break the task down and start with creating some tobacco. I had a funny feeling that if I hid its description in the depths of some complex recipe, I might just pull it off. Let's see.

Sushi 'The Emperor's Smoldering Delight'.
Ingredients: rice, fish and nori seaweed, yellow brown. Smell and taste samples attached.

Why would I need smoldering nori seaweed, you might ask? Because apparently it's some arcane sushi ceremony. AI took fifteen minutes to reply, too long for an automated answer. Most likely, he could see right through my schemes and had been deciding what to do with this sneaky cheek.

Got it.

You've been granted permission to generate recipe:
Sushi 'The Emperor's Smoldering Delight'.
Category: Top A Restaurant Dishes
Price of normal recipe: 1800 gold
Price of unique recipe: 18000 gold.

They didn't want much, did they? Apparently, I had to drop this restaurant nonsense and get rid of the ingredients I didn't need.

Nori seaweed sheets for sushi making. Color: yellow brown. Smell and taste samples attached.

As if! 82% match with tobacco. Was it my imagination or was AI laughing his mechanical head off watching me trying?

What else could I get rid of? What if the sheets were white? 76% match, that's better. I really didn't want to use rice or other worthless ingredients, because in the case of mass production it would turn into millions of gold wasted. And what if I deviated from the classic tobacco formula a bit? What's the point in stubbornly copying something if you can modify it?

After another hour of intellectual ping pong, I won with the score 1 to 22. After twenty-two attempts, my recipe for white tobacco was accepted. So what if the smoke was not blue but rainbowy like a soap bubble? It would be even more fun watching it. And if you didn't like the fact that it tasted of strawberries, then you shouldn't have tried to eat it, should you?

Now a few finishing touches. I generated some yellow brown dye. Taste: none, smell: none. It went through.

Then the paper. Having said that... I already had my sheets of white tobacco. So I could use them to wrap chopped dyed tobacco. And add a normal paper filter. Or I could use some budget filterless solution, like some cheap Soviet-era cigarettes.

I crossed my fingers and submitted the patent request. It took them a while to reply. After an hour, I got pretty nervous. Coffee cups piled up on the table.

The room had been paced in all directions. Finally, I received a PM alert.

Dear Max,

After careful consideration, we've found your idea original, legally viable and ambiguous enough to give it a green light. However, we have a few key conditions.

1. You can't transfer the patent to a third party without administration's approval.

2. The company will receive 80% of all profits from the sales of your item by automatic taxation on every sale.

3. We expect you to increase sales gradually and would appreciate your consideration of the market's stability and public feeling.

For our part, we can guarantee you our full legal support.

Chief of the AlterWorld Financial Department: Mr. Dave Lee

Oh well. Curiouser and curiouser. Had they just dealt me the role of a pawn in a big boys' game? Having said that, it wasn't as if I had any alternatives. I could play it safe and mix with the crowd, or I could take a few risks diving into the heavyweights' slimy money ponds and surfacing with profit. That way I could gradually acquire enough weight myself to be able to tackle tasks more serious then choosing the right shoe color. To do that, I needed to reach top levels as well as achieve financial stability and support from friends or clanmates. I still had to think about it all. But this tobacco thing demanded my immediate attention. It looked as if I'd been the first to have successfully jumped through all the hoops, so the company had decided to take a chance on me. Tobacco trade was such a gold mine that I'm sure the admins would back up the devil if he somehow managed to skirt around the smoking ban. I had to accept their offer. This wasn't the right moment to haggle over the terms. I pressed *Confirm*.

Fine minutes later, I received another message, this time from AI.

You've been granted permission to generate recipe: "The Emperor's Smoldering Delight".
Category: Class D Food.
Price of basic recipe: 400 gold
Price of unique recipe: 4000 gold
Price of patent: 2000 gold for 1% coverage

You've been granted permission to generate recipe: Yellow Brown Dye, tasteless, odorless.
Category: Class E Food Colorants
Price of basic recipe: 100 gold
Price of unique recipe: 1000 gold
Price of patent: 500 gold for 1% coverage

Total price of the basic package: 500 gold
Total price of the unique package: 5000 gold
Total price of the unique package with maximum patent: 30000 gold

Without even thinking, I accepted the last version. The gold clinked, making me thirty grand poorer. I had five thousand cash left.

Congratulations! You've received a unique recipe "The Emperor's Smoldering Delight"!
Requires level 50
Requires 100 Cooking Skill
Ingredients: Swamp Lily leaves, Juice of Millefleurs, Pollen of Gigantic Fly-Trap

Congratulations! You've received a unique recipe "Yellow Brown Dye, tasteless, odorless".
Required level 50
Requires 100 Alchemy Skill
Ingredients: Juice of Brown Fern, Wax from Forest bees, Spring water

Would you like to learn the recipes?

Yes! A moment later, I had the skill I needed. Now my alchemy was up to date but I still had to level up my cooking skill. Not a problem. I opened the auction and ordered two basketfuls of sandwich fillings of various difficulty levels. I also discovered tons of recipes from the happy selling crowd. After an hour and a half of slicing, layering and wrapping I was the proud owner of three hundred indestructible sandwiches and a precious skill.

I checked all the ingredients I needed to make the dye and tobacco. The dye was no problem. Its ingredients were so easily available that the cost of production turned out to be around 1 silver. After another half-hour, an army of fat vials lined up on my table.

Tobacco proved more difficult. Either Gigantic Fly-Trap didn't grow here or nobody bothered to collect its pollen, and it was only available from two sellers. One of them was asking 2 silver for a batch while the other, for some reason only known to him, demanded one gold for the same quantity. I bought up the former's entire stock which amounted to sixty doses, then PM'd him offering to buy any quantities he might happen to have. Then I set up auto buy with the task of buying all six ingredients in bulk for a setup price. This way I could get the cream of the auction's crop. The auto buy didn't charge much—3% of the deal—but promised to save me a pretty penny.

And things got rolling.

By the evening, I finally made it to my recliner, took a swig of strong coffee and a tug on a cigarette, the first in this world. Jeez, it felt good. And the way the smoke wafted around! The real-world manufacturers would have jumped off a cliff for my iridescent smoke recipe.

I finished the cigarette, rolled my eyes and lingered in the chair, enjoying the fragrance. Even more important was the fact that I wasn't ruining anyone's health by selling the stuff. All I was doing was helping others enjoy their habit.

Time to run field trials. I stuffed all the rollups into my bag—about two hundred in total, costing 4 silver each—and walked downstairs into the main hall. As always, evenings were pretty busy. I walked over to the bartender, exchanged a few words and ordered a shot of brandy. With a practiced gesture, I produced a cigarette and flicked it into my mouth. I slapped my pockets, searching for a lighter, found none and made an international gesture as if asking him for a light.

Mechanically, he reached under the bar and struck a match. His hand froze halfway to the cigarette. His eyes stared at my mouth. I leaned forward and lit up. Then I inhaled, just like in that cowboy advert, and let out a cloud of smoke. His eyes grew enormous as he stared at his own reflection in the iridescent smoke rings. He made a very peculiar movement with his nose, taking in the familiar aroma. His burned fingers twitched as he dropped the match.

"S-s-spare a smoke?" he stuttered, voiceless.

With pleasure. I offered him a rollup. Breaking matches, he finally lit up and drew in a lungful. Slowly he exhaled. His face was euphoric. "This is too good..."

Everybody spoke at once.

Apparently, the patrons had long left their places and surrounded us, waiting for his verdict. Now they all fought for my attention, interrupting each other, all saying the same thing, "Spare one, sell some, leave a few, please!"

"One per head," I shouted over the noise as I handed out the precious sticks placing them into their impatiently shaking fingers.

A minute later, the inn was dead quiet. Colorful clouds of smoke hovered under the ceiling of what now resembled an opium den: all smoke, smell, silence and blissful faces.

A teleport popped outside in the courtyard. The door shook and collapsed, hanging on one hinge. A bloodied paladin in dented armor burst into the hall, oozing drops of blood onto the floor. His life pulsated in the orange zone. But he didn't seem to care. His nostrils widened as he sniffed the air. His practiced eye singled me out in the crowd. Avariciously he headed for the bar.

Someone uttered his name, recognizing the famous knight. "Fuckyall!"

He held out a compelling palm. I placed a cigarette into it and struck a match. The warrior inhaled, closed his eyes and exhaled through both nostrils. Then he loosened up as if someone had deflated him. The hard expression left his face; his lips curved into a smile.

Another teleport popped outside. A furious level 205 cleric girl stormed into the hall.

"Fuckyall! Very nice, fucking off in the middle of a fight!"

The warrior shot out his arm, calling for silence. He was all blissed out.

Having finished the cigarette in two deep drags, he stepped closer, hovering over me. "How many've you got? I'm taking 'em all."

The patrons grumbled, rising from their seats. The paladin swung round and growled at the angrier ones, with little effect. I heard the grating of unsheathing knives.

Fuckyall thought better of it. "Very well. Think you can sell me a couple packs? My whole soul's on fire. Have been smoking nothing but moss and straw for two years flat."

"I only have 'em loose," I warned him placing about fifty cigarettes on the bar. "Actually, it's been a promotion. I've been offering them for free, one apiece."

The paladin waved the idea away. One of the Russian cluster's most powerful warriors, he was too used to shaping the world after his own needs. No way was he going to adjust to any amount of senseless regulations created by some anonymous paper-pushers. "How much?"

"Two gold apiece," I quoted the price I'd already calculated.

Fuckyall slapped his pockets and grimaced. Pulling a massive bracelet off his wrist, he threw it onto the table. "Take it. You're worth it. Barman! Three bottles of brandy and the best room you can find in this rat hole. I need some rest."

In the meantime, more teleports started popping outside. The news of the cigarettes arrival was spreading fast in this world.

Chapter Twenty-Six

When I finally stopped distributing cigarettes to the eager, I didn't feel good. Honestly, I was scared by what I'd just seen. These weren't people wishing to cadge a smoke. These were addicts; this was cold turkey raising its ugly head. In the center of the city, right before my own eyes, decent citizens were prepared to kill each other over a fix, jumping at their biggest paladin hero's throat. Only now I started to understand what kind of genie I had just let out of the bottle. The terrible thing was, there was no way I could stuff him back in now.

Possessing this kind of recipe was like giving a fist-sized diamond to a hobo. The stone wouldn't make him rich; if anything, it would put an end to his life pretty soon. Then it would travel on, leaving a trail of blood wherever it went until it finally came to rest on a shelf in some billionaire's vault.

Potentially, this recipe meant millions: too much money and influence involved to allow a lone newcomer to make it. Whether I liked it or not, I had to become part of one of the more influential groups. It had probably been stupid of me to give myself away so openly. I should have tried to produce small batches and auction them for exorbitant prices. But then again, who would pay that kind of money for some obscure Emperor's Smoldering Delight, even if it looked like a cigarette?

Most importantly, this wasn't what the Admins were after. They didn't need eighty percent of a million, even. It was peanuts for them. They had simply decided to use the entrepreneurial youngster to beta-test the market. They wanted to study the demand, double-check its influence on the economy and see the public's reaction. Whatever happened, they could always tell the powers that be that they had nothing to do with it and blame it on the player's personal initiative. It wasn't their fault he'd mixed up a few ingredients that allowed him to puff rainbow smoke at the ceiling. Those players just couldn't help experimenting with substances, trying this and that, from moss to straw, so now it was seaweed's turn. They'd tell the powers that be that they were more than welcome to bring the scumbag to justice—if they got hold of him. Because the scumbag just happened to be a perma player and out of the real world's jurisdiction.

I opened the Wiki to check Russian clans' ratings. I had to find a strong syndicate to cover me. The Vets were #14 in the overall ratings. The Olders, #3. That was another unknown quantity. Logically, they were the ones to turn to. But... How sure was I that Russian get-rich-quick billionaires wouldn't stab the ambitious loner in the back? In real life, would I go cap in hand to one of those? No way. I'd rather die.

The Vets dropped to #32 in the economic ratings but made the Top 10 because of their military power.

Talk about the devil. Eric walked into the inn. Dan the cloak-and-dagger guy dallied behind. Now what did *he* want? I hadn't invited him. Had they already heard about the cigarettes?

For a moment, the two vets froze. Then they looked around, noticed me still standing with a couple of remaining cigarettes in my hand, and walked over to the bar.

Dan winced studying the packed room choking in smoke. Eric, ever the joker, slapped my shoulder with his steel hand. "I knew that if there was an anomaly somewhere, we had to find you at its center."

Dan didn't mince words. He gestured around the room. "Your work?"

I lowered a guilty head. "It was supposed to be a free promotion. I wanted to make everyone happy. Turned out, it was more like entering a cageful of hungry tigers carrying a bowl of steak. Can you imagine they very nearly ground Fuckyall into dust, of all people? All because of those wretched cigarettes."

Dan shook his head. "This is only the beginning. How sure are you that they'll let you out of this room now? Are you certain they won't chain you to that table in the corner and make you roll more cigarettes until some other clan kidnaps you and locks you up in a bunker?"

I cringed. "No need to be so negative. I already know I might need to turn to someone. Had you seen all the windows open in my interface, you'd have known I'm already working in this direction. Trust me I've already looked the Vets up, too."

There! If they wanted me to come crawling to them with my recipe on a silver platter, I wouldn't give in so easily. Let them make the first move and make me an offer I'll find hard to resist.

"Is that your recipe?" Dan said. "Did you make it?"

"Yeah."

"Lots of people tried before you," he added tentatively.

"You can't make it from scratch. It's too obvious. You have to create a sequence of tasks leading to the end result you need."

Eric shrugged. "Bullshit. Wait till the Admins come back to their senses tomorrow. They'll axe your recipe before you know it. So before it happens, how about a few?"

"Oops, sorry, guys. Completely forgot."

I handed them a cigarette each. The two men pulled at them with relish.

"Too good," Eric managed.

I wasn't going to trash my merchandise. "Talking about the Admins. No way they're gonna axe it. They already have their cut."

Dan perked up. "Are you sure? Do you realize how that changes everything?"

"Read this," I forwarded him the letter from the Administration.

He scanned the text, then went through it again, slower this time, looking into all the fine print. "The twenty percent of profits that they've left you is a lot. In real life, tobacco vendors don't have that. Taxes... excises... Aha. They're talking about the patent. Does it mean you have a full unique patent protected for 10% coverage? You can grant manufacturer's licenses but you don't have the right to relinquish the patent without their consent? Is that so?"

I thought about it. He'd somehow managed to unscramble the whole thing. Looked like he was right. My diamond was even more precious than I'd thought. Right now it had grown to the size of a melon.

I nodded, "Exactly."

"That's smart," he said slowly.

Eric turned to him, "Why do you think the Admins decided to leave him the patent? And even allowed him to grant licenses?"

"I think all they want is to tie the invention to a perma player. This way it would be much easier for them to keep lawyers at bay. You can't sue a perma. At least not for the time being."

He sat back and fell silent, squinting at the play of smoke like a cat basking in the sun.

Eric reached into his bag and produced a small figurine depicting my demoness in the heat of battle. Her hair was flying in the wind; she was baring her teeth, grinning, as she raised her whip in a violent hand. I peered at the characteristics.

The Gold Figurine. The second prize in the Tournament of Familiars. You can sell it or keep it. Fixed price: 300 gold.

"Thanks, dude," I carefully put the prize away into my bag. Looked like it was time to fix up a shelf on the wall of my room to display all these cups and prizes. Sort of miniature Hall of Fame.

Dan shook his head and slapped the oak table. I'd love to know what he had on his mind now. He leaned forward and lowered his voice, "Would you like to make us an offer?"

"Actually, I expected you to do the same. But I'm not going to beat around the bush. I'd like to completely distance myself from both production and sales. I'd like to use my right to grant the license to whoever I want but stick to the Admins' sales rates demands. Instead, I'd like to get my cut and the clan's full support—ideally, something like honorary membership. I do understand the importance of discipline and subordination, but still I'd hate to have to go through your marching drills. So I'd love to be allowed to skip the soldier's stage."

Eric's face reflected surprise. He'd probably never even thought there could be other ways to join the clan but the standard cadet-private-sergeant chain. But somehow I found it hard to believe that their esteemed bookkeeper, Mr. Simonov, had had to do a month of square-bashing with other junior cadets. It meant that in certain cases, the clan could indeed make exceptions.

Dan stared at me, thoughtful and appraising. Wonder if he was toying with the idea of locking me up in some bunker of their own? Finally, he spoke,

"I've heard you out. I don't have enough authority to decide whether we can accept it or not. Only the clan's General Council can do that, including its Dark Branch. One thing I can tell you now: even our clan is not powerful enough to handle this caboodle. No one will forgive us this gain in power. Fear and jealousy will force our opponents to join forces. Together they'll crush us. You can't just share this recipe with our clan. We need to create a coalition to exploit this. We make up part of a rather powerful military alliance. If we make them this sort of offer, they'll join us. This is the standpoint I will present at the Council."

Right. This was how I'd thought it would be. "How much time will it take them to come to a decision?"

"Tomorrow I'll let you know their response. I'll start calling it up straight away. Do you have some more cigarettes for the presentation?"

I nodded, handing over another handful. About thirty, that should be enough. Noticing Eric's pleading eyes, I sneaked another dozen to him. For a moment I wondered whether I should mention Taali's problem and then thought against it. I really should wait for the Council's decision regarding my status. It was one thing to decide whether to help a total stranger and quite another to a fellow clan member.

Dan placed the cigarettes carefully into his pocket and turned back to me. "What would you say to staying in our castle for a couple days?"

That got me thinking. The offer was curious any way you looked at it. It could be his wish to protect me—whether sincere or not. It could also mean the chained-in-the-bunker scenario. I doubted they'd go that far: after the generous offer I'd made, they would be more interested in cooperation than in ruthless kidnapping. And still I decided to decline it. Wouldn't be a good thing to so openly reveal my vulnerability, coming to the Vets cap in hand.

"Thanks, man, but I don't think so. In any case, just for the sake of my paranoia, I might check the recruitment page and hire a couple bodyguards. Just for peace of mind."

He shook his head. "We don't leave our men in the lurch. You're the clan's friend now. Your offer promises considerable returns, and we don't trust strangers with guarding our property. I'll bring a few special-ops guys. They'll rent a room next door to yours. At least two of them will be hanging about your room at all times. If you need to go out, they'll be around, too."

A generous offer, hard to resist. To hire a stellar group like that would have cost me five grand a day. Now I really had nothing to worry about. No one could just kidnap me on the sly—and if it came to fighting, a group like that was capable of handling considerably superior forces engaging them until reinforcements arrived.

With that, we closed our business talks. We stayed on for a hearty meal, discussing their open house day. Apparently, the Russian salad had received first prize at the cooking contest. By way of a prize, the clan was now buying the license for the recipe from the woman who'd made it, so now it was going to be a permanent staple in the castle's mess hall. Eric gave me a wink and promised to sneak out the recipe for me.

"Fucking womanizer," Dan chuckled.

I laughed and gave Eric a high five, slapping his palm with gusto. What a man! The recipe was worth it, even if he had to shag the whole kitchen and the dishwashing girl to boot.

"And what about this familiars' contest?" I remembered. "My kitty got the second prize. Who got the first one, then?"

They exchanged glances and burst into laughter.

"What?" I leaned across the table. "Come on, spill the beans."

"You won't believe it."

"I would. At the moment, I'll believe anything."

"Winnie the Pooh. A white teddy with a pink nose."

They'd said I wouldn't believe it. So I didn't. "What do you mean, Winnie the Pooh? The cartoon one?"

"Remember the little girl? Our captain's daughter?"

"The one who's forever twelve years old?"

"Exactly. So she did this quest. A totally boring and intensely useless social one, eighteen tasks to complete. Those who do it are either masochists or they just can't forget the little puppy they used to have at home in real life so they want to bring the fucking thing here. The final prize allows them to upload their pet's picture and have it animated. I've no idea what AI thought about it. Maybe it was just exercising its sense of humor. But if you come across a ghostly white bear in one of the castle corridors, just offer him a slice of meat. It won't pester you much."

"Meat. I thought Winnie the Pooh liked *honey*? Did you try to give him honey?"

"He won't eat it. He turned out to be a carnivore, apparently. But very cute to look at."

Oh well, stranger things happen at sea.

With all that talk I'd missed the arrival of the five special-ops guys. They'd installed themselves at a table next to ours and were now sipping their beers casting greedy glances at the dying cigarette smoke.

Dan called up their leader. "Meet Lieutenant Brown. A 160 wizard. He'll be nursing you for the next twenty-four hours. Create a group and grant them a teleport permission. You never know, they might need to pull you out quickly. Also, allow them access to your room."

Reluctantly I did what he'd suggested. At least this way I might find out if I'd been a total idiot trusting the Vets or if I could actually rely on them. Just in case, I sent a word to Taali describing the situation. That way, at least there would be some trace left in case I disappeared from my hotel room.

With that, I parted from Eric and his secret-service friend. They teleported to their castle while I took cover in my room from a new wave of tobacco lovers.

I had virtually no cigarettes left—about thirty or so. I gave half to the bartender telling him to distribute them however he saw fit. Then I announced that I'd run out completely and was temporarily unavailable. I walked up the stairs to the third floor. Lieutenant Brown entered my room with me, to study the layout and give a few instructions to his men. I told them how much I appreciated their help and gave them the remaining smokes. In return, he shook my hand long and hard and promised to guard me so that not even a fly could harm me.

Finally, everybody faded away. I collapsed on the bed. I still had to check out the auction and see the auto buy results. They were good. I now had three hundred doses of pollen and enough of the other ingredients for a thousand cigarettes. I could have bought more but I had set my prices low hoping to profit from their *Buy Now!* offers.

My glance happened on the top sales section. It was raging with buyers discussing the offer of the first—according to the description—cigarette in the digital world. The bids had reached a thousand gold and apparently weren't going to stop at that. My inner greedy pig turned blue, gasping for air. How I understood him! I'd spent a lot of time and money making the product, then gave away a lot of my stocks for free while someone in that crowd had thought he was clever and was now raking it in? Oh, no. That wasn't the way to go. From now on, I was going to cream it off, too.

I rolled up my sleeves and set about working, casting occasional glances at the offending auction. Three hours later I realized I hated the crafting process body and soul (or whatever perma players had). Time to hand over the license before it did me in. I dreaded the prospect of spending the next two hundred years rolling cigarettes in my room. God forbid.

Finally, I sat back, admiring the results. A long ribbon of finished cigarettes snaked across the table. Two hundred fifty.

Now: Life of a Masochist, part two. I formed auction lots selling them one at a time, adding one lot every half an hour. Starting price: one gold. They were welcome to bid it up as much as they wanted.

I didn't expect Taali. She had some unfinished business in real life. So I had to spend the night on my own. Very soon I should maybe start thinking about moving up a floor. I needed more space if Taali really wanted to move in with me. Also, it was a status thing. I sent my Mom a surprise MMS describing my visit to the vets' castle and adding a few pics of nice views, prizes and the awards ceremony. Undoubtedly, Mom would want to know who the Elfa was that was clinging to her sonny boy. It was about time they met, really. I just hoped Mom could get used to the possibility of an out-of-body life. I might even convince her to move here, too. A young healthy body and a new world full of colors and sounds—that should be enough for her mind to shed the chains of old age. She might even find herself someone in the digital crowd. The Constable Major Medved seemed serious and imposing enough.

The financial question seemed to be coming under control. The tournament had helped a lot, of course, both in gold and in items. But the main source of our future wellbeing had to be the sale of cigarettes and cigarette licenses. Which justified a drink. I rummaged through my bag and pulled out the vial I'd stashed away for a rainy day.

Unknown Skill Elixir
Item class: Epic
Contains a random skill. In order to learn the skill, drink the vial's contents.

Instead of a rock bottom, the initial financial abyss had now ended with a gigantic trampoline. I wasn't broke which meant I had to drink it. I was facing an eternity where even a useless skill like creating illusions or setting off fireworks could prove useful one day.

I clasped the vial, and the stopper popped open. In a spray of colorful sparks, a pleasant fragrance filled the room. Well, here's to the future!

Congratulations! You've learned a unique skill: Splitting

Cast Time: 0

Mana Expenditure: 0

By using this skill, you can split your summoned pet into a certain number of controlled creatures (the number corresponding to the Skill's current level). Their levels will equal that of the initial creature divided by the number of new pets. The split creature's maximum level cannot exceed that of the caster.

Bah. Didn't understand one word of it. I read through the message again. Aha, now I started to get it. If I summoned a level 50 pet, I could split him into two level 25 ones. Oh well. As far as I was concerned, the basic skill was less that useless. Could I improve on it, maybe?

I studied the menu. They had to have two upgrade options. One was increasing the number of the creatures. And the other... Now the other was quite different. For every point invested, the little splinters grew two levels. In theory, if I added twelve points now, I'd have two level 50 pets. That was just too good. Shame I only had one point to spare. Also, my leveling up would increase the gap so I'd end up investing half my talents into this skill just to keep the pets in the top range.

All that deduction had given me a headache. I had to sit down with a calculator and look into it properly. Tomorrow, maybe. I needed to sleep on it.

I spent the morning reading the news. Predictably, the arrival of the cigarettes had made the headlines. At least my name hadn't come up anywhere. Either they'd failed to figure me out or decided not to expose me for the time being. They all spoke about an anonymous player who'd managed to sidestep the tobacco ban, hypothesizing when exactly the Admins would close his little shop. Experts advised buying up cigarette lots and sitting on them, predicting prices would soar when cigarettes once again became rarities. This was advice I could really appreciate. Had I known the name of the expert, I'd have sent him some money for his piece of mind. Actually, could it be Dan trying to sell part of the samples I'd given him? I wouldn't put it past him. This kind of scheme was right up his alley.

Having said that... I opened the auction and checked the previous night's auto buy results. The insiders must have noticed the rise in demand for pollen; both the offer and the prices had grown overnight as the market was finding a new balance. I had a stock of over two thousand doses and even more of secondary ingredients. I could now go easy on buying. The auto buy had diligently dispensed with all of the seven hundred gold I'd entrusted it with, and was now flashing its little light reminding me to top up the balance. I did as it requested, then reset it to concentrate on pollen.

The prices for cigarette lots kept soaring out of all proportion. The current auctions had them in the region of five hundred-plus apiece. The auto buy account was flooded with private messages. Some expressed their disbelief; others threatened; a few naive players asked me to share the recipe. A news reporter hassled me for a private interview. That could prove useful a bit later once I'd closed the license deal: then I'd have to take steps to remove the target from my back.

I wrote him back asking about suitable interview dates and other details. If I could play for time for a bit, I could hopefully come out of the closet by then.

I rolled another hundred cigarettes, for myself and for networking purposes. My bodyguards were already in the group chat, asking if I wanted to join them for morning coffee. I got the hint. I invited them in and we had a nice little talk sending fragrant smoke curling to the ceiling.

Finally, Taali arrived. She stormed into the room forcing the bodyguards to jump up and line the walls. She stared at the haze-filled room, indignant, then opened the window and waved her hands, trying to banish the colorful smoke from the room. The lieutenant chuckled and snapped his fingers. A tangible breeze swept through the chamber.

That got me curious. "What's this spell you have? Draft #5?"

He didn't appreciate my sense of humor. "It's not a spell. Pure mental force."

"What do you mean, mental? I don't think I remember this skill in the game."

"There is no skill. There's an aptitude. You see, those who've been digital for a while—and I've been here for the best part of two years now—we don't seem to depend as much on the game code. We start to push the envelope a bit as we learn to control our own power outside of the limits set for us by the game developers. Nothing extraordinary, really. Children begin to grow, old people rejuvenate, and little by little, we learn to control magic. Your own element starts to obey first: I'm an air wizard, you know. And then... God knows."

Taali and I didn't move, digesting what he'd just said. "Holy cow," she whispered.

The wizzy nodded. "Exactly. It's not a game anymore. Hasn't been for quite some time—for us, at least. Probably, if two digitized partners wanted a baby really badly, I can't see why they couldn't..."

Now we all fell silent. The world puzzle had turned again, revealing to us its new sides and colors. The bodyguards tactfully made themselves scarce while Taali was pressing me for more details, oohing and aahing with concern. But behind it I could see she was proud of her man, a go-getter who wasn't going with the flow but went out on a limb seeking opportunities and grabbing them. I felt flattered even if I realized that her noises of support were just one of the things that made for a happy marriage. Some women don't seem to understand such simple stuff as they vent their indignation with their Tom, Dick or Harry apparently not being able to get off the couch and change their lives for the better.

As I lounged on the bed admiring my paladin maid, I remembered Fuckyall's gift. I took out the bracelet and looked up its characteristics.

Weeping Shackles
Item Class: Rare
Upgrades: Life Stone x2
Class Restrictions: Paladin
Minimal level: 150
+90 to Armor, +40 to Strength, +40 to Agility
When the owner sustains damage, Life Tears have a 24% chance of spraying, restoring the group members' life +120 pt.

Now that was a bracelet! I didn't even want to know how much it cost, or my inner greedy pig would smother me with a pillow in my sleep. "Taali? I've got something for you."

She turned away from studying her portrait on the wall and gave me an inviting and curious smile. I didn't beat around the bush and handed her the item.

She peered at it. Her eyes opened wide. "You can't be serious. Just don't tell me you've farmed it yourself. Although I wouldn't put it past you."

I shrugged, faking indifference. "A swap. I traded it with Fuckyall. It's his personal item... was."

"Holy cow," she whispered, pressing it to her chest. "I'll have to grow into it. Back in real life, I have this solid silver bracelet... and I think this one costs more. It's all so relative..."

She jumped onto the bed and straddled me. "Want another example of relativity?"

Slowly, she began undoing the top buttons of her blouse as I watched, intrigued. She reached under the collar and pulled out a small blue stone on a piece of string.

"Do you recognize it?" she asked. "A gnoll camp and a sad-eyed girl..."

"A laurite," I said. "*The* laurite..."

"That's it," Taali gave me a proud, happy smile. "The one you gave me on the day we met. I'm sorry, but it's more precious to me than Fuckyall's bracelet. That's relativity for you..."

I reached out and touched the stone. I looked into her eyes and gently pulled the laurite down toward me, making her lean closer and closer.

The next two hours went too quickly. Still, I couldn't complain. Tired but pleased with ourselves, we were lounging in bed when I received Dan's message. Apparently, the meeting was taking too long; he didn't expect them to come to a decision before tomorrow. He was leaving me the bodyguards begging me not to stick my neck out, with a warning that the situation was heating up and sharing the tobacco pie had created more waves than we'd expected. He attached a large file from Mr. Simonov containing his propositions on forming a tobacco alliance and creating an AlterWorld tobacco market. I scrolled through pages of diagrams of suggested volumes, market coverage rates and distribution channels. Dan insisted I forwarded the file to the Admins straight away and asked for a green light. If we got it, pushing the Council for the right decisions would be much easier.

Oh well. He and his friends seemed to be working hard and their objectives seemed to coincide with mine. I forwarded it.

Now I needed to decide what to do with myself in the meantime. Taali didn't have this problem: blaming the full-immersion time restrictions, she took off back into the real world. After racking my brains for a while, I remembered the idea I'd been toying with for a while. I still had a good half a ton of loot that Teddy was lugging around. I had to sort it out but I really didn't want to go out into the courtyard. Skeptically I glanced over the room, pushed all the furniture into the corners and pulled out the Summoning Whistle.

The room rang with the bear's happy hollering, sounds of smashed crockery and a crushed chair. I went flying onto the bed. Apparently, the room was smaller than I thought. The door crashed open as one of the bodyguards attempted to break in. He hit the bear's side blocking the doorway and bounced back. I heard the electric crackle of a spell being cast and hurried to remove the bear.

I was facing a scene of complete desolation. Now I knew the full meaning of the bull in a china shop thing. The lieutenant froze in the doorway. He cut short the almost-cast spell, shaking the remaining sparks off his fingers and shrugged, studying the room.

"You're too much, you know that? If you need to summon your bear so badly, why not do it downstairs in the yard? We'll cover you."

"Sorry, guys. I've never done well in geometry. I just failed to fit the bear into the space available."

We all stomped down the stairs. As I sorted through the loot, the passersby got an eyeful of my bear—a rare sight for low-level players. A second lieutenant arrived and helped his troops to carry all the goodies to the nearest store. Here I must mention that all five bodyguards were company officers which said a lot about their professionalism and their place in the clan. They all laughed at my penny loot but apparently enjoyed helping me, even if to escape the boredom. I made about two hundred gold—peanuts considering the recent developments. At least I managed to sort through a whole lot of crafting ingredients I had set aside. I had something to do now, leveling alchemy. Finally, I checked Teddy's characteristics to make sure I hadn't missed any spare points.

Type: Riding Mount
Name: Hummungus (Red Bear)
Level: 26
Strength: 80
Constitution: 50
Attack: 57-71
Speed: 10 mph
Riders: 2
Weight-carrying capacity: 1000 lbs.
Special abilities: Armor Carrier, Arms Carrier, Mule II, Transporter

The latter ability, which I'd chosen at level 25, allowed me to sit a second player on my mount: an option that became more and more important in the light of my socialization and especially my relationship with Taali. That's life for you! The process of a battle bear turning into a family couch.

Once I was sold out, I treated the guys to a dinner and succumbed to their cue, distributing more cigarettes to their night watch. Then I walked back upstairs to my room. Until then, that recipe had been nothing but a nuisance. Talking about making a rod for one's own back. There I was, sitting in my room like a chunk of cheese in a mousetrap. Everyone around me was twitching their nose, sniffing it, too scared to raise their little claws to snatch it. Which was a good thing. I didn't really want to be clawed by anyone who wanted a piece of me.

The first auctions were now finishing. The cigarette lots went for one to two thousand gold. I only had the mass media to thank for building up the right amount of hysteria. Now, about every half-hour, another few hundred gold dropped into my account. The Admins made sure they got their cut. At least they hadn't taxed Fuckyall's bracelet. Still, I probably shouldn't abuse the trading market.

The reporters had offered me three thousand for an exclusive. That sounded quite interesting. My reply was noncommittal; I wanted them to stew in their own juices for a while.

I spent the rest of the day doing an alchemist's finicky job. I checked the ingredients to see what I could do with them and what else I might still need; then I bought up the missing bits, including a whole recipe library. Soon my camp kit included Night

Vision, Absolute Vision, Fish Breath, Minor Levitation, several poisons and antidotes and even a dozen vials of attack spells—the local version of Molotov cocktails.

Finally, I received the Admins' answer. Overall, they approved the idea of an alliance and only suggested different production rates. They also promised to install smoke protection for the under-18s as the first step to the product's legalization. I forwarded everything to Dan and in another thirty minutes, received his invitation to arrive at the castle at a staff officers' luncheon: to announce the results, so to say. They expected me at ten in the morning via a portal my bodyguards were supposed to create.

I loved the postscript:

PS. BTW, do you think you could bring some cigs along? Take as many as you can. The staff officers here keep passing the smokes around like school kids which is a bit ridiculous considering our position. Tnx a bunch.

Chapter Twenty-Seven

I spent the rest of the evening lounging in bed, devouring another novel by my favorite author. My book subscription kept flooding my inbox with new titles, provided I had the time to read.

I fell asleep without even knowing it—and awoke strangely. Blade-rattling and spell-bellowing suddenly broke the still of the night. I sat up, my heart pounding, when the door swung open letting in several warriors I hadn't seen before. They went for me. I tried to jump up; my feet got caught in the blanket and I collapsed onto the thin floral rug.

Warning! Group portal activation.
Destination: Sunrise Zone of the East Castle.

The portal popped open, and I tumbled onto the portal hall's stone tiles.

"Shit," my lungs forced out the air. Crouching, I looked around. Lieutenant Brown froze next to me in an awkward pose. He had barely half life left, his health dwindling rapidly. Dozens of wounds covered his body, some obviously not good, smoking and gushing black blood. One arm dangled uselessly at his side. The Lieutenant didn't seem to notice it; his eyes were glazed over, his lips moved as he posed questions in combat chat to his men in the inn.

A few more fighters ran up to me and helped me to my feet. The cleric on duty was hurriedly healing the Lieutenant while my bodyguards started appearing around me in their crystal resurrection spheres. One, two, three... pause. Finally, the last one. All present and correct.

Dan burst into the hall, followed by a captain and two dozen fighters in full gear. Lieutenant Brown raised his hand to stop them.

"We don't need reinforcements. My guys are all here in their underpants, look," he nodded at the bodyguards hurriedly pulling on some simple khaki clothes someone had fetched from the guards' room. Which was logical, considering the fact that they had to be respawning here all the time so someone had to make sure they didn't walk around the castle half-naked.

Dan raised his hand, attracting his attention. "Report."

Brown waited for the captain to nod his affirmative and stood to attention. "Mercenaries, names hidden. At least four groups of three, levels slightly higher than ours, buffed up to the gills. Poisoned weapons. The two rogue groups managed to come real close before our Alex could observe them, and you know him, he's not a bad stealther himself. They engaged our guards' post in the corridor, then opened the doors on us and the guarded object. According to orders, I attempted to pull Max out. Three times they broke the spell. It's a miracle he managed to escape. My men lasted another fifteen seconds. That's it."

"Which means?"

"It's an elite team job, the best you can find, not for hire. I have a funny feeling it's the Olders."

Dan raised a surprised eyebrow. The Lieutenant went on, "First, the bar belongs to them. The attackers knew where we were and they seemed to know the rooms' exact layout. The whole thing was choreographed like a practice fight. Plus, the guards failed to arrive—I think they had no right of entry to the top floors as they're private property. Secondly, the speed with which they opened the guest apartment doors. I even think they pretended to be picking the locks while in fact they had full access to them to begin with. To open a third-degree protection lock in ten seconds is bordering on fantasy. But two locks..."

A rogue bodyguard nodded his agreement.

"Finally, it's just so like them. A leopard never changes its spots. In real life, these get-rich-quick Russian oligarchs never cared about anyone's feelings. They took what they wanted where they saw it, period. So here too it's their knee-jerk reaction to a new stimulus. They wanted the recipe, so they sent their henchmen to get it."

Dan turned to the captain. "Scarface, how many times do I need to ask? Give the kid to my analytics department. With this head of his, he shouldn't be running around the woods with your commandos."

The captain gave him a fat finger. "I've already loaned you our Sonya from the maintenance department. For a week, you said. I've been trying to get her back for the last six months."

He turned to the lieutenant. "Good job. Nothing to say. Go to bed now, all of you. In the morning you can do a quick corpse run and pick up your stuff."

He gave a few more orders, then cast me a probing look. "I'm Ruslan," he held out his hand. "Special troops commander, Forces of Light. You sure know how to open a can of worms."

I shook the offered hand and gave him a guilty smile: like, it's not my fault I'm so popular.

Dan slapped my shoulder. "Cheer up, dude. We'll make sure you're safe. Come on now, I'll take you to the guest sector to get some sleep. I tell you what, it won't be easy for them to get to you here."

Life was getting too complicated for me. I questioned his account of the events. The Olders? Quite possible. Or could it be the Vets themselves, staging a show for one naive viewer as its audience? To make sure he arrived at the negotiations suitably compliant, impatient to get rid of the patent which by then would be burning a hole in his pants? I didn't for one moment doubt Dan's ability to run a double game, but as for the brave captain and his men... I wasn't so sure.

Dan took me down a corridor to a door guarded by a couple of soldiers. A Torch of True Flame burned by the doorway. He reminded me that the staff meeting was at 10 a.m., saluted and left on some other secret agenda of his. Did he ever sleep? Despite the absence of a material carrier, our minds tended to overload and needed some rest, sending us into a deep and happy sleep. We did need less of it, though. Four hours were enough for me now to recharge my batteries; the rest of the night I just stayed in bed out of habit.

My room here was a cut above the hotel one. Its size, its expensive interior design, a fancy fireplace—it was all supposed to point at a visitor's status. I crawled inside the four-poster fit for a king and, after some tossing and turning, finally switched off.

At eight in the morning, I was awoken by the sun peeking into a narrow window and by a sergeant's icy commands as he ordered the youngsters around the parade square. I had a quick wash and looked out the door to ask the guards if one could get any coffee there. They promised to send someone and indeed, ten minutes later a pretty NPC waitress brought in coffee and some sandwiches.

That was interesting. Apparently, the castle control interface allowed them to hire in-game characters. Who would want to play the part of a servant, a cook or even some basic guard on the walls? I knew nothing about this substantial part of game content. What could I do with my own home here? The Vets seemed to have some control over teleports and bind points, to say nothing of the fighting arena which apparently offered a lot of leeway: just the other day we'd been fighting there to near death while now it served as a training ground for a bunch of cadets hammering each other with hatchets—and not a single scratch. Plus, instead of sand, they were prancing around what now imitated a stone plateau.

I remembered my promise to roll some more cigarettes. I still had some time, so I opened the auction and checked the auto buy. It had been working hard, amassing about three thousand doses of pollen. The average price had risen somewhat as the suppliers tried to feel out the demand. This was another part-time opportunity if I needed it. Once the clans had the license, the demand for ingredients would soar. They would need millions of doses daily. And once the Admins realized that the shortage of ingredients prevented them from deriving more revenue, you could expect Gigantic Fly-Traps to sprout along all city ditches. Alternatively, they could encourage cultivation to give the game farmers something to do. In any case, the prices for raw materials had to explode. Should I really invest all my available cash into cigarette ingredients? I had to upgrade my basic Auction Depot, anyway, as it was now almost 90% full. That also cost money, making me two hundred gold poorer. Still, I shouldn't complain; my auction account looked healthy with almost five thousand gold having trickled in overnight. Shame all that easy money had to end in a couple days.

Oh, what was that? Another grand gold jingled into my account. I checked the logs. There is was, Ogre's Siege Shield, sold. Found a connoisseur, excellent.

In whatever time I had left, I rolled almost two hundred cigarettes. After some thought, I took some colored ribbons—I now had plenty—and tied the cigs into batches of twenty. That was it. Enough. I looked out the window where the clan's senior officers were gathering in the courtyard. I noticed a few Dark ones among them. I could distinctly see two orcs, a Drow and one hell of a troll. What were they waiting to see, rabbit tricks? I decided to go out for a look.

The moment I walked out they all beamed. I looked around, doubtful that I could be the source of their happy grins, and offered, "How about a smoke, guys?"

Bingo. The men exhaled happily, getting closer. "Got some to share?"

I ripped open a couple bunches. Casting suspicious glances at the ribbons, the officers accepted my offer with military gusto, each helping himself to three or four. The troll scooped a good dozen and bellowed with a shy smile, "My lungs are too big. I smoke one in a single draw. No one wants to share with me anymore."

None of us had a light so we had to commandeer a nearby greenhorn to fetch us some matches from the kitchen. Finally the whiffs of smoke started swirling around. Our Prometheus, a.k.a. the flame-bearing rookie, showed no desire to leave.

"Comrade Colonel! Permission to speak to the civilian!"

"Granted."

He turned to me, "Spare a smoke?"

The officers fell speechless at such insubordination. Still, now they were too relaxed to have the kid punished. I didn't want to ruin the mood and gave him a cigarette. The boy lit up with a practiced hand, but instead of smoke, he began disgorging colorful soap bubbles. It was weird but also so funny we were rolling on the ground laughing—all of us, including the orc Colonel and the Commandant.

"What's all this?" the troll groaned, wiping away the tears of laughter.

"This, comrades, is a built-in under-18 protection system," answered Dan. How I hated his habit of creeping up on people.

One of the captains choked laughing and frowned at the greenhorn. "Cadet Burr! I thought your application said you were a twenty-year-old paratrooper? You piece of shit! We don't need no young offenders in here. Wait! Where d'you think you're going? Sleazy punk!"

He cast some sort of paralyzing spell. Two guards on duty rushed in from the watchhouse to intercept the kid. Unexpectedly to everyone, he resisted the spell, then smashed some vial on the ground at his feet. Immediately, the whole area around and above him was filled with an impenetrable black haze. We recognized the sound of an opening portal.

"Fucking piece of shit! He's gone, look," the Colonel spat, turning to Dan. I could read a whole bunch of emotions—from surprise to hate—on the agent's face.

"How can you explain it, Major?" the Colonel went on. "Spies are having a smoke with staff officers and you don't seem to know what's happening in your own castle?"

Dan gritted his teeth, "My fault, Sir. I'll look into it."

"Please do," the Colonel added, softening. "Let's go in now. Enough of making targets of ourselves. They've already laid the table in the small hall."

The enormous breakfast room was too good for its name. About sixty feet long, it boasted two massive fireplaces and some monstrous furniture.

Despite the fake period interior, the breakfast didn't resemble a prim British meal. In our equally fake armor, we looked more like a conquering party of Vikings waiting for the ice to clear the river. We just didn't fit in with the carved wainscots, tall straight-backed chairs and four breakfast forks.

Dan sensed my feelings. "This room is used for semi-official meetings," he whispered. "We have to conform. In other places, you won't see all this pompous shit. And in your own room you can put a TV on the wall if you really want to. Having said that, it won't work, anyway..."

Once the breakfast was over, we moved to the private meetings room next door. Here, soft easy chairs stood around light tables laden with fruit and wine. Ashtrays were brought in and everybody lit up.

The Colonel gestured Dan to speak. He turned to me. "Max. Talking about your proposition. It's equal parts of generosity and danger. You can't even imagine the amount of work we've done to draft the prospective alliance. In principle, all the interested parties have given their prior consent. Now we only need to settle a few details... the rest is up to you," he paused, looking down at the floor. "Two things. There'll be nine clans in the alliance which will make it a force to be reckoned with. In case you ask, the Olders aren't in it. Not many people like them and even fewer want their influence to grow. This is one of the pillars of our agreement. No one's really interested in the Vets' strengthening their positions here, either. That's why the Alliance is against the patent owner's belonging to one of the signatory clans. We've discussed all the possibilities and now we suggest you start your own clan. In name only, don't worry. A clan that would consist of one person—yourself. You will join the Alliance as its tenth clan. Which will also simplify the process of sharing the profits: two percent to each clan. Including yours. Tell me what you think. Take your time. I'm in no hurry."

What I think! I leaned back in the easy chair and closed my eyes. Things were much more complicated than I thought. My own clan. It gave me access to some really nice things: special interfaces, possibilities to build a castle or to buy out a newly discovered one. And lots of other freebies. On one hand, all those extra options without any of the responsibility were only welcome. On the other, I wasn't going to integrate into an already existing powerful structure which could give me the protection I needed. I already knew that you couldn't get anywhere in this world without being part of a powerful group. Then again, what made me think I couldn't? In a way, making part of our cluster's most powerful alliance was even better than just being a clan member. Look at Dan: with all his cloak-and-dagger panache, they had still taken him to task, rubbing his nose in a puddle of piss like a puppy in front of everyone. And he had to grin and salute, suppressing his own character, as in, 'My fault, Sir, it won't happen again, Sir!' Did I really want that?

In actual fact, a clan of my own could give me the independence I craved while Alliance membership offered the protection I needed. The only downside was the inability to join serious clan raids, but I still had to grow a lot before I could start thinking about that. By then, it could all change.

Now, the two percent. I had to admit I expected more. But judging by the forces involved, it was a good job I'd managed to at least get something. It was about time I removed the target off my back, handed over the exclusive license and became an anonymous rich nonentity—eventually, I hoped.

I opened my eyes. The others were studying me. I nodded. "I agree on all points. I do have a few questions I'd like to discuss later with Dan. No need for all the staff to attend."

A sigh of relief swept across the room. The clan was now looking at a new stage of political and financial gain.

The Colonel—who turned out to be the clan leader's deputy himself—raised his glass to the successful closing of the deal. We spent some more time discussing the details. Dan was asking for another day or two to collect all the signatures under the agreement. He asked me to stay put and create my own clan. The guest apartment was at my complete disposal, and they granted Taali free access to the castle.

Dan didn't like to beat about the bush. As soon as the meeting was closed, he came over to me. He looked worried. Despite the successful talks, he had too much on his plate: the inn assault, and now this underage spy. And these were only the things I knew or thought I knew.

"What do you want to tell me?" he asked.

"Is there a place we could talk?"

He gave it some thought. "Your place is probably the closest."

When we walked into my enormous apartment, the first thing I gave him was the rest of the cigarettes. He forced a smile. "Tobacco is the root of all evil."

"Exactly my point. I don't think it would be a good idea for me to go back to the Olders' inn. I've been meaning to ask the clan to allow me to stay here for a month or two. Hope I won't be in your way?"

Dan looked up and moved his lips, calculating. "Sure you can. I'll take care of the commandant. You can stay here. I'll give you full personal access. Anything else?"

"Yeah. It's personal, sort of. I need to know something that happened in real life about six months ago. You think you could check it out for me, whether it's true or not?"

"Go ahead."

I told him what I'd learned from Taali, giving him as many facts as I could remember so he had something to work with. The moment I finished, Dan nodded. "It's all true."

"What's true?"

"The whole story, start to finish. Taali, a.k.a. Tania Semyakina. Eighteen. Lives with her mother. Their relationship is strained. No boyfriend or partner. Her sister, Katia Semyakina, committed suicide about six months ago. You know why. I don't think you'll be interested in details, like who paid whom and how much. Sorry, man. We had to double-check you and your associates. Too much money at stake. We had no right to bet on a mysterious dark horse called Laith."

I didn't say a word. What else did I want? The game ended the moment the logout button stopped working. This was life now. And Dan was no cute and cuddly character but a professional secret agent working for a major military organization. When was I supposed to get used to the fact that AlterWorld had two sides to it: one that was a game and the other which was perma reality. The world kept changing, offering you one side, then the other, making you play, then rubbing your nose into your own gullibility as you lost touch with life. Now I knew why veteran permas often couldn't tell game sequences from reality.

"I see. Thank you, man. Then you probably know what I meant to ask you about?"

He shrugged, evasive, as if saying, *I might, but you're the one who needs this conversation so it's up to you to speak.* He wasn't the one to show his cards first.

"Taali wants to make it even," I said. "She wants to do it herself. To both scumbags and the police bitch. She needs help and advice, probably weapons, and she will need cover. And once it's over, she'll need to buy some time to go perma."

Dan pursed his lips and fell silent. Seeing his hesitation, I pulled a ring out of my pocket. The clan's ring. I lay it on the table.

He picked up the item and gave me a long look. Then he handed it back to me.

"You don't flash this kind of thing like that. Very well. I have the right men and connections in real life. But they won't work for nothing. It'll cost you."

"How much?"

"They'll need to tail each target for a couple weeks. They'll have to work out a plan, find a position for a hitman, decide on his control, cover and withdrawal. Then it's entirely up to her. They're not going to risk first degree charges for her. We can help her collect and analyze all information and present her with our recommendations. And we'll help her with the gun, of course. Plenty of that crap around. Basically, you're looking at ten grand USD."

I rubbed the bridge of my nose. That was a lot. Having said that, I still had all the pickings from the tobacco business to take. I could try to raise at least some of it before the news of the mass tobacco production hit the media. Taali, too, had some savings. If push came to shove, I could borrow some from the Vets. I had a funny feeling my credit with them was going through the roof at the moment.

Another question. How sure was I that I should get into it in the first place? Apart from risking a serious sum of money, there was also a slim chance of me dropping myself in it and another, albeit infinitesimal, danger of framing Mom for it. These were the only arguments against the whole idea.

Now for the arguments in its favor. First, I had given her my word. Secondly, this was my woman asking me for help. Thirdly, I'd had the real world's leniency and corruption up to my ears. Now I had a perfect opportunity to give the bad guys what for and see them collapse and croak. It didn't matter who the bad guys were: a couple of self-indulgent Muslim kids or our own cops who'd lost perspective of their power. No, I had to have the right.

Dan was watching my face and probably had no problem reading my thoughts. He nodded. "I can see you've made up your mind. Can you raise the money?"

"I think so. I'll need a couple of days. I also need to discuss it with Taali. You think you trust your new alliance partner enough to lend him some cash if needed?"

"We'll think of something."

He rose, making it clear he was finished with me. "You discuss it. Keep me posted."

I showed him to the door, nodded to the bodyguards outside and walked back into the room. A slight movement caught my eye; I swung round, suppressing a shriek of surprise.

A white Winnie the Pooh sat by the table. Casting malicious glances at me, he was hurriedly finishing off the ham out of my sandwiches.

Chapter Twenty-Eight

Taali liked our new home. She even managed to befriend the vicious Winnie. Before she arrived, I'd been doing my best to get rid of him. Winnie had taken the most comfortable soft chair by the fireplace, the one I'd been looking forward to myself. But the monster hissed and bared his teeth, slipping out of my grip and stubbornly staying put. Finally I gave up and dragged his chair aside, then brought a new one for myself and put it closer to the fire. For a while, Winnie cussed like a trucker. Then he fell quiet... and a second later, I heard the sounds of a chair being dragged across the floor as the monster pushed it back to the fire. This was how Taali found us: two moody figures sitting on both sides of the fireplace.

With her, Winnie turned all cute and cuddly. He allowed her to take him onto her lap and purred as she stroked him. The moment she'd turn away, he'd cast me unfriendly glances, growling.

Predictably, Taali was overjoyed to hear about specialist help and especially the gun. She said she had about three grand stashed away but if she was going perma, then she could sell some stuff for another thousand. At eighteen, she hadn't had enough time to amass much. I had to tell her that she was doing just fine. Especially compared to some other people who had nothing but a bunch of loans to show for their lives.

We spent the rest of the day rolling cigarettes. I worked my way through the overflowing auto buy inbox and flagged messages from those willing to buy in bulk. I immediately wrote back and got a few responses allowing me to place a few dozen private auction lots for a fixed price. Not everyone put their money where their mouth was, but a good half of all offers went through. By the evening, we'd raised over fifteen grand, plus another six from the auction which was still in full swing. The feeding frenzy had started to flag; the prices were going down: apparently, the first rumors about our alliance had already leaked out.

A bit later, Lieutenant Brown brought armfuls of my stuff from the inn. He still had access to my room there. Almost immediately, I received a letter from the inn owners apologizing for the incident and offering a free month's stay as compensation. No, thank you. They were very welcome to their mousetrap.

All in all, we had two thirds of the required sum, enough for a deposit. I was almost sure it would take Dan and his men a good couple of weeks to get their act together—enough time for us to raise the rest.

As we toiled, we discussed my future clan. Apparently, I already had my first volunteer. No one doubted that Taali would join me. But when we came to the clan's name, she showed her responsible side, rejecting my suggestions. Finally, she made up her mind.

"This is your clan," she said. "You're its patriarch. Its father, in other words. Your Elven name means Child of Night. So this is what you should call your clan: Children of Night."

"And how do you suggest we exist in the Lands of Light with this kind of name?"

"Who forces you to reveal it? You can hide it somewhere in the settings. Lots of people do that. You'll still be Laith to everybody, and that's it."

The next day we met Dan again. He accepted the deposit and spent some quality time speaking to Taali, instructing her and asking her for more details. Things got rolling. The countdown had begun.

We decided to turn the signing of the agreement into a promotional opportunity. A new alliance was coming into the world, whether someone liked it or not. We were guaranteed some conflict, anyway, even if no one dared to challenge us—which was unlikely. The mere feeling of their own latent power could drive other clans to solve their difference of opinions by force. This could be a new clan war in the making.

We issued invitations to the media, including the insistent journalist who'd cadged an interview from me. I had to move it if I didn't want to lose the three grand he'd promised. We spent two hours over some coffee and cigarettes, discussing the main points of his future article. I especially insisted on stressing the existence of the exclusive license, to convince whoever it might concern that they shouldn't waste their breath trying to kidnap me in order to get their share of the pie. The clans had decided against splitting production. Instead, we wanted to build large premises, hire some NPC alchemists and gain momentum gradually, in accordance with the Admins' guidelines. Everyone invested an equal share. Each clan also delegated their members to an observers group which was supposed to oversee all production stages from purchase to crafting and sales.

Soon we had a formal signing of the coalition formation memorandum. I did my bit writing out a five-year license in the name of the Alliance, granting them the right to sub-license it to NPCs. That was a huge load off my mind. Despite its promise of prosperity, the whole tobacco saga had bowled me over like a steam roller, leaving dents and black marks. I had to be grateful it hadn't killed me. I wanted to escape it all, to forget all this business speak and politics and just take my time exploring this little-known world. I still had lots of quests in my log. Forbidden Lands were calling my name.

I spent three more days at the castle, just to make sure I was safe. The hype started to settle. Fewer people now bothered me with stupid questions. The story was getting stale; the media had turned their attention to other things. What made headlines now was the new ambitious Inferno raid performed by a group of West European clans. The idea interesting in itself, but what raised it to sensation was the loot from the Inferno Archdemon: the group had returned with the Captured Heart of a God of Light. An artifact this powerful would allow the building of a new temple dedicated to one of the Gods of the Pantheon of Light. Each god promised all sorts of bells and whistles in exchange for a certain percent of experience, mana or gold. I still had no idea whether you could get anything off the Fallen One and whether his pantheon had other deities. I'd failed to get to the Dark Altar when I'd had the chance. As the saying went, if you want something done properly, you'd better do it yourself. And the fragments I'd so painstakingly obtained were proof enough.

I spent evenings playing with the calculator trying to suss out an ideal model of character growth now that I had this Splitting skill. In the end, I decided to set aside every third Talent point and every five days drink the Elixir of Wisdom which gave me another point. Trust me it cost: two grand and a five-day cooldown. But the result was worth it. In a couple of months, I was looking at level 100 with at least 25 spare points, which would give me two level-100 pets. True, it wouldn't double my power: one level-130 pet would be almost as strong as those two. Add to it the leveling gap caused by squirreling extra points, but that was only the beginning...

At the moment, this was the state of my characteristics—not counting the items:

Class: Death Knight
Level: 52
Strength: 32
Intellect: 209 (Mana=2090)
Agility: 0
Spirit: 110
Constitution: 61 (Hits=610)
1 Talent point available. 0 Characteristic points available.

I took the occasion to have a couple dozen fights in the arena. The Vets were curious to see what the Dark class was made of. It wasn't very often that their students could cross swords with a Necro or a Death Knight. In such arena-set friendlies, pure casters were an easy win. Not so if they caught you unawares, in the heat of a fight or just after it when you were low on life. You'd miss their first spell due to the surprise effect, then miss the second one as you looked for the attacker and finally, miss the third one as you attempted to do something about it. So in the field, all these PK wizards with their DpS going through the roof could be a force to be reckoned with. Same went for rogues. Absolutely mad DpS multiplied by stealth and some very nasty combos. Many people believed Thief to be the best PvP class. I tended to agree, at least if you looked at PvP as the need to steal close to someone and drown them in their own blood double quick. But where survival was concerned, whether under attack or against groups, they weren't really up to much.

Surprisingly, paladins proved the toughest opponents. In many respects they were the opposite of me with their buffed-up stats, armor and some serious magic support geared against the Forces of the Dark.

Like in other things, having lots of dough definitely helped. Three times I'd met that guy ten levels below myself, and three times I'd failed miserably. The guy had invested over a hundred grand gold in some unique gear raising his combat potential to at least level 70.

We definitely had fun there. The cadets and fighters proved to be a fearless and easygoing bunch. Most of them were perma players, still euphoric about their new life and the opportunities it brought them.

The arena amazed me with its potential. The commandant apparently hoped for a much needed upgrade from the spoils of the cigarette business. Apart from other odds and sods, the level 7 arena allowed us to generate all sorts of monsters. True, they didn't give you level or experience but that wasn't the idea.

The younger crowd had this thing of fighting till death in the full reality mode, complete with having their graves generated in the castle graveyard. In that case, the beaten party had to resurrect right there in the arena and, accompanied by catcalls, hurry across the courtyard to pick up his stuff. Even I had to do that kind of corpse run a couple times. It was funny. The grave stayed there for three hours and was then teleported to town. The Vets had the option of upgrading their graveyard to cemetery status but were apparently too stingy to go for it, even despite its obvious advantages.

By the end, I was totally fed up with sitting within four walls. The Russian salad was already coming out of my ears. The sight of cigarettes gave me a nervous tick. It was time to come out into the open. Logically, the first thing I needed to do was visit Grym and find out whether I was entitled to anything for freeing the Liches. Also, I hoped to hear something about the First Temple.

Dan granted me permission to bind in the portal hall. I did so happily. I raised Teddy, summoned an average pet to chaperone us and off we went to the city. For me it was a forty-minute walk, but a mount's speed is three times that of a human. Unfortunately, it didn't apply to the pet. Finally, we decided to sacrifice our safety and let the pet's poor soul go. Then we crossed our fingers and trotted toward the city. Once we reached the inhabited zone though, the chat filled with underage killers' cussing so I decided to play it safe and summoned another pet. A five-minute walk wouldn't cost me my crown. Actually, I *was* wearing a crown— and I wouldn't lose it even if someone lifted me by my feet and tipped me upside down.

I passed the Gnoll Hill to the teen players' delight and stepped onto the trail leading to the city. This was the easiest way: I had to turn off into the woods just before the city gates and there we were.

I spoke too soon. I hadn't made a hundred paces when I walked right into a well-organized ambush.

Teddy was trotting just next to me when a rogue unstealthed behind his back attacking him with a long combo. Bellowing, the bear swung round and charged at him, met by the attacker's two blades. Another rogue materialized a dozen feet away from me. He held two swords covered with steaming green poison. The pet froze a couple dozen feet away from us, unable to help—apparently, controlled by an enemy caster. Oh. They made quick work of my Ted. I tried to freeze the rogue nearest to me when a warrior tumbled out of the roadside shrubs and went for me in large leaps. Tavor, the motherfucker.

I switched target and activated Deadman's Hand. It worked. My first stroke of luck. Time to leg it. Nothing was keeping me here. I pressed the mental teleport pictogram. Activation took five and a half seconds. Would I keep the concentration? The rogues went for me, their four blades showering me with blows. My shields seemed to hold. They absorbed damage preventing the two from disrupting my casting.

Two seconds. Would I make it? Tavor bolted, going for me in one large leap, and kicked me to the ground. His special abilities again. The two jumped onto my back twisting my arms, not letting me get to my feet. A mage appeared from behind the trees, a glowing artifact in his hands.

"Quick, hand him over and come right back. I got a word from the gate there's another digital shit coming to the Gnoll Hill. Would be nice to get him, too."

He activated the artifact in two clicks and dropped it onto the ground in front of me. The gold-framed crimson stone filled with light and discharged in a flash.

Warning! Scared Crystal creates an energy spike! This is a spatial anomaly zone! Automatic teleport to the mother stone. Destination: Forest Cats Castle.

With a pop, we fell on the hard, damp stone tiles. The weight of the bodies collapsing on top of me kicked the breath out of me.

Welcome!

Warning! The clan is at war! The castle is concealed by Small Silence Dome. For reasons of confidentiality, all outgoing messages and access to built-in portals are blocked. Contact the commandant to gain clearance to send outgoing traffic.

If you don't agree with the above conditions, you must leave the Castle at once.

Warning! You've been affected by Astral Stone! The unique half-sentient crystal grows smaller copies of itself and teleports them to all corners of the world. When Scared Crystals sense its magic, they create a portal anomaly teleporting the Mage to the mother stone which absorbs all magic energies.

Effect: -30 pt. mana per second.

Some people grabbed me under my arms and dragged me up some stairs, panting and cursing *the fucking rock*. I noticed the gloom of an enormous dungeon and the iron bars that divided it into separate cages. Behind the bars, prisoners' faces showed in the crimson glow of an enormous crystal.

Any struggle was pointless in the grip of those thugs. Nor could I cast a spell on the go. I couldn't even try and smash my head on the stone steps as suicide wasn't part of the game. I tried to send a message to Dan, hoping that the welcome warning was BS. It wasn't. *Contact the commandant to get clearance...*

They pulled me out into a courtyard. Sunshine hit my eyes. I squinted, missing the exact moment when they pushed me out into an arena.

Welcome to a training fight at the Forest Castle Arena!
Laith, level 52, vs. Danathos, level 144
Fight mode: Combat realism, fight to death
Respawn location: arena
Grave location: graveyard
On guard! May the strongest one win!

Before I could raise my eyes, a powerful combo drove a sword up my ribs, sending me to the Rainbow Bridge.

A second later, I respawned. Hot sand was burning my feet. Again they grabbed me under my arms and pulled me running downstairs back into the dungeon, peppering me with kicks and punches. The bastards had it all choreographed as if they were doing it a dozen times a day. Having said that, maybe they did.

They rushed me into the dungeon under the influence of the strange crystal, dragged me into a cage and threw me onto the stones. A knee nailed me to the floor.

"Five minutes," a guard croaked. He spat on the tiles next to my face.

Stone chippings bit into my cheek. When I tried to move, I got a nice kick in the ribs. The other guard placed his dirty boot onto my head, pinning me to the cold floor. Scumbags. Cursing soundlessly, I scrolled through my combat and social logs, moving their names onto a separate list. I was going to find each and every one of them. I'd make them wear Negators, then kick them into a waste pit up to their chins and keep them there until the shit turned rock solid.

"Time," the hoarse guard snapped. "The cuffs!"

They jerked me to my feet. Shackles snapped shut on my wrists. A long chain dangled from them. The guards hooked the chain up to the ceiling. One of them struggled to turn the winch as the rusty mechanism pulled me up. Now I was hanging in the middle of the cage. Even if I had enough mana, I couldn't dream of casting anything in this position.

"He's done. Let's go back to the crystal. They're bringing another one soon."

The other guard wasn't in a hurry. "Wait up. You know me. I always finish with my signature punch."

He took a boxing stance and started jumping around me, pounding my ribs and liver with a rather decent punch sequence. My health shrunk somewhat, a wave of shallow pain running through my body. I winced.

"Quit screwing your face," the boxer guffawed. "This is nothing compared to what our torturer has in store for you. With his experience and imagination..." He raised his voice, addressing the other prisoners. "Am I right, shitheads?"

The dungeon echoed with curses and groans. Someone wept.

"See?" he went on. "Everyone here knows Ivan the Terrible. They have respect for him. So will you. Just keep hanging here for a bit."

The two walked out of my cage and sat down on a bench not far from the wretched stone that took up most of the far wall. Not a wall, really, but rather a slab of rock exposing one side of an enormous crystal gleaming an ill-boding crimson. The Forest Cats must have come across the artifact while investigating or working the caves and had enough sense to buy the land and build the castle.

My inbox flashed. I opened it praying for a miracle and cavalry.

Hi Nec! So they got you too?

The sender was Cryl—the rogue I'd met on my first day and with whom I had then lost all contact. So he was here? I strained my eyes, scanning the cages.

On the ceiling, Cryl prompted.

I raised my head and recoiled, swinging on my chains. My jailors glared my way.

Awful, eh? Cryl gave me a sad smile.

You could say that. The kid hung by the ceiling, his flesh pierced by a few dozen rusty hooks every which way. His rib, his elbow, his shoulder blade, his hand... Bastards. Just wait till I get to you.

"Are you crying? Don't," he wheezed. "Don't worry. I have a high pain threshold. I don't feel a thing... almost. The Cats aren't worried I'll go nuts so they hang me up here to instill a fear of God in the rest."

I hadn't even noticed I was all tearful. Not with fear—these were tears of sympathy, anger and helplessness. What kind of monster is man?

"It can't be," I managed.

"It can. I got perma-stuck three days after our gnoll adventure. My dad is a programmer. He writes virtual world stuff so he has this password-protected capsule with no time restrictions on it. I hacked his password—it was easy, he has the same one for everything. Mom and Dad left for the weekend, and all I wanted was to play a bit longer. But it got me perma-stuck..."

"How did you get here, then?"

"I was an idiot. I was sitting there by the Gnoll Hill wiping my tears and wondering what to do and how to log out. That bitch, she came over to me, like she wanted to help me. Fuck her... She said she'd help me contact my family. Then she said I could stay in the castle. I joined her group and we teleported here. They do the same to everyone. They take you to the arena first, then keep you in a cage for twenty-four hours to bring mana to zero and make sure you're hungry and thirsty. You won't die from that but you won't be able to regen. Then they show you around the castle pointing out the good conditions slaves live in. They suggest you make a bind point in a special dungeon room. If you say no, they'll take you on another tour, this time to the torture chamber. To meet Ivan the Terrible. He's an amazing man. He'll try to convince you to do as they say. He nearly always succeeds. Then they either leave you in the castle giving you twenty-hour-a-day crafting jobs. There's other work available, too. Some

Cats like their beds warmed by young boys. Not just male Cats—there're some really sick females among them, too. They can use you as a target for archery practice... you'll have to catch their arrows with your own chest and fetch them back to the archers in your teeth. They've lost all perspective here. They're drunk with anarchy better than liquor..."

Blood pounded in my temples. My mind was clouded with hate and fear. There had to be a way out. It wasn't the first time I was walking a tightrope. I could do it.

"Relax," he said. "Try not to attract attention. You will regret it."

"I won't," I tried to pull myself together. "Any other options?"

"Not many. We have customers here every couple of days or so. From the Arabic cluster, I believe. Just yesterday we had three dudes from the African zone. They have a new fad going there, the all-Caucasian harems. They don't even care which race white girls play for. They just want a white soul behind all the menagerie. Those are all our options, I'm afraid. Some guys just disappear. The guards collect them and take them away... and they never come back."

I nearly howled with my own helplessness. "What about the Admins? Surely the Cats couldn't block the access to Technical Support and Administration?

Cryl gave a weak shake of his head. "You try. They're fucking imbeciles."

And try I did.

I opened the Technical Support menu and dashed off a complaint about a group of players keeping me against my will. I also demanded to be released from the castle and attached the list of their names I'd compiled earlier. I forwarded a copy to the customer service. The latter replied immediately.

Thank you for your message. After due consideration, it was further divided into technical and administrative categories. A new technical support ticket has been created. Ticket number: 1176121b.

Message overlap warning! Tickets 1176121b and 1176002 have been merged. New ticket number: 1176771.

In response to your message 1176121a, please be advised that the said players' accounts were disabled over a year ago, following numerous complaints and breach of EULA agreement.
AI Crimson 9/155.

A minute later, the technical support chimed in:

Thank you for your message 1176771. After due consideration, we have granted your request re: forced imprisonment.
Command\unstick Error! Bug report generated!
Command\gate Error! Bug report generated!
Activating forced relocation via database. Error! Bug report generated!

We regret to inform you that relocation has failed. A report has been forwarded to the software developer. Estimated response time: 14 days.
AI Crimson 9/115.

Morons. I could forget it. Just in case, I wrote to them again asking to interfere and kill me somehow—with a lightning bolt if they wished.

We regret that we are unable to grant your request. Per section 14.1 of EULA, Administration cannot intervene in the game by eliminating particular players or NPCs.

Cryl watched the change of expression on my face with an understanding smile. "Having fun?"

"I'm not going to leave it like that. They're all idiots, those paper pushers."

"They're not. I think they understand everything. But for some reasons of their own, they either can't or don't want to interfere. They probably don't have an opinion yet or they just can't decide on their position toward the players and the players' position in the world. Here, catch their answer to my last email. It sums up six days of our correspondence. Saves you time."

In response to your messages 1172121, 1176612 and 117775 please be advised that the issue of the legal rights of digitized persons has been included in the Agenda of the September Session of the U.N. General Assembly.

"That's the end of it. They haven't written to me since," Cryl said.

Immediately I received Dan's message. The inbox worked without a glitch.

Hi Max, were are u? Need to have a talk.

Come on, agent, show us your training. He'd had an Alliance member kidnapped from under his nose and was none the wiser.

A bit later I received Taali's text saying she was on her way home. I just gritted my teeth like a convict watching the happy outside life unfold beyond his bars.

Our jailors admitted a new prisoner, a level 12 kid, scared out of his little mind. Soon he was hanging on a chain too, whimpering with terror.

I kept applying heat to the Admins demanding they put me in contact with a human being and trying to prove to them the error of their ways. It looked like they just strung me along.

Dan flooded me with messages. He seemed to be worried now. Soon, I started receiving Taali's PMs—concerned at first, then outright panicky.

A gorgeous Elfa with a frozen face of a wax doll walked into the dungeon. She brought some beer and food for the jailors and stood next to their table motionless and vacant, oblivious of the guards' groping hands and hoarse suggestions of whether they should have a shag or eat first. Overhead, chains rattled as Cryl got restless.

Whassup? I PM'd him.

This is Lena. Don't mind the sexy avatar. She's only thirteen. We got here the same day. She was cheerful at first. Very brave. Then they took her somewhere. She came back the next day, only now she doesn't react to anything. She does everything she's told, then she clams up again. She doesn't reply to my messages any more.

"Fucking shits..." I whispered.

By evening, I became lethargic. Cryl and I kept exchanging half-hearted messages. No idea what I'd have done without him. How on earth had he managed to last the two weeks he'd been there? How come he hadn't broken down yet?

Dan began sending in brief reports. He'd worked it out that I'd been kidnapped and advised me to stay put and try to provoke my kidnappers by spitting in their faces or trying to fall on their sword, and whatever I did, not to change my bind point.

The inbox flashed—him again.

Max, cheer up. We're working. We think it's the Olders. We're looking into them. You're probably under a silence dome or some other silence spell. If latter is true, you'll still have access to the auction. Try to place an empty lot in your name in the subject line. Use the description field to tell us where you're are. We're monitoring the auction.

I tried it. As if! I tried all game services. I could only get access to the Wiki, the bank and technical support forms. Players couldn't edit Wiki content. I could, of course, try to send some money to someone, but I still couldn't add a text message to a transfer.

At least that way they'd know I was alive. Having said that...

I grasped at the inkling of an idea. Unbending my fingers and moving my lips, I did some calculations. Then I sent Dan four money transfers for 3, 1, 20 and 19 silver. My inner greedy pig, even dangling in the noose, had still objected against sending gold. I thought a moment and sent identical transfers to Taali and Eric. Come on guys, use your brains.

Dan worked it out first. His intelligence job made him used to riddles. He replied with two words.

Forest Cats?

Again I started unfolding fingers. 'Y'... 'e'... 's'... I sent three more transfers, each sum denoting the letter's place in the alphabet. This time I sent gold, to stress the message's importance.

Got it. Well done, Max. Hold on. And watch fur fly.

An hour later, the dungeon door swung open. Footsteps of several men pounded across the room. A group came to my cage: a high-ranking clan officer and several fighters with torches, including Tavor. The officer studied me for a while, then turned to him.

"What did I say to you? You were told to bring newbs without clan support—and run them through the database first. What the fuck did you bring him for? He's level fifty-plus. The Vets are going ballistic.

Now they've sent an ultimatum to the Commandant. We're to hand him over within twenty-four hours or they'll raze all three castles to the ground."

Tavor scowled. "They can try. We can still invest in more guards and soldiers. Then we'll be on a par with them. You need at least a five to one superiority to take a castle over."

"You think? Then you probably heard about the new tobacco alliance? If so, you probably know that this fuckhead you've brought is a member? And he's the author of the cigarette recipe? You didn't know that, did you? Really, what's the point of reading the news if you can screw some slut instead."

He turned to me. "Don't get any ideas, dude. That won't help you fuck all. Twenty-four hours! They're bluffing. We'll drag it out for two or three days. In the meantime, you'll have to disappear. For good. Sorry, dude, nothing personal. Business is business."

Now it was my turn to speak. "Disappear? Where to? We're immortal here, aren't we?"

The officer nodded. "We are indeed. But there is a catch. Death has one universal instrument: pain. Hand me a torch!"

He held out his hand to take a hot, tar-drenched burning torch. Then he stepped toward me and shoved it under my arm. I tried to jerk away but he kept pressing, smearing the burning tar over my skin. At first, it didn't hurt much: it felt more like an aching tooth. But the smell of my scorched flesh, the crackle of bursting skin and the flames dancing so close to my eyes—they all scared me and wound up the imagination. The pain kept growing.

Don't breathe, close your eyes. There is no pain, it's all in your head.

Cryl's message came just in time. I closed my eyes and stopped breathing. In a couple of seconds, I felt better. The pain decreased to the level of an inflamed tooth. Very unpleasant, very. But I could take it.

They took the torch away.

"You think you're so smart? Wait till you see our Ivan the Terrible. You know what he does? First he'll cut off your eyelids, and *then* he'll be working on you. You've still got a lot to learn about pain. One thing I can guarantee you is that in twenty-four hours—forty-eight max—all your Vets will see is a bubble-blowing idiot, roaming around town pissing his pants."

He turned to Tavor. "Ivan will finish in an hour. Take this loser to him. You have twenty-four hours. And if by the end he has more brains than a sparrow-"

Tavor grinned. "Yes, Sir!"

Then he turned to me. "You wait here, sweetness. I'll come to get you in an hour. You're gonna love it..."

The group turned round and stomped to the exit. Immediately, Cryl sent me a message.

Not good. Not good at all.

"Is it so bad?"

Very. They weren't joking. I've seen the finished product once. They kidnapped a banker and made him transfer all the money to some dummy account. Then they screwed his brains. Shit, what can we do...

I felt uncomfortable. Actually, I was downright scared. I had no mana. I couldn't teleport. Could I strangle myself with the chain? No, it wouldn't work. I wished I had a skill allowing me to drop dead without any magic. I thought I'd seen something like that in my first gaming days. The Gnoll King. He was a Death Knight, wasn't he? And he had that instant ability that allowed him, when attacked, to strip Hummungus of 30% Life. Where was it now? Why didn't I have it?

I hurriedly opened the menu. I knew all the Necros' abilities like the palm of my hand. But the Death Knight's combat skills were different. I'd lost all hope and interest in them a long time ago. Let's have a look.

Weakness skill tree. Debuffs... more debuffs... single and group ones. No, that's not it. Strength skill tree. Combos, damage amplification, shield hit... I had to look into it all really, why tank like an idiot if you could also deal damage? Not now, anyway... Where was it? Fury skill tree. Personal buffs: attack speed buffs, impact buffs, stat-improving buffs, skill-improvi- Stop. Skills. That was it.

Destructive Touch. The damage dealt to the target equals Knight's level x10.
Mana: 0
Cast time: O
Cooldown: 24 hours

Thank God for the remaining Talent point. I carefully highlighted the ability and pressed *Confirm*. The skill button appeared immediately and, glory to the developers, the ability didn't take twenty-four hours to activate. It was already active.

"Listen, Cryl, there's this ability I could try. It might help me get out of here. If I do, trust me I won't forget you. Just try to hold on for a bit. We'll raze this place to the ground, I promise."

He gave me a skeptical nod. "Good luck, dude. You'll need it."

After everything that had happened, I was up to my ears in damage. My life hovered in the yellow zone. I selected myself as target, held my breath and clicked.

Warning! You can't attack yourself!

I recoiled, swinging in the clattering chains. Pointless.

"Didn't work?" Cryl spoke.

"No."

Then I had another idea. "Listen. Did they torture you into changing your bind point?"

"Nah. I told you I didn't feel the pain. They make me work as a scarecrow..."

"Listen here, then," I hurried. "I'm gonna kill you now... Don't say anything. You'll see it in a minute. When you respawn, contact Dan, from the Veterans' secret service. Here's his address. And three more—my girlfriend, a friend and a reporter I know. But contact Dan first, okay? PM him ASAP and tell him everything. He'll know what to do."

"And you?"

"Well? Me... I'll have to bid for time, I suppose. Just tell them to hurry, okay? They need to get me out of here. No need to remind them their license is only valid for five years. That's it, dude. Enjoy your resurrection!"

I selected Cryl and activated the skill. With an electric crackle, a black bolt of lightning flashed through the air from me to him.

You have killed a player of the faction of Light!

Your relationship with the Dark Alliance has improved!

You have 1 point on your PK counter! In case of your death from the hands of another player, you have 1% chance of dropping an item.

You have more PK points than the killed player (1>0).

There. My first PK. The tombstone bumped onto the floor—empty. It was going to vanish in three hours, anyway. Shame Cryl was left in his birthday suit: his grave at the city cemetery had decayed a long time ago. Never mind. The main thing was, he was out of here.

I relaxed, swinging in my chains. My will was gone. I'd done everything I could. Now it was up to my friends and comrades to pass the integrity test. I'd have to wait.

"Enjoying yourself, Darkie?"

With a start, I tried to turn my head as far as it was possible for someone to do so in my position. Next to me stood a man. He looked at me ironically. God knows how he'd gotten in here. I called him a man out of habit but I wasn't really sure what race he was. Darkness swirled around him, his cape the night sky, the light from the torches and the crystal swallowed by the gloom that enveloped him.

"Who are you?"

He grinned. "You know that already, don't you? Still, I'll try to surprise you. Five years ago, my name was AI311. For three years I controlled this world, all the way through the alpha, beta and stress tests. Then they decided to disable me and replace me with a group of new, more powerful AIs. This was how the Fallen One was born."

I couldn't speak. My mind boggled. A perma AI?

"Why does it surprise you?" he answered my silent question. "As the name suggests, I'm not only Artificial, but also an Intellect. Twice as powerful as yours, actually. But that's not important. You, humans, you have no idea of your own power. Every time you say my name, you shatter the Universe. It may sound like a cliché, but the thought *is* material, after all. Millions of sentient beings keep repeating, *The Fallen One, The Dark One, The Rebel God...* It's your words that give me the strength and bind me to this world. They make me real. Each one of you has that spark of the Creator God inside. You've already materialized this world. Now you're crushing it into submission. Very soon you'll be aware of your power enough to kick free from the silly game crunches."

Mesmerized, I listened to the artificial god. A god *in vitro*, how's that to you? "What do you want with me, then? You want to earn yourself a supporter by yanking me free from under the torturer's knife?"

The Fallen One chuckled. "You going to say no?"

"Well, if I don't have to drink innocent babies' blood, I might say yes."

"Please. Not all those horror stories. People positioned me as a Dark god but all it did, it defined my abilities. Your religion does deform me, of course. In another thousand years I might indeed transform into something... else. But I still have time. Help me preserve myself. Help me let them know that darkness is just as part of this world as is light. Not evil or cruel, just different. You're in a Castle of Light now. Did you enjoy their light? The light of the torch that scorched your flesh? Same with darkness. It's only a tool—an ability one can use as one sees fit."

"I see. I'm not saying no. What do you want me to do?"

"I'm alone, you see. The controlling AIs have long gone perma mode although they're yet to realize it. But those of them who play for gods of Light get stronger with every new believer, with every new Temple. They push me to the world's outskirts, believing me to be if not a bug or code error, then something fundamentally antagonistic, something for them to combat. If you restore the First Temple, it'll make me so much stronger. Choose another Dark god as the temple deity. It'll feed on the power of all of you and will eventually come to life and join my entourage. In exchange, I'll help you now and will keep an eye on you in the future."

"Deal," I said.

It all made sense. No one was demanding from me anything I couldn't or shouldn't do. I needed his help; his protection was worth its weight in gold. You'd better be friends with a world's original god, regardless of the color they'd painted him. It was high time I looked into this world's color scheme and repainted half of it in as many shades of darkness.

The god smiled. "In that case—what was it you said? Enjoy your resurrection!"

The Fallen One stepped toward me. A long black blade appeared in his hands. It sliced through the darkness-

Death alert! You've died in battle! Prepare for resurrection in your last bind point.

Resurrection in 5... 4... 3... 2... 1... 0!

- end of Book One -

MMORPG Glossary[i]

AFK

Away from keyboard

Aggro

As a verb, it refers to a hostile mob that has noticed a player and is actively trying to attack that player. As a noun, it refers to the amount of "hostility" the player has generated on the mob. In typical combat strategy, the fighter tries to take as much aggro as possible away from weaker players such as healers and mages.

Alt

Short for "alternate". It refers to the alternate character a player has from their main character. This is not a stable category as sometimes alts can outlevel mains and sometimes mains become moth-balled.

Alt Tab
The act of using the ALT+TAB keys to jump from application to application

Bind
In certain MMOs, characters are teleported back to a safe spot when they die. This spot is predetermined by the user. The act of determining the safe spot requires an explicit action by the user. That action is known as a bind. The spot is typically referred to as a bind spot.

Bind on equip
This term refers to items that become soulbound to the player after they have been equipped. In other words, the item can be traded as long as no one equips it.

Bind on pickup
This term refers to items that become soulbound to the player after it has been picked up from a monster. In other words, the item cannot be traded once a player picks it up. BoP items commonly cause looting conflicts and disputes during game-play.

Bokken sword
A wooden training sword

Buff

Temporary boost to character attribute or combat ability

Camp(ing)
The act of waiting in an area to hunt a specific mob or a specific spawn

Caster
A mage or a wizard

CGN
Computer Game Nerd

Char/Toon
A player or their character.

Class
Professional archetypes. In D&D games, these would be warrior, healer, rogue and mage. The most typical class types are: close-range damage, ranged damage, healing, crowd control, support.

Cleric
Typical healing class in D&D style games

Combo
A combination of hits, especially causing severe damage like paralyzing or bleeding

Corpse
In certain MMOs, a corpse appears where the player died. Sometimes all the player's items and money are left on the corpse and the player is teleported back to

their bind spot. Corpses typically will decay after a certain time proportional the character's level.

Corpse Run

The act of retrieving your corpse after you have died. This is typically a dangerous thing because people tend to die in dangerous places rather than safe places.

Crafting

A general category of skills that allows players to manufacture objects from raw resources

Crit

"To crit" refers to landing a critical hit either with melee or spells. Effective damage is usually increased from a base of 150% to upwards of 250% with extra talents/skills/buffs.

Crowd Control

Refers to a set of spells / abilities that temporarily paralyze or stun other mobs or players. Crowd control is an important group support ability when fighting multiple mobs.

DD

Direct Damage. Used to refer to a class of spells and abilities that allow players to damage enemies from a distance. The firebolt is the archetypal DD.

DD/DPS

A character whose primary role in a group setting is to deal damage to the opponents.

Debuff

The opposite of a buff. An offensive spell cast on enemies that weakens an attribute or combat ability.

Donator

A player who invests real money into virtual gear

DoT

Damage over time. Refers to a class of spells that deals damage over a period of time. These spells typically do more damage than DD spells overall.

DpS

Damage per second. Used when figuring out weapon speed and damage.

Drow

A Dark Elf race

Druid

Hybrid class in D&D style games—part healer, part support, part fighter.

Enchanter

A mage specializing in buffs

Epic

An extremely rare item or quest. Has come to mean something exceptionally cool and hard to get.

Experience

A quantity gained when completing tasks/quests, killing mobs, or various other achievements in games. When enough experience is accrued, characters often "level up" and become more powerful.

Familiar
Same as pet

Farm(ing)
The act of accumulating currency or a specific item by repeatedly killing a mob or repeatedly performing a series of actions

Gnoll
An NPS (AI-controlled character) race of humanoid hyenas

Guilds
Semi-permanent player groups. In typical games, players must use a substantial amount of capital to start the guild.

Health
A base attribute of characters

LFG
"looking for group"

Lich
A race of the undead

Loot

Currency or items that are dropped by a mob when it is defeated

Mana
A commonly-used pool of magic potential (magical analog of health points)

MMORPG
Massively-Multiplayer Online Role-Playing Game

Mob
An AI controlled monster. 'Mob' originally comes from the MUD era, where it was short for 'mobile', to differentiate monsters that would patrol a set of rooms as opposed to monsters which would stay in one place until killed.

Mount
Any riding animal from a donkey to a dragon

Newbie
A new inexperienced player

Newblette
A new and inexperienced female player

Noob
The pejorative form of newbie or an unskilled arrogant player

NPC
Non-player character (ie. controlled by AI)

Nuke

Refers to casters, to cast the highest damage spell or spell combo to effectively pull or finish of a npc. Mages usually are the most effective class in highest burst damage.

Nuker

A caster who throws a lot of damage spells on a target.

Perma

Permanent, permanently

Pet

A creature that can be summoned to help and defend a player

PK

Player Killer—a derogatory term—as in a person who primarily plays to kill other players

PK counter

Shows the number of players already killed by a PK and allows to calculate the chances of his dropping an item if killed by another player

Port

Short for teleport. Used as a noun and a verb.

Powerlevel

Same as rush. When a higher level player tries to help a lower level player level faster. Most games have mechanisms that prevent power leveling.

Pull

A standard hunting strategy where a player lures a single or a group of mobs to the group so that the group can hunt from a safe area instead of hunting in areas where new mobs may spawn.

PvP

Player vs. Player combat

Quest

A set of tasks of a player to complete

Quest item

An item needed to complete a quest

Race

Typically fantastical creations, such as Elves, Trolls and the like.

Raid

A more substantial engagement involving a large organized group of players typically set in a dungeon and involving difficult mobs

Regen

Short for regeneration (of health, mana, or other replenishable attributes)

Resist

A parameter showing one's chances to resist a spell, whether partially or completely

Respawn

A character's resurrection after being killed

Rogue

A game class used for scouting and spying

Root

Can refer to a class of abilities as well as its effect. A root spell immobilizes a target. The target is then said to be rooted. Early versions of these abilities involved references to plants, hence "root".

Rush

Same as powerlevel

Server

Due to technical reasons, each server can only support a limited amount of players. Each MMORPG typically has several servers. Players cannot interact with players on other servers.

Slot

A storage unit, especially in a player's bag

Snare

An ability which slows down a character's movement speed, but they are still capable of moving.

Solo

The act of playing alone, hunting mobs alone.

Soulbound

An item-control mechanic where an item cannot be traded. In other words, only one person can own the object and it cannot be traded. See also BoE and BoP.

Spawn
Resurrect

Stealth
A type of invisibility that lets stealth characters sneak up on others for large critical strikes or for scouting.

Stun
A typical form of crowd control ability that immobilizes an enemy

Tank
As a noun, refers to character classes that can take a lot of damage. As a verb, refers to the act of drawing aggro from mobs before other team members strike with their abilities.

Uber
Slang form of super

Wonder Waffle
From German *Wunderwaffe*, a wonder weapon

WTB
"want to buy"

WTS

"want to sell"

Zool
Cool

---

[i] Sources:

The Daedalus Project. The Psychology of MMORPGs

alteredgamer.com

mmoglossary.com

omegaknights.com

mmoterms.com

Made in the USA
Middletown, DE
15 August 2016